Sir Thomas Dick Lauder

Highland Legends

Sir Thomas Dick Lauder

Highland Legends

ISBN/EAN: 9783744764766

Printed in Europe, USA, Canada, Australia, Japan

Cover: Foto ©Andreas Hilbeck / pixelio.de

More available books at **www.hansebooks.com**

HIGHLAND LEGENDS

BY

SIR THOMAS DICK LAUDER, Bart.

Author of "The Moray Floods," "The Wolf of Badenoch," "Lochandu,"
"Royal Progress in Scotland," &c.

TWO VOLUMES IN ONE

LONDON: HAMILTON, ADAMS, & CO.
GLASGOW: THOMAS D. MORISON
1880

RIGHT HON. THE COUNTESS GREY.

DEAR LADY GREY.

With your permission, I now dedicate these volumes to you. I should do so with great diffidence, did I not know that everything connected with Scotland is interesting to you.

By associating them with a name so universally revered I give them value; whilst I afford to myself an opportunity of expressing my admiration of those many virtues and amiable qualities which have rendered it so much beloved in your person by all ranks who have the good fortune to come within reach of their influence; and I have thus also the satisfaction of expressing my warm sense of the kindness I have received from you and Lord Grey ever since I have had the honour of being known to you, as well as of assuring you that I am,

With every possible respect,

DEAR LADY GREY,

Very sincerely and faithfully yours,

THOS. DICK LAUDER.

EDITORIAL NOTE TO THE PRESENT EDITION.

IN this volume the Publishers present to the reading public a new edition of Sir Thomas Dick Lauder's first collection of Highland Legends. Originally published under the somewhat misleading title of "Highland Rambles and Long Legends to Shorten the Way," it has been thought desirable that the title be abbreviated, and made more decidedly descriptive of the volume, as the "rambles" form no important part of the work. In all other respects the present edition is a *verbatim* reprint of the work as it came from the hands of the distinguished Author.

CONTENTS.

HIGHLAND LEGENDS.

SCOTTISH MOORLAND SCENERY.

THE scenery of the less cultivated parts of our native Scotland may, generally speaking, be said to be checkered, as human life is with its events; for as, during our pilgrimage here on earth, evil continually succeeds good, and good evil, so are beauty and deformity seen to alternate with each other on the simple face of Caledonia. A long stretch of dreary and uninteresting hill country is often found to extend between two rich or romantic valleys, so that the lover of nature has to plod his weary way from the one to the other over many a mile of sterile desert; and, if he be a pedestrian, through many a burn, and many a slough too, with little to disturb him, save the sudden *whirr* of the grouse, as he bounds off through the air with the velocity of a cricket-ball,— or the sharp *frisp* of the snipe, as he rises like the cork from a brisk bottle of champagne,—or the wailing *teeweet* of the green plover, who, like some endless *seccatore*, most perseveringly follows his track, unceasingly boring him with his dull flapping and his tiresome cry.

When not broken in upon by any such incidents, these wildernesses are sometimes rather valuable to a solitary traveller. They afford him time for rumination whilst he is traversing them. They give him leisure to chew the cud of reflection, and he is thus enabled to digest the beauties of the valley which he has last devoured, before he proceeds to feast upon the charms about to be presented to him by that to which he is hastening. But whatever may be the advantages to be derived from journeying in any such single state of blessedness, I am disposed to think that the man who has a cheerful companion or two

2

associated with him in his pilgrimage, will not be much inclined to wish them absent in such parts of the way; and as I do not think that either his moral or his physical digestion will be in any degree impaired by society, I am quite sure that his intellectual enjoyment will be thereby much increased.

My own experience convinced me of the truth of this one fine autumnal morning, when, in company with two friends, I left the romantic valley of the Findhorn, to cross the moorlands towards Grantown, a village which may be called the capital of Strathspey. The sun that rose upon us, as we took our staves in hand to begin that day's walk, had continued to display a brighter and merrier countenance than any, perhaps, which I had ever seen showing face within the precincts of this vapour-girt island of ours. Yet vain were his friendly efforts to throw a glow of cheerfulness over the brown heaths and the black plashy bogs almost entirely covering the tame unmeaning undulations of the country before us. A scene apparently less calculated to furnish food for remark or conversation, can hardly well be conceived. But when the imagination is not altogether asleep, a very trifling hint will set it a working; and so it was, that the innumerable grey, ghastly-looking pine stocks of other years, that were everywhere seen pointing out of the peat-mosses, from amidst tufts of the waving cotton grass, and wiry rushes, and gaudy ranunculuses, quickly carried our minds back to former ages by a natural chain of connection, filled them with magnificent ideal pictures of those interminable forests which completely covered Scotland during the earlier periods of its history, and immediately furnished us with a subject for talk.

Author. — You see yonder hill, called the *Aitnoch.* Although it is, as you may easily perceive, the highest in all this neighbourhood, yet an extensive plain on its summit, almost entirely peat-moss, is so thickly set with the stocks and roots of pine trees, such as these you are now looking at, and all fixed, too, like these, in the growing position, that, if the boles and branches were still standing on them, it would absolutely be a difficult matter for a deer, or even for a dog, to force a passage through among them.

Grant. — I should like much to mount the hill to examine

the plain you speak of. Well as I am acquainted with this north country, I never heard of it before.

Author.—It will cost us little more than the additional fatigue created by its rather rough and steep ascent to do so, for it is not quite an hundred miles out of our way.

Clifford.—Phoo ! we are not to be tied to ways of any kind. Let us climb the hill, then, by all means. But, to return to what you were talking about, can you tell us how, and for what purpose, these vast forests were annihilated ?

Author.—The charred surfaces which most of these stocks and roots still exhibit sufficiently prove that fire must have been the grand instrument of their destruction. The logs which originally grew upon them, but which are now found lying horizontally under the present surface, all bear testimony to the same fact in a greater or lesser degree. Many of these, indeed, when dug up, present a very curious appearance, the nether part being left almost entire, whilst the upper side has been hollowed like a spout. This n have been effected by the flames, which naturally continue. to smoulder on the upper surfaces of the fallen trunks, whilst the moisture of the ground where they fell extinguished them below.

Clifford.—Come, that is all very well as to the *how;* now, let us have your *wherefore.*

Author.—As to the causes of the devouring element being let loose among these aboriginal forests we might speculate long enough, for they were probably many and various. Accidental fires may have been kindled by the rude inhabitants, which afterwards spread destruction far and wide, as they often do now in the forests of America. Or they may have been raised with the intention of driving away wild beasts, or of aiding in their destruction, of annoying enemies, or even for the more simple purpose of clearing spots of ground for hunting or for pasture. The causes may have been trivial enough in themselves. You, Grant, who have travelled so much in Switzerland, must be aware of the practice which still prevails there, of burning down large patches of gigantic pine timber on the sides of the Alps, for no other reason than to allow the sun and the moisture to reach the surface of the ground, so as thereby to increase the quantity and value of the pasture growing beneath.

Grant.—Yes, I can vouch for what you say with regard to the practice in Switzerland, and I am much inclined to think with you, that instead of attributing the fall of these mighty Caledonian forests, as many are disposed to do, to some one great and general catastrophe, we ought rather to place their ruin to the account of a combination and reiteration of fortuitous causes, by the increasing frequency of the repetition of which they were rapidly extirpated in detail. Indeed, in support of what I now say, I remember having heard a well authenticated tradition of exactly such an accidental conflagration, which is said to have taken place so late as the year 1640.

Author.—I should be glad to hear the particulars of it. Do you think you can recall them?

Grant.—I think I can, but you will perhaps find the story rather a long one.

Clifford.—Long or short, let us have it by all means. And let me tell you for your comfort, my good fellow, none of Chaucer's pilgrims could have begun a story under circumstances so favourable. A parliamentary speech itself might have some chance of being listened to if uttered to one whilst passing through so dull a country as this—that is to say, without one's gun and pointers.

THE BURNING OF MACFARLANE'S FOREST
OF BEN LAOIDH.

THE sun had not yet disappeared behind the mountains on the western side of Loch Lomond, and the unruffled surface of the lake was gleaming with his parting rays, when the Laird of Macfarlane, as he was returning from the chase, looked down from the ridge of a hill over the glorious scene that lay extended beneath him. His eyes travelled far along the calm expanse of the waters, till they lost themselves in the distance, amid the tufted and clustering islands which lay glittering in the fleeting light like gems on the bosom of Beauty. He then recalled them along the romantic undulations and irregularities of its shores, to dwell with peculiar pride and inward satisfaction on the wide stretch of those rich and smiling pastures which he could call his own, and on the numerous herds of cattle which his vassals were then driving to their home-grazings for the night. All was still and silent around, save when the quiet of the balmy evening air was gently broken by those rural sounds which, when blended together and softened by distance, as they then were to Macfarlane's ear, never fail to produce a musical harmony that thrills to the very heart of the true lover of nature. The lowing of the cattle—the occasional prolonged shouts of the herdsmen—the watchful bark of their attendant dogs, careful to permit no individual of their charge to stray from the main body—the shrill and solitary scream of the eagle, coming from the upper regions of the sky, as he soared to his place of repose amid the towering crags of Ben Lomond—and, lastly, the mingled cawing of the retreating army of rooks as they wheeled away in black battalions, to seek for undisturbed roost among the branches of that forest which then filled the whole country from Loch Lomond to Glen Urchay with a dark and interminable sea of foliage,—such were the sounds

that came in mellow chorus on the delighted ear of Macfarlane. He sat him down on a mossy stone to rest for a
while, that his eyes and his ears might have fuller enjoyment. His faithful sleuth-hounds and braches, overcome
with fatigue, quickly stretched out their wearied bodies in
ready slumber around him ; and his numerous followers
no less gladly availed themselves of their lord's example
to ease their tired shoulders of the heavy loads which the
success of that day's woodcraft had imposed upon them.

Macfarlane was a stern chief of the olden time. Yet,
what heart, however stark or rude, but must have been
subdued and softened beneath the warm influence of those
emotions which such a scene, and such sounds, and such
an evening combined to excite? As he sat apart from his
people he was melted into a mood of feeling which he had
rarely experienced during his life of feudal turmoil. His
thoughts insensibly stole upwards in secret musings, which
gradually exhaled themselves in grateful orisons to that
Heaven whence he felt that all the blessings he possessed
had so liberally flowed ; and although these prayers were
inwardly breathed in the formal and set terms prescribed
by his church, yet his soul more fully and effectually suffused itself into them than it had ever done before. That
mysterious and uncontrollable desire which man often feels
to hold converse with his Creator alone, gradually stole
upon him ; and, having ordered his attendants to precede
him, he arose soon after their departure, to saunter homewards through the twilight in that calm and dreamy state
of religious reflection which had rarely ever before visited
his stormy mind.

As he slowly descended the mountain side that slopes
down to the Arroquhar, the course of the little rill, which
he followed, led him into a grove of natural birches, and
his silent footstep betrayed him into an involuntary
intrusion on the privacy of two lovers. These were his
foster-brother, Angus Macfarlane, and Ellen, a beautiful
maiden, who was about to become his wife. The wedding-
day was fixed, as the Laird of Macfarlane well knew ; and
as his heart was at this moment brimful of kindly feeling,
the sight of this betrothed pair made it run over with
benevolence.

"What ho ! my fair Ellen," cried he, as, chased away by
her modest confusion, her sylph-like form was disappearing

iy among the tender foliage of the birchen bushes like some delicate thing of air, "dost fear the face of thy chief? Knowest thou not that Macfarlane's most earnest wish ever is to be held as the father of his meanest clansman? and think ye that he would be less than a father to thee, sad posthumous pledge of the worthiest warrior that ever followed the banner of Loch Sloy, or for whom a gallant clan ever sung a wailing lament? But ha!" exclaimed he, as he kindly took her hand to detain her; "why dost thou look so sad? By this light, such as it is, it would seem as if the tear-drop had been in that blue eye of thine. My worthy Angus could never have caused this? He loves thee too well ever to give pain to so soft and confiding a heart as thine."

"Angus never could wilfully give me pain," said the maiden earnestly, and throwing down her eyes, and blushing deeply as she said so.

"Ha!" said Macfarlane, in a playful manner, "now I think on't, yours may have been the tears of repentance, seeing that you most wickedly have seduced my trusty master herdsman from his duty this evening, and that he hath left his people and his beasts to take care of one another, that he might come over the hill here to whisper soft things into thine ear, under the clustering woodbine, that wreathes itself through the holly there, and fills the air thus with its delicious perfume."

"My good lord, I would humbly acknowledge my fault, and crave your pardon," replied Angus; "I must confess that I did leave the lads and the cattle to come to keep tryst here with Ellen. But albeit that she had some small share of blame in this, her tears fell not from compunction for any such fault. Say, shall I tell the cause, Ellen?— They fell because of a strange vision which her old Aunt Margery saw last night."

"A vision!" exclaimed Macfarlane seriously; "tell me, Ellen, what did she see?"

"... was last night, my lord," replied Ellen, "that my Aunt Margery came over to my mother's cottage to settle some matters regarding—a—a—I mean, to speak with my mother of some little family affairs, which kept her better than an hour after nightfall, when, as she was crossing the hill again in her way home, she suddenly beheld a red glowing gleam in the sky, and turning to look behind her, the whole of the forest below seemed to be on fire. She rubbed her eyes in her astonishment, and when she looked again the vision had disappeared."

"Strange!" said Macfarlane seriously.

"But this was not all," continued Ellen, with increased earnestness of manner, and shuddering as she spoke, "for by the light that still gleamed in the sky, she beheld a dark object at some distance from her on the heath. It moved towards the spot where she was. Trembling with fear, she stood aside to observe it, and on it continued to come, gliding without sound. A single stream of faint light fell upon it from a broken part of the sky, and showed the figure and the features of—of—of you, Macfarlane."

"What, my figure! my features!" exclaimed the laird, in a disturbed tone; and then, commanding himself, he quietly added, "Awell, and saw she aught else?"

"She did, my lord," added Ellen, much agitated, "for, borne over your right shoulder she beheld a human corse; the head was hanging down, and the pale fixed features were those of—of—my betrothed husband!" Overpowered by her feelings, Ellen sank down on a mossy bank, and wept bitterly.

"Let not these gloomy fancies enter your head at a time like this, Ellen," said Macfarlane, roused by her sobbing from the fit of gloomy abstraction into which her narration had thrown him. "If not altogether an unaccountable and unreal freak of imagination, it can be interpreted no otherwise than felicitously for you. The burning forest is but a type of the extent and the warmth of your mutual affection, and the dead figure of Angus only shadows forth the fact that your love will endure with life itself."

"There needed not such a vision to tell us these truths," said Angus energetically.

"Yet do we often see matters as palpable as these, as wonderfully vouched for by supernatural means," said the chief. "Get thee home then, Ellen; and do thou see her safe, Angus, and let her not suffer her young mind to brood on such dreary and distressing phantasies as seem now to fill it. Be yours the joyous anticipations of the bride and bridegroom three days before they are made one for ever. Ere three days go round your indissoluble union shall be blessed by the happiest influence of the warm sunshine of your chief's substantial favour. Meanwhile, may good angels guard you both !—Good night."

With these words, Macfarlane sought his way home, musing as he went, impressed, more than he even wished to own to himself, with the strange tale he had heard, and when he could contrive to rid himself of it, turning in his thoughts from time to time certain benevolent schemes which suggested themselves to him for the liberal establishment of Angus and his bride.

The next day's sun had hardly reddened the eastern sky, so as to exhibit the huge dark mass of Ben Lomond with a sharp and well-defined outline on its glowing surface, when the herdsmen of the Laird of Macfarlane arose and left their huts, with the intention of driving their cattle across the dewy pastures back to the slopes of the mountains. The thick summer mist still hung over the lower grounds; and the men wandered about hallooing to each other whilst employed in actively looking for the animals of which they had the charge. They had left them the previous evening feeding in numerous groups among herbage of the most luxuriant description. They were well aware that it was much too fragrant not to tie them, by the sweetest and securest of all tethers, to the vicinity of those spots where they had been collected in herds; and they were quite sure that the animals never would have left them voluntarily. But all their shouting and all their searching appeared to be unsuccesful, and the more unsuccessful they were likely to be the more were their exertions increased. All was clamour, confusion, and uncertainty, till sunrise had somewhat dispelled the mist that had hitherto rolled its dense and silent waves over the bottom of the valley; and then one herdsman more active and intelligent than the rest, having climbed the mountain that sends forth its root to form the boundary between the enchanting mazes of the beautiful oak and birch-fringed lakes of Ballochan and the long stretch of Loch Lomond's inland sea, and having looked up Glen Falloch, and far and wide around him to the full extent that his eyes could reach,—

" We are harried !" shouted he in Gaelic to his anxiously inquiring comrades below. " Not a horn of them is to be seen ! I can perceive a large herd of deer afar off yonder, clustered together in the open forest glade, but not a horn

or hide of cow, ox, quey, or stirk, do I see within all the
space that my eyes can light upon ; and unless the muckle
stone, the *Clach-nan-Tairbh*, down below there has covered
them, as tradition tells us it covered the two wild bulls,
when the fury of their battle was said to have been so
great as to shake it down from the very craig upon them,
our beasts are harried every cloot o' them !"

"My curses on the catterans that took them then !"
exclaimed Angus Macfarlane, the master of the herdsmen
—"and my especial curses, too, because they have thus
harried them the very night when I chanced to be wandering ! But if they are above the surface of the earth we
must find them ; so come, lads, look about ye sharply."

Like an eager pack of hounds newly uncoupled, who
have been taught by the huntsman's well-understood voice
that a fresh scent is at hand, the herdsmen now went
dodging about, looking for the track of those who had so
adroitly driven off a *creagh* so very numerous and so
immensely valuable.   Long experience and much practice
in such matters soon enabled Angus to discover the country
towards which the freshest hoof-prints pointed, and in a
short time the whole band were in full and hot pursuit of
the reavers.

"They are Lochaber men, I'll warrant me !" said Angus,
whose sagacity and acuteness left him seldom mistaken ;
and guessing shrewdly at the route they would probably
take, he resolved to follow them cautiously with his assistants, that he might dog their footsteps and spy out their
motions, whilst he sent one back as a messenger to the
Laird of Macfarlane, to report to him the daring robbery
that had been committed on him.

If you have been able to conceive the calm that settled
upon Macfarlane's mind when the placidity of the previous
evening had brought it so much into harmony with all the
surrounding objects of nature, that it might almost have
been said to have reflected the unruffled image of Loch
Lomond itself, you may easily imagine that the intelligence
which he now received operated on him as some whirlwind
would have done on the peaceful bosom of the lake.   The
eyes of the dark-browed chief kindled up into a blaze of
rage, and shot forth red lightnings, and his soul was lashed
into a sudden and furious storm ere the messenger had
time to unfold half of his information.

"What! all harried, said you?—Bid the pipers play *the gathering!* Shout our war-cry of Loch Sloy! We'll after them with what of our clansmen may be mustered in haste. By the blessed rood, we'll follow them to Lochaber itself, but we'll have back our bestial!"

But Macfarlane was not one who allowed his rage to render him incapable of adopting the proper measures for the sure attainment of his object. A numerous party of his clan was speedily assembled, all boiling with the same indignation that excited their chief. Macfarlane himself saw that each man was equipped in the most efficient manner for celerity of movement; and when all were in order, he instantly set forward at their head, taking that direction which was indicated to him by the intelligence which the messenger had brought him.

In their rapid march through the great forest, they threaded its intricacies, partly trusting to their local knowledge, partly to their leader's judgment of the probable route of the reavers, partly guided by the fresh tracks which they now and then fell in with, and partly by certain signal marks which the wily Angus had from time to time left behind him, by breaking the boughs down in a particular direction. Once or twice they encountered some individual of the party of herdsmen in advance, whom Angus had stationed in their way to give his chief intelligence; and at last, as the sun was fast declining towards the west, another man appeared, who came to meet them in breathless haste.

"Well! what tidings now?" demanded the laird.

"They are Lochaber men, sure enough," replied the man.

"Pshaw! I never doubted that," said Macfarlane impatiently; "but, quick! tell me whither you have tracked them. We have no time to lose."

"I'm thinking you may take your own leisure, Macfarlane," replied the man, "for I'm in the belief that they are lodged for the best part of this night, tethered as they are with the tired legs of the beasts." And so he went on to explain that they had been traced into what was then one of the thickest parts of the forest, to a spot lying between Loch Sloy and what is now the wide moss of the *Caoran*, stretching south-east from Ben Laoidh.

"Then they cannot be far distant from the bothy of the

lochan, where I slept when we last hunted in that quarter?" said the chief.

"Sure enough, you have guessed it, Macfarlane," replied the man, "sure enough they are there, and Angus and Parlane, and the rest, are watching them. By all appearance there's a strong party of the limmers, and I'll warrant me they keep a good guard."

"Let them guard as they may, our cattle are our own again," said the chief, with a laugh of anticipated triumph; "Saint Mary! but we'll make these gentlemen of Lochaber pay for their incivility, and for the unwilling tramp they have given both to us and to our beasts! Not a man of them shall escape to tell the tale!"

A general exclamation burst from his followers. "Not a man of them!" was echoed around, and they besought Macfarlane to lead them instantly to the slaughter.

"No!" replied he sternly, "I have said, and I now swear by the roof-tree of my fathers, and by the graves where they rest, that not a man of these vermin shall escape! and Macfarlane has never yet said, for weal or for woe, what he did not make good to the very letter. But no advantage must be lost by rashness. Every precaution must be taken coolly and deliberately, so that not a man of them may ever return to parent, to wife, or to child. Lochaber shall wail for them from one end of it to the other, and the men of that country shall pause long before they again attempt to lay hand even on a cat belonging to Macfarlane."

Having thus checked their impatience, he marched them slowly onwards, without noise, till he discovered a thicket by the side of a brook, where, sheltered and concealed by an overhanging bank, his men could rest and refresh themselves without being observed, and there he patiently halted to wait for the night, and for further intelligence.

Impenetrable darkness had settled over the forest, and the Macfarlanes had sat long in silence, listening eagerly to catch the distant but welcome sound of the lowing of the cattle, that came on their ears faintly at intervals, and assured them that they were now within a short march of their enemies, when the cracking of the withered branches of the firs at some distance a-head of them made them stand to their arms and look sharply out from their ambush. Human footsteps were evidently heard approaching.

Not a word was uttered by those in the thicket, but every eye that peered from it was steadily fixed on a natural break among the trees growing on a bank, that rose with a gentle slope immediately in front of their position, where the obscurity being less absolutely impervious, they might at least be enabled to see something like the form of any object that came, however imperfectly it might be defined. The sounds slowly advanced, till at length one human figure only appeared on the knoll that crowned the bank. It stood for some moments, as if scrutinising every bush that grew in the hollow below. It moved—and then it seemed to stop, as if in hesitation. Macfarlane's hench-man raised his arquebuse, and proceeded to light a match for its lock. The click of the flint and steel made the figure start.

"It is a patrol of the Lochaber men," whispered the henchman, raising the piece to his shoulder to take aim ; "I'll warrant they have got hold of Angus and the rest. But I'll make sure of that fellow at any rate."

"Not for your life !" replied Macfarlane in the same tone, whilst he arrested his hand. "The whole forest would ring with the report, and all would be lost."

Seizing a crossbow from one of his immediate attendants, he bent it, and fitted a quarrel-bolt to it, and, having pointed it at the object on the summit of the knoll, he challenged in such an under tone of voice as might not spread alarm to any great distance, whilst, at the same time, he was quite prepared to shoot with deadly certainty of aim the moment he saw the figure make the smallest effort to retreat.

"Ho, there !" cried the chief.

"Ho, there !" replied the figure, starting at the sound, and turning his head to look eagerly around him.

"Where grew your bow, and how is it drawn?" demanded Macfarlane, in the same tone.

"It grew in the isles of Loch Lomond, and it is drawn for Loch Sloy," was the ready reply.

A long breath was inhaled and expired by the lungs of every anxious Macfarlane, as he recognised the well-known voice of Angus, the master herdsman.

"Advance, my trusty Angus," said the chief; "the brake is full of friends."

Angus had never left his post of watch until he was

satisfied that the Lochaber men were in such a state of repose as to ensure to him time enough to return to meet his chief. He then planted some of his people to keep their eyes on the enemy, whilst he found his way back alone, to make Macfarlane fully aware of their position. The plunderers lay about a mile from the spot where the chief had halted. The great body of them, consisting of some thirty or more in number, had retired into the hunting-bothy, before the door of which a sentinel was posted, to give alarm in case of assault. To prevent the cattle from straying away, they had driven them together into a large open hollow, immediately in front of the knoll on which the bothy stood; and to take away all risk of their escape or abstraction, four men were stationed at equal distances from each other, so as to surround them. The poor animals were so jaded with their rapid journey, that they drew themselves around the shallow little *lochan* or pool in the bottom of the hollow, from which the bothy had its name, and having lain down there, they showed so much unwillingness to rise from their recumbent position, that the watchmen soon ceased to have any apprehension of their running away. The men rolled themselves up in their plaids, therefore, and each making a bed for himself among the long heather, they indulged in that sort of half slumber to which active-bodied and vacant-minded people must naturally yield the moment they are brought into an attitude of rest.

Macfarlane had no sooner made himself perfectly master of all these circumstances, than he at once conceived his murderous plans—took his resolution—gave his orders; and, having cautioned every man of his party to be hushed as the grave, they proceeded, under the guidance of Angus, to steal like cats upon their prey—foot falling softly and slowly after foot, so that if they produced any sound at all, it was liker the rustle of some zephyr passing gently over the heather tops, than the pressure of mortal tread.

Whilst they were proceeding in this cautious manner, Angus, who was at the head of the men, was observed suddenly to raise his crossbow, and to point it in the direction of Macfarlane, who was, at that moment, some ten or fifteen paces before the party. Filled with horror, the men who were nearest to him sprang upon him to prevent so great a treason as the murder of their chief. Angus

was felled to the ground—but his bolt had already flown
—and, with a sure aim too, for down fell among the heath,
weltering in his blood, and with an expiring groan, not the
chief of the Macfarlanes, but one of the Lochaber men.
The quick eye of Angus had detected him standing half
concealed by the huge trunk of a tree, exactly in the very
path of the chief. Three more steps would have brought
Macfarlane within reach of the very dirk of the assassin,
which was already unsheathed, and ready to have been
plunged in his bosom. Amazement fell upon all of them
for some moments. Macfarlane could with difficulty com-
prehend what had happened ; but when he was at length
made to understand the truth, he ran towards Angus. He
was already raised in the arms of those of his friends who
had so rashly judged and punished him, but who were now
sufficiently ashamed and repentant of their precipitation.

" Look up, my brave Angus," said Macfarlane to his
clansman, as he began to revive ; "look up to thy chief,
grateful as he is for that life which thou hast preserved to
him !—Heaven forbid that it were at the expense of thine
own life ; and that, too, taken by the too zealous hands of
Macfarlanes."

" Fear not for me," replied Angus, somewhat faintly, "I
was but stunned by the blow ; and he that gave it me
would have been well excused if he had given me a death-
wound, if I could have been justly suspected of traitorie to
my chief ; and well I wot the bare suspicion of such
villainy is wound enough to me."

" Nay, nay, Angus," said Macfarlane ; "you must not
think so deeply of this accident. The judgment was
necessarily as sudden as the action, and no wonder that it
was faulty. But, how came this stray man to be patrolling
about ? Are we betrayed or discovered, think ye ?"

" I would fain trust that we are not," replied Angus.
" As we watched, we saw one man leave the bothy to go
out and spy around their post, as we guessed ; but, as we
afterwards saw a man come in again, we took him to be
the same, when, I'll warrant me, he has been the fellow
whom the first man went out to relieve. But, if we were
deceived, the fault is luckily cured now, for this is doubtless the very man who"——

" Aye," said the chief interrupting him ; "the very man,
indeed, who would have certainly taken my life, had it not

been for thine alert and timely aid. What do I not owe thee, my trusty Angus! But stay; let him sit down and rest for a brief space, till he recovers his strength, and then, if I mistake not, we shall bloodily revenge his passing injury."

They now again moved forward, with much circumspection, until they at length began to perceive a distant light, which occasionally twinkled in advance of them. As they proceeded, the light became broader, though it was still broken by the intervention of the thick-set stems of the forest. But after groping their way onwards with redoubled care for some hundred yards farther, it burst forth fully and steadily on their eyes, as the trees ceased suddenly, and they found themselves close to the very edge of the open hollow described by Angus, and in the middle of the herdsmen who had been left by him as spies. After using their eyes very earnestly and intently for a little time, they could now perceive the surface of the shallow pool, which lay in the still shadow, in the centre of the bottom below them, and they could dimly descry the dusky mass of cattle lying crowded together around it. As the Macfarlanes stood peering into the obscurity, a low and melancholy voice of complaint would every now and then burst from some individual beast, reminiscent of the rich Loch Lomond pasture from which it had been driven, and bitterly sensible of the sad change of fortunes which a few hours had brought to it. The figures of the four watchmen were as yet invisible; but the whole face of the opposite knoll being free from wood, the door of the hunting bothy was clearly defined, by the bickering blaze of faggots that burned in the middle of the floor within, distinctly displaying the sentinel as he walked to and fro across the field of its light. The thick wooding of the forest that encircled this natural opening came climbing up the rear of the knoll until its tall pines clustered over the back of the bothy itself, and the existence of high grounds rising with considerable abruptness at no great distance, if not previously known, could only have been guessed at by the greater density of the shade which prevailed over everything that was beneath the lofty horizon, the limits of which were easily distinguished by the partial gleam that proceeded from the sky above it. There the clouds were now every moment growing thinner and thinner, as the driving rack skimmed across the face of heaven with a velocity that proclaimed an approaching hurricane.

In obedience to the orders already given to them by their chief, the Macfarlanes retreated a few steps into the thick part of the skirting forest, the dark foliage of which arose everywhere around this naturally open space, and beneath its impenetrable concealment they made a silent movement to right and left, during which they posted single men at equal distances from each other, until they had completely surrounded the hollow, the bothy, and the whole party of Lochaber men, together with their booty. This manœuvre was no sooner silently and successfully executed, than four choice young herdsmen, remarkable for their daring courage as well as for their strength and agility, were selected by Angus. These had well and accurately noted the respective spots where each of the Lochaber watchmen had lain down, and after some consultation, each had one of them assigned to him as his own peculiar object of attack. Having gone around the edge of the wood till each man was opposite to his slumbering enemy, they glided down the sloping edges of the hollow, armed with their dirks alone, and they crept on their bellies towards the bottom, drawing themselves like snakes silently and imperceptibly through the long heather. Full time was to be allowed for each man to reach his prey; and although the period was not in reality very long, yet you will easily believe that it passed over the heads of the Macfarlanes with a degree of anxiety that made it appear long enough. The moment the four herdsmen began to descend into the deep shadow which filled the sides of the hollow, their figures were entirely lost to the view of those who were stationed within the skirt of the surrounding forest. Every heart beat with agonising suspense. The smallest accident might ruin all. An occasional prolonged moan was heard to come from some of the cattle, and all felt persuaded, however contrary it might be to reason, that each succeeding recurrence of it must awaken the slumberers. But at length, whether from the operation of some peculiar instinct, or from some remarkable sense of smell which these creatures have occasionally proved that they possess, it happened that they really did become

3

sensible of the approach of some of those who were wont
to attend on them, I know not; but all of a sudden some
ten or a dozen of them sprang up to their legs, and changed
their long low moan into that sharp and piercing rout into
which it is frequently known to graduate.

"Look out! look out there!" cried one of the Lochaber
watchmen in Gaelic, and half raising himself as he spoke.

"Look out!" cried one of the others laughing, "I'm
thinking that I would need the blazing eyes of the devil
himself to be able to look at anything here."

"What's the matter?" shouted the sentinel at the door
of the bothy; and as he said so, he halted in the midst
of his walk, and bent his body forward in all directions
in his eagerness to descry the cause of the alarm.

"Tut, nothing," replied another of the watchmen, "all's
well, I warrant me."

"Aye, aye," said another, "we're safe enough from all
surprise this night; for, as Archy says, it would need the
fiery e'en of the red de'il himself to grope a way through
the forest in such darkness as this."

"It's dark enough to confound an owl or a bat, indeed,"
said the watchman who first spoke, "but mine are eyes
that can note a buck on Ben Nevis' side of an autumn
morning a good hour before the sun hath touched his
storm-worn top; and, by St. Colm, I swear I saw some
dark-looking thing glide over the lip of the bank yonder."

"It must have been a dark-looking thing, indeed, to
have been visible there," replied his comrade; "but if it
were not fancy, it must have been a fox or a badger."

"Be it what it might," replied the man, "I swear I
saw the back of the creature as it came creeping over the
round of the bank."

"What, think ye, makes the cattle rout so strangely?"
demanded the sentinel.

"That which makes the pipes skirl so loudly," replied
one of the men below, "a stomach full of wind. I promise
you the poor beasts got but a scanty supper ere the sun
went to. And here, unless they can eat gravel or sand
in this hole, or heather as hard as pike-heads, they have
little chance of filling their bellies with aught else but wind."

A noise of talking was now heard within the bothy,
where all had been so quiet previously, and immediately
afterwards the doorway was darkened by the figures of

two or three men, who came crowding out to gaze ineffectually around them. Some talking took place between them and the sentinel; and Macfarlane and his people gave up all hope of the success of the manœuvres they had planned. But after some moments of most painful suspense, the talk of the Lochaber men terminated in a loud laugh, produced, no doubt, by some waggish remark made against some individual of the little knot, after which the figures retired into the hut. The sentinel resumed his silent walk, and the watchmen in the hollow below seemed to relapse into their former state of slumber.

The silence that now prevailed was not less deep and intense than the darkness that sat upon this wild forest scene, where the plunderers lay unconsciously surrounded by their mortal foes. Macfarlane moved cautiously round the circle of his men, to assure himself that all were prepared, and sufficient time having now expired to have allowed the slumber of security to have again crept over his victims, he took a matchlock from his henchman, and stepping forth from under the trees, he pointed it with a deliberate and unerring aim at the sentinel, as he stood for a moment directly opposed to the full light proceeding from the doorway. He gave fire. This was the fatal signal—instantaneously fatal to him against whom the deadly tube was levelled, who sprang into the air and fell without a groan, pierced through the very heart. But it was not fatal to him alone; for ere the report of the shot had re-echoed from the surrounding heights of the forest, or its myriads of feathered inhabitants had been roused by it on the startled wing, the dirks of the four Macfarlane herdsmen had bathed themselves in the life's-blood of the four Lochaber watchmen; so that their living slumbers were in one moment exchanged for those of death. The wild war-shout of " *Lochsloy! Lochsloy!*" arose at once from every part of the ring of the Macfarlanes, who environed the place; and each man keeping his eyes on the light that issued from the bothy, on they ran towards it as to a centre from all parts of the circle. So sudden was the attack, that those within had hardly time to start from their sleep, and to hurry in confusion to the door, ere the Macfarlanes were upon them. The clash of arms was terrific, and the slaughter fearful. At once driven back in a mass, the remnant of the Lochaber men barricaded the doorway in despair, and determining to die hard, they fired many shots from behind it, as well as from a small window hole near it; but discharged as these were from a crowded press of men, where no aim could be taken, no very fatal effect could be produced by them. On the other hand, the assailants could do nothing, till Macfarlane kindled a slow-match, and prepared to thrust it into the dry heather that covered the roof.

"Macfarlane!" cried Angus, eagerly endeavouring to interpose; "for the love of the Virgin fire not the thatch! Think of old Margery's vision!"

Macfarlane did think of it; but, alas! he thought of it too late; for the slow match had been already applied—had already caught fatally; and in one instant it had burst into a blaze, that, amidst the pitchy darkness of that night, would have been a magnificent spectacle, could any one have beheld it without those dreadful emotions naturally excited by the cruel cause that created it, and the horrible circumstances that attended it. In one moment more the whole of the wooden structure was in flames, and inconceivably short was the period in which the tragedy was consummated. Loud and piteous were the cries for mercy; but they fell on ears which revenge had rendered deaf to mercy's call. The half-burned Lochaber men, yelling like demons, rushed in desperation forth from the blazing walls; but dazzled by the glare, they only rushed to certain destruction on the spears of the Macfarlanes, and were hewn down by their trenchant claymores, or despatched with their ready dirks: so that ere a few brief moments had fled away, all those who had been so recently reposing in fancied security, with the full pulses of robust life beating vigorously within their hardy frames, were heaped up in one reeking mass of carnage before the burning bothy.

"Let us rid the earth of these carcases!" said Macfarlane after a pause; for now that the keenness of revenge and the exciting eagerness of enterprise had been fully satiated by success, he was half horror-struck with the ghastly fruits of it, which he thus beheld piled up before him. In obedience to his command, the whole of the dead bodies were immediately gathered together, and thrown within the burning bothy, where they were quickly covered with branches and half-decayed pieces of wood, hastily dragged from the forest, till the fire that was thus created shot up far above the trees in one spiral pillar of flame, bearing on its capital a black smoke that poisoned the air with the heavy and sickening taint with which it was loaded.

The Macfarlanes stood for a while grouped in front of it, in silent contemplation of its fitful changes; but its light showed little of the flush of triumph on their sullen brows. Each man held dark communing with his own gloomy thoughts. Their chief, leaning on the deadly instrument which had given the fatal signal, looked on the scene with a cloud on his brow not less dark than that of the murky smoke itself. Whatever his reflections were, there was a restless and uneasy expression on his countenance. He started, for a dreadful sound came crashing through the forest. It was like that which might well have announced the coming of the demon of destruction or the angel of vengeance; and before he could mutter the Ave-Maria which mechanically came to his lips, that hurricane which the careering rack of the clouds had been for some time unheededly announcing, came rushing upon them with the swiftness of lightning and with resistless force. In one moment the frail wooden walls of the bothy, already yielding to the influence of the combustion, were levelled with the ground; and some six or eight of the tallest pines which stood nearest to them behind, were laid across them with all their branches in one heap by the blast. Macfarlane and his men were driven down on their faces, and compelled to cling to the knoll on hands and knees, like flies to a mushroom top. So tremendous was the violence of the tempest, that they could not rise from their crouching position, nor even dare to lift up their heads without the certainty of being whirled off their feet, and dashed to atoms against the boles of the neighbouring trees. This furious fit of the elements endured not long; but when a sudden lull of nature did allow them to assume the erect position, how terrible! how appalling was the scene they beheld!

The funeral pile which they had themselves kindled for the massacred men of Lochaber, now arose in one broad resistless tower of fire, crowned, as it were, with many a

pointed pinnacle of flame, that appeared to pierce the very
sky, lighting up every part of the surrounding elevations,
nay, every little crevice in the rocks, and every tree, bush,
or petty plant that grew upon their rugged surface. If the
spectacle was grand before, it was now sublime beyond all
imagination. But, alas! the Macfarlanes were occupied
with other contemplations; for the huge fallen pines which
had so much augmented the conflagration, had formed a
train of communication from the burning bothy to the
thick forest immediately behind it; and the flames had
spread so rapidly far and wide on every side, that already
the whole of the surrounding circle of wood presented
nearly one dense and lofty wall of fire through which there
was hardly any door of escape left for them. For one
instant, and for that one instant only, something like
dismay appeared in Macfarlane's eye, as he first gazed
around him, and then cast a glance full of anxious expression towards his faithful clansmen.

"Perhaps I might have shown more mercy," half-
muttered he to himself. "But if it be the will of Heaven
to punish me, oh! why should these poor fellows suffer for
the sin of their chief? My brave men," continued he
aloud, "we cannot stand here. The air already grows hot
and scanty. Follow me, and let us try to burst through
yonder point where the flames seem to burn thinnest.
Come on."

Followed by his people, Macfarlane rushed down the
sloping face of the knoll, with the intention of cutting
across the open space by the most direct line towards the
spot he had indicated; but they had not gone many steps
ere the hurricane again came sweeping over the woods
with all its former fury,—the enormous pines bent and
groaned as if from the agony they were enduring,—the
violence of the conflagration was increased tenfold,—the
wall of fire by which they were environed was speedily
closed in, so as to annihilate every lingering hope of
escape,—and the Macfarlanes were compelled to throw
themselves again flat on the ground, and to scramble down
into the bottom of the hollow, to avoid being scorched up
like moths by the fire which the uncertain whirlwind
darted suddenly hither and thither in different directions,
and to escape the risk of being snatched up into the air
and launched amid the burning pines.

It had happened so far well for the sufferers, that the cattle, terrified by the shouts of the conflict, and still more by the first blaze of the bothy, had fled up the bank from the hollow, and, forgetting their fatigue, they had charged full-tilt through the forest, routing and bellowing in that direction which led to their own Loch Lomond pastures, from which they had been so unwillingly driven. The small space towards the bottom of the hollow, therefore, was thus left entirely disencumbered of them; so that when the Macfarlanes were forced down thither, they were enabled to gather around the shallow pool of water in the centre of the place. There they endeavoured to defend themselves against the flying embers, by rolling up their bodies tight in their plaids. But although they were rid of the cattle, they were not left as the only occupants of the spot; for the place was soon covered with swarms of mice, weasels, adders, frogs, toads, and all the minuter sorts of animals, like them driven into the centre of the circle by the scorching heat of the devouring element that surrounded them. For now the flames raged fiercer than ever, and the dense canopy of smoke that covered the comparatively small space where they lay, was so pressed down upon them by the fury of the blast, that it appeared to shut out the very air; and they seemed to breathe nothing but fire and burning dust and ashes. Their very lungs seemed to be igniting, whilst at every temporary accession of the tempest, the half-consumed tops of the blazing pines were whirled among them like darts, inflicting grievous bruises and burns on many of them.

And now, as if to consummate their afflictions and their miserable fate, the long, dry, and wiry heath that grew within the open space where they lay, was laid hold of by the fire; and the flames, running along the ground from all sides towards the centre, threatened them with instant, awful, and inevitable death. But one resource now remained; and to that they were not slow in resorting. They rolled themselves into the shallow pool, and wallowed together in a knot. They gasped like dying men, and their eyeballs glared and started from their sockets with the agony they endured; and in their utter despair they sucked the muddy water of the *lochan* in which they lay, to cool their burning mouths and throats. Macfarlane felt as if they had been already consigned to the purifying pains of that purgatory through which, as his religion told him, their guilty souls must pass. Their bewildered brains spun round, and strange and terrific shapes seemed to pass before their eyes. Some short ejaculations for mercy were breathed, but not a groan, nor a word, nor a sound of complaint, was permitted to escape from any one of their manly breasts, even although the pool, their last frail hope, was now fast drying up from the intensity of the heat.

After a complication of indescribable torments, which made the passing minutes seem like hours, the force of the hurricane suddenly slackened for a short time, and the thick surface of heath around them having been by this time burnt out, and the trees which grew upon the immediate confines of the circle having had their boughs and foliage consumed and their trunks prostrated, the open space within which they were enclosed grew wider in its limits, and consequently the air became more abundant and freer in its circulation; so that they began gradually to revive. By degrees they were enabled to raise themselves in a weak and half-suffocated state from what was now reduced to little more than the mere mud of the pool. Then it was that their chief, though himself much overcome by the conjunction of his own bodily and mental sufferings, was roused to active exertion by that anxious desire to preserve his people which now sprang up within him, to the utter extinguishment of all consideration for his own person. He was so faint, that it was with some difficulty he could ascend the knoll; but he hastened to climb it, that he might endeavour to discover from thence whether any hope was likely to arise for them. There he found that the bothy, and the fuel and pine trees that had been heaped upon it, had already sunk into a smoking hillock of red-hot ashes, from the smouldering surface of which the ghastly half-consumed skulls of his Lochaber foes were seen fearfully protruding themselves. The undaunted heart of Macfarlane quailed before a spectacle so unlooked for and so unwelcome at such a moment. He started back and shuddered as their blackened visages met his eye, grinning, as it were, with a horrible fiend-like expression of satisfaction at his present misery. He turned from the sight with disgust, not unmingled with remorse, and then sweeping his eyes around the now far-retreating circle of the burning forest, and reflecting on

the imminent destruction which he and his clansmen had
so recently escaped, and looking to the peril by which they
were yet environed, he crossed himself, threw his eyes
upwards, uttered an inward prayer of penitence and
of thankfulness, and then he bravely prepared himself
to take every advantage of whatever favourable circumstances might occur.

After scanning the blazing boundary all around with
the most minute attention, Macfarlane thought he could
perceive one narrow blank in the continuity of the fiery
wall. His knowledge of the forest enabled him to be
immediately aware that the blank was occasioned by a
ravine which he knew was but partially covered with wood,
through which a stream found its way. He took his
determination ; and summoning his people around him,
and pointing out this distant hope of escape, he called to
them to follow him. With resolute countenances they
immediately began to make their difficult and hazardous
way over the torrid and smoking ground, among the red-
hot trunks of the pine-trees which stood half-consumed—
smouldering fallen logs—tall branchless masts, which still
blazed like upright torches, and which were every moment
falling around them, or those which had already fallen, or
which had been broken over, hanging burning in an
inclined position across their way—whilst they were, every
now and then, tripped and thrown down by some unseen
obstacle among the scorching embers; and ever and anon
each returning gust of the hurricane whirled up around
them an atmosphere of ignited dust and cinders, almost
sufficient to have deprived them of the breath of life. But
still, with their heads half-muffled in their plaids, they
persevered, till the increasing heat of the air they inhaled
and of the ground they trod on, and the multiplication of
the difficulties they had to encounter, would have been
enough of themselves to have convinced them of their
approach to the more active theatre of the conflagration,
even if its fiery enclosure, and the groaning and crashing
of the falling timber, had not been but too manifestly
before their eyes and loud in their ears.

The difficulties and dangers of their progress now became
infinitely multiplied. Hitherto their endeavours to keep
together had been tolerably successful ; but now each
individual could do no more than take care of himself, and

every cloud of burning cinders that blew around them produced a greater separation among them, till finally they became so dispersed, that when the chief reached the head of the narrow ravine, through which he had hoped that he might have led them in a body, he cleared the burning dust from his eyes, looked everywhere around him eagerly for his people, and, to his bitter mortification, he beheld no one but his trusty Angus, who, amidst all the obstacles and hazards through which they had passed, had still contrived to stick close to his master. Old Margery's vision came across his mind, and, in the midst of the burning heats to which he was subjected, the blood ran cold to his heart. He cast his eyes down the trough of the ravine, over which clouds of flame and smoke were then rolling, and there, indeed, he did, at transient intervals, behold a handful of his clansmen toiling through the perilous passage. He shouted aloud to bid them stay; but the overwhelming roar of the whirlwind, combined with that of the combustion of the neighbouring trees, rendered his voice altogether powerless. Distressing doubts arose within him as to the fate of those who appeared to be amissing; but the rapid growth of the conflagration around him compelled him to shake off all such thoughts, and summoning up his sternest resolution, he rushed down into the ravine, with Angus at his back, as if he had been rushing to an assault under the spirit-stirring influence of the war-cry of the Macfarlanes. And few assaults indeed could have been so hazardous, for, ever and anon, huge burning pines were precipitated from the steeps above, so that even the water-course itself was in a great measure choked up by their hissing and smoking ruins. But still Macfarlane fought his way onwards amidst burnings and bruises, many of them occasioned by his frequently looking round with anxious solicitude for the safety of his faithful follower; but, in spite of all these difficulties and perils, he had already made considerable progress down the ravine, when, in one instant, he was deprived of all sense by the sudden descent of an enormous pine, which he could neither avoid nor see.

When the chief recovered from his swoon, he found himself lying on his back, in a shallow part of the little stream, which there crept along between two great stony masses. He had been struck down by the spray and smaller branches of the upper boughs of the tree, which,

fortunately for him, had rested across the great stones in
such a manner as to form an arch over his body, and as
this arch naturally produced a rush of air under it, he was
thus saved alike from being crushed to death and from
suffocation. Raising himself on his hands and knees, he
made his way out from under the burning boughs, and got
up so stunned and battered, that some moments elapsed
ere he quite recovered his recollection. Recent events
then crowded fast to his mind, and with these his anxiety
for the safety of Angus recurred more strongly than ever.
He called loudly and frequently on him by name, but the
well-known voice of his faithful follower came not in return.
A lurid light was thrown down into the depth of the ravine
by the conflagration which was spreading widely above.
He moved anxiously around the tree, looking earnestly
everywhere underneath the smoking branches, till at last
the manly countenance of Angus Macfarlane met his eye.
The forehead exhibited a fearful ghastly-looking wound,
and his body was lying so crushed down beneath the
boughs that pressed upon it, as to take away all chance
that a spark of life remained within it. With desperate
strength and anguish of mind the chief drew his claymore,
and hewed away the interposing branches, till he had so
far relieved the body as to be able to draw it forth. He
eagerly felt for the pulses of life, but they were for ever
stilled.

"Alas, alas, my faithful Angus!" cried Macfarlane, "art
thou gone for ever! Alas, thy fate was indeed too truly
read! But I cannot leave thee to feed the devouring
flames, or to be a banquet for the ravens when this awful
burning shall have passed away. Alas! I promised to
provide for thy bridal, and now, since it hath pleased
Heaven to dispose it otherwise, it shall not be said that
thy chief permitted thee to lack funereal rites!"

With these words Macfarlane stooped him down, and
raised the body of Angus upon his shoulders. The way
down the water-course was obstructed by the huge half-
consumed trunks of the fallen pines, which lay in every
direction across, resting irregularly on the large blocks of
slippery stone, with their branches interwoven like hurdles.
But Macfarlane, weakened as he was by the accumulated
fatigue and suffering he had undergone, staggered on under
his burden with an unsubdued spirit, determined to bear

it so long as his limbs were able to sustain his own person. Inconceivable was the toil which he underwent, and many were the hairbreadth 'scapes which he made from instantaneous destruction. But still he persevered with undiminished courage, until his heroic exertions were at length rewarded by his reaching a spot of comparative safety, beyond the fiery barrier which had so long environed him. But here he only stopped to breathe for a moment, for, toil-spent, exhausted, and bruised, and faint as he was, he was still compelled, by a regard for his own life, to urge onwards over the smoother ground which he now trod, with longer and less cautious strides. His way was illuminated for an immense distance before him, by the triumphant conflagration that came roaring after him, and it was still gaining fresh strength every succeeding moment from the furious aid it was receiving from the increasing hurricane.

As he bore his burden resolutely onwards, his uncertain path led him across a mossy patch of heath, where there were but few trees. There the lurid light of the conflagration, reflected as it was from the heavens, was sufficient to show him a white figure advancing hastily towards him. It was a maiden's slender form—she came —she uttered one wild and piercing shriek, and then she sank down amid the long heath. Macfarlane laid the body of Angus upon a small hillock, and ran to her aid. It was Ellen. He flew to a rill hard by, and brought water in his bonnet. She still breathed, but, as he lifted her head on his knee, each succeeding inspiration became fainter and fainter, till her fair bosom ceased to heave, and her lovely features settled into the marble stillness of death. Her frenzied efforts had been greater than her delicate frame could bear, and the severe mental shock which she received had suddenly expelled her pure spirit from its earthly tenement.

Macfarlane leant over her for a time, altogether absorbed in the intensity of those feelings to which human nature compelled him to yield. But it was not long till the increasing roar of the advancing conflagration, which was now fearfully extending the breadth of its line of march, roused him from his stupor. What could he now do? Was he to abandon both, or even one of the bodies of those, the memory of whom he so much cherished, in order to consult

his own safety? or was he to peril his own life for the purpose of performing a pious but by no means an imperatively
necessary duty? He hesitated for a moment—a transient
and accidental gleam disclosed to him the honest countenance of Angus—his heart filled with many an old recollection—his lip quivered—his eyes became moist—he moved
towards the hillock where the body of Angus lay, and,
stooping down hastily, he raised it again to his right
shoulder, and then, passing onwards, he put his left arm
around the slim form of Ellen, and lifting it up, he laboured
on under the weight of both, with the long hair of the
maiden sweeping over the tops of the purple heath as he
went. Louder and louder came the roar of the conflagration behind him. He quickened his steps, toiling on every
moment more and more breathlessly. But again the trees
grew thicker as he advanced, and his way became more
and more encumbered by their stems. The heat of the
advancing flames now came more and more sensibly upon
him, yet still he struggled on, firmly resolved not to
relinquish either of his burdens till dire necessity should
compel him to do so. The moment when this alternative
was to arrive seemed to be fast approaching—nature was
becoming exhausted—when his ears caught a shout which
he well knew must come from some of his own clansmen.
Faint as he was, the chief was not slow in replying to it;
and, to his great relief, he was soon joined by some of
those from whom he had been separated during the earlier
part of their dreadful and bewildering retreat. He was
now speedily relieved of both his burdens, and the flagging
spirits of all of them being in some degree restored by this
meeting, they again pushed on with renewed exertions,
and without a halt, for some miles, during which they
picked up several stragglers, whose bruised and blackened
figures gave sufficient evidence of the dangers and difficulties they had passed through.

Worn out almost to death, this remnant of the Macfarlanes with difficulty climbed the gentle slope of a
considerable eminence that lay in their way, and as they
wound over the summit of it, where the trees grew somewhat thinly, Macfarlane, as he looked behind him, had at
last the satisfaction to perceive that they had now gained
so much on their pursuing enemy as to render them secure
of a safe and easy retreat. Many, I trow, was the cross

that was signed, and the broken thanksgiving that was uttered ere the chief and this fragment of his followers threw themselves down to rest awhile, and to contemplate the awful scene of destruction from which they had so wonderfully escaped, of which their present commanding position gave them a full view.

The flames had now spread for miles in every direction over the thickest parts of the forest, rising over the crested ridges and swelling elevations, and diving into the deepest valleys and hollows. It seemed like one great billowy sea of fire, agitated as it was from time to time by the hurricane, which, as it approached its termination, came in gusts, violent in strength, but short in duration. As each of these successively swept over the blazing woods, its terrible roar was mingled with the fearful crash of thousands of gigantic pines, which were levelled like reeds before it. These, as they fell, tossed up myriads of mimic stars and meteors into the firmament, which, being surrounded by a zone of dense and inky clouds on its horizon, shone from within that circumference to its very centre, like one vast concave plate of red-hot brass. The scene was enough to humble the proudest heart. The very deer were terrified into an unwonted degree of familiarity with man, for a herd of them that came sweeping over the brow of the eminence, flying in terror from the devouring flames, halted by them, and mingled with them, as if to claim protection from them. The dauntless heart of Macfarlane himself sank within him, as the whole desolating circumstances of this terrible night came crowding to his mind. It was wrung by a deep pang as he recalled the horrible spectacle of the massacred men of Lochaber; he wept like a child when he again looked on the inanimate bodies of those whose appointed bridal-day must now become that of their funeral. He groaned deeply as he gathered from his people around him the sad fate of many of those who were not now to be seen among them; and when such thoughts as these could be so far subdued as to permit him to gaze on the red and resistlessly devouring element, which was so rapidly annihilating his forest, he pictured to himself the melancholy devastation it would produce over his wide domains, and the destruction it would occasion to his hunting grounds, and already, in imagination, he beheld the sable livery of mourning that must soon be spread over his hitherto magnificent territory. And how well his anticipations were verified, we know from the fact, that ere many days went round the whole of the forest covering that country for above twenty-five miles in length, and of a breadth corresponding to that extent, was completely burned down, and the mosses which afterwards originated from it, and which still exist, are full of the embalmed witnesses of this terrible calamity.

COMPARATIVELY RECENT DESTRUCTION
OF THE FORESTS.

Author.—Your legend, my dear Grant, is extremely valuable as matter of history. The preservation of the circumstances which fortuitously caused the destruction of one vast extent of forest, enables us easily to imagine those which may have contributed to the annihilation of all the rest.

Grant.—Doubtless, it does.

Author.—It appears that many of those tracts of woodland must have perished at periods much more recent than we should at first sight be led to suppose; and it now occurs to me, that I lately heard enough to convince me that this was the case with the forests covering the bare country you are now looking at. Both of you know enough of it to be aware that the upper part of Strathspey, far beyond those distant hills, is somewhat about eight and twenty or thirty miles from Cawdor Castle; and you know that bare heaths, such as we see before us, now cover the whole of that stretch of country, with two exceptions; I mean that of the picturesque forest of Dulnan, immediately to the south of the Bridge of Carr, and that presented by the now almost exhausted forest of Dulsie, the remnants of which you may see behind us yonder to our right, running along the trough of the river Findhorn, and covering part of the hills to the north of it. In the whole of the space I have mentioned, these are the only fragments of woodland left to interrupt the dull monotony of the moors.

Clifford.—I was over it all this very season. It is not very easy for me to conceive that it could have ever been wooded at all. 'Tis excellent grouse ground every bit of it. But, as to timber, if there be any, it is all buried beneath the heathery sod.

Author.—True. Yet a respectable man, perfectly worthy of credit, assured a friend of mine, that in his grandfather's younger days, the state of this part of the country was very different. The old man he alluded to lived near Aviemore. He sent his son, who was the father of my friend's informant, on some errand to Fort George. He had himself become blind from age, and as he had not travelled that way for many years, he earnestly questioned his son after his return. "What sort of a country is that you have been seeing?" said he ; and when his son had described it as having pretty much the same appearance as it now wears, "Och, hey!" exclaimed the old man, "what a change! When I was a youth, I used to go in underneath the shade of the forest on this side of the woods of Dulnan, and I hardly ever saw the sun again till I got out of it below Cawdor Castle !"

Grant.—That is a very curious fact. Why that would bring the existence of the forests of this part of the country down to within three generations ; and, even allowing that your friend's informant was advanced in life when he told the story, and that his father and grandfather were rather patriarchal in the endurance of their lives, yet I think the evidence you have brought forward would enable us safely to say, that these moors we now look upon were still covered with wood at the beginning of the eighteenth century.

Author.—Such, certainly, ought to be our conclusion. Is it not surprising, then, that I have never been able to pick up any account, legendary or otherwise, of the circumstances which must have produced the extirpation of these forests at a period comparatively so recent.

Clifford.—From the roots and trunks which are left, it would appear that the trees were almost entirely pines.

Author.—The pine is certainly the prevailing tree, but it is by no means the only one. Birches, alders, and hazels are common, and oaks of immense size, some of them three or four feet in diameter for a great way up the stem, are dug up in various parts of these moors, and many of them in situations where it is now matter of astonishment that such monarchs of the wood could have been produced; for they are found high on the hills yonder above Dulsie, as well as in the mosses far up the courses of the rivers Dorback and Divie.

Clifford, with enthusiasm,—With what a different scene I never be now be surrounded, if we could conjure up all these ancient tenants of the soil, like the reanimated bodies of dead warriors from their graves, as told in some fairy tale of my childhood, to live again, and to wave their leafy banners triumphantly over these hills and hollows!

Grant.—It would be a very different scene indeed.

Author.—Aye, truly it would. Conceive the bleak face of these moors so covered, and then carry your imagination back into remote ages, and let us endeavour to people it in fancy with the animals which must have roamed through its endless wildernesses, and couched within the protection of its almost impervious thickets.

Clifford.—What a country for sport !

Author.—Let us picture to ourselves the myriads of birds of all kinds which winged their flight over the boundless ocean of its foliage, as it was blown into billowy motion by the breezes, or which nestled among its branches as it quietly settled itself to repose, and we shall not only have produced out of these wastes a gorgeous landscape, most romantic in its character, but we shall have opened a wide field for the speculations of the naturalist.

Clifford.—Yes; but, talking of the romantic character of your landscape, what would all that be to the ancient figures to be found in it?- Fancy, only fancy the figures! Think of the dress, the arms, the hunting-implements, and the houses of its human inhabitants! Would we could have but one glimpse of them truly as they were !

Author.—If you were to go far enough back for them, you would fill our forests with a race of men, rude as the scenes in which they lived and roamed, and the whole sketch would be one for which we could hardly now find any really existing resemblance, save in the wilds of North America.

Grant.—Your view of the matter is probably correct enough.

Author.—I believe it to be very correct ; and, now I think of it, a discovery was made some eight or ten years ago, which would seem to bear evidence to the former existence of this ideal picture in which we have been indulging. Some labourers, who were employed in digging in a moss on Lord Moray's estate of Brac Moray, to our left there, found a curious bundle, w¹ they took from under ten feet of a solid peat ⌐

The bundle was about two feet long by one foot thick, and in form it very much resembled such a cloak-bag as you may have at times seen strapped behind a horseman's saddle. A careless inspection of it would have led one to believe that it was covered with leather tanned with the hair on it, and it looked, for all the world, like that of one of those strange old trunks which were frequently to be seen bristling like bears among the uncouth baggage on the top of our ancient *Flies* and *Diligences.* When I first saw it, a piece of it had been torn up by the curious peasants who had found it, and the aperture they had thus made enabled us to become instantly acquainted with the nature of the mass within, which proved to be tallow.

Grant.—Tallow !—*Adipocere*, I suppose. That fatty substance into which animal fibre is frequently converted by long immersion in water.

Author.—No such thing, I assure you. It was pure tallow; and the whole appearances connected with it were very easily explained. It was evident that the tallow, fresh taken from the recent carcase, had been pressed into the raw hide the moment it had been stripped from the newly slain animal, and the whole had been stitched or rather laced up with thongs cut from the *skin itself.* The perfect state of the leather into . which the skin had been converted, exhibited a beautiful proof of the extent to which the chemical principle *tannin* exists in peat moss. No modern tan-pit could have performed the process more effectually. Nor were the preservative properties of moss less established by it; for the tallow was quite entire and uncorrupted, and perfectly inodorous and tasteless. On first inspection it presented a hard appearance, so much so indeed, that it might have been mistaken for chalk; but the moment heat was applied, it melted as readily as fresh tallow would have done.

Clifford.—By your account of this strange mass, it might have been valuable for the candlemakers, if not for culinary purposes. Pray, what became of it?

Author.—The noble proprietor of the estate where it was found gave it me at my request; and with his permission I sent it to the Museum of the Edinburgh University. But whilst it remained in my possession, I never could look at it without its bringing to my mind

what we have so often read of in North American travels,—
I mean the Indian practice of killing an elk, or a deer, or
a buffalo, bundling up the tallow of the creature in its
raw hide with all manner of expedition, with the future
purpose of making *pemmican* of it, and so marching off
with it on their shoulders, leaving the flesh to feed the
wolves and the bears. And really I cannot divest myself
of the conviction that the mass of tallow I have described
belonged to a period of the history of this country when
the state of its inhabitants differed but little from that of
those nomade North American tribes.

Grant.—It certainly does appear to give no small degree
of probability to your fancy.

Clifford.—Nay, but might not some of your cattle-lifters
of a much later date have performed all that you suppose
your savages to have done ?

Author.—The circumstance óf the bundle being found
beneath ten feet of solid moss, which had formed over it
since the time it was left there, together with the various
layers of trees found in the same bog, lying one over the
other, would seem to forbid any such apparently modern
explanation, and to throw back the period of its deposition
to a very remote era indeed.

Grant.—Undoubtedly ; and the probability is, that the
tallow was the produce of no vulgar beast, but rather that
of some of the bisons or magnificent wild cattle of the
ancient Caledonian forests.

Author.—Certainly. But I have since had another lump
of tallow sent me, which had all the evidences of a much
more modern origin. It was found on the farm of Drum-
lochan, on the south side of the Findhorn, about a mile
below Dulsie Bridge yonder ; and it was covered by a
little more than two feet of moss. Its form was very
peculiar ; for it was round one way and flat the other,
like a North Wiltshire cheese, which it very much
resembled in shape and size. It had indeed every appearance of having been pressed into a cheese shape
until it had become firm enough to be removed. It had
no covering of any kind on it ; and although in hardness
and consistence it was quite like the matter of the other
mass, yet it must strike every one that its form, and the
comparatively small depth at which it was found, render
it probable that its origin was much more recent. I sent

it to the Museum of the Northern Institution at Inverness.

Clifford.—Ah! I shall be right at last, I find. This
surely may have been the work of some of these free-
booters of whom I have heard you speak,—of some
of those very *limmers*, for example, who, as you once
told me, stole Mr. Russel's cattle.

Author.—Oh no. That story is much too modern even
for this last mass of tallow.

Grant.—Bravo! Have you a tale of cattle-stealing to
tell also? Allons, let us have it. I have a fair right to
demand it of you.

Author.—There is little in my tale; and I fear it will
tell but tamely after yours. Besides, I have already
given an abridgment of it in an early number of a well-
known magazine. But as you may not have seen it, and
as we are now in the very scene where part of its events
took place, we may sit down under the lee of yonder
large stone on the brow of the hill, and I shall there give
you the particulars of it, whilst you are enjoying the
prospect which that elevated position commands.

By the time we had reached the spot I had indicated,
my friends were not sorry to rest a while, and I began as
follows :—

MR. RUSSEL AND THE REAVER.

THE decided though cruel measures which followed the defeat of Culloden, whilst they were sufficient to extinguish the hopes of the Highlanders who had so enthusiastically espoused the cause of Charles, were ill calculated to subdue their warlike spirits. They were driven, it is true, to seek shelter in those rocky and inaccessible fastnesses which their highest glens afforded them ; but there, amidst the wildest and most solitary scenes of nature, they permitted their minds to brood in bitter reflection over all their wrongs—over all those tragedies which history itself has blushed to record—their wives and children massacred amidst the midnight conflagration of their humble dwellings, or perishing in their flight through the snows of winter. But heroism such as theirs was not to be crushed even by such calamities as these,—calamities which were calculated to have bowed down less lofty and indomitable spirits to the very dust. With them the effect was like that which would result from some puerile attempt to curb and arrest the mountain cataract. They were divided, as its stream might be, into smaller and less important bodies, and their power was no longer so forcible as when they were united together in one stream, but each individual portion seemed to gain a particular character and consequence of its own by its separation from the main body, where it had hitherto flowed undistinguished and unobserved.

It was thus that, lurking in little parties, in retreats only known to themselves, among craggy ravines and pine-clad precipices, they now resumed that minor and predatory warfare which they had been wont to wage against the inhabitants of the more civilised parts of Scotland,—I mean that which consisted in plundering those richer districts of their cattle. Perhaps no inconsiderable degree of political animosity may have mingled itself in many instances with the other motives that prompted these

marauding expeditions in the later times of which I am
speaking. But, be this as it may, we must not look upon
those who were engaged in them as we do upon the
wretched cow-stealers of the present day. That which is
now considered as one of the most despicable of crimes was
then, in the eyes of the mountaineer, esteemed as an
honourable and chivalrous profession. In his untamed
imagination no one was looked upon with so much admiration and envy as that individual who might be chosen as
the leader of a daring band to harry the low country of its
live stock; for these proud sons of the Gael had ever held
the inhabitants of the plains in the most sovereign contempt, and they regarded them and their more favoured
pastures in no other light than as so many nurses and
nurseries, destined by Heaven to rear the cattle which they
were born to consume. I can instance one well authenticated example which displays this opinion in its true light.
The Laird of Grant, the great chieftain of the glen of
Urquhart, having had his cattle driven off by a party of
Camerons, and having sent a strong remonstrance to
Cameron of Lochiel himself by a special ambassador, had
his herds immediately restored to him, with a most courteous letter of apology, which, I believe, still exists, assuring him that his stupid fellows had entirely mistaken his
orders, which were, that they should not begin to plunder
until they had reached " *Moray-land, where every gentleman
was entitled to take his prey.*"

It was soon after the middle of the last century that Mr.
Russel, a gentleman of Morayshire, who resided at Earls-
mill, near Tarnaway Castle, to the north of the Findhorn,
and about ten miles from hence, was alarmed one morning
by the unpleasant intelligence, that a strong body of
Highlanders had come before daybreak and carried off the
whole of his cattle from this very farm of the Aitnoch, which
he had at that time taken as a hill-grazing. Mr. Russel
was an extremely active and intelligent man; and although
he did not make all the warlike preparations which your
friend the Laird of Macfarlane did, yet he was not deficient
either in promptitude of decision or in readiness of action.
After putting a few questions to the scared and breathless
messenger, he lost not a moment in summoning and arming his servants; and, instead of taking this way—towards
the Aitnoch, he struck at once diagonally across the

country in a westerly direction, and marched with great
expedition, in order, if possible, to reach a part of the deep
glen of the Findhorn, some miles above Dulsie yonder, in
such time as to enable him to intercept the plunderers.
You may trace with your eye the dark shadow of the glen,
which sinks deep and abruptly into the bosom of those
purple mountains which you see retreating behind each
other in misty perspective. That is the grand pass into
the Western Highlands, and Mr. Russel was well aware
that if he did not succeed in arresting his cattle before the
robbers had made ·their way through it, the boundless
wastes to which it led would render all further search
after them quite hopeless. Having reached the course of
the river, Mr. Russel and his party made their way down
the steep hill-side, forded the stream to its southern bank,
and, carefully examining the ground to ascertain whether
any fresh footprints were to be observed, they took their
stand, satisfied that they had been so far successful.

The spot chosen by Mr. Russel for his ambuscade was in
the midst of that most beautiful range of retired and tranquil scenery known by the name of *The Streems.* There
the hollow glen is so profound and so narrow in many
places, that one of those little clusters of cottages which
are now found here and there sprinkled in the pastoral
bottom has the name of *Tchirfogrein,* a Gaelic appellation
implying that it never sees the sun. There were then no
houses near the place they had selected, but the party lay
concealed behind some huge fragments of rock, shivered by
the wedging ice of the previous winter from the summit of
a lofty crag that hung half across the narrow holm where
they had taken up their position. A little farther down
the river the passage was contracted, and there was no
approach from that point but by a rude and scrambling footpath irregularly worn along the steep face of the mountain,
and behind them the glen was equally confined. Both
extremities of the small amphitheatre thus enclosed were
then, though they are not now, shaded by dense thickets
of birch, hazel, and holly, whilst a few wild pines found a
scanty subsistence for their roots on the face of the crags
in midway air, and were twisted and writhed by lack of
nutriment into the most fantastic and picturesque forms.
The stillness of an unusually calm and breathless air hung
over this romantic scene, and it was lighted by the now

declining sun of a serene summer day, so that half the narrow haugh was in broad and deep shadow, that was strongly contrasted with the brilliant golden light falling on the tufted tops of the trees of a wooded bank on the opposite side of the river.

Mr. Russel and his small party had not long occupied their post when, as they listened in the silence of the evening, they heard the distant lowing of the cattle and the wild shouts of the reavers as they came faint and prolonged up the hollow trough of the glen. The sounds gradually drew nearer and nearer, and increased in volume as they were swelled and re-echoed from the rocks on either side. At length the crashing of the boughs announced the appearance of the. more advanced part of the drove; and the tired animals began to issue slowly from among the tangled wood, or to rush violently forth as the shouts of their drivers were more or less impetuous, or their blows chanced to light upon them. As they appeared individually, they gathered themselves into a group on the level open sward, where they stood bellowing, as if quite unwilling to proceed any farther.

In rear of the last stragglers of the herd Mr. Russel now beheld, bursting singly from different parts of the brake, a party of fourteen Highlanders, all in the full costume of the mountains, and wearing the well-known tartan of a western clan. All of them were armed with the dirk, pistol, and claymore, and the greater number of them carried antique fowling-pieces. Mr. Russel's party consisted of not more than ten or eleven persons; but they were well armed, and they were people upon whom he could depend. Exhorting them to be firm, therefore, he drew them suddenly forth from their ambush, and ranged them up in array upon the green turf. The robbers appeared to be confounded for a moment, and uttered some uncouth exclamations of surprise; but a shrill whistle from their leader made them quickly recover their presence of mind, and they rushed forward in a body, and formed themselves in order of battle in front of their spoil. Mr. Russel and his party stood their ground with determination, whilst the leader of the enemy seemed to be holding counsel with himself as to what he should do. He was a little spare athletic man, with long red hair curling over his shoulders, and with a pale and thin, but acute visage.

After leaning upon his gun for a time, and surveying the party opposed to him with the eye of a hawk, he shouldered his piece and advanced slowly a few paces in front of his men, until he considered himself to be sufficiently within earshot, and, raising his voice,—

"Mr. Russel," cried he, in very correct English, though with a Highland accent, "are you for peace or war? If for war, look to yourself. But if you are for peace and treaty, order your men to stand fast, and let you and me advance and meet each other half way."

"I will treat," replied Mr. Russel; "but can I trust to your keeping faith?"

"Trust!" exclaimed the other in an offended tone, and with an imperious air; "methinks you may well enough trust to the word and honour of a gentleman."

"I am content," said Mr. Russel.

The respective parties were now ordered to stand their ground, and the two leaders advanced about seventy or eighty paces each towards the middle of the open space, with their loaded guns cocked and presented at each other; and having abridged the distance that divided them to some ten or twelve paces, they halted, and the negotiation commenced. A certain sum was demanded for the restitution of the cattle. Mr. Russel had not so much money about him; but he offered to give all he had in his pocket, which amounted to a sum not a great deal short of what the robber had asked. After some little conversation this was accepted. The bargain was concluded, the money was paid, the guns were uncocked and shouldered, and the two hitherto hostile parties advanced to meet each other and to mingle together in perfect harmony.

"And now, Mr. Russel," said the leader of the band, "you must look at your beasts, to see that none of them are wanting."

"They are all here but one small dun quey," said Mr. Russel, after a minute examination of the herd.

"Ha!" cried the Highland leader, darting an angry glance of inquiry around his men, "how is this? Ewan, I would speak with you."

A tall handsome dark man, whom he had thus addressed, then moved a little way apart with him, and a conversation ensued between them in Gaelic, the sound of which could only be heard, whilst ever and anon the leader's eyes

glanced towards one or other of his people ; and his voice
and gestures indicated anything but satisfaction.   At last
he returned towards the group.

"Mr. Russel," said he, "you may make your mind easy
about the dun quey.   On the word of a gentlemen, she
shall be on your pasture before daylight to-morrow morning."

The treaty being thus happily concluded, and the cattle
taken possession of by those who were wont to have the
charge of them, Mr. Russel and the Highland leader shook
hands and parted, and each took his own way, attended by
his followers.

Clifford, interrupting the narrative, Ah ! I have a shrewd
suspicion that the cheese-shaped lump of tallow you spoke
of will turn out, after all, to have been the produce of poor
Dunny.

Author.—Have patience, and you shall hear.

We shall leave Mr. Russel and his people to return
down the glen with the rescued herd, that we may inquire
a little into the motions of the reaver and his men.   They
had no sooner threaded the mazes of the brake which shut
in the upper end of the dell that was the scene of the
strange negotiation I have described, than the leader
halted them, in order to hold a conference.

"Ewan," said he to him who seemed to act as his second
in command, "this is an awkward affair, and you have
been much to blame.   You had charge of the rear, and not
a beast should have strayed.   But your carelessness has
brought my honour into pledge ; and, by all that is good,
you must redeem it.   I have said that the dun quey shall
be on Mr. Russel's pasture in the morning ; and, dead or
alive, she must be there, for a gentleman's word must be
kept."

"I own I have not been so sharp as I should have been,"
said Ewan, with a mortified air ; "but I think I have enough
of cleverness in me to enable me to promise *you*, on the
word of a gentleman, that *your* word shall be made good."

"See that it be so, then," said the leader somewhat
sternly, as he walked slowly away up the glen.   "Take
what strength you please with you, but see that you save
both my honour and your own."

His comrades crowded around Ewan, proffering him
their friendly aid to enable him to search for and recover

the quey. But he courteously declined all their kind offers; and tightening his plaid over his body with the utmost composure, he sprang up the almost perpendicular face of the southern mountain with the agility of a deer, and disappeared over the brow of it, without permitting his breath to come much quicker there than it had done whilst he was in talk with his companions in the deep glen below.

Ewan wandered not over the moors and mosses which you see stretching over the mountain far off yonder like one who was bewildered, or like a hound at fault. Circumstances had arisen to his mind, which had afforded him some clue to the search he had undertaken; and of that clue he had at once laid hold, with a determined resolution to unravel it as speedily as possible to the end. His course, therefore, was taken at once; and it was a most direct one. You see that singular opening in the country between us and Strathspey? Perhaps you may remember that there is a narrow pass there, where a small lake fills the bottom of the defile, and where the face of the mountain that rises over it has all the appearance of having been shaven down by the sword of some giant. The strange tradition of the country indeed is, that it was done by the mighty Fingal, by way of trying the temper of a claymore which he had not yet put to the proof. Well does the weapon seem to have performed its office; and in honour of it the place has ever since been called *Beemachlai*, or the cut of the sword. Ewan then had no sooner breasted the mountain that hung over the Findhorn, than he turned his face directly southward, and took his way in a straight line for the pass; and despite of the ravines and burns, and peat-pots and moss-hags, and all the other difficulties and obstructions that lay in his road, and the darkness of the evening which settled down upon that wild hill to make all these difficulties ten times greater than they otherwise would have been, he, in a wonderfully short period of time, found himself planted in the narrow path that ran between the loch of Beemachlai, on the one hand, and the mountain that rises from its western margin on the other.

But before taking up his post, the cautious Ewan stooped down, and carefully passed his hand over the whole surface of a bare spot, of some dozen or so of square yards in

extent, which he knew must necessarily have been crossed
by every man or beast travelling that way, to ascertain
whether any fresh footprints had been made in the soft
black surface of the moss. His experience in such investigations was so great as to enable him perfectly to satisfy
himself that no animal at least had recently trodden there;
and with this assurance he stationed himself in the very
hollow of the pass, and, seated on a bank, he turned his
head towards the north, whence the path came downwards
along the base of the hill, and kept eager watch both with
eyes and ears. . The moon was at this time but young, and
the sky was partially covered with thin fleecy clouds; so
that when it did rise, it gave but a scanty and uncertain
light, though it was enough to pourtray the bold profile of
Fingal's hill on the calm bosom of the lake, as well as to
enable any one to distinguish a human figure at some little
distance.

Ewan had not remained long in this position, when he
distinctly heard the short sharp cry used by Highlanders
for urging on a bullock. It was occasionally repeated; and
by and bye it was followed by the faint sound of the footsteps of a beast and its driver, which grew upon his ear.
Ewan bent his head towards the ground, that he might
the better catch the figures of both against the sky; and
ere they had already come within fifty yards of him, he
rubbed his hands together with satisfaction to find that
his judgment had not deceived him, and starting up to
his feet, he planted himself directly in the middle of the
path, so that his figure threw a broad shadow across it;
and leaning on his gun, he calmly waited the advance of
him who came. He was a tall—nay, almost a gigantic
man, with an awkward shambling gait; and he held the
dun quey by a long halter with his left hand, whilst he
drove her on with a huge rough stick which he carried in
his right. He halted the moment that Ewan's dark
figure appeared.

" What is it that stands there? Answer, in the name
of God!" cried he in Gaelic, and in a tone that manifested
great alarm.

" Methinks a foul thief like you had little ado with any
such name, Gilliesh," replied Ewan resolutely. "What
devil tempted you to steal the dun quey from our herd?"

" What devil told you that I had stolen her?" demanded

Gilliesh, much relieved to find that he had to deal with
nothing more than mortal flesh.

"Did I not see thee lurking among the birches on the
Doun of Dulsie?" said Ewan; "and did I not know that
thou couldst be there for no good end; and when the
quey was missed, did I not put that and that together to
help my guessing, and have I not guessed rightly?"

"What an you have?" replied Gilliesh; "'tis but a poor
prize I have gotten after all, and hardly worth your tramping so far for. You had surely enough, without grudging
me this bit dwining beast."

"Such base thievery cannot be suffered," said Ewan,
"besides, I have reasons of my own for what I do. Come
away, then, and give me the rope; and bless your stars
that you escape, for this time at least, being hanged by one.
The beast must back with me, and you may take your own
way home to Dulnan side at your leisure, and thank your
good fortune that you get there in a whole skin."

"Well may you speak so bold indeed," said Gilliesh
bitterly, "with that big black gun in your hand, ready to
bring me down in a moment like a muir-cock off a hillock.
But by the great oath, ye would crack less crouse if ye
stood there before me with nothing but your claymore by
your side."

"Ye lie, ye thieving vagabond," cried Ewan, "I'll stand
at all times before you or a better man with this good
sword alone. See here, my gun shall rest against this
rock; and on the word and honour of a gentleman, I'll
never touch stock or lock of it till I shall have chastised
thee to thy heart's content, if thou wilt so have it."

"Be it so," said the crafty Gilliesh; "and I'll tether
the quey to this moss-fir stump here, and let her stand by
to see the stour, and to be the prize of him who may
prove himself to be the better man."

It would have been a sight of some interest to have
watched the preparations for this very extraordinary single
combat. On the part of Ewan they consisted merely in
his placing his gun against the rock with great tranquillity
and with great care, and then drawing his claymore from
its scabbard, and twisting the folds of his plaid tightly over
his left arm, ere he put himself into the proper position for
action. As for Gilliesh, he had no sooner tied the end of
the quey's halter to the moss-fir stump, than he drew a

broadsword of a magnitude so tremendous, as well corre-
sponded with his almost Philistian height. The bare, flat,
mossy piece of ground already noticed was the arena on
which they were to contend; and if it was free from prints
of any kind when Ewan examined it a brief space before,
it was now destined ere long to have enow of them
impressed upon it by the coming struggle. Aware of the
great advantage which Gilliesh had over him from his
superior height, and still more from the greater sweep of
his arm and sword, Ewan approached his adversary very
cautiously at first. On the other hand, numerous, and
rash, and awkward, were the cuts and the thrusts which
Gilliesh attempted to make; but they were given with a
force and a fury that rendered it necessary for Ewan to use
all the skill of which he was master, to enable him to dodge
and to parry them. Now and then their blades came into
fearful contact; and when they did so, the shearing of them
together produced a sheet of flame that gave a temporary
illumination to the deep shadow which a projecting bank
threw over that part of the lake immediately below. As
their desperate play went on, the clashing of the glowing
steel struck terror into the timid animal that had occasioned
the fight; and the powerful efforts which her fear impelled
her to make having at last burst her tether from its fasten-
ing, she fled away beyond hearing of the fray. Meanwhile,
the combat continued to rage, and as it went on the com-
batants gradually shifted their ground until they had
changed places. On the part of Gilliesh this was not done
without its intention; for no sooner did he find himself
within reach of Ewan's gun, than he seized it up, and presented it without scruple at its owner, and without one
shadow of remorse drew the trigger. But the hammer fell
harmless into the empty pan. Ewan sprang upon him in
a moment, and, ere he could recover the use of his sword,
he gave him one desperate cut across the temple
that brought him to the earth with his face bathed in
blood.

"Villain!" cried Ewan, as he stood over his prostrate
foe with the point of his sword at his throat. "Traitor
that thou art, wouldst thou have been a murderer as well
as a thief? Had not a stray stag crossed me at a distance
as I came over the hill, and tempted me to take an idle
chance shot in the twilight, when my haste would not

allow me to load again, I should have been at this moment stretched out a corpse by thy treachery."

"Spare my life!" cried the wretch piteously.

"Spare thy life!" replied Ewan contemptuously, as he quietly picked up his gun, and proceeded to load it; "I have no mind that thy worthless and cowardly life should stain this good sword of mine with dishonour, nor do I choose that it should be the means of cheating the gallows of what so justly belongs to it. Gather thyself up, then, as thou mayest, and take thy way to Dulnan side; for, by all that is good, if thou dost show thine ugly visage again to me, like a grim ghost on the moor, I'll not miss thy big body as I did that of the stray stag, but I'll open a door in it wide enough to allow thy rascally soul to issue forth and to join its kindred malignant spirits of the swamp and the fen."

With these words Ewan threw his gun over his shoulder, and set out in search of the stray heifer. It was some time before he found her, and a still longer time after he had found her before he caught her, and after he had caught her it was but the commencement of a most toilsome night with her, ere he could compel her, tired as she was, to travel through bog and mire to the place of her destination. But be this as it may, Ewan saw that the reaver's word was made good,—next morning the dun quey was seen grazing with the rest of the herd on the farm of the Aitnoch. Nobody could tell how she came there; but the eagerness with which she plucked at the pasture, and her jaded and draggled appearance, afforded sufficient evidence of the length and nature of the night journey she had been compelled to perform.

It was not very long after this that Mr. Russel happened accidentally to have ridden up to his farm here one morning, and, as he was engaged in moving about looking at his stock, his attention was attracted by a long drove of cattle, which he observed straggling up yonder opposite bank of the Dorback branch of the river Divie, to the eastward there, evidently with the intention of crossing at a ford a little way above. At first sight there appeared to be little remarkable in this, for he well knew that to be a common track, travelled by all whose route lay through this country, stretching up the south side of the Findhorn. But the drovers and their herd had no sooner passed the Dorback, and gained its western bank, and begun to advance in a direction pointing towards the course of the Findhorn, than Mr. Russel recognised the same Highland party and the same bold leader from whom he had so recently recovered his own cattle. Some of the men who were about him were led, from certain circumstances, to know that the drove of beasts which they now saw had been carried off from Gordonston, the seat of Sir Robert Gordon, about thirty miles distant in the *Laigh of Moray.* Mr. Russel was in habits of friendship with Sir Robert, and he quickly came to the resolution that he should allow no such hostile and predatory act to be done to him if he could help it, and above all that he should not facilitate it by permitting a passage for the robbers and their booty through his territory. He was here not only in the midst of his own people, but he was, moreover, in the very centre of Lord Moray's estate of Brae-Moray, of which he had the entire management, and accordingly he resolved to avail himself of these circumstances, and he determined immediately to arrest them. With this intention he hastily collected all the dependants who were within his reach, and, before the robbers came up with their booty, he found himself at the head of double their number of well-armed men.

When the party arrived within hearing, Mr. Russel hailed the leader, and at once plainly told him that he could not stand by and suffer the cattle of his friend Sir Robert Gordon to be thus harried, far less could he tamely permit them to be thus driven through his farm. He therefore called upon the robber to halt, assuring him that if he offered to advance with his party, or to persist in driving the cattle one step farther, it should be at his own peril, and he must take the consequences ; for that nothing but force should compel him to give them way.

"Mr. Russel!" cried the leader, stepping before the rest with a haughty air, "this is not what I expected from you after what has already passed between us. You stopped and recovered your own beasts, and nobody could blame you ; but, sir, it is not like a gentleman to offer to hinder me from taking cattle from anybody else."

"My principles are very different," said Mr. Russel, with great coolness.

"I tell you again," cried the little man, "that you will

5

be acting unjustly if you persevere, and that you have no right to do so."

"I am determined to persevere notwithstanding," said Mr. Russel, with great strength of emphasis and firmness of expression.

"Then, sir, I must caution you that you had better take care what you do," said the Highlander.

"I am prepared for all consequences," said Mr. Russel.

"Well, well, sir," said the Highlander frowning, "we cannot help it; you are in your own kingdom here, and you must have your own way; but, I bid you take heed— you'll rue this yet,—look well to yourself." So saying, he called to his followers in Gaelic, who, with much apparent dissatisfaction, abandoned the cattle, and the whole party took the road to the hills, muttering dark threats and half-smothered imprecations against Mr. Russel.

These denunciations were little heeded, and were probably soon forgotten by him against whom they were uttered, or if they were remembered at all it was only to produce greater vigilance on the part of those who had the charge of his stock. But it so happened that, during the course of the ensuing winter, some express business, connected with his charge of Lord Moray's affairs, carried Mr. Russel to Edinburgh. When he was on his return homewards, he arrived late one stormy and tempestuous night at the solitary inn of Dalnacacrdoch, situated, as everybody knows, at the southern extremity of that part of the great Highland road leading through the savage pass of Drumouachter. Seeing that it was quite hopeless to think of prosecuting his journey that night in such weather, he took a hasty supper and went to bed, with the resolution of rising as early next day as the lack of light at that season would permit.

He was accordingly up in the morning, and in the saddle before he could well see his horse's cars, and he set out through the snow for the inn of Dalwhinnie, situated at the northern end of the pass, attended only by a single servant. He had not proceeded far into the wild and savage part of that solitary scene, where high poles, painted black, are erected along the edge of the road to serve as beacons during winter, to prevent travellers from deviating from the road and being engulphed in the snow-wreaths, when by the light of the dawn, he descried a man, at some two or three hundred yards' distance, who came riding towards him. As he came onwards, Mr. Russel had time to remark that he exhibited a thin spare figure which was enveloped in a long dark brown cloak or greatcoat. He rode one of the loose made garrons of the country, of a dirty mouse colour, having no saddle, and no other bridle than a halter made of small birchen twigs, twisted into a sort of rope, called by the common people a *woodie.* In spite of himself, the recollection of the Highland reaver and his angry threats darted across Mr. Russel's mind ; and he was somewhat alarmed at first, when he observed that he who approached carried in his hand, poised by the middle, a very long fowling-piece, of that ancient character and description which gave our ancestors excellent hope of killing a wild duck sitting in the water half-way across a lake of half a mile broad. Mr. Russel instinctively pulled out his pistols and examined their locks, and he made his servant do the same by his ; but the inequality of such weapons, compared with that which I have this moment described, was only thereby rendered the more woefully apparent to both of them. Mr. Russel rode slowly but resolutely on however, with his eyes intently watching every motion of him who came, and who was now drawing nearer and nearer to them. The stranger himself seemed to advance cautiously ; but no sooner had he come close enough to enable him to recognise a human countenance, than he pushed up his shying steed by the application of ardent and repeated kicks ; and, when he had at length succeeded in compelling him forward, to Mr. Russel's no inconsiderable relief, he recognised in him—the landlord of the inn of Dalwhinnie !

"Keep us a', I'm glad I ha'e forgathered wi' ye in time, Mr. Russel !" he exclaimed in a south country tone and dialect, and without waiting for the ordinary preliminary salutations.

"Why, what's the matter?" demanded Mr. Russel.

"Matter !" replied the man ; "a matter o' murder, gif I'm no far mistane."

"Mercy on me ! Who has been murdered?" cried Mr. Russel.

"I didna say that ony body was murdered," answered the man ; "but, an ye persevere on your road through the pass, I'm thinkin' that somebody will be murdered."

"What makes you fancy so?" asked Mr. Russel.

"Were ye no to hae been at my hoose last night?" demanded the Dalwhinnie landlord.

"I did so intend," said Mr. Russel; "but the road turned out to be so much heavier than I had anticipated, that all I could do was to reach Dalnacaerdoch, and that at a late hour."

"It was the yespecial providence o' Heevin that you didna get forrit," said the landlord, throwing up his eyes as if in thanksgiving, "for, if you had, you would have been assuredly a cauld corp at this precious moment."

"A corpse!" exclaimed Mr. Russel, "what has put that into your head?"

"Troth, as sure as ye are noo sittin' on your horse," replied the landlord, "ye wad hae been murdered, though you had had mair lives nor a cat."

"Explain yourself, I entreat you!" said Mr. Russel.

"It's an awfu' story," said the landlord, shuddering at the mere recollection of it. "It was at the dead hour o' the night, ye see, whan we war a' sound sleepin' in our beds, we war a' alarumed wi' a sudden noise and rissellin' in the yard, an' afore we kent whar we wuz, the hoose was filled wi' better nor twa dizzen o' great muckle armed hillan'men, wi' blackit faces. Aweel! they lighted great big lunts o' moss-fir at the kitchen fire, and cam' straught to my bedside, brandishin' their pistols and durks, and lookin' as if they wad eat me up.—'Whar's Mr. Russel sleepin'?' cries they.—'Gentlemen,' says I, 'as sure as death, Mr. Russel's no in this hoose.'—'We ken better,' says they, 'we ken he was to be here this night.'—'Some mistak, gentlemen,' says I, 'I'm dootin' that ye maun hae made some mistak, for Mr. Russel's not only no here, but, an' ye'll believe me, troth I didna even expeck him.'—A' this only made them waur. They threatent and swoore at me like very rampawgin deevils, and then they begud to search ilka hole and bore and cranny and corner in the hoose; an' no contented wi' the hoose, they rummaged a' the oothooses, lookin' even into places whaur it was just simply impossible that a very cat could ha'e concealed hersel', an' forcin' me along wi' them a' the time, half naked, an' near hale dead wi' fear. And syne, whan they could find neither you nor your horses, preserve us a' what

a furious hillant yell they did set up!—they war just
a'thegither mad wi' rage and disappointment; an' some o'
them war for burnin' the very hoose, that they might mak'
sure that ye warna lurkin' somewhere aboot it after a'.
At length, a stiff, stern wee body, wha seemed to be their
captain, scelenced them in a moment; and having spoken
to them for some time in Gaelic, their violence was moderated, or rather it seemed to be converted into downright
hunger and drouth, for they begud to look for bread and
cheese, and ither eatables, and whisky, for themsel's.
Weel I wot, I gied them what they wanted wi' gude heart
and wull, houpin' to get the sooner quite o' them; and
little payment, I trow, did I expeck for my cheer. But
what think ye, sir? As I'm a sinner, they honestly paid
me every farden o' their shot afore they ga'ed awa."

"Have you any notion as to whither they went after
they left your house?" demanded Mr. Russel.

"Some o' our herds war sayin' that their tracks i' the
snaw lay towards Loch Ericht," replied the landlord; "and
gif so be the case, I'se warrant that they have darned
themsel's in some o' the queer hidy-holes aboot the craigs
there awa'. And, I'll be bailed, they'll be ready to come
back again or e'er ye ken whaur ye are, to murder you
clean oot o' hand; for surely they maun contrive somehoo
or ither to ha'e gude information."

"It is certainly most strange how they could have
known so well what my plans were," said Mr. Russel.

"Troth, sir, they're just deevils incarnate," continued
the landlord; "but ye maun on no account think o' gaein'
on, Mr. Russel, for, gif ye do, ye gang to certain death.
Gae ye yere ways back to Blair or Dunkeld, for I'm dootin'
ye'll no be safe nae gate else, and I'll send ower into
Morayshire for some o' your ain fouk, weel accoutred and
furnished, to convoy ye safe hame."

Mr. Russel was no coward, but he well knew the nature
of the Highlanders he had to deal with. And what could
the pistols of two men do against two dozen of well-armed
assassins, springing on them at unawares by the way, or
attacking them in their beds? After some little consideration, therefore, he deemed it most prudent to take the
landlord's advice; and, accordingly, after he had thanked
the honest fellow for the zeal he had manifested for his
safety, and after the landlord had looked suspiciously

around him and scanned the faces of the hills to their very tops with strong signs of apprehension, earnestly praying to God that their interview might not have been overlooked and watched by any of the robbers or their spies, they parted; and Mr. Russel and his servant retraced their steps at a good round pace.

After nearly a week's delay at Dunkeld, Mr. Russel was enabled to renew his journey at the head of a well-armed party of between thirty and forty of his own people, who came to escort him. They travelled along with great caution, but they did not perceive the smallest show of hostility till they got into the middle of the Pass of Drumouachter. Then, indeed, they observed that they were reconnoitred from the rough face of one of the hills overhanging the road, by a body of more than twenty armed mountaineers. They seemed to have issued from the recesses of one of those *Corries*, or ravines, which there yawn over the valley like gashes on the lofty brow of a warrior; and after some minutes apparently spent in consultation, they began to move along the steep acclivity in a line parallel to the road which Mr. Russel pursued. Their dark tartans waved in the wind, and their figures were boldly relieved against the glazed and brilliant surface of the snow they trod on. A certain degree of hesitation seemed to mark all their movements, which appeared to have a manifest reference to those of the party below. Mr. Russel marched on with a steady and resolute pace, his men keeping a sharp lookout in all directions, and being perfectly prepared to resist any sudden attack. But the mountaineers, being conscious of an inferiority of strength which rendered any open attempt on their part quite hopeless, did not venture to assault so large and so well armed a band. After skirting along the hill-sides for five or six miles, they seemed gradually to slacken their pace, till the whole body came to a halt on a prominent point of the mountain, where they remained, following Mr. Russel and his people with their eyes, and probably with their curses also, so long as they remained within sight. Mr. Russel thought it prudent to halt but for a short time at Dalwhinnie; and well was it for him that he did not tarry there all that night, for the house was again surrounded and searched by an overwhelming force, whilst Mr. Russel was urging his way homewards with an expedition that enabled him to reach his residence in perfect safety.

Whether a natural or accidental death, or some other cause, put an end to any further attempts on the part of the vindictive mountaineer, I know not; but certain it is, that Mr. Russel was never more troubled either by him or by his people.

SCENERY OF THE FINDHORN.

Clifford.—In justice to your story, I must say that it is much more interesting than the scene where it was enacted, if we may judge from the specimen at this moment before us.

Grant.—Nay, but take the trouble to carry your eyes entirely over the foreground, and behold the sun gleaming afar off yonder on the broad sheet of the Moray Firth, with those bold dark headlands called the Sutors defending the entrance of the Bay of Cromarty beyond, backed by the blue mountains of Ross-shire and Sutherland in the distance.

Clifford.—These are indeed features that would give dignity to any scene; but you must admit that this unmeaning flat which stretches everywhere from under our feet is sufficiently tiresome, notwithstanding the laudable efforts that are making to cover it with plantations.

Author.—It is monotonous enough, to be sure; but how often do we find inestimable worth concealed under an unpretending exterior. The apparently dull stretch of country before you is a pregnant example of this; for the charms of the river Findhorn that bisects it from west to east are so buried in its bosom as to be quite overlooked from hence. Grant will tell you, that if you were to follow the river upwards through all the mazes of its deep and shadowy glen, you would find that it exhibits scenery of the wildest and most magnificent character.

Grant.—Nay, it is hardly fair to refer him to me; for although I have a full impression of its grandeur upon my mind which will not easily be effaced, I can give him no very accurate account of its pools or its streams, as regards their excellence for salmon angling.

Clifford.—Pho! none of your jokes, Mr. Grant. Although I like fishing and shooting, you know very well that I enjoy wild nature as much as either of you.

Grant.—Ha! ha! ha! I know you do, my dear fellow.

Clifford.—And, moreover, I have so much admired the scenery, as well as the fishing-pools of the river lower down, that if what you now speak of equals that with which I am already so familiar, it must be magnificent indeed.

Author.—I think that it in many respects surpasses all that you have hitherto seen. In truth, I know no river scenery in Great Britain at all to be compared in sublimity to that of the Findhorn about Ferness. Indeed, it rises more into that great scale of grandeur exhibited by some of the Swiss gorges than anything I have ever met with at home. But you must take the first opportunity of visiting it, Clifford. And then, in addition to the treat that nature will yield you during your ramble, and the good fishing which you will certainly have, I think you will be much gratified by the inspection of that interesting relic of antiquity, *The Cairn and Pillar of the Lovers,* which you will find there.

Clifford.—What! ha! ha! ha! some Pyramus and Thisbe, —some Petrarch and Laura,—among your heroes and heroines of the pemmican, I suppose!

Author.—No, no. The lonely obelisk, and the cairn from which it rises, may indeed have stood on the green holm of Ferness, with the rapid Findhorn sweeping around them, for ages. They may have been there whilst the great forests still spread themselves thickly over the country, but you would judge wrong if you supposed them to have co-existed with my savages of the pemmican; for there must have been some considerable approach to civilisation amongst a people who could have cut and transported that great mass of rough-grained sandstone, of which the obelisk is formed, from the nearest quarries of the same rock, some fifteen or twenty miles off, to the spot where it has ever since stood, not to mention the beautiful hieroglyphical carvings with which it has been ornamented.

Clifford.—Is there no legend attached to the monument?

Grant.—There is; and our friend has woven it into a little poem, which he once repeated to me.

Clifford.—Poem! come, let's have it! You need not fear to give it to me now, you know; for there is no birch at hand to punish you for your false quantities.

Author.—To tell you the truth, I am quite tired of repeating the story in prose; so, lame though my stanzas may be, I shall prefer risking your criticism. But you must remember, that it is one thing to climb a rugged heathery hill like this, and another thing to mount Parnassus.

THE CAIRN OF THE LOVERS.

THE raven of Denmark stretched his broad wing,
 And shot his dark flight o'er Moray's fair fields ;
And Findhorn's wild echoes were heard to ring
 With ill-omened croak, and the clash of shields.
  And the yelling shouts of the conflict broil,
  As Dane and Scot met in mortal toil,—
  And cruel and fierce was the battle tide
  That raged on rocky Findhorn's side ;
  And red was his wave, as it wailed away,
  By that plain where his slaughtered warriors lay.

Yet stark stern in death was each hero's frown !
 Each fell not till crushed by an hundred foes !
But, though hordes of Norsemen had borne them down,
 Dire vengeance had soothed their dying throes.
  For the bloody fight had not been won
  Till drooped to the west the slanting sun,
  And his golden beams a bright glory shed
  Around each dying hero's head,
  And lighted his soul with a cheering ray,
  E'er his dim eye closed on the parting day.

But Findhorn's dark heights, and his wizzard wave,
 Were lighted anon by far fiercer rays,
Calling bosoms abroad, that beat warm and brave,
 To muster around the tall beacon's blaze.
  And now, as afar o'er the plains they look,
  Where glistens with flame each winding brook, '
  Red ruin enwraps both tower and town,
  . And wild Norsemen's shouts reach the beacon Doun;
  And by shrieks of woe their hearts are wrung,
  Till each Scottish breast to revenge is strung.

Whose steed-tramp resounds down the woody glen ?
 Who bears, as he rides, his proud crest so high,

His brow circled with gems, as chief of men,
  And gold shining bright on his panoply?
     'Tis Fergus the King! The broad signal fire,
     And the Norsemen's ravage, have roused his ire;
     And, see how his clustering horsemen sweep
     From the forest dark and the dingle deep!
     And, hark to the tread of the many feet
    That crowd to those heights where the waters meet!

Full little does Sewyn, the Norse King, know,
  As his ruthless Danes rifle the peaceful plain,
That the Pass of the Dhuie conceals a foe
  Of far other mould than the shepherd swain.
     And far other herds, and far other flocks
     Than shepherds may feed, lie hid by these rocks.
     He doubts not but all who a spear could wield
     Have fall'n in the strife of one bloody field.
     Onward he presses, and, blindly led,
    Go his Norsemen, with hopes of plunder fed.

The current was rapid, the stream was deep,
  And the cumbered waters foamed high and flashed,
As horsemen and foot, from the shore so steep,
  Through the Dhuie in thick confusion dashed.
     But scarce were they rid of the rushing tide,
     Nor yet had they formed on the meadow's side,
     When by bursting yells the skies were rent,
     With the gleam of arms glowed the firmament,
     And down, like the lightning's fiery shower,
    Came King Fergus' force on King Sewyn's power.

And quailed the black raven of Denmark then,
  And he cowered his wing, and he croaked his fear;
And wide with the eagle's scream rang the glen,
  As eager she snuffed up her feast so near;
     And each Norseman's heart, though ne'er so bold,
     With panic-dread grew sick and cold,
     Nor dared they abide the battle shock,
     But fled away like some startled flock,
     Or some scattered herd of timid deer,
    When the howl of the gaunt mountain wolves they
      hear.

Bu slaughter was wide, and the vengeance deep,
　　hat the Moray-men took of their Danish foes;
　yet deeper revenge did Findhorn reap
As high, in his anger, his billows rose.
　　For he had wailed that his wave before
　　The dye of his children's life's-blood bore;
　　But now, full glutted with hostile dead,
　　He reared him aloft, shook his oak-crowned head,
　　And, roaring with fearful revelry,
　　He swept off his spoils to his kindred sea.

Who sits her and sighs on the castled isle
　　That on Loch-an-Dorbe's dark breast doth float?
And why lights her eye with a radiant smile
　　As the moonbeam falls soft on that little boat?
　　A fairy thing it seems to be,
　　It glides o'er the wave so silently;
　　And like such sprites of witching power
　　It vanished beneath a shadowy tower,
　　As its slender side lost the moonbeam's ray,
　　Nor left it one trace of its liquid way.

That maiden who sat in the castled isle
　　Scanned that little boat with no idle gaze;
And I ween that her eyes with their radiant smile
　　Had hope blent with love in their glowing rays.
　　Malvina she was that maiden fair,
　　King Fergus' daughter, who sat her there.
　　She's gone!—and her pulse may hardly beat,
　　As in silence move her trembling feet
　　To the dungeon where lonely her lover lies,
　　And wastes the night in despairing sighs,
　　The son of King Sewyn in battle ta'en,
　　The gallant Prince Harrold, the brave young Dane.

She unlocked the bolts with a master key,
　　And Prince Harrold sprang forth to his lady's side.
"Love favours our flight!" softly whispered she,
　　"At the postern stairs doth the boat abide."
　　Then they stole away by the shadowy wall.
　　Yet she sighed to quit her father's hall,
　　And her bosom heaved, and she dropped a tear,
　　Whilst her lover essayed to hush her fear,

And she clung to his arm as the little boat
Did o'er the wide lake in silence float.

'Twas a right trusty page that gave them way,
  And he landed them 'neath the greenwood tree,
Where tied to the oak was a courser grey;
  Prince Harrold to saddle sprang merrily.
    The fair Malvina behind him placed,
    With snow-white arms her lover embraced.
    The sun rose to welcome the bonny bride,
    As they fled them straight to the Findhorn's side;
    But its stream was swollen and barred their flight,
  And drove them for refuge to Dulsie's height.

" Go, bring me Prince Harrold," King Fergus cried,
  His royal eyes sparkling with beams of joy,
" My daughter Malvina shall be his bride,
  And Moray be freed from the Dane's annoy.
    Envoy to me hath King Sewyn sent,
    And peace shall their bridal knot cement."
    But Harrold was gone and Malvina fair !
    Yet a sharp-witted page could teach him where,
    And quick spoke the boy; for the King had told
  Such glad tidings, I ween, as made him bold.

" To boat !" cried King Fergus, with eager haste,
  And—" To horse !" when he touched the farther shore,
And furious he spurred through the forest waste,
  As to Findhorn's stream his swift course he bore.
    The lovers from Dulsie's wooded height
    Saw Moray's lord coming in kingly might.
    'Twas better to tempt the swollen tide,
    Than captive be torn from his bonny bride.
    Harrold lifted Malvina to saddle again,
  And down Dulsie's slope urged his steed amain.

Oh, Findhorn shrieked loud to warn them away !
  But louder yet did the water-fiends yell,
Rebellious they laughed at his empty sway,
  As vainly he strove their wild rage to quell.
    And the sire's despairing cry was vain,
    " Malvina ! my child ! oh, turn again !"

But the lovers, twined on the courser grey,
Were swept from his outstretchd eyes away,
And he smote his bosòm and tore his hair
As adown the big stream he sought the pair.

Why tarries the knight in his lonely way
  At yon cairn on flowery Ferness holm ?
Why scans he yon pillar, so rough and grey,
  That rises from out its rudely-heaped dome ?
      'Twas there the love-twined youth and maid,
      Unsevered in death, were sadly laid ;
      And there did King Fergus and Sewyn weep
      When they found them locked in death's cold sleep,
      And Findhorn still lingers around their grave,
  And sighs for their fate with repentant wave.

HILL OF THE AITNOCH.

Author.—See now how innumerable the stumps of the trees are here. They are peeping up through the moss in every direction. Conceive what a thick pine wood this must have once been.

Grant.—You were certainly guilty of no great exaggeration when you said that a deer could hardly have penetrated it whilst it was standing in all its gloomy grandeur.

Clifford.—It is well for our comfort that we can now pass so easily over its fallen majesty; and methinks the sooner we escape from so dreary a scene the better.

Author.—Let us keep more this way, then. A short walk will now bring us to the southern brow of the hill, whence a new scene will open on us.

Clifford, who first reaches the point.—Ha! what have we here? A dark lake,—its waves rolling sluggishly eastward, and breaking gently on a narrow stripe of yellow gravelly beach,—bare rocky hills without a tree,—and an island covered with the ruins of a very extensive castle. What do you call this wild and lonely scene?

Author.—That is Loch-an-Dorbe, with its ruined castle.

Grant.—The remains of the castle seem to be very extensive.

Author.—They are said to occupy a space of not less than an hundred yards square.

Clifford.—This, then, is the very castle whence your Danish prince escaped with his lady-love. Let me tell you, that if their grey steed had not gone with a somewhat freer pace than your verses do, the old king of the castle would have caught them ere they had covered half the way to Dulsie.

Grant.—I'll warrant me those huge round towers and massive curtains have many strange and eventful histories attached to them.

Clifford.—Come, Signore Cicerone, prelect to us about t, if you please.

i

Author.—Loch-an-Dorbe was one of the few royal or national fortresses which Scotland possessed. When Edward the First traversed this country with his army in 1303, he came to Loch-an-Dorbe in the month of September, and occupied it for some time; and Edward the Third considered it as a place of so much importance, that he and Edward Baliol marched all the way from Perth to its relief in August, 1336, when Catherine de Beaumont, widow of David de Hastings, Earl of Athol, and her son were besieged in it by the brave Sir Andrew Moray, then Governor of Scotland. Sir Andrew would have been overwhelmed by the superior force of the English monarch, had he not baffled pursuit by crossing the river Findhorn at the celebrated pass, the Brig of Randolph, so called, as you know, from Randolph, Earl of Moray, Regent of Scotland. Another important historical fact is connected with this castle. It was here that William Bullock was confined. After abandoning the cause of Baliol, and after having risen to high honours under David the Second, he was enviously and maliciously accused of treason; and having been thrown into one of the dungeons within these massive walls, he was cruelly allowed to perish of cold and hunger. We also know that the famous Alexander Stewart, son of King Robert the Second, and who, from his ferocious disposition, was surnamed the Wolf of Badenoch, possessed and inhabited this castle. It was from hence he is supposed to have issued when he made his famous descent into the low country of Moray, and fired the Cathedral of Elgin, reducing that magnificent structure, that *speculum patriæ et decus regni*, as it was called, and many other religious edifices in the town, to a heap of ruins.

Clifford.—Oh, you have told us enough, in all conscience, about that wild beast; "*adesso parliamo d'altro.*"

Author.—I am at a stand, so far as the history of Loch-an-Dorbe is concerned, excepting that I may add, that in more recent times it was possessed by the Earls of Moray, and passed from their hands into those of the Campbells of Cawdor, and thence to the Grants of Grant. I have seen at Cawdor Castle a massive iron gate, believed to have been that of the Castle of Loch-an-Dorbe, which tradition says was carried off from thence by Sir Donald Campbell of Cawdor, who bore it on his back all the way

across the moors till he set it down where it is now in use,
the distance being not less than some twelve or fifteen
miles. But this is a story much too marvellous for belief
in these matter-of-fact days of ours.

Clifford.—It is incredible enough, to be sure. Yet I
have a story, a well authenticated story too, which I think
will almost match it.

Grant.—Out with it then.

Clifford.—No, I promise you you don't get my stories
at so very easy a rate; and for this simple reason, that
they are by no means so plenty as yours. Besides, I have
just been thinking that with this warm breeze, that so
gently ripples the surface of the lake, I could kill a
handsome dish of trouts this afternoon, if trouts there be
within its watery world. Why might we not loiter off
the remainder of the day about this lake?

Grant.—I like the idea much. I perceive a nice looking
cottage on the other side, where I dare to say we may
find lodging for the night.

Author.—That cottage is a shooting-lodge belonging to
the proprietor; and were he there in person, we should
not lack a kind and hospitable reception. But at present
its doors are locked, and its rooms void.

Clifford.—There is a house, then, here on the nearer
shore, immediately below us; why should we not go there?

Author.—'Tis but a smoky uncomfortable place; but it
may do well enough for a shelter for one night, and if
you are content to abide there, so am I.

Clifford.—Pho! as to comfort, I am a soldier, and can
rough it. I have lain out all night to kill the enemies
of my country, and would do no less at any time for a
good day's shooting or fishing.

Author, addressing gilly, who was leading a pony with
panniers,—Go down thither, then, and see our quarters
made as comfortable as may be.

Clifford.—Aye, that will do. Come along, let us to work
without more hesitation or talk. I am all impatience.

Having sent round to borrow the proprietor's boat, we
embarked on the lake, and were soon intensely occupied
in all the exciting anxieties of the angle. Our success
was various and unequal, like that of man in the great
lottery of human life. It was not always when basking
in the sunshine that we were most successful. Sometimes

G

a warm shadow would cross the lake, and the trouts would rise and hook themselves three at a time on our lines. The bottom of the boat became alive, and shone and glittered with the growing numbers of our golden and silver captives. Anon, every cast we made was in vain; and then, when the foolish fish began again to bite, our eagerness was such, that we forgot each other's lines; and the loss of hooks, the destruction of the finer parts of our tackle, and the fracture of delicate top pieces, became the result of our numerous and grievous entanglements. Poor Clifford could not account for a sudden cessation of his luck at the very time that ours appeared to be doubled, and he went on in no very good humour, flogging the water unsuccessfully, whilst Grant and I were catching two and three at each cast; till at last, to his great chagrin, he found that he had been all the while fishing without flies, which were uselessly and most provokingly sticking in the rough coat and around the neck and head of my great Newfoundland dog Bronte, to the poor brute's great inconvenience. He did not fail to make up very quickly for this bad luck, however. Our evening was altogether most delightfully spent; for when we grew tired of the angle, we landed on the island, and wandered among the extensive ruins which cover it. We then sat on the mouldering walls of the castle till we saw the sun sink behind the western hill; after which we returned to the shore, and sought our place of retreat.

It was a small old-fashioned house, once used as a sort of hunting lodge. It consisted of two stories, with little else than one ruinous room in each, the whole being filled with the great smoke that arose from the kitchen fire. But the exercise we had had, added to our hunger, prepared us for being pleased with any accommodation; and after a supper well eked out by a fritto of the delicious trouts we had taken, we drew our stools around the fire, to enjoy a temperate cup of pure Highland whisky, diluted with water from a neighbouring spring.

Grant.—Now for your story, Clifford.

Clifford.—'Tis of a famous Highlander, called John Mackay, of Ross-shire. I got the narrative, with all its nationalities, from an old Scottish brother officer of mine, a certain major of the name of Macmillan, who knew the hero of it well.

Grant.—I should have hardly looked for such a story from a Sassenach like you.

Clifford.—Tut. You know very well that my mother was a Highlandwoman, and that I have moreover always had a strong feeling for Scotland, and especially for the Highlands, as well as for everything connected with these romantic regions, where, let me tell you, I have had some wanderings as well as you.

Author.—We admit your right to tell your story. So now, come away with it without further preface.

Clifford.—If I tell you anything, I must very nearly tell you all honest John's life. Have you patience for so long a narrative?

Grant.—We shall give you the full duration of the burning of these moss-fir faggots. Will that serve you?

Clifford.—I think my story will have expired before them. And by that time we shall all be nearly ready for our blankets and heather; for such, I presume, will be our fate to-night.

LEGEND OF JOHN MACKAY OF ROSS-SHIRE, CALLED IAN MORE ARRACH, OR BIG JOHN THE RENTER OF THE MILK OF THE COWS.

My old Highland major told me, what perhaps you know better than I do, I mean, that some half century or more ago, before sheep were quite so much in fashion in the Highlands as I believe they now are, and when cattle were the only great staple of the country, the proprietors of the glens had them always well filled with cows. In those times it was the custom in Ross-shire to allow one calf only to be reared for each two cows of the herd. Each calf with its pair of cows was called a *Cauret;* and these caurets were let to renters, who, as they might find it most advisable, took one or more of them in lease, as it were, according as their circumstances might dictate; and the renter being obliged to rear one calf for the landlord for each cauret he held, he was allowed the remainder of the milk for his own share of the profit. These milk-renters were called *arrachs;* and John Mackay, the hero of my story, was called Ian More Arrach, from his lofty stature, and from his being one of these milk-renters. According to my informant the major, who personally knew him, Ian well merited the addition of More; for he declared that he was the most powerful man he had ever beheld.

It so happened that Ian went down on one occasion into Strath-Connan, to attend a great market or fair that was held there, probably to dispose of his cheese; and as he was wandering about after his business was over, his eye was caught, exactly like those of some of our simple trouts of the lake here, by the red and tinsel, and silk and wool, and feather glories of a recruiting sergeant and his party. He had never seen anything of the kind before, and he stood staring at them in wonderment as they passed. Nor did his solid and substantial form fail to fill the sergeant's eye in its turn; but if I am to give you a simile illustrative of the manner in which it did so, I must say that it was in the same way that the plump form of a well-fed trout might fill the greedy eye of a gaunt pike. He resolved to have him as a recruit. The party was accordingly halted immediately opposite to the spot where Ian was standing; and after one or two shrill shrieks of the fife, and a long roll of the drum, the martial orator began an oration, which lasted a good half-hour, in which he largely expatiated on the glories of a soldier's life, and the riches and honours it was certain one day or other to shower on the heads of all those who embraced it. The greater part of this harangue was lost upon Ian More Arrach, partly because he but very imperfectly understood English, and partly because his senses were too much lost in admiration. But when the grand scarlet-coated gentleman approached him with a smiling air, and gaily slapping him on the back, exclaimed,—

"Come along with us, my brave fellow, and taste the good beef and mustard, and other provender, that King George so liberally provides for us gentlemen of his army, and drink his Majesty's health with us in his own liquor. Come, and see how jollily we soldiers live !"

His wits returned to him at once, and he quickly understood enough of what was said to him, to make him grin from ear to ear, till every tooth in his head was seen to manifest its own particular unmingled satisfaction, and his morning's walk from his distant mountain residence having wonderfully sharpened his appetite, he followed the sergeant into a booth with all manner of alacrity, and quietly took his seat at a table that groaned beneath an enormous round of beef, flanked by other eatables, on which the hungry recruits fell pell-mell, and in demolishing which Ian rendered them his best assistance. The booth or tent was constructed, as such things usually are, of some old blankets stitched together, and hung over a cross-stick, that was tied horizontally to the tops of two poles fixed upright in the ground. It was the ambulatory tavern of one of those travelling ale and spirit sellers who journey from one fair or market to another, for the charitable purpose of vending their victuals and drink to the hungry and thirsty who can afford to pay for them.

The space around the interior of the worsted walls of this confined place was occupied with boxes, vessels, and barrels of various kinds; and whilst the landlord, a knock-kneed cheeseparing of a man, who had once been a tailor, sat at his ease in one corner reckoning his gains, his wife, a fat, bustling, red-nosed little woman, was continually running to and fro to serve the table with liquor. Many were the loyal toasts given, and they were readily drank by Ian, more, perhaps, from relish of the good stuff that washed them down, than from any great perception he had of their intrinsic merit. His head was by no means a weak one. But the sergeant and his assistants were too well acquainted with all the tricks of their trade not to take such measures as made him unwittingly swallow three or four times as much liquor as they did.

"Now, my gallant Highlander," exclaimed the sergeant, when he thought him sufficiently wound up for his purpose, "see how nobly his Majesty uses us. Starve who may, we never want for plenty. But this is not all. Hold out your hand, my brave fellow. See, here is a shilling with King George's glorious countenance upon it. He sends you this in his own name, as a mark of his especial favour and regard for you."

"Fod, but she wonders tat sae big an' braw a man as ta King wad be thinkin' on Ian Arrach at a', at a'," said the Highlander, surveying the shilling as it lay in the palm of his hand; "but troth, she wonders a hantel mair, tat sin King Shorge was sendin' ony sing till her ava, she didna send her a guinea fan her hand was in her sporran at ony rate. But sic as it be, he taks it kind o' ta man," and saying so, he quietly transferred into his own sporran that which he believed to have come from the King's.

"That shilling is but an arnest of all the golden guineas he will by and bye give you," said the sergeant; "not to mention all those bags of gold, and jewels, and watches which he will give you his gracious leave to take from his enemies, after you shall have cut their throats."

"Tut, tut, but she no be fond o' cuttin' trotts," replied Ian; "she no be good at tat trade at a', at a'."

"Ha! no fears but you will learn that trade fast enough," said the sergeant. "You mountaineers generally do. You are raw yet; but wait till you have beheld my glorious example — wait till you have seen me sheer off half a dozen heads or so, as I have often done, of a morning before breakfast, and you will see that there is nothing more simple."

"Och, och," exclaimed Ian, with a shrug of his shoulders that spoke volumes.

"Aye, aye," continued the sergeant, "'tis true you cannot expect that at the very first offer you are to be able to take off your heads quite so clean at a blow as I can do. Indeed, I am rather considered a rare one at taking off heads. For example, I remember that I once happened to take a French grenadier company in flank, when, with the very first slash of my sword, I cut clean through the necks of the three first file of men, front rank and rear rank, making no less than six heads off at the first sweep. And it was well for the company that they happened only to be formed two deep at the time, for if they had been three deep, no less than nine heads must have gone."

"Keep us a'!" cried some of the wondering recruits.

"Nay," continued the sergeant; "had it not been for the unlucky accident that by some mistake the fourth front rank man was a leetle shorter than the other, so that the sword encountered his chin-bone, the fourth file would have been beheaded like the rest."

"Och, och!" cried Ian again.

"But," continued the sergeant, "as I said before, though you cannot expect to take up this matter by nattral instinck, as it were, yet I'll be bail that a big stout souple fellow like you will not see a month's sarvice before you will shave off a head as easily as I shave this here piece of cheese, and—— confound it, I have cut my thumb half through."

"Her nanesell wunna be meddlin' wi' ony siccan bluidy wark," said Ian, shaking his head, and shrugging his shoulders. "She no be wantan' to be a boutcher. But, noo," added he, lifting up a huge can of ale, "she be biddin' ye a' gude evenin', shentilmans, and gude hells, and King Shorge gude hells, an' mony sanks to ye a'; and tell King Shorge she sall keep her bit shullin' on a string tied round her neck for a bonny die." And so rising up, Ian put the ale can to his head, and drained it slowly to the bottom.

"But, my good fellow," said the sergeant, who had

been occupied, whilst Ian's draught lasted, in tying up
his thumb in a handkerchief and giving private signals
to his party, "you are joking about bidding us good
evening—we cannot part with you so soon."

"Troth she maun be goin' her ways home," said Ian,
"she has a far gate to traivil."

"Stuff!" cried the sergeant; "surely you cannot have
forgotten that you have taken King George's money,
and that you have now the great privilege of holding
the honourable and lucrative situation of a gentleman
private in his Majesty's infantry, having been duly and
volunteerly enlisted before all these here witnesses."

"Ou, na," said Ian gravely and seriously; "she didna
list—na, na, she didna list; troth na. So wussin' ta
gude company's gude hells wanss more, an' King Shorge's
hells, she maun just be goin' for she has a lang gate o'
hill afore her."

"Nay, master, we can't exactly part with you so easily,"
said the sergeant, rising up. "You are my recruit, and
you must go nowhere without my leave."

"Hoot, toots," replied Ian, making one step towards
the door of the booth; "an' she has her nane leave, troth,
she'll no be axan' ony ither."

"I arrest you in the King's name!" said the sergeant,
laying hold of Ian by the breast.

"Troth, she wudna be wussin' to hort her," said Ian,
lifting up the sergeant like a child before he knew where
he was; "but sit her doon tere, oot o' ta way, till her
nanesell redds hersell of ta lave, and wuns awa'."

Making two strides with his burden towards a large
cask of ale that stood on end in one corner of the place,
he set the gallant hero down so forcibly on the top of it,
that the crazy rotten boards gave way, and he was
crammed backwards, in a doubled up position, into the
yawning mouth of the profound, whilst surges of beer
boiled and frothed up around him. Ian would have
charitably relieved the man from so disagreeable a situation,
which was by no means that which he had intended him
to occupy; but, ere he wist, he was assailed by the whole
party like a swarm of bees. The place of strife was
sufficiently narrow, a circumstance much in favour of
the light troops who now made a simultaneous movement
on him, with the intention of prostrating him on the

ground, but he stood like a colossus, and nothing could budge him; whilst, at the same time, he never dealt a single blow as if at all in anger, but ever and anon, as his hands became so far liberated as to enable him to seize on one of his assailants, he wrenched him away from his own person, and tossed him from him, either forth of the tent door, or as far at least as its bounds would allow, some falling among the hampers and boxes—some falling like a shower upon the poor owners of the booth—and some falling upon the unfortunate sergeant. The red-nosed priestess of this fragile temple of Bacchus shrieked in sweet harmony with the groans of the knock-kneed and broken-down tailor, and in the midst of the melee, one unhappy recruit, who was winging his way through the air from the powerful projectile force of Ian More, came like a chain-shot against the upright poles of the tent—the equilibrium of its whole system was destroyed—down came the cross-beam—the covering blankets collapsed and sank,—and, in a moment, nothing appeared to the eyes of those without but a mighty heap, that heaved and groaned underneath like some volcanic mountain in labour previous to an eruption. And an eruption to be sure there was; for, to the great astonishment of the whole market people, Ian More Arrach's head suddenly appeared through a rent that took place in the rotten blanket, with his face in a red hot state of perspiration, and his mouth gasping for breath. After panting like a porpoise for a few seconds, he made a violent effort, reared himself upon his legs, and thrusting his feet out at the aperture which had served as a door to the tent, he fled away with all the effect of a fellucca under a press of sail, buffeting his way through the multitude of people and cattle, as a vessel would toss aside the opposing billows; and then shooting like a meteor up the side of the mountain that flanked the strath, he left his flowing drapery behind him in fragments and shreds adhering to every bush he passed by, bounded like a stag over its sky line, and disappeared from the astonished eyes of the beholders.

It were vain to attempt to describe the re-organisation of the discomfited troops, who, when their strange covering was thus miraculously removed, arose singly from the ground utterly confounded, and began to move about limping and cursing amidst the bitter wailings of the unhappy people whose frail dwelling had so marvellously fled from them. The attention of the party was first called to their gallant commander, who, with some difficulty, was extracted from the mouth of the beer barrel, dripping like a toast from a tankard. His rage may be conceived better than told. His honour had been tarnished, and his interest put in jeopardy. He, whose stirring tales of desperate deeds of arms and fearful carnage had so often extended the jaws of the Highland rustics whom he had kidnapped, and raised their very bonnets on the points of their bristling hair with wonder,—who could devour fire as it issued from the mouth of a cannon,—and who could contend single-handed against a dozen of foes, to be so unceremoniously crammed, by the arm of one man, into a beer barrel, in the presence of those very recruits, and to be afterwards basely extracted from it before the eyes of the many who had listened to his boastful harangues. And then, moreover, to be choused out of the anticipated fruits of his wily hospitality, as well as of a silver shilling, by the flight of the broad-shouldered Celt, whom he thought he had! secured, and of whom he expected to have made so handsome a profit. All this was not to be borne, and, accordingly, wide as was Ross-shire, he determined most indefatigably to search every inch of it until he should again lay hands on him. From the inquiries made on the spot, it was considered as certain that Ian More had gone directly home to his lonely bothy, in a high and solitary valley some dozen of miles or so from the place where they then were; and as one of the recruits knew the mountain tracks well enough to act as guide, he collected the whole of his forces, amounting to nearly double the number of those who had been engaged in the battle of the booth, and after having refreshed and fortified them and himself with all manner of available stimuli, he put himself at their head, and set forward on his expedition at such an hour of the night as might enable them to reach the dwelling of Ian More Arrach before he was likely to leave it in the morning in pursuit of his daily occupation.

Ian More was but little acquainted with the tricks of this world; and no wonder, for the habitation in which he lived, and from which he rarely migrated, was situated in

one of those desert glens which are to be found far up in
the mountains, where they nurse and perhaps give birth
to the minuter branches of those streams, which, running
together in numbers, and accumulating as they roll onwards through wider and larger valleys, go on expanding
with the opening country until they unite to water the
extended and fertile plains in some broad and important
river. The ascent to the little territory of which Ian
More was the solitary sovereign was by a steep and narrow
ravine among rocks, down which the burn raged against
the opposing angles, like a wayward child that frets and
fumes against every little obstacle that occurs to the indulgence of its wishes. Higher up its course was cheerful
and placid, like the countenance of the same child, perhaps,
when in the best humour and in the full enjoyment for
the time being of all its desires, laughing as it went its
way among water-lilies, ranunculuses, and yellow mari-
golds, meandering quietly through a deep and well-swarded
soil that arose from either side of it in a gently curving
slope to the base of two precipitous walls of rock, within
the shelter of which the caurets of Ian More had ample
pasture for a stretch of about a quarter of a mile upwards
to the spot where the cliffs, rising in altitude, and apparently unscalable, shut in the glen in a natural amphitheatre. There the burn issued from a small circular
lochan ; and it was on the farther margin of this piece of
water, and immediately at the foot of the crags behind it,
that the small sod hovel of Ian More Arrach was placed,
so insignificant a speck amid the vastness of the surrounding features of nature as to be hardly distinguished from
the rock itself, especially when approached, as it now was,
in the grey light of the morning, until the sergeant and his
party had come very near to it.

The leader of the enterprise felt that no time was to be
lost in a survey, lest, whilst they were hesitating, Ian
might perceive them, and again make his escape. A simultaneous rush, therefore, was made for the door ; but,
albeit that Ian generally left it unfastened, he had somehow or other been led to secure it on this occasion, by
lifting a stone of no ordinary size, which usually served
him as a seat, and placing it as a barricade against it on
the inside. Their first attempt to force it being thus rendered altogether unavailing,—

"John Mackay, otherwise Ian More Arrach, open to us in the name of King George," cried the sergeant, standing at the full length of his pike from the door, and poking against it with the point of the weapon.

"Fat wud King Shorge hae wi' Ian More," demanded the Highlander.

"Come, open the door and surrender peaceably," cried the sergeant; "you are the King's lawful recruit. You have been guilty of mutiny and desartion; but if you will surrender at discretion, and come quietly along with us, it is not unlikely that, in consideration of your being as yet untaught, and still half a savage, you may not be exactly shot this bout, though it is but little marcy you desarve, considering how confoundedly my back aches with the rough treatment I had from you. Keep close to the door, my lads," continued he, sinking his voice, "and be ready to spring on him the moment he comes out."

Whilst the sergeant yet spoke, the whole hovel began to heave like some vast animal agonised with internal throes. The men of the party stood aghast for one moment, and in the next the back wall of the sod edifice was hurled outwards, and the roof, losing its support, fell inwards, raising a cloud of dust so dense as utterly to conceal for a time the individual who was the cause and instrument of its destruction.

"Ha! look sharp, my lads!" cried the sergeant; "be on your mettle!"

The words were scarcely out of his mouth when the herculean form of Ian More arose before his eyes from amidst the debris and dust, as did the figure of the Genii from the jar before those of the fisherman in the Eastern fable.

"There he is, by Jupiter!" cried the sergeant, involuntarily retreating a step or two. "On him—on him, and seize him, my brave boys!"

The nature of the spot seemed to forbid all hope of escape. The party blocked up the space in front of the bothy, and the narrow stripe of ground that stretched along between the lake on the one hand, and the cliffs on the other, grew more and more confined as it ran backwards, until it disappeared altogether at a point about an hundred yards distant, where the crags rose sheer up out of the water. In this direction Ian More moved slowly off, after throwing on the throng of his assailants a grim smile,

which, however, had more of pity than of anger in it.
Before he had taken a dozen steps the most forward of the
party were at his skirts. He turned smartly round, and
suddenly catching up the first man in his arms, he sent
him spinning through the air into the lake as if he had
been a puppy dog. The next in succession was seized with
astonishment, but before he could shake himself free of it,
he was seized by something more formidable, I mean by
the iron hands of Ian More, who flung him also far amid
the waters after his fellow. A whole knot of those who
followed them sprang upon him at once, but he patted
them off, one after another, as if they had been so many
flies, and that he had been afraid to hurt them ; but, as it
was impossible for him to accommodate his hits with
mathematical precision to the gentleness of his intentions,
some of the individuals who received them bore the marks
of them for many a day afterwards. The ardour of the
attack became infinitely cooled down. But still there were
certain fiery spirits who coveted glory. These, as they
came boldly up, successively shared the fate of those who
had gone before them. Some were stretched out, as chance
threw them, to measure their dimensions on the terra
firma, whilst others were hurled hissing hot into the lake,
where they were left at leisure to form some estimate of
their own specific gravity in a depth of water which was
just shallow enough to save them from drowning. Meanwhile, the object of their attack continued to stalk slowly
onwards at intervals, smiling on them from time to time,
as he turned to survey the shattered remains of the attacking army that now followed him at a respectful distance,
and halted every time he faced them. The sergeant, like
an able general, kept poking them on in the rear with his
pike, and upbraiding them for their cowardice. Meanwhile
Ian gradually gained ground on them, and having produced
an interval of some twenty or thirty yards between himself
and them, just as they thought that he had arrived at a point
where farther retreat was impossible, he suddenly disappeared into a crack in the face of the cliff, hitherto unobserved, and on reaching the place they found that the
fearless mountaineer had made his slippery way up the
chimney-like cleft, amid the white foam of a descending
rill that was one of the main feeders of the lochan, into
which it poured.

"The feller has vanished into the clouds," said the sergeant, shuddering with horror as he looked up the perilous rocky funnel, and, at the same time, secretly congratulating himself that Ian had not stood to bay. "He has vanished into the clouds, just out of our very hands, as I may say. Who was to think of there being any such ape's ladder as this here?"

The party returned, sullen and discomfited, to the strath, and their leader now gave up all hopes of capturing Ian More Arrach either by stratagem or force. But his thirst for the large sum which he expected to realise by producing such a man at headquarters rendered him quite restless and unremitting in his inquiries, the result of which was, that he found out that Lord Seaforth, then, I believe, Lord Lieutenant of the County, might do something towards apprehending the runaway. He accordingly waited on his lordship to request his interference for procuring the seizure of John Mackay, surnamed Ian More Arrach, a deserter from His Majesty's service. Lord Seaforth inquired into the case, and believing that the man had been fairly enlisted, he procured his immediate appearance at Brahan Castle, by going the right way to work with him. There, it so happened, that Lord Rae was at that time a visitor, and Lord Seaforth called in his aid to work upon Ian More, who bowed to the ground in submission to the wishes of his chief.

"This is an unlucky business, Ian More," said Lord Rae, "it seems that you have deserted from the King's service, after having accepted his money, and that, moreover, you have twice deforced the officer and party. Your case, I fear, is a bad one. Depend upon it, they will have you if it should cost them the sending of a whole regiment after you; and then, if you give them so much trouble, no one can say what may be the consequence. Take my advice and give yourself up quietly. I shall write to your commanding officer in such terms as will save you from any very bad consequences; and with the recommendations which you shall have, there is no saying but you may be an officer ere long. All the Mackays are brave fellows; and if all I have heard be true, it appears that you are no disgrace to the name."

Ian was too proud of the interest taken in him by his noble chief, to dispute his advice or wishes for one moment.

He would have sacrificed his life for him. And accordingly, abandoning his mountain-glen and his caurets, he surrendered himself to the sergeant, who implicitly obeyed the instructions he received from Lord Rae to treat him kindly, particularly as they were backed up with a handsome douceur; and Ian was soon afterwards embarked to join his regiment, then quartered in Guernsey.

The regiment that Ian More was attached to was almost entirely a new levy, and the recruits were speedily put on garrison duty, frivolous perhaps in itself, but probably given to them more as a lesson, in order that they might become familiar with it, than from any absolute necessity for it. It so happened, that the first guard that Ian mounted, he was planted as a night sentinel on the Queen's Battery. The instructions given to his particular post were to take especial care that no injury should happen to a certain six-pounder, which there rested on its carriage; and when the corporal of the guard marched Ian up as a relief, he laughed heartily to hear the earnest assurances which he gave, in answer to the instructions he received from the man he was relieving, "Tat not a bonn o' ta body o' ta wee gunnie sould be hurt, at a', at a', while he had ta care o' her."

And Ian kept his word; for he watched over the beautiful little piece of ordnance with the greatest solicitude. It so happened, however, that whilst he was walking his lonely round, a heavy shower of rain began to fall, and a bitter freezing blast soon converted every particle of it into a separate cake of ice, which cut against his nose and eyes, and nearly scarified his face, so that much as he had been accustomed to the snarling climate of the higher regions of the interior of Scotland, he felt as if he would lose his eyesight from the inclemency of the weather; and then he began to reason that if he should lose his eyesight, how could he take care of the gun? His anxiety for the safety of his charge, united to a certain desire for his own comfort, induced him gravely to consider what was best to be done. He surveyed the gun, and as he did so, he began to think that it was extremely absurd that he should be standing by its side for two long hours, whilst he might so easily provide for its security in some place of shelter; and accordingly he quickly removed it from its carriage, and poising it very adroitly on his shoulder, he carried it deliberately away.

Strong as Ian was, the position and the weight of the six-pounder, considerably more than half a ton, compelled him to walk with a stiff mien and a solemn, measured, and heavy tread. He had to pass by two or three sentinels. These were all raw unformed recruits like himself, and full of Highland superstitions. Each of them challenged him in succession as his footstep approached; but Ian was too much intent on keeping his burden properly balanced to be able to reply. He moved on steadily and silently therefore, with his eyeballs protruded and fixed, from the exertion he was making, and with his whole countenance wearing a strange and portentous expression of anxiety, which was heightened by a certain pale blue light that fell upon it from one part of the stormy sky. Instead of attempting to oppose or to arrest such a phantom, which came upon them in the midst of the tempest like some unearthly being which had been busied in the very creation of it, each sentry fled before it, and the whole rampart was speedily cleared.

It was not many minutes after this that the visiting sergeant went his rounds. To his great surprise, he was not challenged by the sentry upon Ian More's post; and to his still greater astonishment, he was permitted to advance with impunity till he discovered that Ian More was not there. But what was yet most wonderful of all the gun of which he was the especial guardian was gone.

"Lord ha' mercy on us!" exclaimed the corporal, "I see'd the man planted here myself alongside the piece of ordinance; what can have become of them both?"

"'Tis mortal strange," said the sergeant. "Do you stand fast here, corporal, till we go down the rampart a bit, to see if we can see anything."

"Nay, with your leave, sergeant," said the corporal, "I see no use in leaving me here to face the devil. Had we not better go and report this strange matter to the officer of the guard?"

"Nonsense,—obey my orders; and if you do see the devil, be sure you make him give you the countersign," said the sergeant, who had had all such fears rubbed off by a long life of hard service.

On walked the sergeant along the rampart. The other sentries were gone also. One man only he at last found, and him he dragged forth from under a gun-carriage.

"Why have you deserted your post, you trembling wretch?" demanded the sergeant.

"Did you not see it, then?" said the man, with a terrified look.

"See what?" asked the sergeant.

"The devil, in the shape of Ian More Arrach, with his face like a flaming furnace, shouldering a four-and-twenty pounder," replied the man; "och, it was a terrible sight."

"By jingo, my boy, your back will be made a worse spectacle of before long, if I don't mistake," said the sergeant.

By this time a buzz of voices was heard. The guard had been alarmed by the fugitive sentries, whose fright had carried them with ghastly looks to the guard-room. The guard had alarmed the garrison, and the whole place was thrown into confusion. Soldiers, non-commissioned officers, and officers, were seen running and heard vociferating in all directions, lanterns and flambeaux were everywhere flitting about like fire-flies, and soldiers' wives and children were heard screaming and crying. The cause of the tumult was reported in a thousand different ways. Some of the least rational of the women and juveniles even believed and asserted that an enemy had landed on the island; whilst those who really were aware that the true cause of the uproar was Ian More's mysterious disappearance, were employed in searching everywhere for him and the six-pounder; but he was nowhere to be found, and wonder and astonishment multiplied at every step.

At length the tumult rose to such a height that the commanding officer was roused, and hurrying on his clothes, he came running to the Queen's Battery to know what all the hubbub was about. The place was filled with a crowd of all ranks, each individual of which was ready to hazard his own conjecture in explanation of this most unaccountable event. All gave way at the colonel's approach. After hearing what had happened, he inquired into the circumstances so far as they were known; he listened calmly and attentively to the various accounts of those who had been making ineffectual search, and having heard all of them patiently to an end—

"This is very strange," said he; "but well as you have searched, it appears to me that none of you seem to have ever thought of looking for him in his barrack-room. Let us go there."

Off went the colonel accordingly to the barrack-room, followed by as many curious officers and soldiers as could well crowd after him; and there, to be sure, snug in bed, and sound asleep, lay Ian More Arrach, with the piece of artillery in his arms, and his cheek close to the muzzle of it, which was sticking out from under the blanket that covered both of them. The spectacle was too ridiculous even for the colonel's gravity. He and all around him gave way to uncontrollable bursts of laughter, that speedily awaked Ian from the deep sleep in which he was plunged. He stared around him with astonishment.

"What made you leave your post, you rascal?" demanded the sergeant of the guard, so much provoked as to forget himself before his commanding officer.

"Nay, nay," said the colonel, who already knew something of Ian, from the letter which he had received from his chief, "you cannot say that he has left his post; for you see he has taken his post along with him."

"Is na ta wee bit gunnie as weil aside her nanesell here?" said Ian, with an innocent smile. "Is she na mockell better here aside her nanesell, nor wi' her nanesell stannin' cauld an' weet aside her yonder on ta Pattry?"

"Well, well," said the colonel, after a hearty laugh. "But how did you manage to bring the gun here?"

"Ou troth her nanesell carried her," replied Ian.

"Come, then," said the colonel, "if you will instantly carry it back again to the place whence you took it, nothing more shall be said about it."

"Toots! but she'll soon do tat," said Ian, starting out of bed, and immediately raising the gun to his shoulder, he set out with it, followed by the colonel and every one within reach; and, to the great astonishment of all of them, he marched slowly and steadily towards the battery with it, and replaced it on its carriage, amidst the loud cheers of all who beheld him.

As Ian was naturally a quiet, sober, peaceable, and well-behaved man, a thorough knowledge of his duty soon converted him into a most invaluable soldier; and nature having made him a perfect model, both as to mould and symmetry of form, the colonel, who took a peculiar fancy to him, soon saw that he was altogether too tall and fine looking a man to be kept in the ranks. Accordingly he had him struck off from the ordinary routine of domestic duty, and drilled as a fugleman, in which distinguished situation Ian continued to figure until his services were terminated by an unlucky accident.

It happened one evening that the colonel of an English regiment dined at the mess of the Highland corps. In the course of conversation this gentleman offered a bet that he had a man who would beat any individual who could be picked from among the Highlanders. One of the Highland officers immediately took him up, and engaged to produce a man to meet the English champion next morning. By break of day, therefore, he sent for Ian More Arrach, and told him what had occurred, and then added—
" You are to be my man, Ian; and I think it will be no hard thing for you who shouldered the six-pounder to pound this boasting pock-pudding."

" Troth na," said Ian, shaking his head, " ta pock-pudden no done her nae ill,—fat for wad she be fighten her? Troth her honour may e'en fight ta man hersell, for her nanesell wull no be doin' nae siccan a thing."

" Tut ! nonsense, man," said the officer, " you must fight him, aye and lick him too ; and you shall not only carry off the honour, but you shall have a handsome purse of money for doing so."

" Na, na," said Ian, " ta man no dune her nae ill ava, an she'll no be fighten for ony bodey's siller but King Shorge's."

" Surely you're not afraid of him," said the officer, trying to rouse his pride.

" Hout na !" replied Ian More, with a calm good humoured smile ; " she no be feart for no man livin'."

" So you wont fight," said the officer.

" Troth na," said Ian, " she canna be fighten wissout nae raison."

" Surely your o 1 honour, the honour of the regiment, the honour of Sco and, the purse of gold, and my wishes thus earnestly ex] essed, ought to be reasons enough with you. But since you refuse, I must go to Alister Mackay ; he will have no such scruples, I'll warrant me."

This last observation was a master-stroke of policy on the part of the officer. Alister Mackay was a stout athletic young man ; but he was by no means a match for the English prize-fighter. Nor did the officer mean that he should be opposed to him; for he only named him, knowing that he was a cousin of Ian More's, and one for whom he had the affection of a brother; and he was quite sure that his apprehension for Alister's safety would be too great to allow him to be absent from the field, if it did not induce him to take his place in the combat. And it turned out as he had anticipated. Ian came, eagerly pressing forward into the throng; and no sooner did he appear than the officer pointed him out to the Englishman as the man that was to be pitted against him; and as the Highlanders naturally took it for granted that the big fugleman was to be their man, they quickly made a ring for him amidst loud cheering.

"Come away, Goliah! come on!" cried the Englishman, tossing his hat into the air, and his coat to one side. Ian minded him not. But the growing and intolerable insolence of the bully did the rest; for, presuming on Ian's apparent backwardness, he strode up to him with his arms akimbo, and spat in his face.

"Fat is she do tat for?" asked Ian simply of those around him.

"He has done it to make people believe that you are a coward, and afraid to fight him," said the Highland officer who backed him.

"Tell her no to do tat again," said Ian seriously.

"There!" said the boxer, repeating the insult.

Without showing the smallest loss of temper, Ian made an effort to lay hold of his opponent, but the Englishman squared at him, and hit him several smart blows in succession, not one of which the unpractised Highlander had the least idea of guarding.

"Ha!" exclaimed the Highland officer, "I fear you will be beaten, Ian."

"Foo!" cried Ian coolly, "she be strikin' her to be sure, but she be na hurtin' her. But an she disna gie ower an her nanesell gets one stroak at her, she'll swarrants she'll no seek nae mair."

The Englishman gave him two or three more hard hits that went against his breast as if they had gone against an oaken door; but at last Ian raised his arm, and swept it round horizontally with a force that broke through all his antagonist's guards; and the blow striking his left

cheek as if it had come from a sledge hammer, it actually
drove the bones of the jaw on that side quite through the
opposite skin, and, at the same time, smashed the whole
skull to fragments. The man fell like a log, dead on the
spot, and horror and astonishment seized the spectators.

" Och hone ! och hone !" cried Ian More, running to lift
him from the ground, in an agony of distress, " She's
dootin' she kilt ta poor man."

Ian was thrown into a fit of the deepest despair and
sorrow by this sad catastrophe, sufficiently proving to every
one around him that his heart was made of the most
generous stuff ; and, indeed, the effect of the horrible
spectacle they had witnessed was such as to throw a gloom
on all who were present, and especially on those who were
more immediately concerned with the wager. The case
was decidedly considered as one of justifiable homicide.
It was hushed up by general consent, and a pass was
granted to Ian to return to Scotland.

As he was slowly journeying homeward, Ian happened
to spend a night at Stonehaven, and, as he was inquiring
of his landlord as to the way he was to take in the morning, the man told him that he might save some distance by
taking a short cut through the park of Ury, the residence
of Mr. Barclay of Ury, who, as you probably know, was
even more remarkable for feats of bodily strength than his
son, Captain Barclay, the celebrated pedestrian.

" Ye may try the fut-road through the park," said Ian's
host ; " but oddsake, man, tak' care an' no meet the laird,
for he's an awfu' chiel, though he be a Quaker, and gif ye
do meet him I rauken that ye'll just hae to come yere ways
back again."

" Fat for she do tat ?" demanded Ian.

" Ou, he's a terrible man the laird," continued the landlord. " What thi: r ye? there was ae night that a poor
tinker body h. d itten his bit pauney into ane of the
laird's inclosures, at it might get a sly rug o' the grass.
Aweel, the laird c. nes oot in the mornin', an' the moment
he spied the beast, he ga'ed tilt like anither Samson, and
he lifted it up in his airms and flang it clean oot ower the
dyke. As sure as ought, gif he meets you, an' he disna
throw you owre the dyke, he'll gar ye gang ilka fit o' the
road back again."

" Tuts ! she'll try," replied Ian.

Soon after sunrise, Ian took the forbidden path, and he had pursued it without molestation for a considerable way, when he heard some one hallooing after him; and turning his head to look back, he beheld a gentleman, whom he at once guessed to be the laird, hurrying up to him.

"Soldier!" cried Mr. Barclay, " I allow no one to go this way, so thou must turn thee back."

" She be sorry tat she has anghered her honour," said Ian bowing submissively, " but troth it be ower far a gate to gang back noo."

" Far gate or short gate, friend, back thou must go," said Mr. Barclay.

" Hoot na! she canna gang back," said Ian.

" But thou must go back, friend," said the laird.

" Troth, she wunna gang back," replied Ian.

" But thou must go back, I tell thee," said the laird, " and if thou wilt not go back peaceably, I'll turn thee back whether with thy will or not."

" Hoot, toot, she no be fit to turn her back," said Ian with one of his broad good-humoured grins.

" I'll try," said the laird, laying his hands on Ian's shoulders to carry his threat into immediate execution.

"An she be for tat," said Ian, "let her lay doon her wallet, an' she'll see whuther she can gar her turn or no."

" By all means, good friend," said the laird, who enjoyed a thing of the kind beyond all measure. " Off with thy wallet, then. Far be it from me to take any unseemly advantage of thee."

The wallet being quietly deposited on the ground, to it they went; but ere they had well buckled together, Ian put down the laird beside the wallet with the same ease that he had put down the wallet itself.

" Ha!" cried the laird, as much overcome with surprise at a defeat which he had never before experienced, as he had been by the strength that had produced it. " Thou didst take me too much o' the sudden, friend, but give me fair play. Let me up and I will essay to wrestle with thee again."

"Weel, weel," said Ian coolly, "she may tak' her ain laizier to rise, for her nancsell has plenty o' sun afore her or night."

" Come on then," said Mr. Barclay, grappling again with his antagonist and putting forth all his strength, which Ian allowed him full time to exert against him, whilst in defiance of it all he stood firm and unshaken as a rock.

"Noo! doon she goes again!" said Ian, deliberately prostrating the laird a second time, "an' gif tat be na eneugh, she'll put her toon ta tird time, sae tat she'll no need nae mair puttens toon."

"No, no," said the laird panting, and, notwithstanding his defeat, much delighted not only with the exercise he had had, but that he had at last discovered so potent an antagonist. "No, no, friend! enough for this bout. I own that thou art the better man. This is the first time that my back was ever laid on the grass. Come away with me, good fellow, thou shalt go home with me."

Ian's journey was not of so pressing a nature as to compel him to refuse the laird's hospitable offer, and he spent no less than fourteen days living on the fat of the land at Ury, and Mr. Barclay afterwards sent a man and horses with him to forward him a few stages on his way.

On his return to Strath-Connan, Ian was welcomed by many an old friend, and he speedily felt himself again rooted in his native soil. He soon re-edified his bothy; but he did so after that much improved and much more comfortable style of architecture which his large experience of civilised life had now taught him to consider as essential. He again took readily to his caurets, and to the simple occupations attendant on the care and management of them, which he forthwith increased to a considerable extent by increasing their numbers; and every day he grew wealthier and wealthier by means of them. The taste which he had now had of society, led him more frequently to visit the gayer and livelier scenes of the more thickly inhabited straths; and it was seldom that a market, a marriage, or a merry-making of any kind occurred, where Ian's sinewy limb and well turned ankles were not seen executing the Highland fling to a degree of perfection rarely to be matched. These innocent practices he continued long after he was a husband and a father, yea, until he was far advanced in life.

If Ian had a spark of pride at all, it was in the circumstance that the calves of his legs were so well rounded, that however much his limbs might be exercised, they always kept up his hose without the aid of a garter, an

appendage to his dress which he always scorned to wear.
One night a large party of friends were assembled in his
house to witness the baptism of a recently born grandson.
After the ceremony and the feast were both over, the
young people got up to dance, and, old as he was, Ian
More Arrach was among the foremost of them. To it
he went, and danced the Highland fling with his usual
spirit and alacrity, snapping his fingers and shouting
with the best of them. But alas! when the dance was
over, he suddenly discovered that his hose had fallen
three inches from their original position, betraying the
sad fact that his limbs had lost somewhat of their original
muscle. This was to him a sad sinking in the barometer
of human life. He surveyed his limbs for some time in
silence with a melancholy expression ; and then, with something like a feeling of bitterness, which no one had ever
seen take possession of him before, he exclaimed,—

"Tamm her nanesell's teeths! She may weel gie ower
ta fling, noo tat her teeths wunna haud up her hose!"

MORNING SCENE.

THE shrill and persevering crow of a cock, who roosted on the rafters immediately over our heads, gradually succeeded in drawing up Grant and myself from the deep Lethean lake of slumber into which both had been plunged, and we arose yawning and most unwillingly from our simple couches, ere yet the sun had peeped above the horizon. With one consent we stole to the outer door in our dressing gowns and slippers, to inhale a few draughts of pure air, and to inform ourselves as to the state of the weather. A perfect calm prevailed, and the landscape was lying under one general sombre shadow, which made it so difficult to distinguish objects, that we could not even trace the exact line of boundary of the still waters of Loch-an-Dorbe. One glow of an aurora hue made the summit of the opposite hill to gleam faintly, but that was enough to produce a corresponding fragment of bright reflection on the bosom of the lake. In the middle of that warm spot rested a little boat with two men in it, one of whom was seated at the oars to keep it steady, whilst the other was standing in the stern eagerly occupied in fishing.

Grant, rubbing his eyes,—Can that possibly be Clifford?

Author.—Let us ascertain whether he is in his bed or not.

Grant.—Aha! his *gite* is empty and cold! What an indefatigable fisherman!

Author.—Depend upon it, we shall not see him here for some hours to come.

Grant.—Then I shall employ the intervening time in repose.

Author.—And I shall follow your good example.

The very profound sleep into which we both of us sank, was at length interrupted by the return of Clifford with a beautiful dish of fresh trouts.

Clifford.—You lazy fellows! See what a glorious

morning's work I have had while you have been snoring away like a couple of tailors. Look how large and how fine they are! There is one now, twice as big as any that was killed last night.

Author.—We are certainly greatly obliged to you for quitting your couch so early in order to procure us so luxurious a breakfast

Clifford.—I don't think that either of you deserve to share in it, though in truth you are already sufficiently punished for your indolence by missing the fine sport I have had, and therefore I shall act towards you with true Christian charity. Come then, my girl, get your fire up and your frying-pan in order, and I'll stand cook.

Grant.—You must have had a delicious morning of it.

Clifford.—Charming! The effect of the sunrise on the lake was enchanting, and the jumping of the trouts around me perfectly miraculous.

Grant.—I am surprised that you could tear yourself away so soon.

Clifford.—I believe I should have been there for some hours to come, had not my barefooted boatman told me that it was time to get on shore, for that the clouds which we saw heaping themselves up to the westward, threatened to discharge a storm upon us.

Grant.—I suspect that the fellow will turn out to be a true prophet. What a dreadful blast that was! Let us hurry out to witness the effects of it.

What a change had now taken place in the scene! The sun was already high above the horizon; but dense clouds hid his face from our view, and threw a deep inky hue over the whole face of nature, excepting only where the western blast took its furious course athwart the wide surface of the lake, lashing it up into white-crested billows, the sharp and fleeting lights of which acquired a double share of brilliancy amidst the general murky hue that prevailed everywhere around. The spray dashed over the island and the grey towers of the castle. The flocks of sea-mews, kittywakes, and other waterfowl that frequented the ruined walls, were whirled about in confused mazes, like fragments of foam carried into the air, and were utterly unable to direct their flight by their own volition. Nothing could be more sudden nor more sublime than this effect! It was so grand, and at the same time so transient, that nothing but the ready eye and the matchless mind of the Reverend John Thomson, of Duddingstone, our great Scottish Salvator, could have seized and embodied it. It passed away as speedily as it had come. A heavy shower of rain fell after it was gone ; and after that had ceased, all was stillness and sunshine.

When we again set out to pursue our way, which led by the margin of the loch, its waters were rippling gently with every light zephyr that fanned them, and sparkling and glowing under the untamed rays of the broad sun, whilst the sea-birds were partly wheeling over the deep with all their wonted variety and regularity of evolution, and partly dipping into the water, and partly resting in buoyant repose upon its swelling bosom.

Having waved our last adieu to Loch-an-Dorbe from the summit of a knoll at some distance from the lower end of it, we took our course across the moorland, where the views on all sides were peculiarly dull and dreary. A black turf hut was now and then visible, proving that it was at least possible for human beings to live in this bare district ; but all signs of cultivation were limited to a few wretched patches of arable ground lying along some of the small burns that here and there intersected the peat-mosses. Nothing could be more miserable than the country, or than the humble dwellings of its natives ; and yet even here we fell in with a picture of human felicity that strongly arrested our attention.

A group of ragged urchins were sporting on a little spot of greensward before the door of one of these hovels, and shouting and laughing loudly at their own fun. The youngest was mounted on a huge gaunt-sided sow, with a back as sharp as that of a saw ; whilst two elder imps, one on either side, were holding him in his seat, and another was urging on the animal, by gently agitating the creature's tail. All this was done without cruelty, and in the best humour. The father and mother had been in the act of building up their next year's stock of peats into a stack, that rested against the weather gable of their dwelling, so that it might do the double duty of sheltering them from the prevailing blast, as well as furnishing them with food for their kitchen fire. But the merry scene that was passing below had become too touchingly attractive to the hearts of both the parents, and their labour was arrested in the most whimsical manner; for the man sat perched on all-fours on the top of the frail edifice he was engaged in rearing, grinning with broad delight at the gambols of his half-naked progeny; and his wife's attention having been arrested whilst she was in the very act of tossing up an armful of the black materials of her husband's architecture, she still stood fixed like a statue, with her arm raised, quite unconscious of the inconvenience of her attitude, and entirely absorbed in her enjoyment of the spectacle, her whole countenance beaming with the maternal joy she felt, and giving way to sympathetic roars of merriment.

Grant.—You see it is not in the power of poverty altogether to extinguish human happiness.

Author.—Nay, no more than riches can ensure it.

Clifford.—How different the hard fortune of that poor creature from the sunshiny lot of those women of quality and fashion whom we have seen figuring in fancy dresses, and glittering like dancing Golcondas, at Almacks; and yet how much more heart and honesty and true mirth there is in that rustic laugh of hers than in all the hollow gaiety of that professed temple of pleasure.

Author.—This merry Maggy of the moor here has indeed received but a small share of the good things of this life, compared with that which has been showered on the proud heads of those wealthy and titled exclusives. But individual happiness must not by any means be measured by the degree of wealth. And then, when we direct our thoughts to our prospects of happiness in a future life, and reflect how apt those favourites of fortune are to be led astray by that very abundance which has been heaped upon them here below, we cannot but congratulate Maggy there as having at least the safer, if not the better, share of the treasures of this world.

Grant.—True; and we have the authority of almost every moral poet, from Horace to our Scottish Allan Ramsay, for the great truth that even happiness in this world is to be more readily found in a comfortable middle state than in either of the extremes,—

> " He that hath just enough can soundly sleep,
> The o'ercome only fashes folk to keep."

Clifford.—Ha! ha! sermons and poetry for pilgrims in

the desert! But then arises the difficult question, what is it that constitutes that *"just enough"* which the poet holds to be the talisman of human happiness.

Grant.—Give economy fair play, and it will make that talisman out of anything.

Author.—And so, on the other hand, extravagance could never possess it, even if the subterranean treasures of Aladdin, or the diamond valley of Sinbad, were to be placed at its disposal.

Clifford.—Your allusion to the Arabian tales puts me in mind of our story-telling; and the subject we have now accidentally got upon brings to my recollection a remarkable story which you once related to me, Grant.

Grant.—You mean the legend of John Macpherson of Invereshie.

Clifford.—The same. Pray tell it to our friend here.

Grant.—If you, who have heard it before, have no objections to the repetition of it, I can have none to the telling of it.

THE LEGEND OF JOHN MACPHERSON OF
INVERESHIE.

The John Macpherson of whom I speak lived in the very beginning of the seventeenth century. He was the same laird who is well known as having got the Crown charter of the lands of Invereshie. He was a tall handsome Highlander, with a somewhat melancholy cast of countenance. His manners were simple and unassuming, and though untaught by any instructor but nature, they were so much the reverse of vulgar that they might have even been called elegant. He was warm in his affections, kind in his intercourse with all around him, extremely bold and determined in any difficult or desperate juncture, and resolute and stern in his purpose when suddenly called on to deal with a matter of deep or stirring moment, and further—though that belonged to him less as anything peculiar than as a characteristic of the time he lived in—he was superstitiously alive to all those incidents or appearances that might chance to wear the semblance of ominous or fatal portent; and such as these did not unfrequently present themselves in days when the fables of Highland demonology reigned over the strongest minds with an absolute despotism.

Living, as Macpherson did, almost entirely among his native mountains, his time was very happily as well as prudently divided between the chase of the red-deer, in which he particularly delighted, and those attentions which he found it necessary to bestow on the concerns of his landed territory; in looking to the well-being of his people, and the health, prosperity, and multiplication of those large herds of cattle which spread themselves over the broad sides of his hills, and brushed through the ancient fir forests or the birchen groves that shaded his glens. In this way his worldly means so increased, that he became an object of no inconsiderable solicitude to such of the

neighbouring lairds and ladies as happened to have unmarried daughters; and so many were the fair parties
presented to his choice, that, being attracted in all directions, he remained hanging, like a bunch of ripe grapes,
in the fluctuating breezes of doubt and indecision, that
threatened in time to dry and shrivel him up into an old
bachelor.

Whilst Macpherson was still in this negative condition,
he happened to visit the castle of a certain chief. The
company were assembling in the great hall to wait for the
banquet, and he stood ensconced within the deep recess of
one of its antique windows, where he had vainly endeavoured to retreat from the assaults of some three or four
most agreeable spinsters, who, being of a certain age, less
scrupulously adopted measures which were much too bold
for their younger rivals to have ventured upon. Having
brought him to bay in a place whence he could not retreat
without rudeness, each commenced the discharge of her
own independent fire against him, whilst, at the same
time, little spiteful shots of malice, both from their tongues
and their eyes, were every now and then interchanged
from one fair competitor to another. This scene was going
on, much to the amusement of the spectators, but very
much to the annoyance of the victim of this persecution,
when a sudden buzz from the company directed Macpherson's attention to the door of the hall, where entered
a lady of surprising beauty and grace of mien. By a
natural impulse, which he could neither explain nor command, Macpherson burst unceremoniously from among his
tormentors, and stepped forward to gaze upon her as she
moved easily up the hall. The intelligent eyes of the
lovely stranger fell upon him, and fixed themselves upon
him with a species of fascination which touched him to the
soul. He was sensibly conscious of the resistless power of
this influence, but at the same time he felt that it was a
fascination of much too agreeable a nature for him to allow
himself to struggle against it. He at once abandoned his
heart to all its ecstasies, as a thirsty fly would yield itself
up to the delicious temptation of quaffing the nectar from
the cup of some beauteous and fragrant flower; and he
gazed on her face with a rapture which he had never before
experienced. Nor was all this very surprising, for she who
thus attracted him had been born and educated in the metro-

polis,—had even mixed in the gay and splendid scenes of
a court, and her dress and manners lent so dazzling an air
to the lustre of her natural charms, that, compared to her,
the native beauties congregated from all parts of the vast
strath of the Spey, fresh and lovely, graceful and intelligent, as fame has ever held its ladies to be, appeared before
her as so many dim and feeble fixed stars in the path of
some brilliant and glorious planet.

Invereshie's natural modesty made him shrink from asking for that very introduction for which his whole heart
burned. But the lady was the niece of his host; she had
recently arrived with the intention of residing with him
for some months, and the introduction came in the ordinary course of etiquette. He was seated by her during
the greater part of that evening. Something more than
mortal as she at first appeared to be in his eyes, he soon
found, on a nearer approach, that she had nothing about
her either overawing or repulsive. He listened to her
Syren tongue with an eagerness which until then had
been quite a stranger to him. The hours flew like minutes.
He suddenly perceived that every guest was gone but himself. He hurried away in confusion, and rode home in a
delirium of delight so perfectly novel to him, that he two
or three times seriously questioned himself by the way
whether reason was still really holding her dominion over
his brain, and the continual presence of the lady's image
there almost convinced him that she had usurped the
throne of that judicious goddess.

Macpherson was soon drawn back to the castle of his
friend by an attraction which was quite irresistible. The
impression made upon him by a first acquaintance was
powerfully strengthened by a second meeting,—a third and
a fourth visit soon succeeded,—and their interviews became
more and more frequent, as he began to perceive, with a
certain air of triumph, that his attentions, offered at first
with becoming deference, were much more graciously
received than those which came from any of his brother
lairds. His hunting expeditions became less numerous,
and even his wonted prudential daily superintendence of
his rural concerns gave way to a new and much more
seductive occupation. He gradually became almost a
constant inmate in his friend's castle. But, in devoting so
much of his time to attendance on her who had thus gained

so overwhelming a dominion over his heart, he consoled himself for this unusual neglect of his affairs, by reflecting that the prize he coveted was so rare as to be universally considered beyond all price—a gem far richer than any of those that adorned his brooch; and that besides all its glitter and sparkle, it was not without considerable intrinsic value also, seeing that, in addition to her other advantages, the lady's *tocher* was such as might well satisfy a much more avaricious man than he knew himself to be.

As for the lady, I have only to say of her, that she was a woman. There are few of the fair sex whose bosoms have not been visited by a certain spirit of romance at one period or other, and, indeed, it may be matter of doubt whether those who have altogether escaped from this visitation are much to be envied. It is that which makes many a town-bred girl sigh for love and a cottage, until such fancies are extinguished by maturer judgment. The soul of her of whom I speak had been deeply embued with this poetry of life, and as yet she had seen no good reason for ridding herself of it. She was all enthusiasm. Invereshie's gay white tartan—his plumed bonnet and jewelled ornaments—his gallant, though unobtrusive, bearing—his firm tread and independent gait—the resolute and heroic character that sat upon his brow, and yielded a calm illumination to his pensive eye—and, above all, the enchanting scenery of his river—the sparkling Feshie—its wild glen, and the prospective witchery of a Highland life, painted as it was with all the glowing colours of her fervid fancy, and with a thousand adventitious attractions which that fancy threw around it, had conspired to do as much execution on her heart as her manifold charms had wrought upon his. The visions of town gaiety and grandeur, which had hitherto filled her young mind, speedily melted away. Rural circumstances and rural imagery occupied it entirely. She suddenly became fond of moonlight walks, of wandering on the banks of the magnificent river that wound majestically through the wide vale where she then resided, and of musing amid the checkered shadows which evening threw over the ruins of an ancient chapel and burial-ground, embraced by one bold and beautiful sweep of the stream at no great distance from the castle.

She was one night seated on a grey moss-covered stone, one of the many frail memorials of the dead which were

8

scattered through this retired spot, her eyes now lifted in
admiration of the glorious orb that silently held its way
through the skies above, and now thrown downwards to its
image trembling in the mimic heaven then floating on the
broad bosom of the stream below, when Invereshie, who had
been called away by some express affair, was returning at
a late hour to the castle.   These were times, be it again
remembered, when superstition held all mankind under
her thrall, and when the boldest Highlander, who would
have fearlessly rushed on death in the battlefield, would
have quailed before the idle phantoms of his own imagination.

Invereshie's nurse had early embued his mind with a firm
faith in all the wildest of these imaginings, and with him
this belief, then so common to all, had grown with his
growth and strengthened with his strength.   The horse
that he rode started aside and snorted with affright when,
on bursting from the deep shade of the grove that partly
embosomed the burial-ground, he first saw the white figure
of the lady before him; and it argued a more than common
courage in the horseman, therefore, that he should have
checked the flight of the terrified animal in order to
ascertain the nature of the object he beheld.   The moonbeams shone fully and clearly on a face which he could not
for a moment mistake; yet their pale light shed so chilling
and unearthly a lustre over its well-known features, that,
taken in combination with the hour and the place, it made
him hesitate for a moment whether he really beheld the
form of her whom he so much loved, or whether that which
presented itself to him was one of those unsubstantial
appearances which he believed evil spirits had power to
assume for the bewilderment and destruction of mortals.
But the sound of the trampling of his horse's hoof had
fallen upon the lady's ear while it was yet afar off; as it
drew nearer, the fluttering of her heart had whispered to
her that it was Invereshie who came; and ere he had
recovered from his surprise, she arose and saluted him in
that voice which had now become as music to his ear.   His
blood, chilled and arrested as it had for a moment been by
superstitious dread, now went dancing to his heart in a
rushing tide of joy.   He sprang from his horse, and eagerly
availing himself of so favourable an opportunity, where all
eyes but those of God were absent, he made a full and

animated confession of his passion; and that little solitary field of the dead, which had been accustomed for so many ages to scenes of woe and bereavement alone, was now once more doomed to witness the pure effusions of two as happy hearts as had ever been united together before its neighbouring altar, now so long dilapidated.

"Macpherson!" said the lady, with that enthusiasm which so strongly characterised her, "never forget this solemn hour and place, and let the image of that bright moon be ever in your memory; for it has witnessed your vows, and beheld thee pledge thyself to me for ever!"

"Never! never can I forget it, lady!" replied Invereshie, with a depth of feeling equal to her own.

"Tis well!" said the lady. "And now it were better to shun the observation of prying eyes. This private converse of ours, at the witching hour of night, when none but spirits of the moon are abroad, might be misinterpreted. We must part here!" And ere he wist, she had disappeared among the brushwood.

"The witching hour of night!" muttered Invereshie to himself, as he stood rivetted to the spot, overpowered by the surprise in which he was left by the strange and sudden manner in which she had vanished from his sight. There was something, he thought, marvellous and supernatural in it. His eyes wandered round the silent churchyard where he had found her seated. A thousand superstitious tales connected with that spot rushed upon his memory. It was there that in popular belief the wicked spirit of the waters often appeared to bewilder lated travellers, and to lure them to their destruction. He thought of the power which evil beings were supposed to have in re-animating the remains of the dead, or of thrusting forth human souls from their earthly habitations, in order that they might themselves become the tenants of the fairest and most angelic forms. His reason and his judgment were in vain opposed to these terrific phantoms of the brain.

"The witching hour of night!" groaned he deeply. The hand which he had but a moment before so warmly pressed, and which had sent a fever of joy through every fibre of his frame, now seemed to have conveyed to him an icy chillness that ran through every vein till it froze his very heart; and as he hurriedly and almost unconsciously

mounted his horse to prosecute his way towards the
castle, his mind was perplexed and tortured by strange
and mysterious doubts and misgivings, which continued to
haunt both his waking and his sleeping dreams during the
remainder of that eventful night.

But as the dawn of morning swept away the fogs which
hung upon the mountain-tops, so did it dissipate the gloomy
visions which had thus for a few hours shrouded the lofty
soul of Invereshie. Reason resumed her judgment-seat,
and a little calm reflection brought a blush of shame into
his cheek, occasioned by what he was now disposed to
believe to have been his own weakness. Every manly
feeling within him was aroused. Arraying himself in his
richest attire, he sought for an audience of his friend
the chief, and readily gained from him an uncle's and
a guardian's consent to his union with her to whom his
vows of love had been so recently plighted. Overjoyed at
Invereshie's disclosure, the chief led him to the great hall,
at that time thronged with guests, and having taken his
seat to preside over the morning's meal, he called for a grace
cup, and, drinking to the health of the happy pair, he
publicly announced the alliance which had been that
morning agreed on.

All eyes were instantly turned on her to whom the
flowing goblet had been so joyfully drained. But whether
it was from the sudden swelling of those emotions naturally
enough arising from this public declaration, or whether it
was owing to some fortuitous cause altogether unconnected
with what was then passing, no one could say; but,
whatever might be the cause, her brilliant eyes had become
fixed and glazed, the roses had fled from her cheeks, and
she fell gently back in her chair, her lovely features
exhibiting the ghastly hue of death. A chill shudder
came over Invereshie's heart. Pushing back the seat
in which he sat, he gazed with horror upon the spectacle
before him. Again was his mind unmanned, and
a vision of the unearthly appearance which the lady
had presented to him when he first beheld her seated
among the graves beneath the moonlight of the previc
night rushed upon his imagination. Overpowered
his feelings, he remained as if unconscious of what
passing around him. Nor was he at all observed am.
the general panic. The women shrieked, the guests aro..

in confusion, they crowded around the lady, and she was borne off to her apartment by the attendants.

For several hours the lady lay on her couch so perfectly exanimate, that every individual in the castle believed that she was dead, and mournful preparations were begun to be made for the funereal obsequies of her in whose animating smiles they had so recently rejoiced, and in whose bridal festivities they had anticipated that they were so soon to participate. Eloquent was the silence of that grief which reigned everywhere within the walls, unbroken save by the sobbing of those who hung around the couch of her who had already lived long enough among them to have gained the hearts of all who had approached her. But ere long it happily gave way to unrestrained joy; for, to the amazement of her attendants, the warm blush of life gradually began to revisit her cheeks,—the heaving of her bosom gently returned,—her eyelids slowly unsealed themselves,—the pulse resumed its former action, —the tide of life speedily carried renewed vigour into every limb,—her eyes regained their wonted brightness,— and, to the unspeakable surprise and delight of every one, she returned to the hall with a light and airy step, and with a sensible accession to her usual gaicty of heart, apparently resulting from its temporary slumber.

But hers was a gaiety that touched no responsive chords in Macpherson's bosom. He had stood as it were appalled, a motionless spectator of the various wonderful changes which had been so strangely produced upon her; and he remained for some time sunk in silent abstraction, ill befitting an ardent lover who had thus had his soul's idol so miraculously restored to him from the very jaws of the grave. Those who were about him marvelled and whispered together. But his moody musings were quickly overcome by the lady's enchanting voice of gladness. The laughing sunshine that darted from her eyes soon dissipated those sombre clouds that overshadowed his brow. He again became the willing slave of every word and glance that fell from her. The fascination under which he was held increased every moment; and not many days went by ere the Laird of Invereshie, surrounded by a great gathering of his clansmen and followers, and proudly riding by her bridle-rein, led her home as his bride to the blithe sound of the bagpipe.

As he approached the mansion of his fathers, Invereshie was met by crowds of women and children and old men, who thronged about the cavalcade with eager curiosity to behold their future lady, whom they greeted with shouts of gratulation that suffused her lovely cheek with blushes of joy, and flushed her husband's brow with a pride which he had never felt before. An event so interesting to all his dependants had made even the most aged and infirm to leave their humble dwellings. Some of those who had come from great distances were mounted on the shaggy little horses common to the country. The creatures were caparisoned in the rudest and most characteristic manner; and they formed many picturesque groups, which every now and then called forth expressions of surprise and delight from her who was the fair cause of their assemblage. One of these was peculiarly striking.

Under an old twisted mountain ash stood a ragged red-headed boy, holding the withy that served as a halter to a pony, whose bones, exhibiting many an angle beneath his rough white skin, showed that he had arrived at an age but rarely reached by any of his long-lived race. From either side of the wooden saddle that filled his hollow back hung a huge pannier of the coarsest kind of wicker-work, and from each of these arose the plaided head and pale parchment features of an old woman. So very withered were these ancient crones, that, worn down and weak as was the animal that bore them, their wasted frames seemed scarcely to add anything, in his estimation, to the weight of the baskets that contained them. There was something, at first sight, indescribably ludicrous in the picture they presented; and the bride, who was by no means insensible to such emotions, could not resist giving way for an instant to the laughter which it excited in her as she drew near to them. It so happened that the line of march of the procession brought her close past the tree under which these strange figures were stationed. No sooner had she come opposite to it, than one of them, remarkable for the length of her grey elf-like locks, which streamed from beneath the uncouth *mutch* that covered her head, reared herself up from amidst the heap of tartan stuff that enveloped her person. Stretching out her bare and skeleton arm, her red and gummy eyelids expanded themselves so as to bring fully into action a pair of piercing black eyes that flashed with a fire which even extreme age had been unable to tame, and which now lent a fearful animation to her otherwise spectral features. She glared into the lady's face with a fixed gaze and a wild expression that blenched her cheek, and at once banished everything like mirth or joy from her bosom. In vain did the lady try to avert her eyes from an object which was now to her terrific,—they seemed as if enchained to it by a power like that of the basilisk; and to add to her misery some accidental obstacle created at that very moment a stop in their onward march. Anxiously did she wish to have taken refuge in conversation with her husband, but he was just then employed in replying to the warm compliments of some humble well-wisher, who addressed him from the opposite side of the way. Meanwhile the bony and toothless jaws of the old woman seemed to be moved by a temporary palsy, created by her anxiety to utter something which the lady dreaded to hear. But her very eagerness apparently deprived her of the power of speech; for though her skinny lips were seen to move, no sound proceeded from them except an inarticulate muttering, the import of which was lost amidst the din and bustle of the crowd. But although the lady gathered not the sense, the lurid lightnings that shot from the eyes of this miserable looking wretch told her that the words, if words they were, could have conveyed no prayer of benediction. A sudden failure of nature came over the lady, and she must have dropped from her saddle to the ground, had not her husband's attention been recalled to her at that moment by the renewal of the onward movement of the march. Altogether unconscious of what had caused this apparent faintness, nor indeed being quite aware of the full extent of it, his arm was ready to uphold her. Her vital spirits rallied at his touch. She recovered her seat, and then calling his attention to the object of her alarm, who was by this time left some short way behind them,—

"Tell me," said she, "tell me, I entreat thee, who is that fearful looking old woman under yonder tree?"

"That," replied he, "is my old nurse Elspeth Macpherson, one who is believed by all to be gifted with more than mortal powers."

"Her eye is indeed terrible!" replied the lady shuddering.

"Why shouldst thou be afraid of her?" said Macpherson, in a graver tone. "She can never be terrible to thee? Great as her wisdom and great as her powers undoubtedly are, they can never come to me or to mine but to succour and to bless. From my cradle upwards hath she been as a guardian spirit to me, averting all misfortunes that might have assailed me; and, twined as thy future fate now is with mine, my love," continued he with a forced smile, "trust me, dearest, that her searching eye will be continually over it and on it."

An involuntary tremor seized the lady at the very thought of her fate being under the control of an eye the piercing and unfriendly influence of which was still so strong upon her mind. She forebore to reply; but she could not exclude a train of very unpleasant reflections, which even the rapidly succeeding circumstances of the gay Highland pageant, in which she performed so prominent a part, failed for a while in removing. For some time, too, her husband rode by her side wrapped up in silence and abstraction, till rousing himself from what appeared to be a dreaming fit, he addressed to her some kind expressions, which fell on her soul like balm, and by degrees regaining her wonted cheerfulness, she at length rode onwards distributing sunshine and sweetness on all sides, in return for the many warm welcomes that were showered on her, till she was finally lifted from her saddle at the door of her future home, by the nervous arm of the enraptured Invereshie, amidst the deafening shouts of his friends and retainers.

Invereshie's hospitable board was spread with more than its usual liberality on this joyful occasion; and, according to the custom of the time, its feast and revelry endured for many days. As his lady's previous nurture and education had accustomed her to much nicety of domestic arrangement, and to many luxuries then altogether unknown in the Highlands, he exerted himself to the utmost to lessen the disagreeable effect of that change which he was conscious she must experience on her first entrance into his family. He strove to anticipate every wish; and when he had failed in anticipating her wishes, he spared neither pains nor expense to gratify them the moment she had breathed them. He procured comforts and rarities of all sorts from great distances, and at a cost which he would have considered most alarming, had he not trusted that it would cease with the departure of the guests who thronged his house to welcome his newly married wife. But time wore on, and the lady seemed to have no inclination to get rid of either.

There is a prudent and useful old saying—"begin with a wife as you mean to end with her." It would have been well for Macpherson that he had acted upon this principle. Instead of boldly bringing down his lady's ideas at once to that pitch which would have been in rational harmony with his own habits, as well as with his circumstances, to which her strong attachment to him would have most probably insured her ready submission, he had himself done all in his power to give a false colour to things, which he now felt it a very delicate and difficult matter to attempt to remove. Meanwhile she went innocently enough on in obedience to that bent which her education had given her, in the full persuasion that she was only doing that which her duty, as his wife, prescribed to her. Yielding to her resistless importunity and attractions, the neighbouring gentry were drawn around her, as if by some magic spell; and many of them became, in a manner, domesticated at her husband's hearth. Then every succeeding day brought to the old house some new friend from afar, whom she had been dying to make acquainted with that man of whom she was so proud, and to whom her whole heart was now devoted, that she might prove how much she had gained by relinquishing the world for a prize so inestimable; and for the entertainment of persons so cultivated as these were, it naturally followed that more refined schemes of pleasure and amusement were devised which, whilst they gratified Invereshie at the time, by exciting universal admiration at the tasteful genius of his lady who had conceived them, made him afterwards wince at the large and repeated demands which were made on his treasury, for purposes altogether foreign to the whole pursuits of his former life, and which the whole tenour of it had led him to consider as vain and unprofitable. He wondered that her ingenuity could be so enduring, and still comforting himself with the hope that each particular instance of it that occurred must necessarily be the last, he was still doomed to be astonished every succeeding day by new and yet more expensive projects. Amidst all this bustle and occupation, her speech was ever of the delights of her HIGHLAND SOLITUDE, as she called their residence, whilst her thoughts seemed to be unceasingly employed in endeavours to invent means of depriving it of all claim to any such title, by filling it with as large a portion as she could of the gay crowd and vanities of a city. Of all these vanities none were so galling to the honest heart of Invereshie as the arrival of a certain knot of gallant rufflers from the court—men of broad hats jauntingly cocked to one side, and balanced by long feathers of various hues—who flaunted it in silken cloaks, and strutted it in long-piked shoes; all of which, in his eyes, seemed to sort but ill with the manly Celtic garb worn by himself and his Highland friends. But much as it irked him to be compelled to receive such popinjays as these, and irritated as he frequently was by their unblushing impudence, he submitted calmly to that which the rules of hospitality dictated, and even repressed all outward appearance of his dissatisfaction; and he was rendered the more ready to impose this restraint on himself, by the reflection that most of these gay gallants were in some way or other related to or connected with his wife; and he felt that, as her kinsmen or friends, they claimed the full extent of a Highland welcome. But these southern summerfly cousins were no sooner gone than they were succeeded by clouds of fresh and yet more thirsty insects of the same genus; and these tormentors not only contributed, in their own persons, largely to augment the consumption of those luxuries which had been so recently introduced into his house, and to the promotion of those extravagancies which were conceived and executed more especially for their amusement; but the more simple natives of the glens also were soon taught by their infectious example to relish them quite as much as they did.

Invereshie was long silent under all this; but he did not suffer the less deeply in secret on that account. The ardent love with which he adored his wife, and that certain mistaken chivalrous notion of delicacy, which has been already noticed as operating so strongly on his feelings, long prevented him from attempting to restrain the expenses of so fascinating a woman, who had brought him money enough to furnish at least some apology for the expenditure she occasioned. But ample as her *tocher* had once appeared to him, he soon began to see that it was melting rapidly away under those immense drains which she was daily applying to it; and at length, with more of love than of chiding in his tone, he ventured to speak to her on the painful subject which had so long oppressed him. But alas! whilst he did speak to her, her very eye unmanned him, and what he did bring himself to say was couched in terms so gentle and so general, as neither to convey to her any very useful or impressive lesson, nor even any very definite idea of the extent to which she had erred. The lady flung her snowy arms around his neck, bedewed his face with her tears, and made many earnest and sincere protestations, all of which she sincerely intended most sacredly to fulfil. Macpherson was enraptured. He blamed himself for what he called his severity—kissed away the precious drops from her eyes with a more than ordinary glow of affection. They were the happiest pair in the universe, and in a few days her extravagance was going on at its usual rapid pace, whilst she was all the while in the most perfect belief that she was giving the fullest attention to his wishes.

Many were the scenes of this description that afterwards, from time to time, took place between Invereshie and his lady. The kind of life into which he was now so unwittingly and unwillingly plunged, allowed him few moments for sober reflection. But when such moments did occur, they were bitter ones indeed. At such times gloomy and harrowing recollections, and dreadful and appalling doubts would steal over his soul, putting his very reason to flight before them, and his flesh would creep, and his hair would bristle, whilst his mind was thus yielding to its own speculative misgivings as to the mysterious nature of that fascination which could thus drag him on to certain ruin in despite of his own better judgment. But resolute as was his natural character, and deep as were his determinations at such times, they were all put to flight at once by the first bewitching love-glance of his lady's eye.

Things had gone on in this way for months, growing worse and worse every day, when Invereshie, oppressed

by that gloom which now clung more frequently and
more closely to him, set out one morning very early to
join some of his neighbours in a distant chase of the
deer.   He was that day more than usually successful;
and his attendants having been left behind to bring home
the spoils, he was compelled to return in the evening
alone.   The sun was getting low as he came down into
the upper part of his own deep and precipitous Glen
Feshie, and the shaggy faces of its eastern mountains
were broadly lighted up by its rays, thus rendering the
crags on its western side, and the shadows they threw
across the wooded bottom, doubly obscured by the blazing
contrast.   As the laird advanced, he came suddenly in
view of a cottage perched on the summit of a little knoll,
and sheltered by one huge twisted and scathed pine alone,
the bared limbs of which permitted the spot to be
gladdened by a lingering sunbeam, to which the dense
forest that surrounded it forbade all entrance elsewhere.
This was the habitation of his nurse, whose strange
appearance has been already described.   She and the old
crone her sister, who was believed to be scarcely less
gifted than herself, were seated on settles at the door,
availing themselves of what yet remained of the glowing
light to twine a thrifty thread with distaff and spindle.
The laird seldom passed this way without visiting old
Elspeth; and on this occasion he turned from his direct
path the more readily, because his conscience accused
him that he had somewhat neglected her of late.   The
continual round of dissipation in which he had been for
some time whirled, had not permitted him once to see
her since that accidental glance he had had of her on
the day she appeared at his marriage pageant.   On that
occasion, too, he felt that she should have been a guest
at that table where his humbler friends were entertained;
but he remembered that although she had been invited,
she did not appear.   The recollection of that joyous day
shot across his mind like the gleaming lightning of a
summer night, only to be succeeded by a deeper gloom,
arising from the recurrence of all that had passed since.
Unperceived by the frail owners of the cottage, he wound
his way towards it with a sinking heart.   In approaching
it, he was compelled by the nature of the ground to make
a half circuit around the knoll, which thus brought him

up in rear of it; and he was about tó discover himself to the two old women, by turning the angle of the gable of the little building, when his steps were almost unconsciously arrested by hearing his own name pronounced, and he halted for a moment. It was his nurse who was speaking to her sister emphatically and energetically in Gaelic; and that which he heard might have been nearly interpreted thus:—

" Och hone, Invereshie ! " exclaimed she in a shrill tone of lament, as if she had been apostrophising him in his own presence. " Och hone ! what but the black art of hell itself could have so cast the glamour o'er thee, my bonny bairn, that thou shouldst sit and see thy newly-chartered hills and glens melt from thy grasp as calmly and silently as yonder pine-clad rock beholds the sunshine creep away from its bosom, and never once come to seek counsel, as thou wert wont, from these lips which never lied to thine ear."

" Witchcraft ! " muttered her sister ; " wicked witchcraft is at work with him."

" Witchcraft ! " cried the nurse with an emotion so violent as fearfully to agitate her whole frame; "witchcraft, said ye ? The prince of darkness is himself at work with him. The foul fiend, in a woman's form, is linked to him. Bethink thee of her moonlight wanderings by the waters, —her unhallowed midnight orgies among the graves of the dead, where they say she is still seen to walk while he is sleeping,—her sudden death, for death it was, on that ill-starred morning which proclaimed their union,—the strange reanimation of the corpse by the foul fiend that now possesses it,—the momentary sinking, and terror, and confusion of that wicked spirit when he quailed before the gaze of mine own gifted eye, shot from beneath the shade of the spell-dispersing rowan-tree ;—bethink thee of these things, sister Marion, and wonder not that mine unwilling lips should have been urged to mutter a curse where my heart would have fain poured forth a blessing."

"I saw, I saw," replied the other crone, "thine eye was, indeed, then most potently gifted, sister, and thy will was not thine own."

" Och hone, och hone ! " wailed out the nurse again, " that I should live to see my soul's darling thus rent away from the care of Heaven, handed over to the powers of hell, and doomed to destruction both here and hereafter! Och hone, willingly would I give my worthless life if I could yet save him! Och hone, if I could but pour my burning words into his ear, so that his eyes might be opened, and that he might stent his heart-strings to the stern work of his own salvation."

The unhappy laird had already heard enough. He felt as if the deadly juice of upas had found its way into his veins. His whole frame was, as it were, paralysed. He leaned against the gable of the cottage for some moments, during which he was almost unconscious of thought or of existence; and then, with his limbs failing under him, he staggered, giddy and confused, down the side of the knoll into the pathway below, and sank exhausted upon a mossy bank, where he lay for a time in a state nearly approaching to insensibility. Starting up at last with an unnatural effort which he had no reason left to guide, and regardless of all pathway, he hurried along by the brink of the stream with a fury as wild as that which impelled its rushing waters. Slackening his pace by degrees, as his bewildered recollection began to return to him, he at length stopped, and resting against a rock, his scattered thoughts returned thickly upon him. At first he resolved to go back to hold converse with his nurse, but ere he had well conceived this idea, he rejected it as an idle waste of time; for the fresh recurrence to his recollection of all she had uttered flashed conviction too strongly on his mind to render any further question necessary. Those dark and mysterious doubts which had so long tortured him from time to time during his moody musings, now reared themselves into one gigantic, horrible, and overwhelming certainty, to dwell on which, even for an instant, filled him with an agony that brought large drops of cold perspiration to his brow. His jaws chattered against each other, and a cold shudder ran through his whole system, like that which precedes the last shiver of death. Again, a burning fever seized his brain, and he struck his forehead with the palm of his hand, and he wept and groaned aloud. Relieved by this sudden burst of affliction, he started from his resting-place, and knocking violently on his breast, as if to summon up all of man that was yet left within him,—

"Invereshie!" cried he, addressing himself in unconscious soliloquy, "Invereshie! where is thy boasted resolution?

Whither hath thy courage fled? But it shall come to thee now!" said he, setting his teeth together, and clenching his hands. "Hah! nor mortal nor demon shall keep me in this unhallowed state of enchantment, if it be in the power of fire or of water to break the spell. Let me think," said he again, striking his forehead, as if to rouse up his sharpest intellect; and then after a pause, during which he strode for a few turns backwards and forwards beneath the deep shadow of the rock, "I have it!" he exclaimed, and he urged on his steps with reckless haste towards his home.

The distant murmurs of its mirth and its revelry came on his ears whilst he was yet above a bowshot off,—an arrow itself could not have rent his heart more cruelly. He flew forward, and brushing almost unnoticed through the crowd of serving-men in gay attire that obstructed his entrance, he sought a lonely chamber, where, 'in darkness and in silence, he sat brooding over his misery, and nursing the terrible purpose that possessed him. Every now and then his soul was stung to madness by the shouts of mirth, the music, and the other sounds of jollity which, from time to time, arose from the festal hall below, until, unable longer to bear the torture he suffered, he rushed forth again into the woods. There he wandered for some hours to and fro, torn by his contending passions; for love was still powerful within him, and would, even yet, often rise up for a time to wrestle hard with the wizard Superstition, who had now so irrecoverably entangled and bemeshed his judgment. But ever as the recurrence of the tender emotion was felt within him, he summoned up his sterner nature to exorcise it forth as something unholy. At length the broad moon arose, lighted up the bold front of the lofty Craigmigavie, spread its beams over the far-stretched surface of Loch Inch, shed a pale lustre on the distant Craigou, the Macpherson's watch-hill, and fully illuminated the wild scenery and the sparkling waters of the Feshie, and the noble birches that wept over its roaring rapids, and its deep and pellucid pools.

It is not for me to say what were these mysterious associations which came over the mind of Invereshie as he beheld the ample disc of the glorious luminary arise over the mountain top, and launch itself upward to hold its silent and undisturbed way through the immensity of ethereal space. They seemed to bring an artificial calm to his bosom. But it was the calm of a mind irrevocably wound up to a determined purpose. And now, with his arms folded with convulsive tightness over his breast, as if to prevent the possibility of that purpose escaping thence, he stalked with a steady and resolute step towards the house.

It was now midnight. The revelry which had raged within its walls was silent, and the guests, wearied with the feast and the dance, and the tired servants, were alike buried in sleep. John of Invereshie stole to his lady's chamber. She, too, had retired to rest, and that deep and quiet sleep which results from purity and innocence of soul had shed its balm upon her pillow. Her lamp was extinguished, but the moonbeams shone full through the casement directly on the bed where her beautiful form was disposed, and touched her lovely features with the pale polished glaze of marble. Had it not been for her long dark eyelashes, and those raven ringlets that, escaping from their confinement, had strayed over her snowy neck, she might, in very deed, have been mistaken for some exquisitely sculptured monumental figure. For one moment Invereshie's purpose was shaken. But it was for one moment only; for as memory brought back to him the lonely churchyard, her appeal to the moon, the mysterious events that followed their nocturnal meeting, and all those after circumstances which had combined to produce that awful and to him infallible judgment which accident had led him to hear his old nurse pronounce, his dread purpose became firmly restored to his mind. He stretched forth his hand and griped the wrist of the delicately moulded arm that lay upon her bosom. The lady awoke in alarm, but instantly recognising her husband, her fears were at once tranquillised, and springing from her recumbent posture, she threw herself on his neck. Surprised thus unexpectedly into her embrace, Invereshie stood silent and motionless. Love thrilled through every fibre with one last expiring effort. Aware of the potency of its influence over his heart, he threw his eyes upwards, and—ignorant and unhappy man!—blinded by the dark and bewildering mists of the wild superstition that had dominion over him, he actually prayed to Heaven to give him power to go through with his work; and then, with a fixed composure, gained from that fancied aid which he imagined he was thus experiencing, he calmly and quietly turned to the lady.

"Dost thou see yonder moon?" said he; "never was there sky so fair, or scene so glorious. The night, too, is soft and balmy. Say, will ye wander forth with me a little while to note how the eddies of the Feshie are distilled into liquid silver by her beams?"

"Let me but wrap me in my robe and my velvet mantle, and I will forth with you with good will," replied the lady, quite overjoyed to be thus gratified by her husband in the indulgence of her romantic propensity for such walks. "How kind in you, my love, to think thus of my fancies when rest must be so needful for you." And having hastily protected her person from the night air, she slipped her arm within her husband's, and with a short light step, that but ill accorded with the solemn and funereal stride of him on whom she leaned, she tripped with him down stairs and across the dewy lawn.

"It is, indeed, a most glorious scene!" exclaimed the enraptured lady. "But, in truth, thou saidst not well, Invereshie, in saying that never was there sky so fair or scene so glorious." Then smiling in his face, and sportively kissing his cheek, she innocently added, "I trust thou art no traitor."

"Traitor!" exclaimed Invereshie, with a sudden start that might have betrayed him to any one less unsuspicious.

"Aye, traitor in very deed!" replied the lady laughing. "Traitor truly art thou if thou canst forget the lonely churchyard where you bound yourself to me for ever, and that broad moon which then shed over us her *magic influence!*"

"*Magic influence!*" groaned Invereshie in a deep and hollow tone of anguish.

"Alas! are you unwell, my dearest?" earnestly exclaimed his anxious and affectionate wife. "I fear you have already done too much to-day; and your kindness to me would make thee thus expose thyself when thou wouldst most need repose. See yonder dark cloud, too, pregnant with storm. Look how it careers towards the moon; might not one fancy that some demon of the air bestrode it? Had we not better return to bed? Thou art not well, my love. Come, come, let us return."

9

"No !" replied Invereshie, in a tone calculated to disguise his feelings as much as possible. " I shall get better in the air. A sickness, a slight sickness only ; a little farther walk will rid me of my malady."

The lady said no more ; and Invereshie walked onwards with a slow, firm, but somewhat convulsive step, treading through the checkered wood by a path that wound among green knolls covered with birches of stupendous growth, and that led them to the rocky banks of the Feshie. There they reached a crag that projected over a deep and rapid part of the stream. Its waves were dancing in all the glories of that silver light which they borrowed from the bright luminary that still rode sublimely within a pure haven in the lowering sky, its brilliancy increased by contrast with the dense, and pitchy, and portentous cloud that came sailing sublimely down upon it, like a huge winged continent.

"Invereshie !" cried the lady, her feelings strongly excited by the grandeur and beauty of the scene ; and bursting forth in rapturous ecstacy, " do we not seem like the beings of another world as we stand on this giddy point, with the moon thus pouring out upon us all its potent enchantment ?"

"Now God and Jesu be my guides but I will try thine enchantment !" cried Invereshie.

Steeling up his heart to the deed, and nerving his muscular arms to the utmost, he lifted the light and sylph-like form of his lady. One piercing shriek burst from her as he poised her aloft,—a benighted traveller heard it at a distance, crossed himself, and hurried onwards with trembling limbs,—and ere the lady had uttered another scream, Invereshie had thrown her, like a breeze-borne snow-wreath, far amid the bosom of the waves. The wretched man bent forward from the rock, his fingers clenched, his teeth set together, and his eyeballs stretching after the object which his hands had but just parted with.

"Holy Virgin, she floats !" cried he as he beheld her, by the light of the moonbeam playing on the ripple that followed her form as it was hurried down the stream, supported by her widespread mantle.

"Help ! oh help ! my love ! my lord !—'twas madness !— 'twas accident !—but oh ! mercy and save me !—save or I am lost for ever !"

"She floats!" hoarsely muttered Invereshie, drawing his breath rapidly, and with a croaking sound in his throat that spoke the agonising torture he was enduring. "Ha! she floats! by Saint Mary then was the old woman right! Ha! she struggles at yonder tree!" He sprang from the rock to the margin of the stream, and scrambled towards the spot whither the eddy had whirled the already sinking lady. She had caught with a death-grasp by one frail twig of an alder sapling, though her strength was fast failing. Invereshie's eyes glared over her face as her head and her long dripping hair half emerged from the water.

"Help!—oh save!—oh help!" was now all she could faintly utter, whilst her expiring looked fixed itself upon her husband.

"Help, saidst thou? thou canst well help thyself by thy foul enchantments!" cried Invereshie. "Blessed Saint Michael be mine aid! thou hadst well-nigh taken from me my all, fiend that thou art; thou may'st e'en take that twig with thee, too!" and drawing from his belt his *skian dhu*, he sternly divided the sapling at its very root. As it parted from its hold, the lady disappeared amid the rough surges of the rapid stream, and the blindness which superstition had thrown over him fell at once from her distracted husband.

"Holy angels, she sank!" exclaimed Invereshie with a maddening yell that overwhelmed for a moment the very roar of the flood. "My love! my wife! O murderer! murderer!"

He rushed wildly among the waters to save her. But the impenetrable cloud which had been all this time careering onwards, at that very instant blotted out the moon from the firmament, and left his soul to the midnight darkness of remorse and despair.

A STRANGER APPEARS.

OUR friend Grant's sad story of John Macpherson of Invereshie and his unhappy lady produced so powerful an effect on his auditors, that we continued to walk on in silence for some time after he had concluded, each of us musing after his own fashion. We had been accidentally joined by a stranger, a stout made athletic little man, in an old-fashioned rusty black coat and waistcoat, corduroy breeches, and grey worsted stockings. In one hand he carried a good oaken stick, and in the other a little bundle, tied up in a red cotton handkerchief. This personage walked sturdily forth from a small house of refreshment by the wayside a few minutes before our friend had commenced his narrative ; and we had been too much occupied with our own conversation at the time of his appearance to notice him further than by exchanging with him the customary "*good day to you*" of salutation. But the stranger, having taken even this much as a sufficient introduction among pedestrians travelling in the same direction in so lonely a country as that we were then passing through, ventured to continue to keep pace with us in such a way as to be all the while within earshot of what was said. To the story of John Macpherson he listened with most unremitting attention ; and to our no small surprise he was the first person to open his mouth to make a comment upon it, now that it was ended. After taking a short trot of several yards, to bring himself abreast of our friend the narrator, and at the same time taking off a very well worn hat with an air of marked respect towards him whom he was addressing, he spoke as follows :—

Stranger.—Might I be so bold, sir, as to offer a few remarks, critical, historical, and explanatory on the fragment of Macpherson history which you have just finished rehearsing?

Grant (*somewhat surprised*).—Certainly, sir ; I shall be very glad to hear them.

Stranger (*with a grave and solemn air*).—Why, then, courteous sir, whilst I am altogether wishful to render unto your tale every such praise as may be justly found to be due to it as the produce of one remarkable for that sort of inventive genius which caused Homer to contrive so pretty a story out of the bare *facks* of the Trojan War, and which enabled Virgil to interest us so much with that long tale which he tells, by exaggerating those few dry adventures which befell the Pious Æneas as he fled from Troy to found a new kingdom in Italy, yet must I honestly admit that I cannot compliment the historical fragment which you have given furth to your friends for being parteeklarly verawcious.

Clifford.—Bravo! Well done, old fellow. Ha! ha! ha! You beat Touchstone all to sticks. Never heard the lie more ingeniously given in my life.

Stranger (*with great earnestness, and very much abashed*). —Howt no, sir. Upon my solemn credit, I meant no such-an-a-thing. I only meant to convey to this gentleman, and that with all due respect and courtesy, my humble opinion, that in a grave piece of history, having reference to a brave and honourable Highland clan, the true yevents should be closer stuck to than it may be necessar to do where the subject matter is nothing better than such dubious and unimportant trash as that which the auncient Greek and Latin poets had to deal with.

Grant (*a little nettled*).—And what reason have you to suppose that this is not the true and authentic statement of the facts of John Macpherson's history as they really occurred? I gave them as I got them from another. You do not suppose that I altered or invented them?

Stranger (*with an obsequious inclination of his body*).— Howt away, no, no. No such-an-a-thing. If you got them from another I have no manner of doot but you have rehearsed them simply as ye had them, without adding, or eiking, or paring, or changing one whit. But, nevertheless, the real facks have been sorely and most grievously tampered with by some one.

Grant.—Indeed. And how came you to know anything about this Macpherson story? and what is your authority for saying that the facts have been tampered with?

Stranger (*with oracular gravity*).—Firstly, or, in the first place, I beg to premeese, that I am a schoolmaster; and therefore it is that I am greatly given to accurate and par-teeklar inquiry.   Secondly, or, in the second place, having daily practeesed myself into a habit of correcting the errors of my scholars, it is not very easy for me to pass silently by the blunders of other folk.   And, thirdly, or, in the third place, and to conclude, I am a Macpherson myself; and as it is natural that I should on that account be all the more earnest and punctilious in expiscating the facks connected with the history of that great clan, so is it also to be pre-sumed that I may have had greater opportunity for con-ducking such an investigation.   And so, having premcesed this much, I may add, by way of an impruvment on tho subject, that I shall be just as well pleased to correct your version of this history as I should be to correct the theme of any of my own boys.

Grant (smiling).—I am truly obliged to you for this gratuitous offer of your tuition.

Stranger (whom I shall now call Dominie Macpherson).— Not in the very least obliged to me, sir.   The greatest pleasure of my life is to instruct tho ignorant ; and in yespecial I deem it a vurra high honour and delight to me to have this opportunity of instructing such a gentleman as you.   Proud truly may I be of my scholar.

Clifford (with mock gravity).—The master and the scholar, methinks, are quite worthy of each other.

Dominie (with a bow to the speaker).—I am greatly obli-gated to you for the compliment, sir (*then turning to Grant with a more confident and self-satisfied air than he had hitherto ventured to assume*).—Firstly, or in tho first place, then, sir, you must be pleased to know that John Mac-pherson of Invereshie did not espoose a south country woman ; for his wife was a Shaw of Dalnabhert, on Spey-side there.   Secondly, or in the second place, the leddy never had any such extraordinar fascination over him as you have described her to have ; for she was in reality so ill-natured a woman, that she and her goodman were con-tinually discording and squabbling together.   In the third place, or, as I should say, thirdly,—and it being one of the few conditions in which your tale in some sort agrees with the true history,—she was undoottedly so great a spend-thrift, that many was the bitter quarrel that arose 'twixt her goodman and her, because of her extravagances.   But, fourthly, or in the fourth place, the worthy John Macpher-

son did not throw the lady into the Feshie; and this is a
fack which I would in yespecial crave you to correct in any
future edition, seeing that it brings an evil and scandalous
report upon the said John, and would seem to smell of
murder, when the true parteeklars of the history, known
to me from the time I was a babe, are as follows, to wit :—
It happened one day that the dispute between them ran to
a higher pitch than common, and the lady left the house
with the intention of fleeing to her father at Dalnabhert.
There was neither bridge nor boat upon Feshie at that same
time ; but the woman was so demented with rage that she
plunged into the water with the determination of wading
through. Well, she had not gone three steps into the
ford when she was carried off her legs entirely; but her
body being buoyed up by reason of her petticoats, of which
it is said that she was used to wear not less than four (my
grandmother, honest woman, did the same), she floated
down the stream into the deep water, until being brought
by the swirl of an eddy near to a jutting out rock, she
caught at a twig or branch that grew near the edge, and
held by it like grim death. And here I must admit that,
fifthly, or in the fifth place, Macpherson did of a surety
apply the edge of his *skian dhu* to the bit twiggy she had
a grip of. But, then, most people charitably believe that
it was nothing else but pure courtesy that induced him to
do so to the lady; for, as appearances most naturally
caused him to believe that she had taken to the water with
the full intent of making away with herself by drowning,
he thought that the least that he as her husband could in
common civility do, was to render to her what small help
he could towards the effecting of her purpose. And then,
as to his parting with her in these memorable words—
which, to the great edification of all the wives of Badenoch,
have since become a proverb in that country, to wit, "*you
have already taken much from me, you may take that with
you too*," it must strike you as being most evident, gentlemen, that if Macpherson was to part with his lady at all,
he could not have parted with her in terms more truly
obliging, or with words more generously liberal. But the
most extraordinary and most important deviation from
fack, of which the author of your romance has been guilty,
yet remains to be noticed ; for, in the sixth place, or
sixthly, Macpherson, who seems in the whole matter to

have had no other intention than that his lady should get a good *dookie* (as we say, *Scottice*) in the Feshie, whereby to extinguish the fire of her rage, did not only most gallantly jump into the water to try to save her life, but he actually did save it, or at least the lady's life was saved somehow or other, seeing that she was afterwards the mother of Æneas Macpherson of Invereshie, the direct ancestor of the present worthy Laird of Invereshie and Ballindalloch.

The modest yet dignified air of triumph which the schoolmaster gradually assumed, as he thus went on unfolding fact after fact, and which was considerably augmented as he approached the conclusion of this his critical oration, very much amused us all.

Grant (with an assumed gravity).—I see that I have not only to do with a gentleman of liberal classical acquirement, with one, too, who, blessed with great acumen, has made the art of criticism an especial study, but with a person who is also great as an authority touching the particular historical point which is now in question. And yet, daring as it may be in one of my inexperience to enter the arena with an opponent so powerful, I may perhaps be permitted to observe, in defence of that version of this piece of history of which I have been possessed, that the apparent discrepancy between it and that which you are disposed to consider as the true statement, is, in truth, little or nothing in importance, and may, after all, be very easily reconciled. For, if we attend to the circumstances, we shall find, firstly, or in the first place, that there is nothing before us that may render it impossible for us to believe that Miss Shaw of Dalnabhert might not have received a boarding school education at Edinburgh, as many young ladies of Badenoch unquestionably do, yea, and an education, too, which might have well enough fitted her to have mingled in the gaieties of a court. Secondly, or in the second place, as to the *discordings* which you say took place between her and her husband, I think you must do me the justice to recollect that these were alluded to in my narrative, though they were delicately touched on, as you will allow that all such family quarrels should be. But even if you do not admit the propriety of this, you must at least grant that if I fell into an error at all in this respect, it was less an error of fact than of decree. In the

third place, or thirdly, the evidence of both authorities
is agreed as to the fact of the lady's extravagance, as well
as in the important circumstance that her extravagance
was the cause which ultimately led the parties to the brink
of the river Feshie. Fourthly, or in the fourth place, the
conflicting statements in the two several reports regarding
the mode in which the lady first got into the water will
appear to be of little or no moment when we give to them
a due consideration. We are nowhere informed that any
one was present but Macpherson and his wife; and when
we reflect that these two individuals must have been at
the time in a state of excitement and agitation so very
great as altogether to deprive them of the power of judging
distinctly of anything, it would be quite vain for us to look
to either of them for any accurate statement as to how the
matter occurred. All accounts, however, are agreed as to
the use made by Macpherson of the *skian dhu*. As to your
sixthly, or in the sixth place, I think you will be disposed
candidly to admit, that as my informant saw fit to carry
his narrative only to a certain point of time, so as to break
off at the *black cloud* and *the despair*, it is not only perfectly
possible, but extremely probable, that he meant to tell, in
his second chapter, of the happy recovery of the lady from
the waters of the Feshie,—of the perfect reconcilement of
the pair,—of her reformation in all respects,—of the re-
trenchment of her expenditure,—of the disappearance of
all dandies with plumed hats and piked shoes,—of the
happy birth of the young Æneas,—and of his merry
christening, with many other matters which the historian
has now left us darkly to guess at.

The astonished critic was utterly confounded by our
friend's reply, so solemnly and seriously uttered as it
was; and after one or two "*hums*" and "*has!*" and a
"*very true!*" or two, he fell back some footsteps in rear
of us; and notwithstanding divers malicious attempts
made on the part of Clifford to bring him once more into
the fight, he relapsed into an humble and attentive
listener.

Author.—Your tale, Grant, brings to my recollection a
circumstance which, as tradition tells us, happened after
the celebrated *Raid of Killychrist.*

Grant.—I am not aware that I ever heard of the Raid
of Killychrist, celebrated though you call it.

Author.—I believe the outline of the story of that raid has been given somewhere or other in print by a literary friend of mine, though, to tell you the truth, I have never as yet had the good fortune to see it. But I will cheerfully give you my edition of it, such as it is, if you are willing to listen to it.

Clifford.—But stop for one moment ; and, ere you begin your story, tell me, if you can, what that strange scarecrow looking figure is, which we see standing in yonder green marshy islet near the edge of the small lake immediately before us?

Author.—That figure has excited much speculation. It for some time greatly puzzled myself. I passed by this way more than once in the belief, from the cursory view I had of it, that it was a solitary heron. But my curiosity was excited at last, by observing that it was invariably and immovably in the same spot in the islet, whilst I discovered to my no small wonder, that the islet itself was never found by me twice successively in the same part of the little lake, being sometimes stationed in the middle of it and at other times somewhere towards either end, or near to either of the sides.

Clifford.—Come, come! ha! ha! ha! you are coming magic over us now. You don't expect that we are to believe any such crammer as this!

Author.—I assure you that what I state is strictly and literally true, though I must admit that you have some reason for doubt until you have a further explanation ; and I am glad that I have it in my power to give it to you as it was given to myself by an intelligent man who lives in this neighbourhood. What you see is in reality a floating island.

Clifford.—A floating island! I know that you Scots are said to be fond of migration ; but I had no idea that any part of your soil was in the habit of making voyages either for profit or pleasure.

Author.—Nay, nor does a Scot himself often move from any station where he finds himself comfortable, except it may be for the purpose of migrating into some other which may hold out yet greater advantages than that which he possesses. But this whimsical islet shifts its position without reason, exactly like an idle Englishman, who, without any fixed object, moves from one spot of Europe to another, he cannot himself tell why, and merely as the breezes of caprice may blow him about.

Grant.—A Roland for your Oliver, Master Clifford! But (*addressing Author*) tell us how you account for this strange phenomenon?

Author.—The mass, as you see, is not very large. Its extent is only a few yards each way. It is composed of a light, fibrous, peaty soil, which was probably originally torn from its connecting foundation by the influx of some sudden flood, aided by a contemporaneous and tempestuous wind. Being once fairly turned adrift in the lake, we can easily conceive that its specific gravity must have been every succeeding day lessened by the growth of the matted roots of the numerous aquatic plants that grew on it, till it rose more and more out of the water, and became at length so very buoyant as to be transported about by every change of the wind.

Clifford.—Bravo! You have lectured to us like a geologist; and I must confess, with as much show of reason in your theory as those of many of these ante-diluvian philosophers can pretend to. But you have yet to play the part of the zoologist, and to give us some account of that strange animal, human being or beast, alive or stuffed, as it may be, that so strangely stands sentry yonder in the midst of it. One might almost fancy it to be one of Macbeth's weird sisters.

Grant.—It has indeed a most uncouth and ghostly appearance when seen at this distance. It looks so much like some withered human figure, where we cannot easily reconcile it to reason that any human figure could possibly be.

Author.—Yes; and when we think what its effect must be when it is seen by a stranger, sailing slowly over the surface of the little lake, impelled by a whistling wind, at that hour when spirits of all kinds are supposed to have power to burst their cerements, when the moon may give sufficient light to display enough of its wasted and wizard looking form to beget fearful conceptions, without affording such an illumination as might be sufficient to explain its nature, we may easily believe that many are the rustic hearts that sink with dread, and many are the clodpate heads of hair that bristle up "like quills upon the fretful porcupine," whilst whips and spurs are employed with all manner of good will on the unfortunate hides of such unlucky animals as may chance to be carrying lated travellers past this enchanted lake towards their distant place of repose.

Clifford.—I can well enough conceive all this. But you have yet to tell us what the figure really is.

Author.—Notwithstanding its imposing appearance, it is nothing more, after all, than a figure made of rushes and rags carelessly tied about a pole by some of the simple shepherds of these wilds. It is comparatively of recent creation; but I understand that the islet is by no means of modern origin, though I am led to believe that, like other more extensive pieces of earth, it has undergone many changes since its first creation. It must have been liable to be increased and diminished by various natural causes at different periods of its history.

Dominie Macpherson (half advancing into the group, with a chastened air, and more obsequious inclination of his body than he had ever yet used.)—If I may make so bold as to put in my word—ha—hum. If I might be permitted to make so bold as to speak, I can assure you, gentlemen, that the bit island yonder has long existed. I have known these parts for many a long year; and I can testify to the fack, from my own observation, added to and eiked out by that of men who were old when I was born. Superstitious people call it the witches' island, and believe that the weird sisterhood hold it under their yespecial control and governance.

Clifford.—Much better sailing in it than in a sieve. But have you gathered none of the adventures of the Beldams to whom you say it belongs?

Dominie.—God forbid, sir, that I should say it belongs to such uncanny people! But truly there is a very strange story connected with it.

Clifford.—A story, Mr. Macpherson, pray let's have your story without delay, if you please, that we may forthwith judge whether you are to rank higher in the world of letters as an historian or as a critic. *"Perge Domine!"*

Grant.—You will gratify us much, sir.

Dominie.—I shall willingly try my hand, sir; and if you find not the sweetness of Homer or Maro in my narrative, at least you shall be sure of that accuracy as to fack which so much distinguished the elegant author of the Commentaries.

Clifford (with mock gravity).—Doth the narrative touch your own adventures, my friend? Are you, like Cæsar, the historian of your own deeds?

Dominie.—Not so, sir; but I had all the facks from my father, who knew the hero and heroine, and all the persons whose names are mentioned in it.

Clifford.—Ha! you have a hero, then, and a heroine too? Why that, methinks, looks somewhat more like romance than history.

Grant (smiling).—Be quiet, Clifford! You forget that you are all this while keeping us from our story. Pray, sir, have the goodness to begin.

The schoolmaster bowed; and taking a central place in the line of march, he proceeded with his narrative in language so mingled with quaint and original expressions, that I cannot hope, and therefore do not always pretend, to render it with the same raciness with which it was uttered.

LEGEND OF THE FLOATING ISLET.

I MUST honestly tell you, gentlemen, that my story hath much the air of a romance, as well as much of love in it, and many of the other ingredients of such like vain and frivolous compositions; but you shall have the facks as told me by my much honoured father, who, being a well-employed blacksmith, not many miles from the spot where we now are, may be said to have been the chronicler of the passing yevents of his day.

Awell, you see, it happened that a well-grown, handsome, proper looking young shepherd lad, called Robin Stuart, had possessed himself of the young affections of a bonny lassie, the daughter of Donald Rose, one of the better sort of tenants of these parts. Their love for one another had grown up with them, they could not well say how. Its origin was lost in the innocent forgetfulness of their childhood, as the origin of a nation is buried in the fabulous history of its infancy; but, however born, this they both felt, that it had grown in strength and vigour every day of their lives, until with Robin it began to ripen into that honest and ardent attachment natural to a manly young heart, which was responded to on the part of bonny Mary Rose by all the delicacy and softness that ought to characterise the modest young maiden's return of a first love. But however natural it was for the tender heart of the daughter to beat in unison, or, as I may say, to swing in equal arcs with that of her lover, just as if they had been two pendulums of like proportions and construction, it was equally *selon les règles*, as the modern men of Gaul would say, that the churlish and sordid old tyke of a father, who had been accustomed to estimate merit more by the rule of proportion than anything else, exactly perhaps as he would have valued one of his own muttons according to the number of its pounds, should have stormed like a fury when he actually deteckit the *callant* Robin Stuart in the very *ack* of making love to his daughter in his own house !

A desperate feud of some years' standing had made Donald the declared enemy of Robin's father, old Harry *the herd of the Limekilns,* a cognomen which he had from the circumstance of his cottage being placed on the side of yonder hill of that name, so called from a prevailing tradition that the lime used in the building of the Castle of Loch-an-Dorbe was brought in the state of stone in creels on horses' backs from the quarries near to Grantown, and burned there. Old Harry was a poor man and a herd, whilst Donald Rose was wealthy, and especially prided himself on being a *Duniwassel,* or small gentleman, so that there thus existed three most active awgents, to wit, enmity, avarice, and pride, which combined to compel him to put an instantaneous stop to all such proceedings between Robin Stuart and his daughter Mary. Without one moment's delay, he thrust the young shepherd, head and shoulders, violently forth from his door, and smacking the palm of his hand significantly and with great force and birr on his dirk sheath, so as to cause the weepon to ring again—

"I'll tell ye what it is, my young birkie," said he, in a voice like thunder, "gif I catch ye again within haulf a mile o' my dochter, ye sall ha'e a taste o' sweetlips here! An' as for you, Mary, an' ye daur to let siccan a beggarly chield as that come within a penny stane cast o' ye, by my saul but I'll turn ye out ower my door hauld wi' as leetle ceremony as I ha'e done the same thing to Rab himsell yonder!"

But, as one of the ancient heathen poets hath it, love is a fire which no storm can extinguish; it feeds itself with hope, and only burns the brighter the more it is blown against by adverse blasts. You know, gentlemen, how Pyramus and Thisbe contrived to hold secret converse together. Though Robin and Mary had no crack in a wall through which to pour the stream of their mutual love,—nay, although their respective dwellings were some mile or two separate from each other, yet many were the private meetings which the youth and maiden contrived to obtain, during which they employed their time in fostering their mutual hopes, and in strengthening their belief that better and happier days were yet in store for them. And happy indeed would have been those days of their anticipation, if they could have proved happier than were those stolen hours which they thus occasionally enjoyed together.

Now, it happened one beautiful day, in the beginning of summer, that Donald Rose rode off from his door to go to a distant market, whence there was no chance of his returning till late at night. The old saying hath it, that when the cat is away the mice will play. This was too favourable an opportunity to be lost by a pair of young lovers so quick-sighted as Robin and Mary. It had been marked by both of them for some weeks before it came; and the farmer's long-tailed rough grey garron had no sooner borne his master's bulky body in safety along the ticklish and treacherous path that went by a short cut through the long moss, and over the distant rising ground, than Robin Stuart, true to his tryst, appeared to escort his bonny lassie on a ramble of love. No one was at home to spy out their intentions but old Mysie Morrison, the good-natured hireling woman of all work; and she was too much taken up with her household affairs to trouble her head about watching the young lad and lass. Indeed, if she had thoughts of them at all, she was too much attached to her young mistress, and too well acquainted with her secret, and too shrewd to betray her either by design or by accident.

As you may see, gentlemen, there was no great choice of pleasure walks in this bleak *destrick*, but the two young creatures were so taken up with each other, and so full of joy in each other's company, that the dreariest spot of it was as a rich and blooming garden in their delighted eyes. They tripped along merrily together, and bounded like roe deer over the heathery knolls, scarcely knowing, and not in the least caring, which way they went, until they found themselves by the side of the little *lochan* which we have but just left behind us. It was then the season when the wilderness of this upland country was clad in a mantle of wild flowers, and thereabouts especially they grew in so great variety and profusion that it seemed as if the goddess Flora had resolved to hold her court in that place. There, then, they resolved to rest a while; and Robin, producing the simple contents of a little wallet which he carried under his plaid, they sat down together and feasted luxuriously.

When they had finished their meal the lovers began to

waste the hours in idle but innocent sport. They roamed
about here and there, gathering the gaudy flowering plants
that grew around them ; and after filling their arms with
these wildling treasures, they again seated themselves side
by side, to employ their hands in arranging and plaiting
them into rustic ornaments. Whilst thus occupied they were
too happy and too much taken up with their own pleasing
prattle to think of the progress of the sun, who was all
this time most industriously urging his ceaseless journey
over their heads, without exciting any of their attention,
except in so far as his beams might have lent a livelier hue
to the gay garlands they were weaving for each other, or
yielded a fresher glow to the cheeks, or a brighter sparkle
to the eyes, of those who were to wear them.

Whilst they were thus so happily and so harmlessly
occupied, they went on, with all the innocent simplicity of
rustic life, repeating over and over again to each other
their solemn vows of eternal love and fidelity, as if they
could never have been tired of these their sweet and sooth-
fast asseverations, whilst, at the same time, they uttered
them with a copiousness of phraseology and a variety of
dialogue truly marvellous in such a muirland pair as they
were. It would have absolutely astonished all your writers
of *novelles* to have overheard them, and it would have
puzzled any of these fiction-mongers to have invented
the like.

"Oh that your father was but as poor and as humble as
mine, Mary!" exclaimed the youth at last, "or, rich and
proud as he is, that you could leave him and content
yoursel' wi' bein' a poor man's wife!"

"Na, Robin!" replied she, shaking her head gravely,
and then laying her hand upon his arm, and looking up
wistfully into his eyes, "you would never ask me, my
father's ae bairn, to leave him noo that he has grown auld,
and that my dear mother has left us baith and gane to
heeven! Gif, indeed, he could be but brought to look wi'
a kind ee on you—then—then"—continued she, with a
faultering tongue, whilst she blushed deeply, and threw
her eyes down amidst the heap of flowers that lay at her
feet, —"then, indeed, we might baith be his bairns."

"Oh! I wish again that he were but a poor man!" cried
Robin enthusiastically, "for then might thir twa arms o'
mine mak' me as gude a match in his een as a' the bit

10

tocher he could gie might warrant him to look for. Weel and stoutly wad I work for sic a prize as you, Mary!"

" An' weel wad I be pleased that ye should ha'e it, Robin, little worth as it is!" said Mary, with an expression of undisguised fondness. "Though I could na gie up my father, I could gie up a' my father's gowd, gif it wad but bring you hame to help him. And gif it warna for him," added she, with a tear trembling in her eye, " I trow I could gang wi' you to the warld's end, an' I war never to see anither human face!"

" O Mary!" exclaimed Robin, in a transport, " I could live wi' you in a desert. I could live wi' you in some wee uninhabited spot in the midds o' the muckle ocean, aye, though it war nae bigger than the bit witches' island there afore ye, aye, and as fond o' flittin' as it is too, and that we sould never leave its wee bit bouns."

There was something so absurdly extravagant in the very idea of two people being confined together to a space of a few yards square, to live the sport of every varying breeze that might blow over the surface of the deep, that Mary's gravity was fairly overcome, notwithstanding the high pitch of devoted feeling to which she had been wound up at the moment. She could not control herself; and she gave way to loud peals of laughter, in which her lover as heartily joined her. "See!" cried she, the moment she could get her breath, whilst she pointed sportively to the little floating islet which was at that moment lying motionless, and almost in contact with the shore near to the spot where they were sitting, " see, see, Robby, how our wee bit fairy kingdom is waitin' yonder to bid us welcome!"

" Come, then, my queen, let us take possession o 't then in baith our names!" cried Robin, in the same tone, and gaily and gallantly seizing her hand at the same time, he, with great pretended pomp and ceremony, led her, half laughing, and half afraid, towards the place where the island rested.

At the time my story speaks of the borders of the loch were less encroached upon by weeds and rushes than you have seen that they now are, and the island lay, as if it had been moored, as mariners would say, in deep water close to the shore. It was, therefore, but a short step to reach it, and Robin easily handed the trembling Mary into it with as much natural grace, I 'll warrant me, as the pious

Æneas himself could have handed Queen Dido. The lassie's
light foot hardly made its grassy surface quiver as it reached
it ; but, full of his own frolic, and altogether forgetful for
that moment of the precarious and kittle nature of the
ground he had to deal with, he sprang in after her with a
degree of force which was far from being required to effect
his purpose, and so great was the impetus which he thus
communicated to the floating islet, that it was at once
pushed several yards away from the shore. With one joint
exclamation of terror both stood appalled, and they silently
beheld the small fragment of ground that supported them
moving, almost insensibly, yet farther and farther towards
the middle of the loch, so long as any of the force which
Robin had so unfortunately applied to it remained, and
then it settled on the motionless bosom of the deep and
black looking waters, at such a distance even from the bank
which they had just left as to forbid all hope of escape to
those who could not swim.

Fled indeed, gentlemen, was now all the mirth of this
unlucky pair. Poor Mary was at once possessed by a
thousand fears ; and even the firmer mind of her companion, though sufficiently occupied with its anxiety for
her, was not without its full share of those individual
superstitious apprehensions naturally produced by the
place where they were, and which secretly affected both of
them. Neither of them could resist the belief that supernatural interference had had some share in producing their
present distress. But whatever Robin's private thoughts
may have been, he was too manly to allow them to become
apparent to Mary. Plucking up some long grass and sedges,
therefore, and making them into a large bundle, he took
off his jacket, threw it over it, and by this means made a
dry seat for her in the very middle of the quivering and
spongy surface of the islet. Then casting his red plaid over
his shoulder, he stood beside her, now bending over her to
whisper words of comfort and encouragement into her ear,
and by and by stretching his neck erect, that his eyes might
have the better vantage to sweep around the whole circuit
of the dull and monotonous surface of the surrounding
wastes. How mixed, yet how antagonist to each other
were the ideas which now passed rapidly through his mind !
At one moment he felt a strange and indescribable rapture
as the mere thought crossed him that this small floating

spot of earth did indeed contain no other human being but
himself and her whom he would wish to sever from all the
world besides, that she might be the more perfectly dependent on himself alone, and therefore the more indissolubly
bound to him ; and then would he utter some endearing
words to Mary. Then, again, the shivering conviction would
strike him, that although there was no *human* being but
themselves there, there might yet be other unknown and
unseen beings in their company that neither of them wist
of, and he looked fearfully around him, scanning with suspicious eye, not only the whole surface of the lake, but
every little nook and crevice of the shore. And then bethinking him of night, he lifted up his eyes with anxious
solicitude from time to time, to note the position of the
sun, whose progress he and his fair companion had previously so much disregarded ; and great was his internal
vexation when he perceived how rapidly his car was now
rolling downwards, not, as the auncient poets would say,
in his haste to lay himself in the lap of Thetis, but as if he
had been eager to escape behind yon great lump of a muirland hill yonder to the westward.

But a yet more trying discovery soon began to force
itself upon his attention. The islet on which they stood
seemed, as he narrowly measured it with his eye, to have
sunk some inches into the water ! Already in idea he
felt its bubbling wavelets closing over his own head and
the dear head of her whom he so much loved ! His heart
grew sick at the very thought. Summoning up courage,
however, he contrived to allow no outward sign to betray
his feelings to Mary ; and taking certain marks with his
eye, he set himself to watch them with an anxiety so
intense, and with a look so fixed, that he was unable
rationally to reply, either by word or sign, to anything
that the poor lassie said to him, so that she began at
length to entertain new apprehensions at the wild expression which his countenance exhibited. By degrees, however, she became more assured, for, after long and accurate
observation had led him to believe that at least no very
rapid change was taking place, his features gradually
relaxed, and hers were for the time relieved by that very
sympathy which had so enchained them.

And now the sun was fast approaching the horizon, and
Robin's eyes were eagerly employed in endeavouring to

penetrate even the most distant shadows that were rapidly
settling down upon the hills, behind which he was about
to disappear, whence they began to spread themselves over
the wide extent of brown moors and black mosses that
stretched everywhere around them. As the light passed
away, his glances flew more hastily in every direction, in
the vain search for some human being. Above all, he
earnestly surveyed the road where he for some time
sanguinely hoped that he might discover some one returning from the market, who might yet lend them an aid,
though he felt that it quite defied him to form any rational
conception as to what the nature of that aid could be.
Again, he would most inconsistently shrink back, and
instinctively shut his eyes, as if that could have concealed
his person, from very dread that Donald Rose might
come home that way and discover them in this their
distressing and dangerous situation, for he was fully aware
that he had but little chance of rising in the old man's
estimation by having thus had the misfortune to bring the
life of his only child into so great peril. As he thus
ruminated, he remembered that although this was not old
Donald's shortest way home, yet it was that which he was
most likely to take towards night, as being the best. And
he moreover distinctly perceived, that if he did come that
way before it was dark, he could not fail to discover them.
For as the rugged and irregular muirland road wound
round nearly one-third of the whole margin of the little
loch, by reason of its having to cross the bit brook that
issues from its western extremity, it was self-evident that
no one could travel that way without having his eyes
intently fixed, for a considerable time, in a direction that
must compel him to survey the whole surface of the sheet
of water, so that not a duck or a dab-chick could yescape
them. And what if the farmer did not come? Might they
not be discovered by some other hard-hearted person, who,
instead of assisting them, might be so wicked as to carry
the news of their situation directly to old Rose, whose rage,
he felt persuaded, would be enough to burn up the waters
of the loch. Such a finis to the adventure was the least
misfortune they could look for from the malice of those evil
spirits of the islet, by whom he believed that he and Mary
had been thus entrapped. Anxious as he had at first been
to descry some one, he now longed for night to fall down

on them and render them invisible. Then the utter hope-
lessness of eventual concealment occurred to him, for he
reflected that the farmer must return home at some hour
during the night; that when he did so return, he must
find his daughter absent, and that his ungovernable fury
would not be diminished by the tormenting suspense in
which he would be kept regarding her until next day,
when they should certainly be discovered. Robin's mind
was tossed to and fro among such unpleasant thoughts as
these, till they were all put to flight by the overwhelming
force of that superstitious dread which taught him to
believe that night would soon give an uncontrolled
power to those evil beings who had thus so cruelly used
them.

"Oh, for a breeze of wind!" cried poor Robin in his
agony, as a thousand formidable and ghastly shapes began
to dance before his disturbed fancy. And—

"Oh, for a breeze!" sighed the soft and tremulous voice
of Mary Rose, whose mind had all this while been silently
following the same irregular train of thought, and sym-
pathetically participating in the distressing emotions
which had been agitating her lover.

And now the sun went down in a blaze of glory beyond
the western hills, and his last beams took leave of the
surface of the water, after having shed a radiance over it,
as well as a cheerful glow over the countenances of the
two lovers, that but ill assorted with the misery of soul
which they were enduring. By degrees a soft summer
exhalation began to arise from the bosom of the loch, as
well as from all the neighbouring pools, peatpots, and
marshes. But balmy, and cheering, and invigorating as it
was to all the parched offspring of nature that grew in this
desert, which opened their bosoms to receive it, and gratefully exhaled their richest perfumes, it chilled the very
hearts of the lovers, as night fell darkly and dismally
around them.

"Robin," said Mary in a voice that quivered from the
effects of the chilling damp, combined with those secret
terrors which were every instant taking more and more
powerful possession of her, in spite of all her reason and
resolution to resist them. "Robin, put on your jacket,
you will starve."

"Mair need for me, Mary, to gie ye this plaid o' mine,"

replied he in a tender tone. "Here, tak' it about ye, my dearest lassie, and keep up a gude heart."

"Na, I'll no tak' nae mair aff ye," said Mary gently, refusing to allow him to throw the plaid over her.

"Let me—let me gie ye haulf o't then," said he, with a modest hesitation.

After some little further discussion, the matter was at last arranged, for Mary stood up by Robin's side, and the ample plaid having been thrown over both of them, somewhat in the manner of a tent, the edges of it were held together by her lover's nervous arm, so as in a great measure to exclude the cold damp air. If it was not altogether shut out, Robin at least for some time felt none of its influence, for, finding himself thus the sole protector of his beloved Mary, his heart burned within him with love and pride, and all thoughts of evil spirits were banished for a time.

Things had not been long accommodated in this manner, when Mary complained that her feet began to grow cold and wet, and the change in Robin's thoughts may be conceived when he too became convinced that the water was certainly somehow or other gaining upon them. The darkness was now such as to render it impossible for him to make any such minute observation as he had done before. He could only now guess vaguely, and his whole frame shivered with horror as the suspicion crossed him, that the unusual weight which the islet now bore having pressed it downwards, the upper and more porous parts of it, which were formerly comparatively dry, had imbibed a greater quantity of water than usual, and the specific gravity of the whole being thus increased, it was gradually sinking, and must soon be altogether submerged. I say not that the poor lad reasoned thus upon pheelosophical principles, but, nevertheless, he did come to the conclusion that this treacherous bit of ground was sinking fast. How long or how short a time it might possibly take before the awful catastrophe should arrive, was more than he had any means of determining. He had nothing now left but to nerve himself with resolution to enable him to conceal his fears and his horrors from Mary, though, at the same time, he could not help clinging to her with an earnestness and a wildness of manner that did anything but allay her terrors. Dark as the night was, all those superstitious fancies which had disturbed their minds were banished by the overpowering conviction of speedily approaching dissolution which individually possessed them in secret. The black gulf by which they were environed seemed, in the mind's eye of each of them, to be yawning to swallow them up; and the thought that they should die in each other's arms, was the only consolation that visited their afflicted souls in that awful moment.

"Let us pray to the Lord!" said Mary solemnly, "for our death-hour is come!"

Robert, who would now have deemed it to be a sinful ack to speak to her of hope, which he had himself so utterly abandoned, immediately obeyed her command. You know, gentlemen, that it is the glorious preevilege of our Scottish peasantry to receive education from the pious and well conducked teachers of our parochial schools. Even the youngest men are thereby exerceesed in prayer, so that it becomes so much of a habit with them, that they are at all times prepared to pour out their souls in extemporaneous offerings to the Deevine Being. You can easily understand, therefore, that at such a moment when convinced that he himself, and she whom he loved beyond all yearthly things, were about to be summoned to the footstool of their Creator, his prayer was solemn, yearnest, simple, and sublime. So certain did the sealing of their doom now appear, that he put up few petitions for present help in this world. The whole force of his supplication was directed to their salvation through the merits of a Saviour, in that on which they were so soon to enter, and Mary clung closer to him as he spoke, and continued to follow all his expressions, now internally and now audibly, with a fervour that sufficiently proved the intensity of her faith and hope.

Whilst the poor creatures were thus employed a dim gleam of light from the eastern horizon seemed as if struggling through the dense fog that hung over the loch, and soon afterwards a gentle passing breath of air was distinctly felt by both of them. It murmured around them, and fanned them, as it were, for a moment, and found its way even within the hollow of the plaid. Its voice was to them as the voice of their guardian angel, and it refreshed their drooping souls, although they knew not very well how it did so. In a very few minutes afterwards, however, the mist being broken up by the influence of a full moon that had just risen, began to collect itself into distinct spiral columns, which dissipated themselves one after another, as if they had been so many spirits melting into air. The long wished-for breeze then at length came singing most musically as it skimmed over the surface of the perfumed heath. And it had not long curled the hitherto still surface of the loch, till Robin and Mary began to perceive that the half-drowned island was sensibly increasing its distance from the shore whence they had taken their departure. There was something very fearful in this, and the poor lassie clung closer to her lover. But with all their fears it now seemed as if Hope was sitting beckoning to them on the opposite shore, towards which the breeze was so evidently, though so slowly, propelling them.

The moon now shone forth in full radiance, and speedily dissipated the broken fragments of the fog that yet remained. One mass only, denser than the rest, still hung poised over their heads, naturally maintained in that position by the attraction of the damp floating earth they stood on. To their great joy they perceived that the breeze was increasing, and that their motion was gradually accelerating.

" Mary, my dear," cried Robin, " keep a gude heart ; I'm thinking that we'll maybe mak out yet. Let's hoize up the plaid till it catches mair o' the wund."

And, accordingly, they raised their arms and kept the plaid high over their heads, till it was bellied out by the breeze like the lugsail of a herring buss, and their velocity was tripled.

They were thus moving gallantly onwards, in anxious expectation that a very few minutes more would moor them in safety to the shore, so that there might yet be time for Mary to hurry home before her father should arrive to question her absence, when they suddenly perceived a horseman riding along the road which *sweep't* around the end of the loch they were now nearing so fast. What think ye, gentlemen, was the astonishment, dread, and mortification of the poor lassie and her lad when they beheld the moonbeams reflected from a face as broad and as pale as the disc of the luminary from which they had been last projected? It was Donald Rose himself! As their supporting bit of earth drifted onwards with them, they stood together for a moment petrified with surprise and fear, whilst they beheld him check his horse, and turn his head towards the loch, as if to gaze at them; and then, with one shriek from Mary and a deep groan from Robin, which might have made a good treble and bass for the psalmody of the martyrs, both the two of them, by one simultaneous movement, sank down together among the rank grass and water-weeds in which they were standing, and the folds of the plaid collapsing around them, both were completely shrouded beneath it. There they lay, abandoning themselves to their perverse fate, and fearing to move or speak, until, in a very few seconds, they were drifted to the very spot where they too well knew that the enraged farmer must be already standing like a roaring lion ready to devour them; and they were thus prostrated, as it were, at the very feet of him whose ungovernable rage they had so much reason to wish to have avoided.

The floating island had touched the terra firma for some seconds, but still the conscious pair dared not to peep from beneath the covering that enveloped them. They lay, as I might say, as quiet as two mice in a bag of meal. They uttered not a word. They hardly even dared to breathe. But tremblingly in need of support under circumstances so very trying, the poor lassie Mary clasped her Robin about the waist with an energy equal to the terror she was moved by. It was the feeling of this her utter dependence upon him for support and defence that first subdued Robert's own fears, and awakened him to a sense of his own dignity as a man.

"An' ye'll hae but a thoughty o' patience, Maister Rose, I'll tell ye a' aboot it," said he, commencing his peroration from beneath the plaid, somewhat *sotto voce*, as the degenerate modern Romans would say. But gaining greater boldness as he heard the sound of his own voice, and that his words remained as yet unanswered, he went on to speak, gradually raising his tone as he did so, and at the same time erecting his person by slow degrees from his abject attitude, though without unveiling himself.

"Ye may think as ye like, Maister Rose, but I canna help lovin' Miss Mary; I maun love her spite o' mysell, an' gin ye wad hae me no to love her nae mair, ye maun just dirk me here at aince. But for the sake o' a' that's good !" continued he, blubbering from very emotion, "dinna offer to hurt ae hair o' *her* bonny head, for by my troth an' ye do, Maister Rose !"——

These last words were uttered in so loud and impassioned a key, that it sufficiently indicated the nature as well as the resolute determination of the threat that was intended to follow, even if the furious action of the uplifted arm and clenched fist had not left it quite unequivocal. So violent was the effect, that the plaid which had risen along with the speaker, and which had up to this point continued to muffle his head and eyes, was suddenly thrown off.

"Gude keep hus a' he's gane !" cried Robin with a stare of horror. "As I'm a leevin' man !—as I houp and believe I am"—continued he, pinching his own arms and thighs as he said so, to convince himself of the fack that he really was alive, "it was your father's wraith we saw, Mary !"

Half fainting from the effect of the complication of terrors which had surrounded her, Mary Rose was hardly conscious of what Robin had said, and he for his part having gained that self-command of which the sudden nature of his alarm had for a moment deprived him, now bit his lip and studiously avoided uttering one word that might convey to her the least inkling of that conviction which had just then flashed upon him, or that might distress her mind with any share of that superstitious dread which at this moment so completely filled his own.

"He's gane indeed, dear Mary," said he as he gently assisted her to rise ; " let's be thankful that we're safe on dry land, and let me help you hame to your ain house as fast as I can, and may the Lord be aboot us !"

Adjusting his plaid over her, and placing his arm around her slender waist to support her tottering steps, he guided her homewards by the light of the moon through the rugged moor by a short path. Often as they went did each of them secretly remember how auspiciously the morning sun had shone upon them as they had danced lightly together over the blooming heather ! But they were both too much sunk by the unfortunate issue of their day's adventures, believing as they, poor things, foolishly did, that the powers of evil themselves had combined to thwart them ; they were too much sunk, I say, to be able to utter much more than monosyllables to each other, or such words at least as were expressive of gratitude to

Heaven for having permitted them to yescape with life, whilst an indefinite dread of the fate that awaited them hung secretly lowering over each of their minds.

Lights blazed within the white-washed windows of Donald Rose's cottage as it appeared on a knoll before Mary's dizzy eyes. Whether these might indicate her father's presence or not, she could not daur to guess. The poor lassie was so feared, that she hesitated to approach the door herself; yet she felt that there was still greater danger there for Robin, and, with a delicate pressure of the young lad's hand, she bade him tenderly farewell.

"Robin, haste ye hame to the Limekilns," said she. "Ye maunna face my father. Leave me to face him mysell."

"No!" said Robin boldly and with peculiar emphasis, "I ha'e noo faced *mair* than your father, Mary; and sae I'm no ga'in' to flee your father himsell, though he does wear a durk. Gif he *be* comed hame, ye may the mair want my help to meet him."

Fearfully alarmed for the consequences, and still more apprehensive for her father's wrath against him than against herself, she endeavoured to argue with him on the folly of his rashness; and whilst they were both engaged in an animated and somewhat imprudently loud discussion on this subject, they were startled by the voice of Mysie Morrison, who came suddenly upon them from the cottage.

"Bless ye, my bairns, is that you?" exclaimed this good domestic. "What i' the warld has keepit ye sae lang oot daffin'? An' is that the end o' a' your courtin' after a', that you're to come hame an' end it that gate wi' a collyshangy?"

"Has my father come back frae the market yet, Mysie?" tremblingly demanded Mary.

"Na, he's no come hame yet," replied the old woman, "and I'm thinkin' that he'll no be comin' hame the night noo. I'se warrant he's been weel set wi' some drouthy customer, an' he'll hae staid whar he wuz. But come ye're ways in, my bairns, an' get some meat; I trow ye maun be clean starvin'."

With Robin's recollection of the spectre which he had beheld riding by the loch-side he had little heart, at that hour, to cross the wide muir that lay between Donald Rose's house, where he then was, and his father's cottage on the hill of the Limekilns. He much preferred the risk of meeting Donald's substantial body of flesh and blood, dirk and fury and all, within the four walls of a well lighted up room, to having his moonlight path crossed upon the heath by the terrific simulacrum or wraith which had already blasted his sight. In addition, therefore, to the seducing attractions which Mary's society held out to him, coupled with those urgent admonitions which he was receiving at that moment from hunger and thirst, he had thus some vurra strong and powerful secret reasons for preferring to remain, to which he did not choose to give utterance. Mary, for her part, was sorely buffeted between her wishes and her fears. She had every desire to do that hospitality to her lover which her own faintness began to remind her must now be so highly necessary to him. On the other hand, she had the strongest apprehension that her father might suddenly return, in spite of all that Mysie had said to the contrary, and she thus hung for a moment in dootful equilibrio, as a body may say, between the two opposing forces which were thus operating on her. But Mysie, who was much less timorous, having done all she could to assure her that there was no danger of a surprise, she at length hushed her fears and tacitly yielded to her wishes. She and Robin, therefore, were soon seated over some comfortable viands by a blazing hearth, whilst Mysie, with a judgment and prudence that might have well befitted an attendant of Queen Dido herself when she took refuge from the storm with the Trojan king in the cave, retired to make security doubly sure, by setting herself to watch at the window of the neighbouring apartment, where, by the light of the moon, she might see her master return, so that she might give *timeous* notice to Robin Stuart to yescape by the back-door, whilst old Rose was occupied in putting his horse into the stable.

This was well enough arranged in the old woman, gentlemen. Caius Julius Cæsar himself could not have made better dispositions to have prevented a night surprise. But, as our immortal bard, William Shakespeare, hath it, in the words which he hath put into the mouth of the lively Rosalind, time goes at different paces with different individuals. Upon this occasion it certainly went fast enough with Robin Stuart and Mary Rose. For, though their minds were for a short time crossed occasionally by very fearful

visions of the past, of some of which they dared hardly to
speak to each other, yet these were soon banished altogether
by their mutual smiles, and by the ardent and endearing expressions which they went on interchanging together. Swift
flew the minutes, and their conversation was still waxing
more and more interesting. They were seated close together ; and, as their tender dialogue became more intensely
moving, Robin's arm had unconsciously found its way
around Mary's waist, whilst hers had fallen carelessly
over his shoulder, and had accidentally carried with it the
folds of his plaid, which she had not yet thrown off. The
cheerful gleam from the blazing moss-fir faggots threw a
strong effect of light from the ample chimney over their
figures. They indeed believed, from their inaccurate calcu-
lation, that this their felicity had endured for some short
half hour only, whilst, by the drowsy account of old Mysie,
who had sat nodding, and every now and then catching
her head up to save it, if she possibly could, from dropping
irrecoverably into the lap of Morpheus, the god of sleep,
four good hours had gone by. As the truth probably lay
between, I shall take the mean of these two extremes, and
therefore I may say, with some degree of confidence, that
about two hours had yelapsed when she at last yielded to
the soporific influence, and fell into a sleep so profound,
that ere it had endured for ten minutes, ten cannons or ten
claps of thunder could hardly have awakened her; and whilst
matters were in this state the door of the apartment where
Robin and Mary were so comfortably seated as I have just
described them to be,—the door of the apartment was suddenly opened, and Donald Rose himself, covered with mud
from neck to heel, and with a countenance pale and haggard
as death, entered,—followed, gentlemen, still stranger to
tell, by—Harry Stuart, the herd of the Limekilns ! The
surprise by which the lovers were thus taken was perfectly
complete. Their presence of mind was altogether gone.
They started up together at once, without even attempting
to unfold or withdraw their arms from the different posi-
tions which they had respectively assumed, whilst the
drapery of the plaid hung over both of them, mingled with
the garlands which they still wore. They stood as if they
had been converted into statues.

"Gude keep us a' frae evil !" cried Donald Rose the
moment he entered, whilst, to their utter astonishment,

he started back as he said so, his eyes glaring at them with
a ghastly look of fear and horror that was much too natural
not to be perfectly genuine. "Gude keep us frae a' evil,
are ye wraiths or are ye real? The same plaid! the same
garlands! and the same guise! Speak! speak! what
are ye? But I see," continued he, after a pause, during
which he recovered himself a little; "I see, Gude be
thankit! that ye *are* baith flesh and bluid."

"Aye, flesh and bluid we are," said Robin Stuart, summoning up all his resolution and speaking in a determined
tone. "We are flesh and bluid truly, and I trust that we
shall soon be one flesh and one bluid too! Our souls are
already as one! sae let not ane auld man's avarice rend
asunder twa leal hearts already joined by Heeven!"

"Joined by Heeven, indeed, Rabby!" replied old Rose,
with a solemn and mysterious air; "and Heeven forbid
that sic a miserable vratch as I am sould daur to interfere.
What Heeven hath joined let not man put asunder! O
bairns! bairns!" continued he, as he swopped himself
down into his great oaken elbow chair, as if quite overcome
with fatigue both of body and mind; "och, bairns! bairns!
what ane awfu' gliff I hae gotten this blessed night! As I
was on my road hame frae the market—an' at a decent hour,
too,—for the drover an' me had but three half mutchkins
a-piece whan we pairted at Grantown—whan I was on my
road hame, as I was sayin', an' just as I was gaein' to pass
round this end o' the Witches' Loch, to cross at the bit
fuirdy yonder, what does I see, it gars my very flesh a'
creep again to think on 't—what does I see, I say, but your
twa figures, as plain as I see ye baith at this precious
moment, in thay very garments ye hae on, an' wi' thay
very garlands about your necks, an' shouthers, an' breasts,
an' baith claspit thegither, as ye war just yenoo whan I
came in. I say, I saw ye baith in that very guise, an' in
that very pouster, comin' skimmin' o'er the surface o' the
deep water o' the loch, wi' that very red plaid aboon ye
baith for a sail. But, Gude proteck us a'!—what think
ye?—The full moon was just risen in the east, an' her very
light was shinin' through the twa spirits, an' aboot them
there was a kind o' a glory, just like unto the mony coloured
brugh that ye hae nae doot aften seen about the moon
hersel'. Och me, it wuz a grusome sight! I wish I may
e'er won ower wi't!"

Robin and Mary exchanged intelligent glances with each other during this part of old Rose's narrative; but he was too much overpowered with what he had seen, and too full of his subject, to observe what passed between them.

"Tak a wee drap o' this, father," said Mary, handing him a brimming cuach; "you will bo muckle the better o 't."

"Thank ye, thank ye, my bonny bairn !" said the farmer, giving her back the empty cuach, and kindly patting her head as he did so. "I'm sure, my dauty, it was ill my pairt to cross ye as I did. But, stay!—whaur was I?— Weel, ye see, just as the twa speerits war comin' *whush* athort the loch upon me far faster than ony wild duke could flee,—the very dumb brute that I was on started back wi' fear, whurled aboot in a moment, an' whuppit me awa' back o'er the moss in spite o' mysel', regairdless o' ony road; and I trow I never stoppit till I wuz on the t'ither side o' Craig Bey, whar, by good luck, I forgathered wi' Harry o' the Limekilns there—fear, like death, will pit oot the fire o' the auldest feud; and whan Harry heard the cause o' my flight,—for whan he met me I was fleein' like a muir-cock down the wund,—I say, whan Harry heard o' what an a sight I had seen, an' he bein', as it were, in some degree conneckit wi' it, as weel as mysel', I trow he wuz as glad to hae me wi' him as I wuz to hae him wi me, wi' the houp o' keepin' aff waur company. Harry had nae better wull to gae by the Witches' Loch than I had, and sae we cam' ower by the short cut through the lang moss thegither. A bonny road, truly, for sic an afu' late hour o' the night, for a' that we had the moon, as ye may see well eneugh by the dabbled state o' my trews. I'm sure my puir beast 'ill no be able to crawl the morn after a' the gliftin', an' galloppin', aye, an' I may say soomin' too, that he has had, for I hae some doots gif there be ae moss hole atween Craig Bey an' this hoose that he has na' had to swatter through."

"Let me get dry stockin's for ye, father," said Mary.

"Na, my dauty, its no worth while for a' the time !" replied Donald. "An' noo, Harry, man," continued he, turning to his companion, who had been all this while standing near the door, "cum ben, man, an' sit doon ; what

for dinna ye sit doon ? An' noo, I say, although ye *are* but
a poor man, Harry, an' no just sae weel come by deschent
as I am, wha, as ye are maybe awaur, am come o' a
cousin sax times removed of the Laird of Kilravock himself, which a' the warld kens to be ane o' the maist
auncientest families in Scotland,—I say, though ye are no
just descended frae siccan honourable forebears, yet ye are
ane honest man."

" I trust that I am sae, neebour," said Harry modestly,
but with his head yereck, as ane honest man's always
should be.

" Aweel, aweel !" cried old Rose impatiently, " as I was
gaein' to say, we's just owerlook a' thae things, an' souther
up a' oonkindness that may hae been atween us, an' sae
we'll mak' the best o't, an' hae your laddie an' my lassie
buckled thegither as soon as the minister can mak' them
ane. Come, man, gie's your hand on't !"

" Wi' a' my heart !" replied Harry Stuart, with a good-
natured chuckle ; " an' I'll tell ye what it is, Carl, maybe
ye'll find after a' that the son o' Harry the herd o' the
Limekilns is no just sae bare a bargain as ye wad hae
yemagined. The herdin' trade gif it maks little it spends
less ; an' I hae na been at it for better nor fifty years
without layin' by a wee bit pose o' my ain ; an' gif a gude
bien bit hill farmie can be gotten for the twa, I'se no say
but I may come doon wi' as muckle as may buy the best
end o' the plenishen an' stockin'."

" That's my hearty cock !" exclaimed old Rose, slapping
Harry soundly on the back. " Mary, my dauty ! I was
sae muckle the better o' the wee drap ye gied me yon time,
that I think neither Harry nor me wad be the waur o'
anither tasse."

It would be yequally vain and unnecessar, gentlemen,
for me to attempt to describe the happiness of the two
lovers, or the general joy of that night. If Homer or Maro
were alive, and here present, they would fail to do justice
to such a theme. I may shortly conclude by simply telling
you, however, that Mysie's slumbers were rudely broken
by the stentorian voice of her master,—that she was
speedily put to work at her yespecial occupation in the
kitchen,—that the rustic feast was quickly spread,—that
the bowl circulated, or, rather, to speak with a due regard
to fack, that it passed backwards and forwards very

11

frequently from lip to lip of the two thirsty seniors,—that the young couple were in Elysium,—that the old men were garrulously joyous,—that Mysie was frantic, and danced about like a daft woman, and that the sun peeped in upon them from the distant eastern hills ere they even began to think of terminating their revels.

DOMINIE DELIGHTED.

Grant.—Why, sir, you are quite as great as a story-teller as you are as a critic.

Clifford.—Homer or Maro could never have held a candle to you ! Why your floating island would beat a steamer. But, joking apart, we are really much obliged to you for the very interesting story you have told us.

Dominie (bowing).—I am yespecially proud and happy that you are pleased with it, sir.

Author.—We are all very much indebted to you indeed,. for you have helped us very agreeably over the most. dreary part of our road.

The good man rose an inch or two higher than he had. hitherto appeared, and his cheek glowed with satisfaction.

We had now come to the Pass of Craig-Bey, where the Grantown country opened to us. A rocky hill arose on. our right, wildly wooded with tall Scottish pines, whilst, on our left, the ground declined into a hollow, through which the dark streamlet that drains the extensive peat-bog, whence the villagers of Grantown are supplied with fuel, throws itself into a deep rocky ravine, along which our road skirted. At some distance to our left, and on the farther side of the glen, a beautiful smiling portion of Highland country arose in swelling grounds, simply culti-vated, amidst natural birchen groves ; whilst every now and then we had a transient view directly downwards, where the stream threw itself into a fairy little holm, surrounded by tall castellated rocks, richly tinted with warm coloured mosses, and rising picturesquely from among woods of golden-leaved aspen and birch.

Clifford.—Is there no story connected with that beautiful spot below ?

Author.—The place is called Huntly's Cove. It has its name from some cavity in the crag, which is said to have been the place of concealment of George, second Marquis of Huntly, in the time of Charles I.

Clifford.—I forget his history at this moment.

Author.—He was married, if I remember rightly, in 1609, to the Lady Anne Campbell, eldest daughter of Archibald, seventh Earl of Argyll; and he was, therefore, brother-in-law to Archibald, the eighth Earl of Argyll, who so strenuously exerted himself in the cause of the people against King Charles I., and who, as you may recollect, was appointed by the Convention of Estates, 16th April, 1644, commander-in-chief of the forces raised to suppress the insurrection of his brother-in-law, this very Marquis of Huntly of whom we are now talking. The Marquis, you know, rose in arms for the King in the north; but Argyll marching against him, dispersed the Royalists, and obliged Huntly to fly to Strathnaver, in Sutherland. Huntly again appeared in arms in 1645, and refused to lay them down even when commanded by the King, who was then under the control of the Parliament of 1646. He was exempted from the pardon granted on the 4th March, 1647, and he was that same year taken prisoner. I remember the peerage account of him states that his capture took place in *Strathnaver*—a blunder occasioned by the circumstance of his having fled to that district of country upon the first-mentioned occasion. It was in *Strathaven* that he was taken, and the similarity of names assisted in producing the confusion. Before his capture he lay concealed in *Strathaven*, or as it is very commonly called *Stradaun*, and when more than ordinarily alarmed by an increased activity in the search for him, he used to come over to hide himself here for greater security. I think it was an ancestor of the present Sir Neil Menzies of Castle Menzies who took him, but the legendary circumstances have escaped me, if I ever knew them.

Grant.—Thus it is that some of our most curious and valuable traditions are lost.

Clifford.—It is truly provoking that it should be so. As we have Roxburghe, and Bannatyne, and Maitland Clubs for the preservation and printing of old writings, would it not be a meritorious thing to establish a Legend Club, the object of which should be to proceed systematically throughout every part of the British dominions to collect and write down all the legendary and traditionary matter which may yet remain?

Grant.—There is no doubt that an immense mass of

materials might thus be gathered together for the use of the novelist and playwright.

Clifford.—Nay, nay, Grant; but joking apart, I do think that although the great mass might be rubbishy enough, and, perhaps, much fitter for the compounder of melo-dramas than for anything else, *croyez moi on doit cepen-dant trouver des perles, on plutot des diamants, dans ce grand fumier.* And then when you think that the numerous fitful beams of light which might proceed from these recovered diamonds should be concentrated into one focus, it is not very impossible that history itself might receive some fresh illumination from the flame that might be kindled.

Author.—Your scheme is amusing enough, and by no means undeserving of attention; but I conceive that the utility of such a society as you speak of would very much depend upon the efficiency of its secretary.

Clifford (with an arch look).—Why, no doubt, it would so. And therefore I should propose to confer that impor-tant and distinguished post upon our new acquaintance, Mr. Macpherson here, seeing that he is so much given to searching out the truth of such things, and that he has, moreover, proved himself to be so able a narrator of them after he has found them out.

Dominie (his eyes glistening with pride and delight as he again advanced to fill that place in the line of march which he had occupied during the time we were listening to his tale).— What could be more to my mind than such an occupation! And yet, sir, seeing that I am already planted as a teacher of youth in a comfortable house in Caithness, with a small garden and a cow's grass appended thereto; to all which there falls to be added a salary, which, though small, yet sufficeth for my mainteenance, who have no wife or " charge of children," as Lord Chancellor Bacon hath it, save that of the children of other people, whence there arises to me not expense but yemolument, it would be well to know what sum of money by the year might be incoming to the holder of that secretaryship of which you have spoken; seeing that prudence bids us be sure that we move not our right foot until our left be firmly set down.

Clifford.—As to the matter of revenue, I fear there would be more of honorary dignity than of edible income attached to the situation. I would, therefore, earnestly advise you, since I now learn that your lot has already been so pleasantly cast, to hold your right foot fast in Caithness, where, were the society to go on, you might be appointed one of its honorary corresponding members.

Dominie.—Thank you, sir, your advice is good. I could by no means afford to throw away my cow's grass and potato-yard to the dogs, to say nothing of my salary, without something better. I shall therefore e'en hold as I am.

Clifford.—What mountain is that which I see rising blue and grand yonder in the eastern distance?

Grant.—I have now a right to step forward as your cicerone, Clifford, for this is the country of the great clan to which I belong. Yet I must confess that I have no great knowledge of its history. I can at least tell you, however, that the mountain you are inquiring about is Ben Rinnes, the hill which rises over the ancient house of Ballindalloch, at the junction of the rivers Avon and Spey. Ballindalloch belongs to an old family of the Grants.

Dominie.—I could tell you a curious legend about the building of the Castle of Ballindalloch, were it not deemed presumption in me to tell of the Grants in presence of so accomplished a member of the clan.

Grant.—Sir, I shall cheerfully trust to you to do justice to the Grants, and especially to the Grants of Ballindalloch; for since the Macphersons are now engrafted on the family of that house, I think you will be disposed to say nothing that may be in anywise to their disparagement.

Dominie.—God forbid that I should. They have always been kind friends of mine.

Clifford.—I protest against any more stories till after dinner. I presume we shall find an inn at Grantown, and I therefore beg leave to move that all lengthened communications be adjourned until we are fairly set in to be comfortable for the evening.

Grant.—Agreed. Now, then, follow me in at this gate that opens to our left here, and through this plantation, and I, as your cicerone here, shall show you something worth looking at.

We had no sooner burst from the confinement of the trees, than a wide and extensive and grand prospect opened to us. From the immediate foreground the eye ran gently down some sloping cultivated inclosures, till, passing over the widespread woods by which these were surrounded, it swept with eagle flight across the wide valley of the Spey and the endless forests of Abernethy, and rested with joy and with a feeling of freedom on the blue chain of the Cairngorum mountains, rising huge and vast above these minor dependent hills that were congregated about their bases. To the left our view was bounded by tall groves of timber-trees, chiefly beeches, and after penetrating these, the lofty bulk of Castle Grant presented itself within an hundred yards of us.

Clifford.—I think it will not be considered as any breach of the rule we have just laid down, if you should give us an outline, in three words, of the history of this the feudal residence of your chiefs.

Grant.—All I can tell you regarding it is, that it has been the seat of the chief of our clan ever since the fourteenth century, when the surrounding lands were taken from the Cumins and bestowed on the Grants by the Crown. Another large *cantle* of the ancient possessions of the Cumins came into the family by the marriage of Sir John Grant with Matilda or Bigla, the heiress of Gilbert Cumin of Glenchearnich.

Dominie.—True, true, sir, I have a curious story about that. You see, gentlemen, Gilbert Cumin, whose cognomen was Gibbon More"——

Clifford.—You will forgive me for interrupting you, sir, but you will recollect, that although we allowed Grant to tell us what he knew about the castle, we have just laid it down as a rule, that we are to have no more *long* stories upon empty stomachs. Let us hasten to see the interior of this chateau, and then to Grantown and to dinner with what appetite we may. You shall dine with us, and I shall book you for there giving us Gibbon *More*, or any *More* you may be possessed of.

Dominie.—Your pun is most excellent, sir, ha! ha! ha!— your reproof is most just, and your invitation most kind, and readily accepted. And as I can be of little use to you here, gentlemen, perhaps I shall be most benefeecially employed, both for your interest and my own, by stepping my ways on to Grantown, and looking to the preparation for your accommodation and entertainment at the inn.

Author.—No, no, sir, we have already secured all that

by the gilly who has preceded us with the pony. We cannot part with you so, your information may be useful to us.

Clifford.—This huge pile seems to have been built at various periods, and with no great taste. That tower is the only picturesque part about it.

Grant.—That is called the Cumin's Tower, and it is perhaps the only very old fragment of the building. The most modern part is the northern front, the style of which is quite inappropriate.

Clifford.—Come, let us hasten to discuss the interior; my appetite at present is sufficiently sharp, yet it is for something more digestible than granite and mortar.

We hurried through the castle, admired the great hall, some fifty feet by thirty in size, and were particularly delighted with some of the old family portraits, which are extremely curious as to costume.

Clifford.—What a fierce old white-bearded fellow that is in the bonnet and tartan plaid, drawing a pistol as if he was about to shoot us. I should not like to meet in a wood with such an one as he appears to have been, unless I met him as a friend.

Dominie.—That is old Robert Grant of Lurg. I can tell you many a story about him. He was surnamed old *Stachcan*, or the Stubborn ; and—a "——

Clifford.—Unless you are determined to deserve that surname, as well as ever the said Robert Grant did, you had better attempt no more stories till after dinner, my good friend. And now, methinks, we have seen enough of these bearded, belted, and bonneted heroes ; and if you have no objections, I think we may as well proceed to march into quarters for the night.

A walk of little more than a mile brought us to the village of Grantown, and a period of time something less than a couple of hours found us all seated, after a very good dinner, round a cheerful fire, each preparing to light his cigar, and moderately to sip the fluid that was most agreeable to him.

Clifford (opening his tablets).—Let me see what my book says. Ha!—Legend of the Raid of Killychrist—Building of Ballindalloch—Gibbon More—Old Stachcan ! The raid comes first—the raid stops the way,—so drive on with the raid if you please.

Author.—Since you desire it, I shall do so, in order, as you say, to get it out of the way. But I must tell you that the Raid of Killychrist does in fact form so small a part of that which I have to narrate to you, that I might rather call it the Legend of Allan with the Red Jacket.

Clifford.—Pray call it what you please, but *quocunque nomine gaudet,* let us have your legend, if you please, without further loss of time.

LEGEND OF ALLAN WITH THE RED JACKET.

As a prelude to the legend of the Raid of Killychrist, or Christ's Church, I must condemn you to listen to a considerable portion of the previous history of the great rival clans of MacDonell and MacKenzie, which led to that event. A deep-rooted feud had existed for many years between these two neighbouring Highland nations, as I may well enough call them. So savage was their mutual hatred, that no opportunity was lost, upon either side, of manifesting the bitterest hostility towards each other. They were continually making sudden incursions with fire and sword into each other's territory,—burning cottages—destroying crops—driving away cattle—levying contributions on defenceless tenants—carrying off hostages, and massacring such unfortunate individuals or straggling parties as might happen to fall in their way, without always showing much regard to age or sex. It was one unvarying history of rapine and bloodshed, uninterrupted except at such times and for such periods when both parties happened to be too much exhausted to act on the offensive.

It was fortunate for the MacDonells, that about the beginning of the seventeenth century Donald MacAngus MacDonell of Glengarry, chief of the clan, had so harried the MacKenzie country in one dreadful and destructive raid, and had so swept away its wealth and thinned its people, as to have rendered them comparatively innocuous for a number of years; for, during the lapse of these, he became so old and infirm, as to be not only quite unable for any very active or stirring enterprise, but he would have been unequal to the defence of his own territories against the inroads of his neighbours. He had two sons, but neither of them was old enough to relieve him of the cares and fatigues incidental to the government of such a clan. Angus the eldest, indeed, although only some fifteen or sixteen years of age, was extremely bold and impetuous. Like the most forward and best-grown eaglet of the aerie, he would have often rashly braved, with unpractised wing, the storms which raged around the cliff where he was bred, had it not been for the wholesome restraint which the old man was with difficulty enabled to put upon him, and which he could hardly enforce, even with the assistance of his nephew, Allan MacRaonuill MacDonell of Lundy, who being then in the prime of life, acted as captain or chief leader of the clan Conell.

Allan of Lundy, so called from the loch of that name near Invergarry, was the pride and darling of the clan, and it was not wonderful that he should have been so, for he possessed all those qualities which were likely to endear him to Highlanders in those savage times. He was remarkable for his great activity of body, for his wonderful agility in leaping, and his extraordinary swiftness of foot, and endurance in running. But these were not the qualities which the clansmen most especially prized in him ; for, whilst he was kind to every one who bore the name of MacDonell, he was ever ready to visit those who were their enemies with the most ruthless and remorseless vengeance. He delighted in wearing a splendid jacket of scarlet plush richly embroidered with gold, and when the day of battle came, the brave MacDonells always looked to that jacket as to a rallying point, with as much devotion and con- fidence as they looked to the banner of the chief himself, for they were always certain to see it in the front of every charge, and in the rear of every retreat. It was from this that he acquired his most distinguished cognomen, that of *Allan with the red jacket.*

It was not surprising that a youth of a haughty and impetuous temper, like that of Angus MacDonell, could ill brook the well intended admonitions which he received from a cousin, upon whose interference in the affairs of the clan he was taught, by the vile insinuations of certain sycophantish adherents, to look with a jealousy which was but an ill requital for all Allan of Lundy's affection towards him. That affection, though it came from a bosom which was capable of nursing that fierce and cruel spirit which animates the tiger, was deep and sincere. It was an affection which had its basis in gratitude, in love, and in veneration for the old chief, his uncle, who had been to

Allan as a father, and, therefore, it was born with the birth of the boy Angus. It was an affection which had grown stronger and stronger every day with the growth of its object, on the development of whose character the future happiness and glory, or misery and disgrace, of the clan, must depend. It was an affection, in short, which nothing could shake, and which even the often unamiable conduct of Angus towards him could never for one moment chill.

It happened one rainy and tempestuous night, that whilst a party of clansmen, returning from some distant expedition, were approaching the gate of Invergarry Castle, they suddenly encountered a tall man wrapped up in an ample plaid. He started when the MacDonells came upon him.

"Friend or foe?" cried the leader of the party.

"A friend!" coolly replied the other, "unless you are prepared to tell me that the days are past when a MacIntyre may claim hospitality from a MacDonell."

"The day can never come when a MacIntyre shall not be welcome to a MacDonell," replied the other. "Are they not but as a limb of the goodly pine stock of clan Conell? say, what wouldst thou here?"

"I am a wayfaring man," answered the stranger, "and all I would ask is shelter and hospitality for an hour or twain, till this tempest blow by."

"Thou art come in the very nick of time, my friend," said the MacDonell, "for, hark! the piper has gone to his walk, and he is already filling his drone as a signal for us to fill our stomachs. The banquet is serving in the hall, so in, I pray thee, without more delay; trust me, we are as ready as thou canst be for a morsel of a buck's haunch, or a flagon of ale."

The old chief of the MacDonells had already occupied his huge high-backed chair on the *dais*, at the upper end of the hall, and his eldest son Angus, and his cousin Allan of Lundy, the captain, and the other chieftains of the clan, had taken their seats around him, and the greater part of the places at the board had been filled, as rank might dictate, down to the very lower end of it, when the stranger was announced,—

"Give him entrance!" cried the hospitable old chief. "This is a night when the very demons of the storm seem to have been let loose to do their worst. No one would drive his enemy's dog to the door in such a tempest. Were he a MacKenzie we could not see him refused a shelter from so bitter a blast. A MacIntyre, then, may well claim a hearty welcome."

The door of the hall was thrown open, and the stranger entered. He doffed his bonnet, and bowed respectfully to the chief, and to those assembled, yet his countenance remained partly shrouded by the upper folds of his plaid, which had been drawn over his head as a shelter from the fury of the elements, and it now hung down thence so as entirely to conceal his person. There was enough of him visible, however, to show that he was a tall, broad-shouldered, and very athletic man, in the prime of life, with large fair features, small sharp eyes, overhanging eyebrows, severe expression, and a profusion of yellow hair and beard that very much assisted in veiling his face. The retainers who were nearest to him eagerly scrutinised his plaid, as such persons were naturally enough wont to do ; but it was so soiled with the mud-water of the mosses in which it seemed to have been rolled, that knowing as some of them were in the tartans of the different clans, they could not possibly make out the set of that which he wore. They saw enough, however, to satisfy them that it was green, and as they knew that to be the prevailing hue of the tartan of the MacIntyres, they examined no further.

" Friend, thou art welcome !" said the chief ; "a MacIntyre is always welcome to a MacDonell. Take your seat among us as your rank may warrant, and spare not the viands or liquor with which the board abounds—*Slainte!*" and with this hospitable wish of health and welcome, he emptied the wine cup which he held in his hand.

"Thanks!" said the stranger, bowing his head with an overstrained politeness; and without more ado he seated himself in a retired and rather darksome nook, near the lower end of the board, where he immediately engaged himself deeply, and without any very great nicety of selection, with such eatables and drinkables as came within his reach, so that he speedily ceased to be any further interruption to the conversation which had been begun at the head of the table, to which everyone had been most attentively listening when he came in.

"What sort of hunting had you to-day, Angus?" said Allan of Lundy.

"I brought down a royal stag," replied Angus, with an air of sullen dignity.

"That was well," replied Allan of Lundy; "it was as much as I did."

"And why should I not do as much as you, cousin?" demanded Angus somewhat peevishly.

"When you come to your strength, Angus, you may perhaps do more," replied Allan.

"My body," said Angus haughtily, "aye, and my mind, too, are strong enough for everything that a chief of Glengarry may be called upon to perform. And now I think on't, father," continued he, turning towards the chief, "I grow tired of this wretched mimicry of war which I have so long waged against the deer of our hills. I would fain hunt for bolder game. It is time for me to be hunting the *Cabar Fiadh** of the MacKenzies! Why should our ancient enmity against them have slept so long? We seem to have forgotten the disgrace of that ignominious day, never to be washed out but in rivers of MacKenzie blood, when fifty galleys of our clan fled from before the Castle of Eilean Donan, defended as it was by no other garrison than Gillichrist MacCraw and his son Duncan alone, when a single arrow from the boy's quiver pierced our chief, and dispersed his formidable armament. Let us hasten to wipe away so foul a disgrace."

The speech of the young chief of Glengarry had been repeatedly cheered during the time he was speaking; and he finished amidst vociferous applause. The stranger in the green plaid halted in his meal to bend an anxious attention to everything he uttered.

"Angus," said the old chief, "you have spoken unadvisedly, boy. These are subjects fitter for the private chamber of council than for the festive board. You, moreover, seem to have forgotten that the quiet which the MacKenzies are forced to keep, is owing to some successful enterprises of my own, from the humbling effects of which they have not even yet recovered."

* *Cabar Fiadh*, the head of the wild deer, the crest of the clan MacKenzie.

"If that be the case, father," cried Angus energetically, "let us keep them down when we have them down! Let me finish what you so nobly began. Promise me that you will grant me to lead a raid against these *stags-heads*. Promise me, dear father!"

"A raid! a raid led by the young chief!" cried the vassals, starting up from the table as one man with enthusiastic shouts.

"Aye," said Angus, "and the young chief shall not go unattended. Every warrior of the name of MacDonell, nay, every marching man who can trace one drop of his blood to the clan Conell, shall share in the glory to be gathered in the first raid of Angus MacDonell against the MacKenzies!"

"All shall go! all shall go!" cried the clansmen who were present.

"Aye, all shall go!" cried the young chief, warming more and more with the applause he was receiving. "And here, as a good omen of our success, here have we this night a MacIntyre among us. You, sir," continued he, addressing himself to the stranger in the green plaid, "you shall bear a message from me to your chieftain. Tell him to whom you owe service, that the tenth day of the new moon shall be the day of our gathering. It is long since our war-cry of *Craggan-an-Fhithick* has rung in a MacKenzie's ear!"

"Craggan-an-Fhithick!" shouted the clansmen.

"Tell him to whom you owe service, that Craggan-an-Fhithick shall once more rend the air," said Angus; "and that the young chief of Glengarry shall lead a raid against the MacKenzies, of the fame of which senachies and bards shall have to speak for ages to come."

"I shall surely bear your message to him to whom I owe service," said the man in the green plaid, after rising slowly, and making a dignified but respectful bow. And then putting on his bonnet, and gathering his plaid tightly about him, he paced solemnly and silently out of the hall, and departed.

"Methinks you have been somewhat rash and hasty in this matter, Angus," said the chief, with a cloud on his brow. "I have as yet given no consent. What think you of this affair, Allan of Lundy?"

"Much as I am wearying to wreak my vengeance on

the MacKenzies," replied Allan of Lundy, " I do think that my young cousin has been somewhat precipitate in this matter. A year or two more over his head would have confirmed his strength, and made him fitter for enduring the fatigue of such an enterprise. He is too young and unripe as yet to be gathered by death in the bloody harvest of the battlefield. The loss of one of so great promise would be a severe blow to our clan."

"The loss of me, indeed ?" cried Angus, with a lip full of a contempt which it had never before borne towards Allan of Lundy, and which Allan of Lundy could not believe had any reference to him. "If you did lose me you would only thereby be the nearer to my father's seat."

"Speak not so, Angus !" said Allan with a depth of feeling to which he was but little accustomed. . "Speak not so, even in jest."

" Come then, MacDonells," cried Angus again, " let our gathering be for the tenth day of the new moon, and let the dastard MacKenzies once more quail before our triumphant war-cry of Craggan-an-Fhithick !"

" Craggan-an-Fhithick !" re-echoed the clansmen, with a shout that might have rent the rafters ; and deep pledges instantly went round to the success of the expedition.

At this moment Ronald MacDonald, the chief's younger son, a shrewd boy of some eight or ten years of age, entered the hall,—

" What has become of the stranger in the green plaid ?" cried he eagerly.

" He is gone," answered several voices at once.

" Then was he a foul and traitorous spy," said the boy. "When my brother was speaking about the raid, I perceived that he was devouring every word he was uttering. His grey eye showed no friendly sympathy. I resolved to watch him, and the more I did so, the more were my suspicions strengthened. I was struck with the dirty state of his plaid. As it was green it might have been MacIntyre. But to make sure of this I borrowed old nurse's shears, and whilst he was intent on what Angus was saying, I contrived to get near to him unperceived; and I clipped away this fragment, which nurse has since washed—and see !" said he, holding it up to the light of a lamp that all might have a view of it. "See ! it has the alternate white and red sprainge of a base and double-faced MacKenzie!"

"MacKenzie, indeed, by all that is good!" cried the old chief. "Out after him, and take him alive or dead!"

"Fly!—after him!—out! out!—let us scour the country! —haste, haste!—out, out!" were the impatient cries that burst from every one in the hall, and in an instant there was a rushing, and a running, and a mounting in haste, and a flying off in all directions. Shouts came from different quarters without the castle walls; and by and by all was silence, for those who had gone in various ways after the fugitive were already out of hearing; and after a night of fruitless toil, they returned in wet and draggled parties of two and three, each expecting to hear those accounts of success from others which they themselves had it not in their power to give, and all were equally disappointed.

It now suits my narrative best to leave the Castle of Invergarry for a while, in order to notice what passed some little time afterwards in that of Eilean Donan, where Kenneth MacKenzie, Lord Kintail, was seated in his lady's apartment trifling away the hours. A page entered in haste.

"My lord," said he, "Hector Mackenzie of Beauly is here, and would fain have an audience."

"Hector of Beauly!" exclaimed Lord Kintail, "what, I wonder, can he want? With your leave, my lady, let him be admitted. Hector," continued his lordship as his clansman entered, "where have you come from, you look famished and jaded?"

"'Tis little wonder if I do, my lord," said Hector, "for the last meal of meat that I ate, and though good enough of its kind, it was but a short one, was in the Castle of Invergarry."

"The Castle of Invergarry!" cried his lordship in astonishment.

"Aye, in the Castle of Invergarry, my lord," continued Hector; "and if my meal there was short, I have had a long enough walk after it to help me to digest what I ate."

"Are you in your right mind, Hector?" demanded his lordship. "Quick, explain yourself."

"I cannot say that I altogether intended to honour the Glengarry chief's board with my presence," said Hector,

12

drawing himself up; "but having some trifling occasion of my own to pass through the Glengarry country, I rolled my plaid in a moss-hole, and took the wildest way over the hills; and thinking that I mi⸱   noticed amidst the darkness and howling of ⸱   tempestuous night, I ventured so near to the castle, that before I knew where I was, a band of MacDonells were suddenly upon me. Seeing that there was nothing else for it but to brave the danger, I had presence of mind enough to pass myself for a MacIntyre, was invited into the castle, sat at the same table, and feasted with the old raven and his vassals, and heard that young half-fledged corby Angus MacDonell plan and arrange a raid of the whole clan Conell and its dependent families against the MacKenzie country. Taking me for a MacIntyre, he told me to bear his message to him to whom I owed service. To give obedience to his will, therefore, I have travelled without stop or stay, or meat or drink, save what I took from the running brooks by the way, in order that I may now tell you, my lord, to whom I owe service as my chief, that the MacDonells' gathering is to be for the tenth day of the moon, when their fire and sword will run remorseless through our land."

"Hector, you are a brave man," said Lord Kintail, "you shall be rewarded for this. Meanwhile hasten to procure some refreshment and repose; for assuredly you must sorely need both."

I presume that it is scarcely necessary for me to tell you that Lord Kintail and his lady had a speedy and very anxious consultation together. She was a woman of very superior talents, of quick perception, and equally ready in devising expedients as prompt in carrying them into execution. It was at once agreed between them, that this was too serious and impending a danger to admit of delay in preparing to resist it. Feeling, as they did, that the clan had not yet altogether gathered its strength since the last sweeping raid which old Donald MacAngus, chief of the clan Conell, had committed on their territories, both saw the necessity of losing no time in procuring all the foreign aid they could obtain. It was therefore agreed between them as the best precaution that could be taken, that Lord Kintail should forthwith set out for Mull to procure auxiliary troops from his friend and kinsman MacLean.

Preparations were instantly made accordingly in perfect secrecy for his departure; and in the course of little more than an hour after the communication of Hector's intelligence, his lordship's galley stood out of Loch Duich and through the Kyles of Skye, and left the straits with as fair a north-eastern breeze as if he had bought it from some witch for the very purpose of wafting him to Mull. But secrets are difficult to keep; for notwithstanding the privacy of all these arrangements, not only Lord Kintail's destination, but the cause and object of his voyage, was known. Had the discovery been traced, perhaps it might have been found to have originated with my lady's woman, from whom it gradually spread, until it was quickly whispered, with every proper and prudential caution as to silence, into every ear in the Castle of Eilean Donan, whence it spread like wildfire over the whole district.

The MacDonells, too, could have their scouts as well as the MacKenzies. When the hubbub occasioned by the hurried and hopeless chase after the false MacIntyre had subsided, a patient, painstaking, and most sagacious Highlander set off to try what he could make of it; and having once found a trace of the track the MacKenzie had taken, he never lost sight of it again, until he had followed him so far into the enemy's territories, that he had to thank a most ingenious disguise which he wore for saving his neck from being brought into speedy acquaintance with the gallows-tree of Eilean Donan. This man returned immediately to Invergarry with the intelligence that the projected raid of the MacDonells was as well known in Kintail as it was in Glengarry, and that Lord Kintail himself had gone to Mull to procure the powerful aid of his cousin MacLean.

Young Angus of Glengarry was furious when he found that all his schemes, so well laid as he thought they had been, for establishing his own glory and that of the clan, had been thus baffled.

"If that yellow-bearded buck's-head shall ever chance to cross my path again," said he, "young as my arm is, he shall have a trial of my sword."

"Thy spirit is good, boy," said Allan of Lundy; "'tis like that of your father and your grandfather before you. But it will be wise in you to check its rashness, until your sinews are better able to back it up. That same Hector

MacKenzie whom we saw here among us, is moulded for
some other sort of work than to give and take gentle
buffets with a boy."

"Thank thee, kind kinsman, for thy care of me," replied
Angus, in anything but an agreeable tone.

"'Tis true what Allan says," observed the old chief. "I
rejoice in thy spirit, boy; it recalls to me mine own early
days. But for the sake of the clan Conell, to whom your
life is precious, and," added he, with a voice that age, or
perhaps some strong feeling operating upon age, made
falter, "and for the sake of your old father, who doats
upon you, for the sake of your sainted mother, let me not
have to mourn over the too early fate of her first-born !"

"I shall not be rash, I shall be prudent, father," replied
Angus, considerably touched by the old man's appeal.
"But why should we not hasten to strike some blow ere
their succours shall have time to arrive ?"

"There is something in that," said Allan of Lundy.
"And since my young cousin so burns to flesh his maiden
sword, there can be no safer way of his doing so, or with
the certainty of a more easy victory, than by making a
sudden attack on the shores of Loch Carron."

"Safety ! easy victory !" muttered the young chief,
with an expression of offended dignity and ineffable contempt. "But 'tis well," added he, too much filled with
joy at having any enterprise at all in prospect, to allow
any other feeling to occupy his mind for a moment; "let
us not lose time in talk. If we are to move with the hope
of a surprise, it were fitting that not one moment be lost.
Let all within reach be speedily summoned. By to-
morrow's dawn we must march to Loch Hourn, where our
galleys are lying. Said I not well now, father ?"

"Let it be so then, my son," said the chief, with a sigh
which he could not check; "and oh! may all that is good
attend and guard you !"

The sun rose with unclouded splendour over the mountains to the eastward of Loch Carron, and poured out a
stream of golden radiance over the surface of its waters,
which were gently lifted into tiny waves by a western
breeze. The whole of this Highland scene was glowing
and smiling. The early smoke was tinged with brighter
tints of orange, blue, and yellow, as it curled upwards from
the humble chimneys of the cottages which were scattered

singly or in small groups among irregular shreds of cultivation, that brightened the strip of land bordering the shore. The whole happy population was astir, and little boats were pushing forth from every creek amidst the sparkling waves, their crews eagerly engaged in preparing their nets and lines for fishing. Already had some of the old men taken their seats on their accustomed bench, to inhale the fresh breath of life from the pure morning air, and to look listlessly out to sea, that they might idly speculate on the wind and the weather. It was hardly possible that eye could have looked upon a more peaceful scene.

Suddenly some two or three boats, which had gone down the little frith during the night, for the purpose of reaching a more distant fishing ground by the early dawn, were seen returning with all sail, and toiling with every oar. Curiosity first, and then alarm, brought out the inhabitants from the interior of their lowly abodes. The nearer fishing-boats drew their lines and half-spread nets hastily in, and there was one general rush, each individual crew making towards that point of the shore which was nearest, without any regard to the consideration whether it was the point most adjacent to their home or not. By this time all eyes were straining seaward, to discover what it was that created all this panic, when, one after another, there came sailing round the distant point, galley after galley, till a considerable fleet of them had appeared, their white sails filled with the favouring breeze, and shining with a borrowed lustre from the rich stream of light that poured aslant upon them from the newly-risen sun.

What a scene of dismay and confusion now arose! Clamorous discussions began among the timid spectators,—all action seemed to be paralysed. None appeared to think of arming, where the force of the armament that was advancing was manifestly so resistlessly overwhelming. There were but few who had any doubts as to what clan it might probably belong; and these doubts were speedily removed as the fleet came on, by the appearance of the displayed red eagle, with the black galley that formed the bearings on the broad banner of Glengarry, together with the crest of the raven on the rock, with the appalling motto of *Craggan-an-Fhithick.*

And now a bugle was heard to blow shrilly from the

leading vessel, and in an instant the several galleys darted off from one centre towards different parts of the loch ; and the defenceless inhabitants of the hamlets and cottages might be seen abandoning their dwellings and flying inland.   And no sooner did the prow of each vessel touch the bottom, than the armed men which it contained were seen rushing breast-deep through the tide towards the shore, the broadswords in their hands flashing in the morning light.   One band was led by the brave young chief of Glengarry, shouting his war-cry, with the faithful and affectionate Allan of Lundy by his side, intent on little else but to protect his precious charge from harm.

There were but few men of the MacKenzies there to make a stand, and those who tried to do so were scattered, overpowered, and cut down.   Wild were the shrieks that arose, as the miserable and comparatively defenceless people, leaving their wretched houses and boats to destruction, and their effects and cattle to be plundered, fled away towards the mountains.   The impatient Angus no sooner reached the dry land, than he rushed impetuously after the flying MacKenzies,—and soon indeed did he overtake the rearward ; but it was composed of the women, the aged, and the young, and these he passed by and left unharmed behind him to press on after those who might be more worthy of his sword.   On he hurried for miles after the fugitives, calling on them from time to time to halt and yield to him but one fighting man as an opponent.   But his appeal was in vain ; and tired, and disappointed, and chagrined, he stopped to breathe, and he gnashed his teeth in a disappointment which even the friendly counsels of Allan of Lundy could not allay.

" I'll warrant I could soon catch those caitiffs who are disappearing so swiftly over the hill-top yonder," said he ; " but I care less to-day about taking the life of a MacKenzie or two, than I do about keeping the MacKenzies from taking thine."

" Thank ye, cousin," replied Angus, his mortification by no means moderated by this well-meant speech.   " I hope this arm will defend the citadel of my life's blood from all harm without other aid."

As Angus returned slowly towards the shore, he was somewhat shocked to discover that some of his followers had been less scrupulous in the use of their swords than

he had been; and he met with spectacl— ...uich informed
him of deeds of atrocity and of blood wantonly perpetrated.
He beheld those cottages in flames which were lately
smoking in peace; and his heart smote him that he was
now too late to prevent that carnage in which the grey
hairs of the old were blended in one common slaughter
with the fair locks of the young and helpless.

There was no glorious triumph or splendid achievement
to gild the horrors of this day, or to stifle that disgust
which they naturally excited in a young man even of those
times. Little pride or pleasure had he in the miserable
articles of plunder which he saw his ruthless clansmen
bearing off with blood-stained hands to their galleys; and
he sat him down with Allan of Lundy, in a faint and
feverish state of disquietude of mind, on one of those
patriarchal benches which had been so lately and so
placidly occupied by some of those elders of the hamlet
whose lips were now cold, and whose hearts had now
ceased to beat. I need not tell how long the young chief
was compelled to tarry there, in the endurance of thoughts
that bid defiance to all repose of mind, until he beheld the
various bands of skirmishers return each to its own vessel,
after having spread ravage and devastation, and fire and
sword and murder, far and wide around that which was
lately so happy a district.

It happened that the Lady Kintail had gone on the
battlements of her Castle of Eilean Donan, in order to
enjoy the fresh air and the beautiful scenery of those twin
sea-lochs which branch off from one another at the spot
near to which that rocky island lies which gives name to
the building that stands upon it, when, as she cast her
eyes northward, she beheld a scattered crowd of people
rushing down towards the point which creates the narrow
ferry of Loch Ling. Some boats were moored there, and
as she saw them hastily loose and put to sea to cross over
to the castle, her anxiety to know what news they bore
became so great, that she hurried down to the little cove
where the landing-place was, that she might the sooner
gain the intelligence they brought.

"The MacDonells!" cried these scared and unhappy
people. "The MacDonells are upon us, lady! They have
burnt and harried all Loch Carron! and, och hone! we are
ruined men!"

"Och aye, my lady! och hone! we're all harried, and murdered, and burned!" cried some half a dozen of them at once.

"Answer me like rational men," said the Lady Kintail impatiently, "and do not rout and roar like a parcel of stray beeves. How is 't say ye? the MacDonells!"

And then proceeding to question them, she, by degrees, gathered from them that which had at least some resemblance to a true statement of what had happened.

The lady was nothing daunted by all she heard. Her first step was to despatch certain trustworthy scouts to reconnoitre, and to bring her accurate information how matters stood; and then she retired to hold counsel with some of those leaders among her clansmen in whom she had most confidence. With their advice and assistance every precaution was immediately taken to secure the safety of the castle, as well as to receive into it such a garrison and stock of provisions as might enable her to hold it out until her husband's return, against whatever force might be brought to attack it; and her heroic heart beat so high with the resolute determination of resistance, that she felt something like a pang of disappointment when her scouts returned with intelligence that taught her to believe she had no reason to expect any assault. One of her people, who was no other than Hector of Beauly, brought back the most perfect information regarding the motions of the enemy. They were already glutted with slaughter, cumbered with spoil, and, in a great measure, sickened of their enterprise; and, from the top of a hill, he had seen their galleys weighing to stand out of Loch Carron.

"They are tired of their raid for this time," said the lady with bitterness. "It has been undertaken, I'll warrant, but as a first fleshing for that young corby of an evil nest, —that Angus MacDonell; and his young beak having been once blooded by this mighty exploit done against women, old men, and children, he will be carried home to croak his triumph to his dotard old sire, and then he will be mewed up in safety till his wings grow long enough to admit of his flying in earnest. Would I had a good man or two who would deliver him a message from me, as he passes homewards through the Kyle Rhea in his dastard flight to Loch Hourn."

Now, as we have no map here, I must remind you that
there are three sea-lochs on that part of the coast of
Scotland, all of which debouche into the western sea. Of
these Loch Carron is the most northerly, and Loch Hourn
the most southerly, and that Loch Duich, which lies
between both, opens through the expansion at its mouth,
which is called Loch Alsh, into the narrow strait between
the Isle of Skye and the mainland, which is called the
Kyle Rhea.

"Would I had a good man or two who would deliver a
message from me to that young chough Angus MacDonell
as he passes through the Kyle Rhea," repeated the lady.

"That most willingly will I, most noble lady," cried
Hector of Beauly. "Have I not carried one message from
the young Glengarry to my lord, and shall I not claim the
honour of carrying that which the Lady Kintail has to
send to the young Glengarry?"

"Thanks, gallant Hector!" replied the lady. "Then
shalt thou speak it from the mouth of a cannon! Trust
me thou shalt make him hear on the deafest side of his
head."

Then calling him aside, she quickly explained to him the
scheme she had conceived; and desiring him to select the
individuals whom he should most wish to have in his party,
and to choose the boat which he considered best fitted for
such an expedition, she ordered two small cannon to be
put on board, together with sufficient ammunition for their
use; and as no time was to be lost, he and his brave and
well-armed companions leaped immediately into the little
craft, and pushed off. They pulled with all their strength,
and with the utmost expedition, down through Loch Alsh
to that isolated rock called the *Cailleach*, which lies close
off the eastern angle of the Isle of Skye, and near to the
northern entrance of the narrow strait of the Kyle Rhea.
There they secretly ensconced themselves to await the
return of the MacDonells.

The night fell cold and calm, and the moon arose clear
and bright, illuminating every part of these narrow seas,
and every headland and rock that projected into them from
either shore. It was in the latter part of the year, and by
slow degrees some fleecy clouds arose from the horizon,
and, after spreading themselves like a film of gauze over
the expanse of heaven, they thickened in parts into denser

masses, whence, as they passed overhead, some small, thin, and light particles of snow began to fall gently and rarely, such as the sky usually sends down as its first wintry offering to the earth. This was enough to complete the concealment of the party, hid as they were beneath the shadowy side of the rock, without much obscuring the surface of the sea elsewhere. There then they lay, with everything prepared, waiting impatiently for their prey.

At length a distant sound of oars was heard, for there was not a breath of air in these land-locked seas to render a sail available; and the breaking of the billows on the shore, though hoarse, was neither so loud nor so frequent as to disturb the listeners. All ears, and all eyes, too, were on the stretch. The measured sound of the oars grew stronger, keeping time to a low murmuring chant which proceeded from those who pulled them, more for the purpose of preserving the regularity of the stroke than for any music that they might have made. By and by a galley appeared, dimly seen at some distance, and, as it drew nearer, it was at once known to be that which contained young Angus MacDonell from the broad banner that floated over it, though there was not light enough to descry the bearings of Glengarry.

"Now, my gallant cannoniers," said Hector to those who had the charge of the small pieces of artillery, "be prepared. Remember, when I give the word, you go first, Ian, and then you are to follow, Hamish, in about as much time as you might easily count ten without hurrying yourself. But fail not to attend to my word. In the meanwhile, see that you level well."

On came the young chief's galley. It approached the rock with a course which pointed to pass it clear at some fathoms distance to the eastward of it. But whilst it was yet in progress towards it, Hector, with great expedition and adroitness, pointed his first piece, and watched his time; and his fatal

"Now!" resounded over the surface of the deep.

Ere yet the lint-stock had been applied to the touch-hole, the galley was seen to quiver. Every motion of it indicated the alarm that had already been struck into its crew and helmsman by this ominous word. But the *boom!* of the first gun followed with the quickness of lightning; and the accuracy of the shot was told by the crashing of the

balls with which it had been crammed upon the timbers of
the hull and upper works, as well as by the cursing and
confusion of the people on board, the groans and plaints
of the wounded, and the swerving of the galley from its
course.

"That has done some small work, I'll warrant," said
Hector, as he stooped to point the second piece. "Are you
ready, Hamish? Now!"

And *boom!* went the second gun with yet more decided
effects. In the panic produced by this shot the helm was
left to itself, the oars were abandoned, the galley swung
round with the tide, and in a few seconds it was driven
full upon the rock.

"Angus of Glengarry!" cried a voice like thunder. "I,
Hector MacKenzie, bore thy message to him to whom I
owe service, and I have now brought thee the answer!"

Singling out the young chief, and springing upon him
like a tiger, he stabbed him to the heart with a left-handed
blow of his dirk, ere the unhappy youth had recovered his
footing from the shock which the little vessel received on
the rock. The next moment saw his corpse floating on the
waves.

But Hector's broadsword was instantly needed to defend
his own head. Desperate was the conflict which Allan of
Lundy maintained with this hero of the MacKenzies.
There was something awful in the wild yells of the com-
batants, the clashing of their claymores, the groans of the
dying, and the choking and gasping of the drowning. The
very sea-birds, which had been roused in clouds by the
flash and roar of the two cannon shots, and which had
soared about for some moments, screaming in affright at
this rude and unwonted intrusion upon their solitary
slumbers, now winged themselves in terror away. The
crew of the galley were in a few seconds overpowered from
the vantage ground possessed by the assailants, as well as
by the sudden nature of the assault itself; and the slaughter
was dreadful. The fearless Allan of Lundy fought furiously
hand to hand with Hector, backed as the MacKenzie champion was by those who came to aid him after putting their
own opponents to death. Terrific were the blows he dealt
around him, and murderous were the wounds inflicted by
the broad blade of his sweeping sword. But the number
of those who were thus opposed to him individually went

on increasing as his people fell around him, until all were gone; and he saw that he must be overwhelmed and taken if he should any longer attempt to continue his resistance. At once he took his resolution, and bounding boldly into the air, he dived into the bosom of the sea, leaving his astonished enemies filled with doubt and suspense as to his fate.

"He's food for the fishes like the rest of them," said some of the MacKenzies.

"The foul fiend catch him but yonder he goes!" cried one of them, as he saw him rise to the surface at some distance from the rock.

"To your oars, men of Kintail!" cried Hector, "to your oars, I say, and let him not escape!"

Meanwhile, stoutly did Allan of Lundy breast the tide, and so great was the confusion that prevailed among the Kintail men, that ere they could push off the boat, man the oars, and make her start ahead, the powerful swimmer had made considerable way against the billows. Soon, however, would they have diminished the distance he had gained, and soon would he have been the prey of those who thirsted so eagerly for his life, had not the other galleys at that moment appeared; their prows bearing gallantly onwards with the favouring tide, making the sea foam and hiss again with the sweep of their numerous oars, and the rapid rush of their course. In an instant the Kintail boat altered the direction of her head, and shot away off in an easterly direction; her rowers bending to their work like men who were anxious to escape from a pursuing danger. Allan with the red jacket was easily recognised amid the waves; but ere they could get him into the galley that first came up, the boat of the MacKenzies was already lost to their eyes in the gloom that brooded over the more distant part of the straits. Hopeless of overtaking her, the MacDonells, after bewailing the calamity that had befallen them, and looking for some time in vain for the remains of their young leader, pursued their sad and darksome voyage, with the pipes playing a wailing lament, until they reached Loch Hourn, whence most of them were to prosecute their melancholy march back to Invergarry Castle.

The lady of Kintail was no sooner informed of the success of her enterprise, than she despatched a quick-sailing boat to the island of Mull to bear the news to her lord. This boat was observed to pass southwards by the MacDonells, as they were lying by for a short repose. The object of its voyage was quickly guessed at, but Allan of Lundy judged it unwise to interrupt it.

"It is toiling to work out our revenge," said he to his people. "It goes to invite the lord of Kintail homewards. See that ye who are to tarry here keep a lively watch for him, and so shall his blood pay for that of our lamented young chief. Would that I could have remained to have wreaked my vengeance on his head! But I have other duties to perform,—I must go to soothe a bereaved father's sorrow. Alas! how shall I break the news of this sad affliction to the old man!"

I need hardly tell you that the old chief of the Mac-Donells remained in a state of extreme mental anxiety after the departure of Angus with the expedition. He felt that not only the honour of the clan, but the honour and the life of his son, were at stake. He was restless and unhappy; yea, he cursed himself and his feeble limbs because he had not been able to go, as he was once wont to do, at the head of his people. Twenty times in the course of every hour did he fancy that he heard the triumphant clangour of the pipes played to his son's homeward march, and as often was he disappointed. At last something like their shrill music at a distance did strike upon his ear.

"Hah!" cried he with an excited countenance, "heard ye that?—my boy comes at last. Heard ye not the sound? Though I be old, yet is mine ear sharp when it watches for the coming of my gallant boy! Help me to the barbican, that I may behold him! Well do I remember the time when I first came back in triumph! It was on that memorable occasion when——Merciful Heaven!" exclaimed he after a pause, occasioned by the unexpected appearance at that moment of Allan of Lundy, who had come on before the rest, and who now entered the hall with downcast and sorrowful looks, and with his arms folded across his bosom. "Merciful Heaven! Speak Allan! Tell me why look ye so sad? Where is my Angus? Where is my boy?"

"Alas! alas!" said Allan of Lundy, "I cannot—cannot tell thee that it is well with him."

"What!—wounded?" cried the old chief; "so was I in my

first field.   He must look for such fate as fell to the lot of those who have lived before him."

" Alas ! alas !" cried Allan of Lundy, weeping at the old man's words, " Alas ! his fate has indeed come too soon !"

"Hush!" said the old chief, suddenly starting and stretching his ear to listen.   " What strains are these the bagpipes are playing ?—a *coronach !* Ah ! then am I a bereft father !   Oh ! my boy !—bereft !—bereft !—bereft !" and, springing convulsively from his chair, he smote his breast violently, his head turned round to one side, his neck suddenly stiffened, his eyes rolled fearfully, and then protruding themselves from their sockets, they became horribly fixed and glazed, his breath rattled in his throat, and sinking back into his chair, he had died before Allan of Lundy could rush forward to his aid.

Now indeed did the *coronach* raise its wild lament on the pipes, the. women mixing with it their wailings, and the men their groans.   It was for their old chief—their ancient strength, Donald MacAngus MacDonell, and for the young and promising flower of their hopes, Angus, the eldest son and heir of Donald.   The days of mourning, though not long, were sad, and the funeral obsequies of the chief were performed with all the solemnity, and pageantry, and ceremonial that were due to them, whilst those of his son were denied to them by the unhappy nature of his death.

The council of the clan had already determined that Allan of Lundy should govern for the young Ronald, who being in boyhood was deemed quite unfit for so weighty and important a charge.   The experienced warrior assumed the important trust with his usual boldness and confidence, though altogether overpowered by that honest and unfeigned grief which oppressed his heart for the loss of those relatives whom he had so long held dear.   But his warlike and revengeful spirit was not long suffered to remain so clouded, for he had hardly been installed in the situation, to which the universal suffrages of the clan had raised him, when a breathless messenger from Loch Hourn entered the hall.

" What news ?" cried Allan impatiently—" say, has the young blood of our lamented Angus been avenged ?   Has the red tide from Kintail's heart been mingled with the angry currents of the narrow seas ?"

"Alas, no !" replied the messenger, "no such good fortune has attended us ! "

"How then ?" demanded Allan, "methinks that if your leader had but followed the simple guidance which I gave him ere we parted, our grief might have been now somewhat assuaged by the thought that we had made that woman a widow who hath caused our woe, and that clan mourners who were rejoicing over the grief which they have wrought to us. But speak quickly, what hath happened ? "

"Your counsel was strictly followed," replied the messenger. "Our fleet of boats were all ready to be launched, and our men were lying prepared to embark at the first signal. Whilst all were on the watch, a galley appeared in sight, and we began to hurry on board. Suddenly we perceived that she was steering directly for the island where we lay, and we all went on shore again in the belief that she was the vessel with those friends we looked for from Ardnamurchan."

"Quick, quick ! what then ?" cried Allan of Lundy.

"On she came with her prow direct towards the port," replied the messenger, "and she continued to keep it so till she came within hail of the very entrance of it. Then the pipes played up *Cabar Fiadh*, and, ere she tacked to bear away again with all her oars out and hoisting her canvas to the uttermost, a hoarse voice came thundering from on board,—'The Lord Kintail here sends you his greeting by the hands of his captain, the captain of Cairnburgmore;' and in the same moment they poured out so murderous a storm of bullets from their falconets upon us who were then actively launching our boats to be after her, that many of our men were killed and wounded. The confusion among us was great, and she escaped to so great a distance before we were ready to pursue, that all pursuit became vain."

"Curses be on her and on her crew !" cried Allan of Lundy, gnashing his teeth in bitterness ; "it seems as if some fiend helped them ! Curses be on Cairnburgmore ! and curses be on the freight his galley carried ! But I will be revenged on these MacKenzies ! Here I swear," continued he, drawing his sword and striking it against the banner of the MacDonell that was then floating at the upper end of the hall. "Here do I solemnly swear to

make so terrible a reprisal on the MacKenzies, that men's
flesh shall creep upon their bones as they listen to the tale
of it; and yet shall it be but as an earnest of what I shall
inflict on that accursed clan for the grief and sorrow they
have so lately wrought us!"

These then, gentlemen, were the circumstances that
preceded and gave birth to the celebrated Raid of Killychrist, and after so long a preliminary history, I shall now
hasten to give you the particulars of that horrible piece of
atrocity.

It was Saturday, and the most active preparations were
instantly ordered by Allan of Lundy to be made for a
night-march. He had heard that there was to be a
numerous gathering of the MacKenzies next day in the
church of Killychrist, or Christ's Church, a short mile or
two above the little town and priory of Beauly. Putting
himself at the head of a determined band of followers
therefore, he took his way across the mountains with
inconceivable expedition, so that he found himself, early
on the Sunday morning, in the heart of the MacKenzie
country, and crossing the river Beauly, he was soon at the
church of Killychrist, and he surrounded it with his
MacDonells before any of his miserable victims were in the
least aware of his presence.

The church was filled with all ranks of the clan, but
there was a great proportion of the higher class among
them. Psalms were singing, and all within the sacred
building were absorbed in that attention or abstraction
which attends real or pretended devotion.

Suddenly the doors were taken possession of by the
armed MacDonells, with the grim and unrelenting Allan
of Lundy at their head. In an instant the nasal chant
of the psalmody was drowned by the screams of the timid,
who already saw nothing but death before them, and by
the exclamations of those who sought to make resistance,
and to fight their way through their foes. But utterly
impervious were the serried spear points that bristled
through the low-arched doorways, as well as through every
narrow lancet window of the holy fane; and stern and
resolute, and utterly devoid of feeling, were the war-scarred
countenances of those whose ferocious eyes glared in upon
them.

All was now panic and confusion among the MacKenzies,

who filled the area of the church, where individuals crowded and jostled so against each other, that few could draw a dirk, much less a claymore from its sheath. Meanwhile shouts were heard without, and immediately afterwards those of the MacDonells who kept the doors and windows gave way for one single instant; but it was only to admit of the approach of a number of their comrades, who speedily threw in heaps of blazing faggots together with stifling balls of rosin and sulphur, and other combustibles. In an instant the ancient carved screens and other woodwork of the interior were ignited, and the very clothes of the unfortunate people caught fire; and still heaps upon heaps of inflammable materials were hurled incessantly inwards, until all within was in one universal blaze.

"They have light enow within I trow,—they lack not light from without," cried the remorseless Allan of Lundy; "shut and fasten the doors and windows, and block them up with sods."

His orders were speedily obeyed, and those within were now left to their agonising fate; but well I ween that the fancy of no one can imagine what were the horrors conveyed in those sounds that came half stifled from within the walls of that church. Even to Allan of Lundy they became utterly intolerable.

"Alister Dhu!" cried he to the piper, "play up, man! —up with your hoarse melody, and drown these sounds of torture and death that fill our ears, as if we had been suddenly transported to the regions of hell. Play up, I tell you!"

The piper instantly obeyed his command, and blew up loud and shrill; and, after having made his instrument give utterance to a long succession of wild and unconnected notes, altogether without any apparent meaning, he began his march around the walls of the church, playing extemporaneously that pibroch which, under the name of Killychrist, has ever since been used as the Pibroch of Glengarry. For a brief space of time, the horrible sounds which came from within the building continued to mingle themselves with the clangour of the pipes; but by degrees these became fainter and fainter, and the piper had not made many circles around the church till the shrieks, the groans, and the wailings had ceased; their spirits had

13

been released from their tortured bodies, and all was silent within its walls.

Allan of Lundy had no desire to unbar this scene of horror, that he might look upon his work ere he went. The preservation of his people, moreover, required that he should retreat as expeditiously as he possibly could. He was well aware that the whole MacKenzie country must very speedily be alarmed; that all of the clan who were within reach would be immediately in arms, and that the body of MacDonells which he had with him would be as a mere handful compared to that of his foes, if he should allow them time to assemble. He moved off therefore with the utmost expedition; but, with all the haste he could use, he could not shake off the MacKenzies, who collected in irregular numbers and followed him, harassing his rear and his flanks, whilst, like a lion retreating before the hunters, he marched on boldly, endeavouring to beat away the assailing crowds by halting from time to time as he went, and charging back upon them with resistless fury, making many a brave MacKenzie bite the dust. But still they continued to increase in force by fresh accessions.

At length he had recourse to a manœuvre which he hoped might have distracted the attention of his foes. He hastily divided his little band into two parties, and having given secret orders to a trusty leader to start off at the head of one band in the direction of the Bridge of Inverness, and so to pursue his way homewards by the south side of Loch Ness, he commanded the other to follow himself, intending to hold directly onwards over the hills by the route which they had come during the preceding night. This plan so far succeeded, that the MacKenzies were for some time much baffled and perplexed. But after some considerable delay, they recovered themselves so far as to divide their men also in the same manner; and one large body, under the command of Murdoch MacKenzie of Redcastle, followed hard after the first party of the MacDonells, whilst MacKenzie of Coull pressed onwards on the retreating steps of the captain of Glengarry.

Availing himself of the temporary check which his pursuers had thus met with, Allan of Lundy and his party made extraordinary exertions, by which they gained so much ground on their pursuers, that they fairly left the MacKenzies out of sight. They were thus enabled to rest for a little while, like a tired herd of chased deer, in the hills near the burn of Altsay. But their repose was short. The pack of their enemies, who were following on their track, soon opened in yells like those of hounds when they came in view of them, and they were compelled to stand to their arms. A very sanguinary skirmish was the consequence, fought with great success on the part of the MacDonells, who slew numbers of their enemies; but this availed them little, for still the MacKenzies came crowding and gathering on in fresh numbers, whilst the ranks of Glengarry were every moment growing thinner and thinner. Retreat, therefore, became again expedient.

Allan of Lundy made one desperate charge that scattered his foes over the hill-side, and then his bugle unwillingly gave the word of command for his brave MacDonells to retire. They did so with the utmost expedition, and at the same time with all the steadiness and coolness which became them. But as they moved on, many among their number were, from time to time, prostrated and sprinkled, man by man, on the earth, by the distant shots fired at them by their pursuers; and many a gallant clansman fell whilst endeavouring to cover from harm the scarlet-clad body of his leader, that conspicuously attracted the aim of his enemies. At length the number of the MacDonells became so much reduced, and the pursuit waxed so hot, that even a show of resistance was rendered utterly vain.

"Men of Glengarry!" cried Allan of Lundy, "nothing now remains for us but flight. But ere we fly, let us make one more furious onset against these cowardly *Bodachs.* Let us first scatter them to the four winds of heaven, and then, when I give you a bugle blast, see that ye in your turn flee off suddenly apart, and so let each try to find his own way home. I shall shift well enough for myself. Now charge on them."

Unprepared for this instantaneous assault, the effect of it was tremendous. Many of the MacKenzies were slain, and the whole of the remainder were dispersed like a flock of sheep. The MacDonells had hitherto kept together like a ball; but no sooner did they hear the shrill blast of Allan of Lundy's bugle, than they burst asunder, and each individual bounded off in that direction which seemed to offer him the best chance of baffling his pursuers.

As hounds are astonished and divided by the sudden appearance of a trip of hares starting all at once from some well-preserved patch of furze, so were the MacKenzies confused by this new expedient of their enemies. For some time they stood confounded, until at last they gathered into little irregular bands, each of which followed that fugitive to whom the eyes of those that composed it were accidentally directed. But the splendid scarlet jacket of Allan of Lundy, which was as well known to the MacKenzies as to the MacDonells, and which upon this occasion particularly struck them as participating in the hue of that element which had recently done so cruel work upon the miserable wretches at Killychrist, drew on him the fixed attention of by far the greatest body. This was exactly what he wished for, as he saw that in this way even his flight would be the means of contributing to the safety of his men.

"After the firebrand!" cried a powerful and athletic champion of the MacKenzies. "It is Allan with the red jacket himself. After him! See where he flies along the slope! But I'm thinking that there is something yonder afore him that will bring him to a check!—after him! after him!"

Like greyhound freed from the slips, did this leader of the MacKenzies, and a great mass of those who followed him, burst away after Allan of Lundy, who seemed to devour the very ground by the rapidity of his flight, and the crowd of those that were after him very soon showed a long tail like that of a comet.

The MacKenzie champion who had cheered them on to the pursuit, soon shot far-a-head of the great body of his party, some five or six of whom only could keep at all near him. He was well aware that the MacDonell had taken a course which must lead him to a fearful ravine,— a yawning chasm, something not much less than twenty feet in width, that seemed to sink black and fearful into that eternal night which may be supposed to exist in the bowels of the earth. The very stream that was heard to rush through it was there invisible. It was this that the MacKenzie leader had counted on as certain to prove a check to the flying Allan of Lundy. But little did he know that the bold hero of the MacDonells, trusting in his wonderful powers, had taken this very course with the

hope of being thereby enabled to rid himself entirely of his
pursuers. As Allan flew with a velocity that seemed to
vie with that of the heathcock as he skims over the
heather tops on a hill-side, he looked now and then over
his shoulder to ascertain the state of the pursuit; and
perceiving as he came within a few yards of the ravine,
that the MacKenzie leader was considerably in advance of
the handful of stragglers who toiled after him, he halted,
and planted himself firmly in a position to await his
assault. Nor was this halt of his altogether unseasonable;
for his breathing came somewhat hurriedly for a few
moments; but before his enemy came near to him, his
lungs were again playing easily; and if his erect bosom
heaved at all, it did so more with indignation and contemp-
tuous defiance, than from over-exertion. The MacKenzie
champion came to a stop within ten paces of him whom he
had been pursuing.

"Now!" cried he, whilst his words came thick and
half-smothered by the exhaustion under which he laboured.
"Now! now, Allan of the red jacket!—Now I have
got ye!—The last time we met, you escaped from this good
claymore by diving like a duck. Do so now, if you can.
Dive now, if you dare, or stand like a man, and face
Hector MacKenzie of Beauly,—Hector MacKenzie who
slew"——

"Villain!" cried Allan of Lundy, "you need say no
more. I thank thee for thus recalling to me thine
accursed visage and name. The very sight of thee gives a
new edge to this reeking blade of mine."

Allan of Lundy rushed furiously at his foe, who advanced
a step or two to meet him. A terrible single combat
ensued. But active and adroit as the MacDonell leader
had ever proved himself to be as a swordsman, he found in
Hector MacKenzie of Beauly a cool, an experienced, and
a powerful opponent. Conscious that his adversary had
at that moment the advantage of him as to wind, and
being aware that some five or six stark fellows of his
own clan were fast nearing the scene of action, he saw
that his game lay in protracting the fight, till numbers on
his side might make his enemy an easy prey. He contented himself therefore with guarding and parrying the
furious and not always well-directed cuts and thrusts of
Allan of Lundy, until his aid should arrive to render his

victory sure. They did come up at last, panting like overrun blood-hounds; and the brave MacDonell had just presence of mind enough to see that if he meant to save his life from that certain destruction that awaited it, from the fearful odds by which he was so speedily to be surrounded, he had no time to lose. With one desperate cut, which, though guarded, made his adversary reel beneath the very weight of it, he turned suddenly from him, and ran three or four steps towards the ravine—halted—threw back on his enemies a withering look of rage and scorn, and then darting towards the yawning gulf, he sprang over its fearful separation with the bound of a stag, and uttering a taunting laugh, he quietly leant upon his sword on the opposite bank to await the issue. The followers of Hector MacKenzie shuddered involuntarily as he sprang, but impelled by the rage of disappointment, Hector himself flew towards the chasm. He checked for a moment on the very brink, with his plumed bonnet thrown back, and his arms and sword high in air; and then casting one wild and searching look into the abyss that yawned beneath his feet, he retreated a few steps, and nerving himself with all his resolution, he flew at the desperate leap.

"He is over!" shouted one MacKenzie.

"God be here, he is down!" cried another.

Neither of them were accurately right. He had failed in clearing the chasm by a single inch. His toes scratched away the loose earth and moss, and down indeed went his feet. His naked claymore dropped from his hand; but he caught at a young birchen sapling that grew from the very verge of the rock. It bent like a rope with his weight, and he hung over the black void into which his trusty weapon had disappeared, and down which it was still heard faintly clanging as it was dashed from side to side in its descent. Allan of Lundy looked remorselessly downwards upon the wretched man whose eyes glared fearfully amidst his convulsed features, as with extended jaws he uttered some incoherent and guttural sounds, which even the horrors of his perilous situation and impending fate could not compel his indomitable spirit to mould into anything like a petition for mercy from a MacDonell.

"Hector of Beauly!" cried Allan of Lundy, "would that thou hadst but reached this solid ground claymore in hand! Then, indeed, might my revenge have been sweeter and more to my mind. But thy weird will have it so, and vengeance may not longer tarry. You it was who reft from us young Angus, the hope of our clan; and this day hast thou taken many of my brave fellows from me, and many trophies too hast thou taken. So thou mayest e'en *take that too!*"

With one sweep of his claymore he cut the sapling in twain; and the agonised visage of his powerful foe dropped away and disappeared from his eyes. No shriek was heard; but Allan of Lundy started involuntarily backwards as a heavy muffled sound came upwards from the descending body, as it grazed against the successive projections of the chasm; and when the prolonged plunge that arose from an immeasurable depth below, told him of the utter annihilation of what had so lately been a man as full of life, of action, and of courage, as he still felt himself to be possessed of.

Allan of Lundy stood for some moments as if transfixed to the spot. Wheresoever he gazed around him, the glaring eyeballs and the convulsed features of Hector of Beauly still haunted his imagination. But at length a shot from an arquebuse, that passed very near to him, and cut down a tall plant of *bracken** immediately behind him, brought him back to his recollection. He then saw that a great mass of the pursuing MacKenzies had already joined those two or three men who had so closely followed Hector of Beauly, and these were now gathered on the opposite side of the ravine, raging with fury for the loss of their champion. He felt that it was no time or place for him to halt to be a butt for them to shoot at. He sprang again like a deer to the hill. But as he climbed its steep face, many were the bullets that were sent whizzing after him. By one of these random shots he was wounded in the leg, not very severely, but so as to produce a considerable effusion of blood. The MacKenzies saw that he was hit, and like huntsmen marking the effect of their discharge against a deer, they stood for some moments to observe him as he made his way up the hill-side.

"He flags!" cried one.

* Fern.

" He faints!" cried another.

" IIe is mortally wounded !" cried a third.

" He moves on !" cried a fourth.

"Away ! away !" cried another. "Away to the ford above the waterfall. He cannot last long. We shall soon come up with him."

But the game was of a very superior description to what those who hunted him supposed; and they soon found that he was not quite so easily secured as they had calculated. Before they had made their circuit in order to cross the stream that poured itself headlong into the ravine which had been so fatal to their champion Hector of Beauly, the red jacket of Allan of Lundy had disappeared over the hill-top. But he had left his blood upon his track. A consultation was held as to what was best to be done.

" Let us have Rory Bane's trusty sleuth-hound," said one of them. "See! yonder is his cottage on the other side of the moss."

The advice was approved of, and with one consent they hastened to procure the dog. The animal was no sooner put upon the trail of the fugitive, than he was like to pull down the man who held his leash. But the steady Highlander kept his hold of him, for he was well aware that if once let slip the keenness of the animal would lead him on hot foot till he overtook the MacDonell, in which case the creature's death would be sealed long ere they could come up to lend him their aid. In order to benefit by his sagacity, they required to keep with him, and they found it hard enough work to do so. With his leash stretched till its collar almost choked him, he went bounding and yelling after the chase, whitening the very heath as he passed along with the foam of his mouth, and keeping not only the man who held him, but all those who were with him, going at a desperate pace. But still the temporary breathing which the Glengarry leader had enjoyed at the ravine, and the long start which he had gained whilst his pursuers were making their circuit to avoid it, and going out of their way to procure the dog, together with the time which the hound took in picking up the scent in parts where Allan of Lundy had forded the mountain streams, enabled that hero, who was so swift and enduring of foot, to reach

the great valley of Loch Ness, even before the deep baying
of the hound had first struck upon his ear.

Then it was that a shout rang from the echoing face of
the mountain that overhung the lake, for his red jacket
had been descried by his pursuers, and they redoubled
their speed. But Allan of Lundy was now incapable
of increasing his. The blood that had continued to drop
from his wound as he ran had now left behind it that
incipient faintness, which the MacKenzies vainly thought
had fallen on him at the time when they saw that the
shot had told on him. But many miles of rough ground
had he since fled over with little diminution of speed;
and now the blue waters of Loch Ness stretched as it
were from his feet far up between its retreating mountains.
And only now it was that he felt a growing weakness,
that told him that the chase could not endure a much
longer time. Yet still he urged his flying steps, and still
the baying of the hound, and the shouts of his pursuers,
came nearer and nearer to his rear; and now and then a
bullet would whistle among the foliage of the bushes
that grew to right or left of him, or would tear up the
turf in his very pathway, as circumstances gave those
who followed him a chance view of him, whilst the echoes
reverberated the sound of the discharge which had sent it.

Already had he fled for some miles along the rocky
and wooded faces of those mountains which arise from
the northern side of Loch Ness, stopping from time to
time for a few seconds on some knoll-top, to inhale the
western zephyrs that blew on him with refreshing coolness
from the wilds of Invergarry. But his exertions were
so great and so long protracted, that even these his
native breezes ceased to afford sufficient renovation to
his wearied lungs and beating temples. He felt himself
growing fainter and fainter, and this, too, when his pursuers, many of whom had but recently joined in the chase,
were every minute gaining upon him more and more.
Yet still he laboured on until even the very mountains
seemed to conspire with his enemies against him. His
path became reduced to a narrow and confined track,
by the crags which towered above him on one hand, and
the precipices that stooped sheer down into the loch on
the other. All chance of escape seemed now to have
departed from him. In his despair he flung a hasty glance

over the waves that danced below him, and, as he did so, he descried a little boat about half-way across the sheet of water, with two or three individuals in it employed in fishing. The shouts of the MacKenzies now pressed closer and closer upon him. Like a stricken stag, he took his desperate resolve, and scrambling down to a pointed cliff that jutted out into vacancy over a deep and still part of the lake, he stood for a short time to breathe on its giddy brink. The yells of his enemies rent the air as they rushed wildly onwards to secure their prey, whilst the hound gave forth his deep bass to complete their terrific music. They were almost upon him. He cast his eyes once more downwards, then clasped his arms tightly over his breast, drew in one full draught of breath; and as the MacKenzies were clambering hurriedly along the dangerous path with their eyes fixed eagerly and intently upon his figure, they were astonished and confounded to perceive Allan of Lundy's well-known scarlet jacket shooting like a falling star through some fifty or sixty feet of air into the profound below! So perfectly had he preserved his perpendicular position during his descent, that he entered the water like an iron rod, so as scarcely to produce a ripple; and the simple action of stretching out his arms having instantly brought him like a cork to the surface, he was seen breasting his way towards the distant boat, with a vigour only to be accounted for from the circumstance, that the action he now used had brought a fresh set of muscles into play. Several random shots were fired at him by the MacKenzies but unsuccessfully; and he was soon beyond the reach of their bullets.

Grouped upon the point whence he had thus so miraculously sprung stood his panting and toilworn pursuers, wondering at this extraordinary effort of his desperation; whilst the disappointed sleuth-hound continued to rouse the echoes with his prolonged howlings. And now they eagerly watched the fate of him whom they not unnaturally believed to have escaped from their weapons only to be drowned in the unfathomable depths of the loch. For the little boat was still far from him, much farther than any strong swimmer could well hope to reach; and although he swam stoutly enough at first, they began to perceive that he was striking out more and more heavily, as if death was fast shackling his powerful sinews.

But now again, to their grievous disappointment, they saw that those in the boat had perceived him, and were pulling lustily towards him.

It happened that the owner of the boat was no other than Fraser of Foyers, who had come out from his own place near the celebrated waterfall of that name, on the south side of the lake, to waste a few idle hours in fishing. He was the staunch ally of the MacDonell; and although he was at a considerable distance from the spot at the time, the meteor descent of the red jacket had struck his eyes so forcibly, that he immediately suspected that something had befallen Allan of Lundy, whose garment he guessed it to be. Having ordered his men to row in the proper direction, he soon began to recognise the red speck forcing its way through the water, and leaving a long line of wake behind it, while the hostile tartans that waved from the verge of the cliff, and the echoes that were awakened by the baying of the hound and the shouts of the men, told him enough of the story to induce him and his rowers to strain every nerve to save the gallant captain of Glengarry. And great as were their exertions, they were no more than were necessary for effecting their object; for they reached him as he was on the eve of sinking from very exhaustion. Fraser of Foyers had no sooner saved his friend, than he stood up in his boat and gave three hearty cheers, and then hoisting his tiny white sail, he availed himself of a favourable breeze, and bore away for the upper end of the lake, whilst the MacKenzies followed it with their eyes, and continued to pour out maledictions upon it, till it was lost in the yellow haze of the sunset in the western distance.

The captain of the MacDonells returned to Invergarry Castle, to brood over the dire, though dear-bought revenge he had reaped in this terrible raid. His heart was especially filled with savage joy whilst ruminating on the dreadful death which he had bestowed on him who had killed his cousin Angus MacDonell. But these triumphant thoughts soon gave way before that ideal phantom of Hector of Beauly, which never ceased to haunt his fevered imagination, and which exhibited the last despairing, yet resolute look of that bold man, ere Allan of Lundy had cut the only remaining hold he had of earth, and sent him, as it were, into the very bowels of the infernal regions.

Nor did the cries which arose from the burning church of
Killychrist ever leave his ears.

But few of the MacDonells who partook of this expedition survived with their leader.   Even those who went
round by the Bridge of Inverness did not escape; and it
was somewhat remarkable that they died by a fate worthy
of those who had been engaged in so cruel an expedition.
Having been overcome with fatigue, they stopped to refresh
themselves in a house of public entertainment near
Torbreck, where they supposed that they were beyond all
risk of further attack.   But they were woefully mistaken;
for MacKenzie of Redcastle having followed them thither
with his party, suddenly surrounded them, and burned
every one of them to death.

FEUDAL HEROES.

Dominie.—That same Allan with the Red Jacket was surely a terrible chield. I'm thinking that his moral and religious yeddication must have been *vurra* much neglected.

Clifford (gravely).—I should strongly suspect so.

Dominie.—Something might surely have been made of him by subjeckin him to proper early nuture and restraint.

Clifford.—Aye, there is no saying what might have been made of him if you had had the flogging of him, Mr. Macpherson.

Dominie.—Preserve me, sir! no salary upon yearth could have tempted me to undertake the flagellation of such a birky.

Clifford.—Why, to be sure he might have rebelled a little under the lash; and if he had once run away from you, you would have been somewhat troubled to have caught him again. He would have been a grand fellow for a steeple-chase. He would have beaten the world on foot across a country.

Dominie.—These MacKenzies and MacDonells were fearful chaps. I have many a story about them.

Grant.—I have a few myself; and a legend which a friend gave me of a MacDonell of Glengarry and a Lord Kintail has this moment occurred to me, suggested by its similarity in certain circumstances to part of that to which we have been listening.

Author.—Will you favour us with it?

Clifford.—If he does, it must be by my especial licence. Our friend, Mr. Macpherson, is first in my book. But as I see he has lighted a fresh cigar, and as Grant has smoked his to the stump, he may e'en end it by throwing it into the fire, and commence his tale without further loss of time.

Grant.—I bow to your supreme will.

Clifford.—Pray make it short, if you please, for I begin to be rather sleepy, and I should be sorry to affront you by yawning. Besides, I mean to be up betimes to-morrow to try for a salmon.

GLENGARRY'S REVENGE.

My legend has to do with that very Castle of Eilean
Donan with which yours has already made us so well
acquainted. The time of the action was about the early
part of the seventeenth century, and the great actor in it
was a very celebrated MacDonell of Glengarry, whose name
I have forgotten, but who is said to have been remarkable
for his gigantic figure and Herculean strength. The Lord
Kintail of that period was a great favourite with the Court,
so that he thereby rose to great power and influence, which
he very naturally employed, according to the laudable
custom of those days, in humbling his enemies. Amongst
these, none bore him a larger share of animosity than his
hereditary foes, the MacDonells of Glengarry. It was not
in their nature tamely to submit to the dominion which
Kintail was permitted to exercise, with comparative
impunity, over some of the other clans. On the contrary,
they were frequently disposed not only to resist themselves, but they also very often found means to stir up
others to resistance, and in this way they sometimes
furnished Kintail with specious grounds for accusing them,
when all apology for doing so might have been otherwise
wanting.

It happened that the chief of Glengarry was on one occasion engaged for some days in a hunting expedition in that
range of his own country which surrounds the sea lake of
Loch Hourn, already so often mentioned in the last legend.
The sun was setting on a mild and beautiful evening, and
the breeze was blowing softly from the sea, when, as Glengarry was returning from the chase, attended by a small
party of his followers, he espied a couple of galleys standing
in towards the very part of the shore where stood the little
group of black bothies, that at such times formed his
temporary place of encampment. Doubtful whether the
approaching vessels might contain friends or foes, he deemed
it prudent to put himself and his people into ambush

behind some broken ground, where they might lie concealed until they could patiently observe the progress and
the motions of those who came, and so judge as to the
result.

"Knowest thou the rig of those craft, Alaister More?"
demanded Glengarry of his henchman, as they peered
together over the black edge of a moss bank, and scanned
the approaching sails with earnest eyes. "Whence may
they come, thinkest thou?"

"I would not say but they may be Kintail's men,"
replied Alaister.

"Kintail's men!" exclaimed Glengarry, "what would
bring Kintail's men here at this time?"

"I'm not saying that I am just exactly right," replied
Alaister, "but I'm thinking it looks like them."

"Curses on them!" said Glengarry bitterly, "they are
bold to venture hither while I am here."

"They are so, I'm thinking," said Alaister; "but it
may be that they have no guess that Glengarry is here.
But, troth, that Kintail holds his head so high now-a-days,
that I'm judging his men think themselves free to thrust in
their noses just where they like. He's king of the north-
west, as a man might say."

"Accursed be his dastard dominion!" said Glengarry,
with bitterness of expression; "and shame upon the
slavish fools that yield their necks as footstools to his
pride. Is't not galling to see it? Is't not galling to see
men of wisdom and bravery, such a man as my staunch
friend and ally, MacLeod, for instance, yielding so ready
an obedience to one whom all should unite to oppose,
overthrow, and crush as a common enemy."

"That's very true that you're saying, Glengarry!"
observed Alaister; "but I'm thinking that they are not
all just blessed with your spirit. If they had been so, I'm
judging that the MacCraws could not have been left as
they were without help but what they got from you."

"By all that is good, it was our help alone that saved
them," cried Glengarry in an animated tone. "Half of
them would have been hanged on the gallows-tree but for
our interference. The MacKenzies had no reason to pride
themselves on the event of that day, nor had we any cause
to boast of the zeal of those whom we have been wont to
reckon among our allies."

"Troth, you're not wrong there, Glengarry," said Alaister. "So I'm judging that we must even go on to trust to our own MacDonell swords in all time coming; and we have reason to be thankful that their blades are not just made of cabbage stalks."

"Thank God, indeed, that they are made of better metal!" said Glengarry, smiling proudly. "And small as this our party is, would, with all my heart, that these were Kintail's men, with Kintail himself at the head of them!"

"I should not be that sorry to see Kintail," said Alaister.

"We should give him a hotter welcome than this cold coast might lead him to look for," said Glengarry.

"We'll not be slow in giving him that same, I'm thinking," said Alaister.

"Stay! dost thou not make out a banner yonder?" demanded Glengarry.

"I'm thinking I do see something like a banner," replied Alaister.

"With this failing light we cannot hope even to guess at the bearing with which it may be charged," said Glengarry, straining his eyes, "but if that be a banner, as I believe it to be, then is there certainly a chief there. Look to your arms, MacDonells, and let us be prepared for what may happen!"

By degrees the galleys drew nearer and nearer; but as the night was falling fast, their forms grew less and less distinct as their bulk swelled in the eyes of the Mac-Donells, till at last they came looming towards the shore like two dark opaque undefinable masses, which were suddenly reduced, by the displacement of their sails, to about one-fourth part of the size they had grown to. For a time they were rocked to and fro until their keels became fixed in the sand by the receding tide. The dusky figures they contained were then seen pouring out from them, and passing like shadowy spectres across a gleam of light that was reflected on the wet sand from the upper part of the sky; and they showed so formidably in numbers, as to render some short council of war necessary before assaulting them with an inferior force, not from any fear of defeat on the part of him who took this precaution, but dictated by his prudence to prevent all risk of the escape of those whom they were about to attack.

Whilst Glengarry was thus concerting his measures, the
rangers were seen moving in a body towards the cluster
of huts, which stood at something less than an hundred
yards from the water side, and they speedily disappeared
within their walls, and lights soon afterwards began to
start up within them, as if they were preparing to make
themselves comfortable for the night. Glengarry observed
this, and in order that he might lull all apprehension of
attack, he resolved to give them full time to employ themselves in cookery, or in whatever other occupation they
might find to be necessary.

The broken ground which concealed the MacDonells
was charged by a small rill, that ran between banks of mossy
soil, in a diagonal line, and opened on the sand at a point
almost opposite to the spot where the two galleys were
lying. No sooner was the chief of Glengarry satisfied that
the time was come when the assault could be most opportunely made, than he led his handful of men silently down
between the hollow banks of the brook, so as to get unperceived between the enemy and their vessels. So far
everything went well with them, but as they debouched
from the mouth of the water-course, the partial light that
gleamed from the upper part of the sky glanced unexpectedly on the blades of their naked claymores, and
instantly a loud bugle blast blew shrilly from on board the
nearer of the two galleys.

"Dunvegan! Dunvegan!" cried a loud voice from the
bothies, after the bugle had ceased.

In an instant their little black heaps gave forth their
living contents, some armed, and others with blazing
torches of moss-fir, plucked suddenly from the great fires
they had kindled.

"'Tis MacLeod!" said Glengarry in a peevish tone, that
sufficiently betrayed the disappointment he felt that his
well-concerted scheme of attack was thus rendered useless.
"'Tis but MacLeod, then, after all!"

"Hoo!" said Alaister, "sure enough it's MacLeod, and
no one else. So we'll be supping, I'm thinking, and
drinking together like friends, instead of fighting like
wild cats."

"Would it had been otherwise!" said Glengarry,
"much as I love MacLeod, I would at this moment
rather a thousand times have encountered the Lord of

14

Kintail. By the rood, but I ther, was more i' the humc
dealing in blows than pledgir we ng in beakers! But si
could not be Kintail, I rejoice ords in that it is MacLeod, fe
could desire no better foe t ful th an the one, I can ha
worthier friend than the othe

"Both good of their kind hey a surely, I'm thinking,'
Alaister. proud

Nothing could exceed the jmy he oy and cordiality of th
friends at thus meeting so une lf at the ectedly. The fattest
of the chase was dragged towards a fire ntail, kindled
culinary purposes in one of the huts, steaks out fror
haunch were added to the fare which MacLe this od's pe
were preparing, and after a hasty and unceremonious linus,
the two chiefs retired with some of those in whom they
reposed most confidence, into a separate bothy, where they
might have leisure for full converse over a cup of wine.

"To what happy accident am I to attribute our meeting
thus in Knoidart?" demanded Glengarry.

"If I had not chanced thus to meet you here," said
MacLeod, "I should have gone on to Invergarry Castle,
as I originally intended. But it is well that I am saved
so long a journey."

"Nay, by all that is friendly, that is not well said of
you, MacLeod," said Glengarry. "But I shall not be
baulked of your visit. We shall break up hence, and set
forward thither before to-morrow's dawn. If there be
deer on my hills, fish in my streams, steers in my pastures,
or wine in my castle-vaults, thou shalt be feasted like a
prince as thou art."

"That may not be," said MacLeod, "for this is no time
for you to devote to friendship and feasting. Thou
knowest not that the object of this voyage of mine was no
other than to warn thee of certain wicked plots that are
about to be brought to bear against thee."

"What! some evil machinations of the accursed Kintail,
I warrant me," said Glengarry.

"Thou hast guessed, and guessed rightly too," replied
MacLeod.

"Cowardly villain that he is!" cried Glengarry, "what
has he done?"

"Thou knowest that he is in high favour at Court," said
MacLeod. "They even talk now of his being made an
earl. But be that as it may, he hath somehow or other

acquired the means of using the King's ear. And foully
doth he misuse it, by pouring poison into it to further his
own ambitious and avaricious views, to the injury of the
innocent."

" 'Tis like the cold-hearted knave," said Glengarry.
" But what, I pray thee, hath he said of me?"

" I know not what he may have said of thee," answered
MacLeod, " but I know that he must have sorely mis-
reported thee, seeing that through certain channels he
hath persuaded his Majesty to arm him with letters of fire
and sword and outlawry against thee."

" What said'st thou?" cried Glengarry, choking with
his rising anger; " did I hear thee aright? Letters of
outlawry, and of fire and sword, put into the hands of
MacKenzie of Kintail, to be executed against *me!* Oh,
impossible !"

" What I tell thee is too true," said MacLeod.

" The dastard dare not use them!" cried Glengarry,
grinding his teeth from the violence of his rage.

" Backed by the King, as he now is, he may dare do
anything," said MacLeod.

" I defy him though he be backed by the King," cried
Glengarry in a fury; " aye, and though both were backed
by the black monarch of hell? God forgive me for coupling
the name of a sovereign whom I would fain love and honour,
if he would but let me, with those of MacKenzie of Kintail, and that devil whom he delights to serve."

" Moderate your passion, Glengarry," said MacLeod,
"and listen to me quietly, until I put thee in possession
of all that is brewing against thee."

" I am calm," said Glengarry.

" It is my duty as a friend of thine to tell thee, then,"
said MacLeod, " that a meeting is summoned for three
days hence at the Castle of Eilean Donan of all those whom
Kintail chooses to call the King's friends in these north-
western parts, who are called together for the ostensible
purpose of giving him counsel how best to put in force
those letters against thee, which he affects to be deeply
grieved to have been charged with."

" Hypocritical villain !" cried Glengarry.

" I am one of those friends of the King who are thus
summoned," said MacLeod, " and my present object was
to prove to thee, that although I may be so ranked, I am

not the less a friend of thine. I wished to make thee fully aware of the whole state of matters before I go to Eilean Donan to swell, as in regard to my own safety I must needs do, that majority which he looks for to strengthen his hands against thee."

"Thou hast proved thyself a friend indeed," said Glengarry, after ruminating a few seconds. "Thou hast proved thyself to be that old and steady friend of mine which I always have believed, and ever will believe thee to be. And now it is my turn to ask thee, whether thou hast ever found me in one instance to fail thee?"

"Thou hast never failed me, Glengarry," said MacLeod, "and I trust our clans shall be ever linked together like one bundle of rods."

"Aye!" said Glengarry, with a bitter laugh, "a bundle of rods which I trust may one day be well employed in scourging this pitiful tyrant of the north-west. I love thee too much to demand thine open aid at present. But haply thou mayest well enough find some excuse for not going to this meeting thou speakest of. An excuse, mark me, to be sent after the day is past. Thou canst be grievously ill, or anything may serve as an apology, if an apology should be required; for I have friends at Court, too, and I may yet find the means so to bring things into proper joint, as to render apologies more necessary from Kintail than from us. All that I ask of thee then is, that you may not appear at this nefarious assemblage at Eilean Donan."

"MacDonell," replied MacLeod, "I know the risk I run, but I am ready to incur any risk for so old a friend as thou art, especially in a case where the securing aid in arms rather than in council is so evidently the object of Kintail in calling us together. Say no more then; we shall weigh hence for Dunvegan by to-morrow's dawn, and be assured nothing shall drag me thence to be marshalled against thee in any way."

"Thank thee—thank thee!" said Glengarry, cordially shaking MacLeod by the hand. "This is no more than I expected of thy generosity and good faith. Thy kind and friendly information shall not be thrown away upon me. I shall start for Invergarry Castle by to-morrow morning's sunrise. But thou shalt hear from me without fail. And if thy little finger be but brought into jeopardy, thou shalt have my neck to answer for it."

This important conversation between the two chiefs being now ended, they gave themselves up to the enjoyment of that good fellowship and revelry which arose between their two clans. Small was that portion of the time subjected to the rule of night which was by them devoted to slumber, and soon were they both astir each to pursue his separate way; and as the rising sun was glancing on the arms of Glengarry and his people as they wound inland over the muirland hills, they looked back towards Loch Hourn, and beheld the galleys of MacLeod winging their way for Skye, under a favouring land breeze, that seemed to have been begotten by the genial beams of morning, which then poured a flood of brilliant light after them as they flew over the trembling surface of the waters.

The tide was fully up around the little island which gives name to the Castle of Eilean Donan, and the ferry-boat was moored on the landward side of the strait, when the shades of night began to descend upon it, and upon the whole of the surrounding scenery, on the evening of that day which was fixed for the gathering that Lord Kintail had summoned.

"A plague take this MacLeod," said the boatman in Gaelic to his assistant, as they sat glued to their benches, listening with envy to the sounds of mirth that came to their ears from within the castle walls. "A plague upon this MacLeod, who keeps us waiting here in the cold when we might be warming our toes at a blazing fire, and cherishing our noses with a goodly flagon of ale!"

"A plague upon him, with all my heart," echoed the other man. "Is it for him alone that we are condemned to tarry here?"

"Aye, Donald," said the master, "MacLeod is the only man awanting, it seems; and, sure enough, I think there be plenty without him. Hast thou ever before seen such an inpouring of eagles' wings into the Castle of Eilean Donan? There is surely something a-brewing."

"Whatever may be brewing, Master Duncan, we seem to have but little hope of drinking of it," said the man, laughing heartily at his own joke.

"Faith, Master Donald, they may be brewing some *browst* which neither you nor I would be very eager to drink," replied the master; "I would rather be turning up a creaming cup of the castle ale than have aught to do with any such liquor. But hold, heard ye not the tread of men ? Come, loose the rope, and to your oars. That will be MacLeod at last. Who comes there ?" cried he, as he dimly perceived a small party of men approaching the spot where the boat lay.

" MacLeod !" cried a voice in reply, and immediately a tall and bulky figure, completely enveloped in an ample plaid, advanced, and after having given some secret directions to his followers, to which the impatient boatmen neither cared nor tried to listen, he stepped solemnly and silently alone into the boat, and was speedily rowed across.

The hall of Eilean Donan was that night crowded beyond all former precedent. The feast was already over, and Lord Kintail was then presiding over the long board, where flowing goblets were circulating among the numerous guests, who were all his friends or allies, or who at least feared to declare themselves to be otherwise. But fully aware of the uncertain materials of which this great assemblage was composed, the chief of the MacKenzies had most prudently intermingled the stoutest and bravest individuals of his own clan among these strangers ; and, as was customary in these rude times, each man sat with his drawn dirk sticking upright in the board before him, ready for immediate use, in case of its services being required ; and this precaution was the more naturally adopted upon the present occasion, because every one at that table was jealous and doubtful of those sitting to right and left of him.

On a sudden the door of the hall was thrown open, and a huge man strode slowly and erectly into the middle of it. He was muffled up in a large dark plaid, of some nameless tartan ; and it was so folded over the under part of his face as completely to conceal it ; whilst the upper part of his features was shrouded by the extreme breadth of the bonnet he wore. His appearance produced a sudden lull in the loud talk that was then arising from every mouth, the din of which had been making the vaulted roof to ring again. The name of "MacLeod" ran in whispers around, and Lord Kintail himself having for a moment taken up the notion that had at first so generally seized the company, he signed to his seneschal to usher the stranger towards

the upper end of the table where he himself sat, and where
a vacant chair on his right hand had been left for the chief
of Dunvegan.

The stranger obeyed the invitation, indeed ; but he sat
not down. He stood erect and motionless for a moment,
with all eyes fixed upon him.

"MacLeod !" said the Lord Kintail, half rising to acknowledge his presence by a bow, "thou art late. We
tarried for thee till our stomachs overmatched our courtesy. But stay, am I right? art thou MacLeod or not ?
Come, if thou art MacLeod, why standest thou with thy
face concealed ? Unfold thyself and be seated ; for there
are none but friends here."

"I am not MacLeod !" said the stranger, speaking distinctly and deliberately, but in a hollow tone from within
the folds of his plaid.

"Who art thou, then, in God's name ?" demanded Kintail, with some degree of confusion of manner.

"I am an outlawed MacDonell," replied the stranger.

"A MacDonell !" cried Kintail, with manifest agitation.
"What wouldst thou under this roof ?"

"I am come to throw myself on thy good faith, Lord
Kintail, with the hope that thou mayest be the means of
procuring a reversal of the hard sentence which hath been
so unjustly passed upon me and my clan."

"I must first know more of thee," said Kintail. "I can
give no promise until I know who thou art."

"I said I was a MacDonell," replied the other.

"That is a wide name," said Kintail. "Heaven knows
that for the peace of the earth it holds too many that bear
that name."

"That may be as men may think," said the stranger,
with greater quickness of articulation.

"What MacDonell art thou, then ?" demanded Kintail.
"Pray, unmuffle thy face."

"One MacDonell is like another," said the stranger carelessly.

"That answer will not serve me," said Kintail. "I must
see thy face. And methinks it is a bad sign of thee, that
thou shouldst be ashamed to show it."

"Ashamed !" said the stranger, with emphasis—and
then, as if commanding himself,—"In times of feud like
these," added he, after a pause, "thou canst not ask me to

uncover my face before so promiscuous a company as this, where, for aught I know, I may have some sworn and deadly personal enemies, who may seek to do me wrong. But give me thy solemn pledge, Lord Kintail, that I shall suffer no skaith, and then thou *shalt* see my face."

"I swear to thee before this goodly assemblage," said Kintail, "that whoever thou mayest be, or whatever enemies of thine may be amongst us, thou shalt be skaithless. Nay, more; for thy brave bearing thou shalt have free assoilzieing from outlawry and all other penalties, be thou whom thou mayest, with one exception alone."

"Whom dost thou except?" demanded the stranger, eagerly advancing his body, but without unveiling his face.

"Glengarry himself," said Lord Kintail.

"By all that is good, Glengarry may well be a proud man by being so distinguished," said the stranger, with great energy both of voice and of action. And then, after a short pause, he made one bold step forward, and throwing wide his plaid, and standing openly confessed before them all, he exclaimed in a voice like thunder,—"*I am Glengarry!*"

There was one moment of fearful silence, during which all eyes were turned upon the chief of the MacDonells with the fixed stare of people who were utterly confounded. Then was every dirk plucked from the board by the right hand of its owner, and the clash which was thus made among the beakers and flagons was terrific; and the savage looks which each man darted upon his neighbour, in his apprehension of treachery, where each almost fancied that the saving of his own life might depend on the quick dispatching of him who sat next to him, presented a spectacle which might have frozen the blood of the stoutest heart that witnessed it. But ere a stroke was struck, or a single man could leave his place, Glengarry sprang on Kintail with the swiftness of a falcon on its quarry; and ere he could arm himself, he seized his victim with the vice-like gripe of his left hand, and pinned him motionless into his chair, whilst the dirk which he had concealed under his plaid now gleamed in his right hand, with its point within an inch of the MacKenzie's throat.

"Strike away, gentlemen," said Glengarry calmly; "but if that be your game, I have the first cock!"

The MacKenzies had all risen, it is true. Nay, some of them had even moved a step forward in defence of their chief. But they marked the gigantic figure of Glengarry; and seeing that the iron strength he possessed gave him as much power over Lord Kintail as an ordinary man has over a mere child, and that any movement on their part must instantly seal his doom, each man of them stepped back and paused, and an awful and motionless silence once more reigned for some moments throughout the hall.

"Let any man but stir a finger!" said Glengarry in a calm, slow, yet tremendous voice, "and the fountain of Lord Kintail's life's-blood shall spout forth, till it replenish the goblet of him who sits in the lowest seat at this board! Let not a finger be stirred, and Kintail shall be skaithless."

"What wouldest thou with me, MacDonell?" demanded Kintail, with half-choked utterance, that gave sufficient evidence of the rudeness of that gripe by which his throat was held.

"Thou hast gotten letters of outlawry and of fire and sword against me and against my clan," said Glengarry.

"I have," said Kintail. "They were sent me because of thy rescue of certain men of the MacCraws, declared rebels to the King."

"I ask not how or whence thou hadst them," said Glengarry. "But I would have them instantly produced."

"How shall I produce them, when thou wilt not suffer me nor any one to move?" said Kintail.

"Let thy chaplain there—that unarmed man of peace— let him produce them," said Glengarry.

"Go then, good Colin," said Kintail to the chaplain, "go to yonder cabinet, thou knowest where they lie. Bring them hither."

"This is well!" said Glengarry, clutching the parchments with his armed hand from the trembling ecclesiastic, and thrusting them hastily into his bosom. "So far this is well. Now sit thee down, reverend sir, and forthwith write out a letter from thy lord to the King, fully clearing me and mine in the eyes of his Majesty from all blame, and setting forth in true colours my own loyalty and that of my brave clan. Most cruelly have we been belied, for before these gentlemen I do here swear that, as God shall be my judge, he hath nowhere more faithful subjects."

"Use thy pen as he dictates," said Kintail, "for if he speaks thus, I will freely own he hath been wronged in the false rumours which have been conveyed to me, and through me to his Majesty."

"'Tis honest at least in thee to say so much, Lord Kintail," said Glengarry, "and since thou dost grant me this, thine amanuensis here may as well write me out a short deed pledging thee to the restitution of those lands of mine which were taken from me, by the King's order, on former false statements of delinquency. And be expeditious, dost thou hear, lest thy good lord here may suffer too long from the inconvenience of this awkward posture in which thou art thyself detaining him by thy slow and inexpert clerkship."

"Write as thou art bid, and as expeditiously as may be," said Kintail, sincerely coinciding with Glengarry's last recommendation. Accordingly, the papers were made out exactly as he desired, signed by Kintail, and then placed in the capacious bosom of the MacDonell chief.

"All this is so far well," said Glengarry. "Now swear me solemnly that I shall be permitted to return home without molestation, and that thou wilt faithfully, and truly, and honestly observe all these thine engagements."

"I swear!" said Kintail, "I solemnly swear that thou shalt pass hence and return into thine own country, without a hair of thy head being hurt; and I shall truly and faithfully observe everything I have promised, whether in writing or otherwise."

"Then," said Glengarry, quietly relinquishing his grasp, sheathing his dirk, and coolly seating himself at the board as if nothing had happened; "then let us have one friendly cup ere we part,—I would predge to thy health and to thy rooftree, my Lord Kintail!" and, saying so, he filled a large goblet of wine and drained it to the bottom, turning it up when he had finished, to show that he had done fair justice to the toast.

"Glengarry!" said Kintail, "thou shalt not find me behind thee in courtesy. Thine to be sure hath been in certain respects somewhat of the roughest to-night, and I must own," continued he, chafing his throat, "that a cup of wine never could come to me more desirably than at this moment, so I now drink to thee as a friend, for enemies though we have ever been, thy gallant courage has won my full applause."

"And I repeat the pledge, and in the same friendly guise, Kintail," said Glengarry taking him by the hand, and squeezing it till this demonstration of his new-born friendship became almost as inconvenient to the chief of the MacKenzies, as the effects of his ancient enmity had so lately been. "And now I must bid you all God-speed in a parting draught,—*Slainte!*"

"One cup more, Glengarry, to *Deoch-an-dorrus!*" said Kintail.

"With all my heart," said Glengarry, and this last pledge was a deep one. Again he squeezed Kintail's hand, till he made the tears come into his eyes. "Be assured," said he, "thy letter to the King is in safe hands, my Lord Kintail, for I shall see it delivered myself."

"Lights and an escort there for Glengarry!" cried Lord Kintail; and the bold chief of the MacDonells, bowing courteously around him to all that were assembled in the hall, left them full of wonder at his hardihood, whilst he was marshalled with all due ceremonial and honour to the boat, and ferried across to his impatient people. He found that his little knot of MacDonells, with Alaister More at their head, had been kept so long in a state of anxiety, and they had begun to doubt and to fear so much for his safety, that they were on the very eve of resolving to endeavour to break into the castle, that they might ascertain what had befallen him, or to die in the attempt.

"My horse, Alaister!" cried Glengarry, as soon as his foot had touched the shore; and throwing himself into the saddle, he let no grass grow at his heels till he reached the capital, and was presented at Court, where he speedily re-established himself in the good opinion of his sovereign.

LONG YARNS.

Clifford (yawning).—Now, Mr. Macpherson, your story comes next, and if it is but of brevity as reasonable as that which we have now heard,—aw !—aw—I think,—aw-ah-ahaw !—that in justice to you, we are bound to hear it ere we go to bed—a—aw-aw.

Dominie.—I cannot positively say what my story might measure out to in the hands of ane able story-teller. Some clever chield like Homer, or Virgil, or Sir Walter Scott, for example, any one of whom could spin you a thread as if they were working it off by the hundred ells, with that machine once vurra much used by the Highland wives, called the *muckle wheel.* But, plain man as I am, you can never expeck me to tell anything but the bare facks. Yet I must not let you yemagine, gentlemen, that there is any fack at all in the foolish fairy story I am now going to tell you.

Clifford.—Why, Mr. Macpherson,—aw—aw—ha ! if I have any of my logic left in me at all, I think I can prove that *de facto* you have no story to tell. As thus :—

You tell nothing but *facks.*

In your story there is no *fack.*

Therefore you have nothing to tell.

Quod erat demonstrandum. Ergo, as a corollary, I think we had better—aw—aw—a—go to bed.

Grant.—Very ingeniously made out, Clifford. But we know from experience, that logic and common sense are not always equal to the same thing, and therefore they are not always equal to one another. So, to cut the argument short, I now move that Mr. Macpherson do forthwith begin his story.

Author.—I second the motion.

Clifford.—Well, I shall—aw, aw—light another cigar, and if he does not finish in the smoking of it, I for one shall bowl off to bed.

Grant.—Come then, Mr. Macpherson, pray take the start of him.

THE LEGEND OF THE BUILDING OF
BALLINDALLOCH.

As you go down the avenue leading from the bridge to the
present house of Ballindalloch, gentlemen, you cross a
small rivulet that rushes headlong with a cheerful sound
from the wooded banks rising on your right hand, the
which, after finding its way under the road through what
is commonly called a *cundy* bridge, throws itself over the
rocks directly into the pellucid stream of the Aven, that
accompanies you on your left. If you should chance
to go down that way, and if you should be tempted
to trace that little rill upwards through the wild shrub-
bery, and among the tangled roots of the venerable oaks
and other trees which shoot up everywhere in fantastic
shapes from its sides, and by throwing their outstretched
arms across its bed here and there, produce a pleasing
contrast of checkered light and shade, you will find many
a nook amid its mazes which a fanciful yemagination
might set apart as a haunt befitting those frisking
creatures of the poet's brain, Oberon and Titania, and
where the sly tricks and *pawky* gambols of Puck and the
fairy folk might well be played. I think, indeed, that I
could almost venture to assert, that no one truly filled
with what may be termed the romance of poetry, could
well pass a few hours' vigil in the thick retirement of that
lovely and sequestered grove, with the full moon piercing
through the openings in the canopy of foliage, and shining
directly down the little ravine where that musical rill
flows, its beams converting the rushing waters into silver,
and the dewdrops of every leaf, flower, or blade of grass,
on its banks, into diamonds, without looking to come
pop upon some tiny fairy palace, or to be charmed by
some witching sight or sound, that, for the time at least,
may make him forget that he is a mortal. This opinion
I venture to pronounce on the mere internal yevidence
afforded by the spot itself, as well as by the recollections

of my own feelings when I chanced to wander up the place under similar circumstances, with this simple addition, to be sure, that I had been at a wedding that night, and had consequently a small drop of toddy in my head. But be that as it may, the vulgar supposition that it is inhabited by supernatural beings is borne out by the corroborative testimony of very ancient tradition. From time immemorial it has been called *the Castle Stripe*, and the origin of this name is linked with some old foundations which are still to be seen on the summit of the bank above, the legendary history of which I am now going to tell you.

It is believed that several centuries have passed away since the Laird of Ballindalloch proposed to build himself a castle or peel-tower for his more secure abode in times when the prevalence of private feuds required strength of position and solidity of structure ; and having, doubtless, first and foremost sat down, like a sensible man, to count the probable cost of his contemplated edifice, he next, with yespecial prudence, set about considering where he should find the best site to yerect it on; and after a careful examination of his domains, he at last fixed on the vurra spot now occupied by those old foundations I spake of. This place possessed many advantages in his eyes, for, whilst it was itself overlooked by nothing, it not only commanded a pleasant prospect over all the haughs and low grounds of his own property, but it also enjoyed a view of the whole of the lands of Tullochcarron, lying on the opposite side of the Aven; and between that river and the Spey, above their point of junction, and this the good man considered a thing of very great importance at a time when that property was in the hands of another laird, with whom, if there was not then a quarrel, yet nobody could say how soon a quarrel might arise.

This very weighty matter of consideration being thus settled in his own mind, he began his operations with vigour. Numerous bodies of masons and labourers were applied to the work. In a few days the foundations were dug and laid, and several courses of the masonry appeared above ground, and the undertaking seemed to be going on in the most prosperous manner, and perfectly to the laird's satisfaction.

But what was the astonishment of the workmen one morning, when, on returning by sunrise to their labour, they discovered that the whole of the newly built walls had disappeared, aye, down to the vurra level of the ground! The poor fellows, as you may guess, were terrified beyond measure. Fain would they have altogether desisted from a work over which, it was perfectly plain, that if some powerful enemy had not the control, some strange and mysterious fatality must certainly hang. But in those days lairds were not men to whom masons, or simple delvers of the ground, could dare to say nay. He of whom I am now telling you was determined to have his own way, and to proceed in spite of what had occurred, and in defiance of what might occur; and having sent round and summoned a great many more workmen in addition to those already employed, he set them to the work with redoubled vigilance, and ere the sun of another day went down, he had raised the walls very nearly to the height which they had reached the previous evening before their most unaccountable disappearance.

But no sooner had the light of a new morning dawned, than it was discovered that the whole work had again disappeared down to the level of the ground. The people were frightened out of their senses. They hardly dared to go near the spot. But the terrors which the very name of the laird carried with it, swallowed up all their other terrors, as the serpent into which the rod of Moses was converted swallowed up all those that sprang from the rods of the magicians of Egypt; and as the laird only became so much the more obstinate from all these mysterious thwartings which he met with, the poor people were obliged to tremble in secret, and immediately to obey his will. The whole country was scoured, and the number of workmen was again very much increased, so that what by cuffing and what by coaxing (means which I find it vurra beneficial to employ by turns to stimulate my own scholars to their tasks), nearly double the usual quantum of work was done before night. But, alas! the next morning's dawn proved that the building of this peel-tower of Ballindalloch continued to be like unto the endless weaving of the web of Penelope, for each succeeding morning saw the work of the previous day annihilated by means which no human being could possibly divine.

"What *can* be the meaning of all this?" said the laird to Ian Grant, his faithful henchman, vexed out of all patience as he was at last by this most provoking and perplexing affair. "Who *can* be the author of all this mischief?"

"Troth I cannot say, sir," replied Ian. "The loons at the work think that it is some spite taken up against us by the *good people*." *

"Good people!" cried the laird in a rage. "What mean you by good people? More likely fiends, I wot."

"For the love of the Virgin use better terms, Ballindalloch," replied Ian. "Who knows what ears may be listening to us unseen."

"If I did not know thee to be as brave a fellow as ever handled a broadsword, I would say shame on thee, Ian, for a coward!" cried the laird. "Hark, ye! I would not wilfully anger the *good people* more than thou wouldst do. But I cannot help thinking that some bad people, some of my unfriends, some secret enemies of mine, of mortal mould, must have, somehow or other, contrived by devilish arts to do me all these ill turns."

"It will be easy to find that out, sir," said Ian, "we have only to plant a good guard all night on the works."

"That was exactly what I was thinking of, Ian," said the laird, "and I was a fool not to have thought of it before. Set the masons to their task again, then, without delay, and see that they be not idle, and take care to have a night-watch ready to mount over the work the moment the sun goes to bed. I'll warrant me we shall find out the scoundrels, or if we do not, we shall at least have the satisfaction of putting a stop to their devilish amusement."

None of Ballindalloch's people, however brave, were very much enamoured of any such duty, however honourable it might have been considered. But his orders were too imperative to be disobeyed, and so some dozen or twain of stout handlers of the old broad-bladed Scottish spear were planted as sentinels to patrol around the walls during the night. These gallant fellows took care to carry with them some cordials to keep their spirits up, and by a liberal use of them, the first two or three dreary hours of darkness passed off with tolerable tranquillity and comfort, and as time wore on, and their courage waxed stronger and stronger, they began to be of the laird's opinion, that

* *Good people*, the propitiatory name usually given by the superstitious peasants to the fairies.

however wonderful previous yevents had appeared to be, there had in reality been nothing supernatural in them; and, moreover, whatever might be the nature of the enemy, they were by no means disposed to venture to molest the brave defenders of the new walls.

Full of these convictions, their contempt of all earthly foes increased, as their dread of unearthly enemies sub-sided; and as there was an ancient and wide-spreading oak-tree growing within about forty or fifty paces of the walls, they thought that they might as well retire beneath the shelter of its shade, as some protection from the descending damps. This they were the more readily induced to do, seeing that from thence they could quite easily observe the approach of any suspicious people who might appear. Nay, they even judged that the cowardly enemy who might otherwise have been scared by observing so stout an armed band about the walls, might now be encouraged to show themselves by their temporary concealment.

"Come away now, Duncan man," said one of these heroes to a comrade, after they had drawn themselves together into a jovial knot, close to the huge trunk of the oak. "Come away, man, with your flask. I'm wondering much whether the juice that is in its body be of the same mettlesome browst, as that which came with so heart-stirring a smack out of the vitals of Tom's leathern bottle."

"Rest its departed spirit, Charley! it was real comfortable and courage-giving stuff," said another.

"By Saint Peter, but that's no worse!" said Charley, tasting it and smacking his lips, "Hah! it went to my very heart's core. Such liquor as this would make a man face the devil."

"Fie! let us not talk of such a person," said Tom. "I hope it is enow, if its potency amounteth even so high, as to make us do our duty against men like ourselves."

"Men like ourselves!" cried Charley. "I trow such like as ourselves are not to be furnished from the banks of either Aven or Spey, aye, or from those of any other river or stream that I wot of. Give me another tug of thy most virtuous flask there, Duncan. Hah! I say again that the power of clergy and holy water is nothing to this. It would stir a man up to lay the very devil himself. What sayest thou and thy red nose, old Archy Dhu?"

15

"I say that I think thou art speaking somewhat unadvisedly," replied Archy, stretching out his hand at the same time, and taking the flask from Charley as he was about to apply it to his lips for the third time in succession.

"Stay thy hand, man. Methinks it is my turn to drink."

"Silence!" said one who had command over them. "Can ye not moderate your voices, and speak more under breath? Your gabbling will spoil all."

"Master Donald Bane hath good reason with him, gentlemen," said Archibald Dhu, in a subdued tone. "For my part, I shall be silent;" and well might he say so, seeing that at that moment he turned aside to hold long and sweet converse with the flask.

"I tell ye, we must be quiet as mice," said Master Donald. "Even our half-whispers might be heard by any one stealing towards the walls, amidst the unbroken stillness of this night."

The night was indeed still as the grave. Not a leaf was stirring. Even the drowsy hum of the beetle was hushed, and no sound reached their ears but the tinkling music of the tiny rill that ran through the little runnel near them, in its way towards the ravine in the bank, and the soft murmur of the stream of the Aven, coming muffled through the foliage from below; when, on a sudden, a mighty rush of wind was heard to arise from the distant top of Ben Rinnes, which terribly grew in strength as it came rapidly sweeping directly towards them. So awfully terrific was the howl of this whirlwind, that the very hairs of the heads of even the boldest of these hardy spearmen stood stiff and erect, as if they would have lifted up their iron skull-caps. Every fibre of their bodies quivered, so that the very links of their shirts of mail jingled together, and *Aves* and *Paternosters* came not only from the mouths of such brave boasters as Charley, but they were uttered right glibly by many a bold bearded lip to which, I warrant me, they had been long strangers. On came the furious blast. The sturdy oak under which they had taken shelter, beat every man of them to the ground by the mere bending of its bole and the writhing of its boughs and branches. Wild shrieks were heard in the air amid the yelling of the tempest, and a quick discharge of repeated plunges in the Aven below an-

nounced to them that some heavy materials had been
thrown into it. Again, the whirlwind swept instantaneously onwards; and as it was dying away among the
mountains to the north of the Spey, an unearthly laugh,
loud as thunder, was heard over ther heads.

No sooner had this appalling peal of laughter ceased,
than all was again calm and still as death. The great oak
under which the discomfited men of the watch lay, heaped
one on another, immediately recovered its natural position.
But fear had fallen so heavily on these bruised and
prostrate men-at-arms, that they dared not even to lift
their bodies to the upright position; but creeping together
around the root of the tree, they lay quivering and shaking
with dread, their teeth chattering together in their heads
like handfuls of *chucky* stones, till the sun arose to put
some little courage into them with his cheering rays.
Then it was that they discovered, to their horror and
dismay, that the whole work done by the masons during
the preceding day at the new building had been as completely razed and obliterated as it had ever been upon any
of the previous nights. You may believe, gentlemen, that
it required some courage to inform their stern master of
the result of their night's watch; and with one consent
they resolved that Ian Grant, the laird's henchman, should
be first informed; and he was earnestly besought to be
their vehicle of communication.

"Psha!" cried the laird impatiently, when the news
reached him. "I cannot believe a word of this, Ian. Tho
careless caitiffs have trumped up this story as an apology
for their own negligence in keeping a loose watch. I'll
have every mother's babe of them hanged. A howling
tempest and an elrich laugh, saidst thou? Ha! ha! ha!
Well indeed might these wicked unfriends of mine, who
have so outwitted these lazy rascals, laugh till their sides
ached, at the continued success of their own mischief. I'll
warrant it has been some of Tullochcarron's people; and
if my fellows had been worth the salt that they devour at
my expense, assuredly we might have had the culprits
swinging on the gallows-tree by this time. So our men
may e'en swing there in their stead."

"If Tullochcarron's people have done these pranks,
they must be bolder and cleverer men than I take them
for," said Ian calmly. "But before wo set these poor

fellows of ours a-dancing upon nothing, with the gallows-
tree for their partner, methinks we may as well take a peep
into the stream of the Aven, where the wonderful clearness
of the water will show a pebble at the depth of twenty feet.
Certain it is that there came a strange and furious blast
over these valleys last night; and there may be no harm
in just looking into the Aven, to see if any of the stones of
the work be lying at the bottom."

"There can be no harm in that," said the laird, "so let
us go there directly."

They went accordingly; and to the great surprise of
both master and man, they saw distinctly that the bed
of the river was covered over with the new hammer-
dressed stones; and yet, on examining the high banks
above, and the trees and bushes that grew on them, not
a trace appeared to indicate that human exertions had
been employed to transport them downwards thither from
the site of the new building. The laird and his attendant
were filled with wonder. Yet still he was not satisfied
that his conjectures had been altogether wrong.

"If it has been Tullochcarron's people," said he doubt-
ingly, "they must have enlisted the devil himself as
their ally. But let them have whom they may to aid them,
I am resolved I shall unravel this mystery, cost what it
will. I'll watch this night in person."

"I doubt it will be but a tempting of powers against
which mortal man can do but little," said Ian. "But
come what come may, I'll watch with thee, Ballindalloch."

"Then haste thee, Ian, and set the workmen to their
labour again with all their might," said the laird, "and
let the masons raise the building as high as they possibly
can from the ground before night; and thou and I shall
see whether we shall not keep the stones from flying off
through the air like a flight of swallows."

The anxious laird remained all day at the work himself;
and as you know, gentlemen, that the master's eye maketh
the horse fat, so hath it also a strange power of giving
double progress to all matters of labour that it looketh upon.
The result was, that when the masons left off in the
evening, the building was found to have risen higher
than it had ever done before. When night came, the
same watch was again set about the walls; for the laird
wished for an opportunity of personally convicting the

men of culpable carelessness and neglect of duty. To make all sure, he and his henchman took post on the embryo peel-tower itself.

The air was still, and the sky clear and beautiful, as upon the previous night, and, armed with their lances, Bellindalloch and his man Ian walked their rounds with alert steps, throwing their eyes sharply around them in all directions, anxiously bent on detecting anything that might appear like the semblance of treachery. The earlier hours, however, passed without disturbance; and the confidence of the laird and Ian increased, just as that of the men of the guard diminished when the hour began to approach at which the entertainments of the previous night had commenced. As this hour drew near, their stolen applications to their cordial flasks became more frequent; but sup after sup went down, and so far from their courage being thereby stirred up, they seemed to be just so much the more fear-stricken every drop they swallowed. They moved about like a parcel of timid hares, with their ears pricked up ready to drink in the first note of intimation of the expected danger. A bull feeding in the broad pastures stretching between them and the base of Ben Rinnes bellowed at a distance.

"Holy Mother, there it comes!" cried Charley. In an instant that hero and all the other heroes fled like roe-deer, utterly regardless of the volley of threats and imprecations which the enraged laird discharged after them like a hailstorm as they retreated, their ears being rendered deaf to them by the terror which bewildered their brains, and in the twinkling of an eye not a man of them was to be seen.

"Cowards!" exclaimed the laird, after they were all gone. "To run away at the roaring of a bull! The braying of an ass would have done as much. Of such stuff, I warrant me, was that whirlwind of last night composed, of which they made out so terrible a story."

"What could make the fellows so feared?" said Ian. "I have seen them stand firm in many a hard fought and bloody field. Strange that they should run at the routing of a bull."

"And so the villains have left you and me alone, to meet whatever number of arms of flesh may be pleased to come against us! Well, be it so, Ian; I flinch not. I am resolved to find out this mystery, come what may of it. Ian, you have stood by me singly ere now, and I trust you will stand by me again; for I am determined that nothing mortal shall move me hence till morning dawns."

"Whatever you do, Ballindalloch," replied his faithful henchman, "it shall never be said that Ian Grant abandoned his master. I will"——

"Jesu Maria! what sound is that?" exclaimed the laird, suddenly interrupting him, and starting into an attitude of awe and dread.

And no marvel that he did so; for the wail of the rising whirlwind now came rushing upon them from the distant summit of Ben Rinnes. In an instant its roar was as if a tempestuous ocean had been rolling its gigantic billows over the mountain top; and on it swept so rapidly as to give them no further time for colloquy. A lurid glare of light shot across the sky from south to north. Shrieks,—fearful shrieks,—shrieks such as the mountain itself might have uttered, had it been an animated being, mingled with the blast. It was already upon them, and in one moment both master and man were whirled off through the air and over the bank, where they were tossed, one over the other, confounded and bruised, into the thickest part of a large and wide-spreading holly bush; and whilst they stuck there, jammed in among the boughs, and altogether unable to extricate themselves, they heard the huge granite stones, which had been that day employed in the work, whizzing through the air over their heads, as if they had been projected from one of those engines which that warlike people, the ancient Romans, called a balista or catapult; and ever and anon they heard them plunged into the river below, with a repetition of deep hollow sounds, resembling the discharge of great guns. The tempest swept off towards the north, as it had done on the previous night; and a laugh, that was like the laugh of a voice of thunder, seemed to them to re-echo from the distant hills, and made the very blood freeze in their veins. But what still more appalled them, this tremendous laugh was followed by a yet more tremendous voice, as if the mountain had spoken. It filled the whole of the double valley of the Aven and the Spey, and it repeated three times successively this whimsical command, "Build in the Cow-haugh!—Build in the Cow-haugh!—

Build in the Cow-haugh !" and again all nature returned
to its former state of stillness and of silence.

"Saint Mary help me !" cried Ian from his position,
high up in the holly bush, where he hung doubled up
over the fork of two boughs, with his head and his heels
hanging down together like an old worsted stocking.
"Saint Mary help me! where am I? and where is
the laird ?"

"Holy St. Peter !" cried the laird, from some few feet
below him, "I rejoice to hear thy voice, Ian. Verily,
I thought that the hurricane which these hellish—no—I
mean these *good people* raised, had swept all mortals but
myself from the face of this earth."

"I praise the Virgin that thou art still to the fore,
Ballindalloch," said Ian. "In what sort of plight art
thou, I pray thee ?"

"In very sorry plight, truly," said the laird, "sorely
bruised and tightly and painfully jammed into the cleft
of the tree, with my nose and my toes more closely
associated together than they have ever been before, since
my first entrance into this weary world. Canst thou
not aid me, Ian ?"

"Would that I could aid thee, Ballindalloch," said Ian
mournfully; "but thou must e'en take the will for the
deed. I am hanging here over a bough, like a piece of
sheep's tripe, without an atom of *fushon** in me, and
confined, moreover, by as many cross-branches as would
cage in a blackbird. I fear there is no hope for us till
daylight."

And in good sooth there they stuck maundering in a
maze of speculation for the rest of the night.

When the morning sun had again restored sufficient
courage to the men of the watch, curiosity led them to
return to ascertain how things stood about the site of
the building which they had so precipitately abandoned.
They were horrorstruck to observe, that in addition to
the utter obliteration of the whole of the previous day's
work, the laird himself, and his henchman Ian Grant,
had disappeared. At first they most naturally supposed
that they had both been swept away at once with the
walls of the new building on which they stood, and that
they could never hope to see them again, more than they

* Strength.

could expect to see the stones of the walls that had been
so miraculously whirled away.   But piteous groans were
heard arising from the bank below them; and on searching
further, Ballindalloch and his man Ian were discovered
and released from their painful bastile.   The poor men-
at-arms who had formed the watch were mightily pleased
to observe that the laird's temper was most surprisingly
cooled by his night's repose in the holly bush.   I need not
tell you that he spoke no more of hanging them.   You
will naturally yemagine, too, that he no longer persevered
in pressing the erection of the ill-starred keep-tower on
the proud spot he had chosen for it, but that he implicitly
followed the dread and mysterious order he had received to
" Build in the Cow-haugh !"

He did, in fact, soon afterwards commence building
the present Castle of Ballindalloch in that beautiful haugh
which stretched between the Aven and the Spey, below
their junction, which then went by the name of the
Cow-haugh; and the building was allowed to proceed to
its conclusion without the smallest interruption.

Such is the legend I promised you, gentlemen, and
however absurd it may be, I look upon it as curious; for
it no doubt covers some real piece of more rational history
regarding the cause of the abandonment of those old
foundations, which has now degenerated into this wild
but poetical fable.

SOMNOSALMONIA.

Clifford (asleep).—Ha! ha! ha! There he comes! What a noble fish! Didn't I tell you I would do for him? Ha! there—there now—I shall land him beautifully at last.

Author.—Why, he's asleep, Grant; give him a good shake, will you.

Clifford (half-awaking).—Oh! oh! oh! what are you at? Will you throw me into the water, you scoundrels? Hah! what are you at? Aw—a—a! what a magnificent salmon I had caught when you snapt my line. Eh!—hah—aw—a—aw. I believe I have been dozing.

Grant.—Nay, not dozing only, but snoring; and, finally fishing in your sleep.

Clifford.—Then am I a fool—aw—a—a—to stay here awake doing nothing, when I might go to bed and there so happily continue the sport which you so cruelly interrupted,—aw—a—aw, so good night to you,—I'm off.

Taking up his candle, Clifford quickly disappeared, and following his example, we broke up for the night; and having agreed to devote the next day to our friend's favourite sport, we invited our new acquaintance, the schoolmaster, to dine with us again.

Next day Grant and I spent five or six hours in thrashing the river without being gratified even with a single rise, whilst Clifford killed no less than three large salmon and one grilse. We expected that he would have crowed mightily over us, and we accordingly exhibited great humbleness of aspect in his presence. But he was magnanimous beyond our hopes.

Clifford.—Don't be downcast, my dear friends, your fate had been mine and mine yours, had we only exchanged our fly-boxes in the morning. Your flies have been made by some Cockney for fishing in the New River. These Limerick hooks are the things; they never fail. You shall try them next time, and I'll warrant your success.

Clifford picked out the best fish for our dinner, and after

a liberal provision of those ingredients which are supposed
to contribute to the sociality of an evening,

Author (to Clifford).—Come along, Mr. Secretary, how
stands your book ?

Clifford.—Mr. Macpherson is down two or three times
over. But, for aught I know, he may have told all his
tales last night while I slept. By the by, I have to
apologise to him for having done so.

Dominie.—Hout no, sir, I am sure I am well pleased if
my tales can in any manner of way contribute to your
happiness, whether it may be by exciting your interest or
mirth, or by lulling you to sweet repose. I am not the
first story-teller whose tales have had a soporific yeffeck.

Clifford.—Can you favour us then ; you will yourself
recollect which of your stories comes first in the list.

Dominie.—'Pon my word, sir, my memory does not serve
me in that respeck. But I have another story altogether,
in which the Laird of Ballindalloch was also concerned ;
and, as it has been brought to my mind, nay, I may say,
into my vurra mouth at this moment, by the pleasing
flavour of Mr. Clifford's excellent fish, on which we have
all dined so heartily, I may as well give you that.

Clifford.—You are a perfect mine of legendary lore, Mr.
Macpherson.

LEGEND OF THE LAST GRANT OF TULLOCHCARRON.

In my legend of yesternight, gentlemen, I think I told you, that one of Ballindalloch's yespecial reasons for selecking the site he did for his peel tower was the commanding view which he thence enjoyed all over the lands of Tullochcarron, lying above the fork of the Aven and the Spey, and which then belonged to another family of Grants, with whom he was liable to be frequently at daggers drawn. It is of the last laird of Tullochcarron, that I am now going to tell you.

In the earlier part of his life, this laird of Tullochcarron lost a younger brother, who was killed while fighting bravely by his side in a feudal skirmish with a former laird of Ballindalloch. Tullochcarron had a strong affection for this brother, and would have been inconsolable for his death, had he not left an only son behind him, called Lachlan Dhu. Tullochcarron was then unmarried, and he therefore instantly transferred all that which had been his fraternal affection to his orphan nephew. Accordingly, he set himself to nurture the boy with all the care and solicitude he could bestow, and with the full intention of making him his heir. But you are well enough aware, gentlemen, that yeddication in those days must have been a mere farce. Indeed, judging from the worthy Dame Julian Berner's Boke of St. Alban's, the which, I take it for granted, was the gentleman's *vade mecum* in its day, it was worse than a farce, nothing being taught there but hawking and hunting, and the mysteries thereof; as, for example, how to physic a sick falcon, and such like follies, with all the foolish vanities of coat armour, and the frivolities of fishing. Eh! I beg your pardon, Mr. Clifford! I see you are not just altogether pleased with that observe of mine. But I meant no offence,—as sure as death I did not. Where was I? Well, as the lad, Lachlan Dhu, grew up, certain indications of ane evil disposition began to manifest themselves, and these unpromising buds did so bourgeon through time, that after trying to prune away the wicked shoots that sprang from them, and finding, as is often the case, that they only sprouted forth the thicker and the stronger for the lopping, like the poisonous heads of the hydra, the good Tullochcarron found himself compelled to abandon his kind intentions towards the young man, so far as regarded the heirship. But he still continued to make his house his home, and likewise to show him all such kindness as an uncle might be expected to use towards a nephew.

Being thus disappointed in his views of a successor, the worthy man set himself to the serious consideration of another plan, and having cast his eyes about him, they fell upon a fair leddy, whom he resolved, with her consent, to make his wife, and accordingly, after a reasonable court-ship, they were married. No couple could have been happier than they were, and his joy was, in due time, rendered complete by the birth of a son and heir, who was called Duncan. But, alas! what is yearthly felicity? Fleeting as the wintry sunbeam on a wall. His beloved wife died soon after the birth of her infant boy, whom she left as the only remaining hope of his family.

Lachlan Dhu had nearly reached manhood before his uncle's marriage, but Tullochcarron had taken especial care, from the very first, never to allow his nephew to know that he ever had any intention of leaving him the succession of his estate. There was therefore no ostensible cause for disappointment or jealousy in Lachlan. But the youth was sharp enough to have seen the position in which he had so long stood, and to have drawn his own conclusions; and certain it was, that jealousy and disappointment did follow his uncle's marriage and the birth of his cousin Duncan. But young though he might be, he was already so profound a master of the art of dissimulation, that he not only most perfectly concealed them, but he actually contrived to produce so great a seeming change for the better in his own character, that he gradually succeeded in vurra much effacing the recollection of his former errors and iniquities from the memory of his kind and forgiving uncle.

Duncan Bane, as the young Tullochcarron was called

from his fair complexion, was, in every respect, a contrast
to Lachlan Dhu, or Black Lachlan. Tullochcarron had
committed his infant boy to be nursed and fostered by a
respectable lady, a distant relation of the family, who,
though low in circumstances, was high in piety and virtue.
To this lady the infant Duncan opportunely came to supply
the place of a child she had just then lost, and as the little
fellow drew his nourishment from her bosom, all the
strength of a mother's attachment fell in tender sorrow
upon him ; and he who never knew any other mother,
repaid it with corresponding affection. Tullochcarron was
too conscious of the failure in his attempt at yeddication,
in the instance of his nephew, to risk a repetition of it in
the still more interesting case of his son. He therefore
gladly left the tutoring of the boy to the care of his excellent nurse, who appears to have been as intellectually
gifted as any woman of those barbarous times could have
been. It is true that she must, in all probability, have
been tinctured with some portion of the learning of Dame
Julian. For, although nothing remains to establish that
the young man had studied hawking and hunting, the
legend certainly informs us, that he had a complete knowledge of, and an ardent love for,—hum—ha—I would say
for that art of which it would ill become me to speak dis-
praisingly, seeing that we have had this evening so much
reason to thank Mr. Clifford for having so ably and
successfully exerceesed it. But—what was much better—
under her godly care the boy's heart was filled with all
the best feelings of religion and humanity. He was
amiable, generous, and kind-hearted, and ever ready on all
occasions to sacrifice his own little interests to those of
others ; and he was so utterly devoid of guile himself, that
he felt it almost impossible to imagine its existence in
others. It was not wonderful, therefore, that he grew up
with the warmest attachment to his cousin, Lachlan Dhu,
who was the very prince of deceivers, and who well knew
how to put on the mask of kindness. He allowed no
opportunity of gaining his young cousin's affections to pass
unprofitably, and so unremitting was his attention to the
young Duncan, that he even succeeded in throwing sand
into the eyes of old Tullochcarron himself, who began to
thank Heaven for the happy change that had taken place
on his nephew, and to trust that he might yet look to

him as the future protector of his son's youth and inexperience, in the very probable event of his being called from
this world before his boy had grown to the years of manhood.

But the old man was still a hale and hearty carle when
his boy's seventeenth birthday came round. He had
indeed been a marvellously stout and healthy man all his
life. The only disease, indeed, with which he had ever
been afflicted was an almost insatiable appetite for food,
which no endeavours of his own could restrain. It was a
never-ending ravenous hunger, for which the poor man
was by no means morally responsible, and from the
gnawing effects of which he must have died, if it had
not been frequently and largely administered to. Nor
did he ask for dainties, although there certainly was one
species of food which he preferred to all others when he
could get it in its season, and that was—salmon. Tullochcarron's complaint, as you may very naturally conceive,
grew with his growth, which was immense, and increased
with every additional year that he lived. But, old as he
was, and enormous as he became in bulk, his great strength
remained unimpaired, and he was still able to move about
with wonderful activity in the superintendence of his
concerns.

I have already told you, that although he and Ballindalloch were not at absolute war, yet there did exist between
them that ancient grudge and jealousy, left by the ill-
salved, though apparently bandaged up wounds of a peace,
patched together when both parties had suffered too much
to continue the war. And although the then existing
Ballindalloch was not the man in whose reign and under
whose attack Tullochcarron's much-loved brother had
fallen, yet those were times in which the son was made
answerable for his father's sins. The then laird of Ballindalloch, therefore, succeeded to all that secret animosity
which his father had so industriously laboured to earn.
Thus, as one might say, the military precaution, as well as
the civil management of Tullochcarron's little kingdom,
required ane active superintendence and administration.
But although he now scrupled not to employ his nephew
in all duties where he thought his services might be useful
to him, and although he had even begun of late to give
occasional occupation to his son, yet, as they used to say

in those days, he was *aye upon the head of his own affairs himself*, watched everything with his own eye, and gave every order of importance from his own mouth.

Lachlan Dhu, then, having but little else in which to employ himself, spent most of his time in the [chase, and the venison which he slew was always sure to procure him a blessing from his hungry uncle. As for Duncan Bane, his whole attention was directed to fishing, and the salmon which he caught were always sure to be more highly prized than the best buck that his cousin ever brought from the forest. In strict attention to the fack, as well as in justice to the character of the youth himself, I must tell you, that the desire of procuring savoury dishes for his father, to whom his devoted attachment was excessive, was one great reason, as well as in some measure an apology,—that is, I mean, a-a to say, Mr. Clifford, if fishing ever required any apology at all, which I must confess your excellent salmon of this day hath led me vurra much to doot; I say it was a good reason for his following out that quieter sort of sport, instead of that of the chase, which some of your wild Nimrods would look upon as by much the more active and manly. But I must likewise inform you, that there was also a secondary cause that contributed to make him prefer this occupation to all others. This cause, you will doubtless consider of inferior strength to the other; but still it is a cause which is in itself supposed by many to be very powerful in some of its effecks; the cause I mean was—love.

Anna Gordon was the eldest of three orphans who were left to the care of their aunt, who was the vurra lady whom I have already introduced to you as the nurse and female preceptor of the youth Duncan Bane. Anna was but a year younger than the young laird of Tullochcarron. They had grown up together, and had loved one another like companions, until their attachment insensibly assumed a warmer character. The penury to which the Gordons and their aunt had been reduced by circumstances, had hitherto induced Duncan to keep the mutual passion that subsisted between him and Anna a secret from his father, who never ceased to talk of some splendid alliance for his son as one of his most favourite schemes. But as this love of the young man for the lady waxed stronger, his fondness for fishing was most strangely and marvellously augmented in a similar proportion. Were I to attempt to guess at the cause of this whimsical combination of two predilections apparently so inconsistent with one another, I should say, that he began daily more and more to take to fishing, because it furnished him with an apology for more frequently visiting his nurse's cottage, that was situated on a beautifully wooded knoll rising on the north bank of the river Aven. It was, moreover, an amusement which he could pursue without losing the society of her he loved. For as he loitered along the river's bank with his angle-rod in his hand, Anna Gordon was ever at his side; and I am doubting much that they wasted many a good hour in idle talk rather than in fishing. But I am no more than the simple historian of their tale, therefore it is no business of mine to defend either him or her from the charge which you will of necessity bring against both of them for such a mis-spending of their precious time. However, I'm thinking, gentlemen, that they must have had some peculiar pleasure in one another's conversation, or they never would have stolen secretly away thus by them two selves, as they were continually wont to do, even escaping from Anna's little sister and brother. The boy, poor little fellow, had been born deaf and dumb, and could have understood no other language but that of the eyes; and let me tell you, gentlemen, that learned as I am in tongues, both ancient and modern, that is one of which I must confess myself to have no knowledge, though they do say that there is much eloquence in it when it is rightly comprehended. It was not always an easy matter to *jink* these two children, for Duncan Bane had been so kind to both of them, especially to the poor dumb boy, that wherever he went, they ran after him like two *penny doggies;* and as he had too much good feeling in his composition to allow him to treat them harshly, he was often obliged to steal their sister Anna away from them when he wished to have a private saunter with her.

The lovers had one day escaped from them and all the world in this manner, for Duncan was anxiously desirous to be alone with Anna, that he might learn from her why it was that her fair brow wore an unwonted cloud upon it, and why her large blue eyes seemed to have been dimmed by recent tears. He was impatient till they reached a grove by the river's side, which was their ordinary place of retreat when they wished to be free from all vulgar or prying eyes.

"Anna," said the youth, the moment they had got within its shade, "something unpleasant has befallen thee; though thy face cannot be robbed of its loveliness, yet it wants to-day that smile which is wont to be the sunshine of my heart."

"I must try to call it up, then," said she, with an effort to be playful that could not be mistaken. "I would not have thy heart chill if I can help it."

"Nay, but I entreat thee to tell me what has vexed thee, my love!" said he tenderly. "If I cannot relieve thy distress, let me at least share it with thee!"

"I would fain tell thee, Duncan," replied she, "for I would fain shut up no secrets from thee in that heart which is so entirely thine; but"——

"But what, my dearest?" cried Duncan impatiently; "do not keep me longer in suspense. There ought, indeed, to be no secrets with either of us that are not shared between us."

"There never shall be any on my part," said Anna, throwing down her eyes. "And yet—and yet I have much difficulty in uttering what I would now tell thee."

"Keep me on the rack no longer, my love, I beseech thee!" said Duncan.

"I *will* take courage to tell thee, then," said she, "but thou must first give me a solemn promise."

"What! of secrecy?" said Duncan. "Methinks thou mayest safely enough trust to me in that respect."

"The promise I would exact of thee goes somewhat beyond that of mere secrecy," said she gravely. "Thou must promise me that thou wilt not *act* upon what I have to tell thee, but in such manner as prudence may permit me to sanction."

"And dost thou think, my Anna," replied Duncan, "that I could ever do, or desire to do, anything that thou couldst wish me not to do?"

"But promise me, solemnly promise me!" said Anna, persevering with unwonted eagerness in her demand; "do promise me, I entreat thee!"

"Well, well, I do promise thee,—thus solemnly promise thee," replied Duncan, kissing the hand which he held. "And now, come! relieve my anxiety, what is this gloomy

16

secret? This is the first time I have seen traces of tears in thine eyes since the death of the poor thrush I gave thee."

"The present matter is somewhat more serious," said Anna, with a gravity and dignity of manner which he had never seen her assume before. "Your cousin, Lachlan Dhu, dared this morning to address me in odious terms, which he called love. I answered him with a scorn and a reproof which I had hardly believed my young, weak, and untaught tongue could have used to one of his manhood. But the Blessed Virgin lent me language; and he stood so abashed before me, that I trust I have reason to hope that he will not again dare to repeat his offence."

"My cousin Lachlan!" exclaimed Duncan, overwhelmed with astonishment. "My cousin Lachlan, didst thou say? Did my ears hear thee aright? Impossible!"

"I grieve to say it is too true," said Anna Gordon.

"O villain, villain!" cried Duncan. "Most deep and consummate villain! Can so much apparent goodness be but the mask of deceit and villainy? But—I must straightway question him! I will drag him from the disguise which he wears, and—and then!"

"Remember that solemn promise which you have this moment made to me," said Anna, calmly taking his hand. "You see how wise it was in me to secure it. To be the innocent cause of awakening feud between kinsmen of blood so near, would indeed be a heavy affliction to me; and were any of that blood to be spilled—were thy blood to flow—but thou must keep thy solemn engagement to me; and thou must now pledge me thy word, that never till I give thee leave to do so wilt thou, even by a look, discover to anyone what I have now told thee."

"Anna," said Duncan, after some little hesitation, "I will promise you what you desire; but my promise is given on the faith of a counter-pledge, which I now expect to have from thee. Promise me, on thy part, that no such cause of offence shall be again offered to thee that thou dost not instantly tell me of it."

"My present frankness should be my best pledge that I will do as thou wouldst have me," said Anna. "But the promise thou hast given me must then be held as consequently renewed."

"I am content," said Duncan. "I am content to trust that you will not tie me down too rigidly."

Guileless as Duncan Bane naturally was, he felt it no easy task to commence and to carry on a train of dissimulation with one with whom he had been on terms of open and unreserved intercourse of mind from his childhood, as I may say, save on the one subject of his love alone. Duncan dreaded that the very next meeting he should have with his cousin would throw him off his guard. He, therefore, proceeded forthwith to school himself as to the face and manner he should wear, and the words he should utter? and so successfully did he do so in his own judg-ment, that, after the first interview with his cousin was over, he congratulated himself that the deep dissatisfaction which he secretly felt had been entirely shrouded from him who had excited it. And certainly, whether it was so or not, the crafty Lachlan Dhu gave him no reason to believe that it was discovered.

It was on the vurra night after this, however, that the Laird of Ballindalloch was seated in the cap-house of the great round tower of the castle he had so lately built, engaged in some confidential talk with his faithful hench-man, Ian Grant, when his favourite old sleuth-hound, that lay beside his chair, raised up his long heavy ears and growled ; and soon afterwards a step was heard ascending the narrow screw stair leading to the small apartment where they were.

" See who is there, Ian," said the laird, in answer to a gentle tap at the door.

Ian obeyed, and on opening it one of the domestics appeared to announce that a stranger, who refused to tell his name, had been brought, at his own request, to the castle guard-room, having expressed a wish to be admitted to a private conference with the laird.

" A stranger demands to have an interview with me after the watch is set, and yet refuses to tell who or what he is !" cried Ballindalloch. " By Saint Peter, but this smells of treachery, methinks ! Yet let him appear, we fear him not; let him appear, I say," repeated he, waving off the attendant. " Ian," continued he after the man was gone, "look that your dirk be on your thigh."

" My dirk is here, sir, and sharp," readily replied the henchman, as he moved towards the door, and planted himself beside it, to be prepared to strike, if any sudden emergency should require him to do so.

Again steps were heard ascending the stair, the door opened, and the doorway was filled by the bulky figure of a man, whose dark features were almost entirely hid by a blue Kelso bonnet of more than ordinary breadth, and the ample web of a large hill plaid, of the red Grant tartan, put on as Highlanders know how to do when they would fain conceal themselves, completely enveloped the whole of his figure, as well as the lower part of his face, leaving little more visible than the tip of his nose and his dark moustachios. For some moments he stood silent before Ballindalloch.

"Speak!" said the laird at length. "Thy name and thine errand at this untimeous hour!"

"Ballindalloch," replied the stranger, looking around him, and glancing at Ian, "thou shalt have both incontinently, but it must be in thine own particular ear alone."

"Leave us then, Ian," said Ballindalloch, waving him away, whilst at the same time he stretched forth his hand to lift his claymore within easier reach of the place where he sat. "Leave us, I say, Ian! I would be private with this stranger."

"Uve! uve!" said Ian under his breath; then he moved, hesitated, shrugged his shoulders, looked at the stranger as if he would have penetrated him, plaid and all, to the very soul; then he shifted his position—yet still he did not quit the chamber, but stood and threw an imploring look of remonstrance towards the laird.

"Begone, Ian!" said Ballindalloch in a voice of impatience; and Ian at last vanished at the word.

"Sir stranger!" said Ballindalloch, "I hope I may now ask thee to rid me of all this mystery."

"I am most ready to do so, Ballindalloch," said the other, laying aside his bonnet and plaid, and showing himself, to all appearance, entirely unarmed.

"Lachlan Dhu Grant of Tullochcarron?" exclaimed the laird with astonishment; "what stirring errand has moved thee hither at such an hour?"   •

"I come to thee but on peaceful private conference," replied Lachlan Dhu, with a respectful obeisance: "and I use this secrecy because it is for the interest of both of us, that what I have to treat of should reach no other ears but our own."

"Proceed," said Ballindalloch, "thou mayest speak safely here, for in this place we are beyond all earshot."

"I need not tell thee, Ballindalloch," continued Lachlan Dhu, "I need not tell thee, I say, that which is sufficiently notour to all, that mine uncle, old Tullochcarron's patrimony, would have been mine as a fair succession, had he not married on purpose to disappoint me."

"I know this much," said Ballindalloch, not altogether dissatisfied to see something like discontent in what he naturally held to be the enemy's camp. "Perhaps thou hast had but scrimp justice in this matter."

"Justice!" exclaimed Lachlan Dhu, catching eagerly at his words. "Justice! I have been deeply wronged. Bred up and cockered by the old man for a time as his successor, as if it had been with the very intent of throwing me the more cruelly off, and rendering the blasting of my hopes the more bitter, from the very fairness of those blossoms which his pretended warmth of affection had fostered!"

"'Twas not well done in the old man," said Ballindalloch; " but now, methinks, 'tis past all cure."

"Nay," said Lachlan Dhu sternly, "I hope there is yet ample room for remede."

"As how, I pr'ythee?" said Ballindalloch.

"Mark me, and thou shalt quickly learn," said Lachlan Dhu. "But first of all I must tell thee, that I now come to offer myself to thee as thy vassal on this simple condition, that thou wilt give me thine aid and countenance against all questioners to help me to keep what shall be mine own after I shall have fairly won it."

"And how dost thou propose to win it?" demanded Ballindalloch, with a grave and serious air that seemed to argue a most attentive consideration of a proposal in itself so inviting to him.

"By secretly ridding myself of mine uncle's sickly stripling boy, whenever favouring fortune may yield me fitting opportunity," replied Lachlan Dhu, approaching his head nearer to Ballindalloch, and sinking his voice to a low sepulchral tone, and with a coolness that might have befitted a practised murderer.

"What!" exclaimed Ballindalloch, with an air of surprise. "What hath the youth done to deserve so much of thy hatred?"

"Twice hath he crossed my path," continued Lachlan

Dhu, his features blackening, and his dark eyeballs rolling as he spoke. "He hath twice crossed my path; first when he came into this world, and now a second time by thwarting me in my love."

"And what have I to do with all this?" demanded Ballindalloch.

"Much," replied Lachlan Dhu earnestly. "I am now thy sworn vassal. The feudal superiority of Tullochcarron will henceforth insure to thee friendship and strength, where thou hast long had to deal with open or secret foes, and "——

"Thou speakest as if thou wert already Laird of Tullochcarron," said Ballindalloch, interrupting him.

"That young *foulmart* once disposed of, I soon shall be," said Lachlan Dhu, with fiend-like expression. "Mine uncle's time cannot now be long, even were nature left to take its course; or,—it may be shortened. Sudden death to a man of his gross form and *purfled* habit could never seem strange; and then "——

"True," said Ballindalloch calmly; "but how can I aid thee in thy scheme?"

"I lack no present aid while I have this arm," replied Lachlan Dhu; "it is the support and defence of thy faithful vassal, Lachlan Dhu Grant, Laird of Tullochcarron, that I require of thee, if unhappily some unlucky circumstance should awaken idle suspicions against him."

"I trust I shall always know how to defend my vassals," said Ballindalloch proudly.

"Then am I safe," said Lachlan Dhu; "but in the meanwhile secrecy is essential to our purpose."

"I hope I have prudence enough to know how to conduct myself in all cases of delicacy," replied Ballindalloch.

"'Tis well," said Lachlan Dhu, again folding his plaid around him, and putting on his bonnet. "Now I must begone; for time presses. Farewell! I shall trust to thee, and thou mayest trust to me."

"I shall not forget what is due to thee, when thou art my vassal," said the laird, "nor shall I ever forget what ought at all times to be expected from Ballindalloch. Here, Ian Dhu, see this stranger safe beyond the walls and outposts."

The night I speak of seemed to be quite pregnant with

strange visitations; for, at a still later hour, after old
Tullochcarron had himself seen that the guard at the
barbican of his small place of strength was on the alert,
and had secured the iron doors of the entrance of the peel-
tower, and had finally retired to his apartment to go to
rest, he was surprised to see a packet lying on his table,
of which no one of his attendants could give him any
account. It was tied with a morsel of ribbon, the ends
of which were secured with wax, but without any impression. It was simply addressed :—
"To Tullochcarron."
And on cutting it open, he found that it contained the
following letter, with a broad seal at the end of it.
"Tullochcarron,—I write this private communication,
to tell thee that thou hast a traitor in thy house, that thou
dost nourish a viper in thy bosom that would sting thee.
The life of thine only son is certain to be taken, if thou
dost not secure it by the instant seizure of thy nephew,
Lachlan Dhu. Thine own murder will speedily follow.
The cold-blooded villain came to me secretly under the
cloud of this night, and did unfold his devilish plans,
offering to me the feudal superiority of thy lands of
Tullochcarron, provided I should protect him as my vassal
against all after question. I seemed to listen, and yet I
evited direct promise; and I now hasten to certiorate thee
of these facts through ane trusty messenger, who engages,
by certain means best known to himself, to have these
placed upon thine own private table before thou sleepest.
This traitorie is as yet alone known to thee, to me, to the
foul faitour who planned, and to the devil who prompted
it. And that thou mayest have no doubt left in thee of
the truth of what I have here written, I do hereto affix my
sign-manual, as well as the seal, the which is attached
to the last instrument of pacification that passed between
our houses.—Ballindalloch."
You may conceive, gentlemen, that this letter, read alone,
at midnight in his chamber, dreadfully alarmed old
Tullochcarron. He started from the large oaken chair in
which he had seated himself to peruse it, and snatching his
lamp, he rushed to his son's apartment, where he held up
the light, and gazed with fear and trembling on his son's
couch, almost expecting to see his boy foully murdered,
and weltering in his blood. Stretched on his bed, he did

indeed find him; but his eyes were closed in the sweet slumbers that attend the pillow of pure and spotless youth. He gazed on him in silent anxiety for some time, till he was really certain that he breathed; and then the old man's lip quivered, and his eyes were dimmed by the big drops that rapidly distilled over his eyelids. Stooping gently down, he kissed Duncan's cheek, and then quitting the room upon tiptoe, he called up an old and tried domestic.

"Hamish," said he, "I had a strange and troubled dream, as I dozed in mine arm-chair."

"Thou didst sup somewhat of the heaviest, Tullochcarron," replied Hamish. "After so many pounds' weight of salmon, 'tis but little wonder if the foul hag on her nightmare should have been riding over and over thee."

"Psha!" said Tullochcarron in a vexed tone and manner that showed he was too seriously affected to be trifled with. "My dream touched the safety of thy young master. Hark ye! I bid thee watch his couch, and let no one approach it with impunity."

"My young master!" said Hamish with energy. "These grey hairs shall be trodden under foot ere the latch of his door shall be touched."

"I know thy fidelity," said Tullochcarron. "Be sure thou givest me the alarm if aught extraordinary should occur."

Having taken this hasty precaution, the old Laird of Tullochcarron again seated himself in his arm-chair to read over for the second time the alarming communication he had received. Ballindalloch's name and seal were the first things his eyes rested on after opening it. Doubts and suspicions instantly flashed across his mind.

"What a silly fool am I after all," said he, "to let any information from such a quarter so agitate me! What truth is to be expected from a house so full of hereditary enmity against mine of Tullochcarron! And is not Lachlan Dhu the son of that very brother of mine who worked so much sore evil to the house of Ballindalloch? And is he not at this moment the best, the stoutest, and the sharpest arrow I have in my quiver? And are not these reasons enough to prompt such a secret enemy to urge me to whet my knife against him? Dull old idiot that I was! but now I see it all! I see it all! What a trap was I about to run my head into! But stay, let me think what is best to be done. Prudent precautions with regard to my son can do no harm. I shall put him well on his guard; and that secured, the best thing I can do is to bury the contents of this paper in mine own bosom."

With such determinations as these, Tullochcarron retired to rest; but his repose was disturbed and put to flight by visions which were not altogether to be laid to the account of the heavy meal he had taken ere he retired to rest. He was early visited by his son Duncan.

"Father," said the young man, "how was it that old Hamish took post in my chamber last night? I found him sitting by my bedside at daybreak this morning, and all the explanation I could extract from him was that he had the laird's orders for being there."

"He had my orders my dear boy," said Tullochcarron, pressing his son to his bosom, and kissing his forehead. "A strange dream had come over me, that alarmed my foolish old heart about thy safety."

"A dream about me!" said the young man smiling. "What harm couldst thou dread for me, father?"

"I dreamed that thy life was threatened, boy," said his father; "and therefore it was that I made Hamish watch thee."

"My life in danger, father!" exclaimed Duncan, "and from whose hand?"

"From the hand of thy cousin Lachlan Dhu," replied his father. "Hast thou any cause to dread that my dream might have aught of reality in it?"

"My cousin Lachlan Dhu!" exclaimed Duncan, with unfeigned surprise. "Nay," continued he, after some little hesitation, during which he remembered the promise he had given to Anna Gordon; "why should I think that Lachlan should wish to injure me?"

"Why *should* we think it, indeed?" exclaimed the old man, with considerable emotion. "Both I and mine should look for anything but hostility from Lachlan Dhu, if there be any faith or gratitude left in man. Let us then think no more about it."

"Trust me, I shall think no more of it," said Duncan.

"Aye!" said the old man again; "but yet I'd have thee to be cautious. I would entreat thee to guard thyself as if there were danger. Thou hast a dirk and a hand to use it, boy! Thou hast a claymore and an arm that can wield it; and though thou art as yet but a stripling, still thou art the son of old Tullochcarron! But let faithful Hamish be thy constant henchman, and then my heart will be at ease."

"I will defend mine own head as a true Tullochcarron should do, if dirk or steel can do it," said the youth energetically, and by no means relishing the idea of his motions being watched, and his person eternally haunted by an attendant. "But I have nothing to fear, and Hamish might be better employed than in following me in all my idle wanderings."

Duncan thought with himself that he had perhaps better grounds for entertaining some suspicion of evil intentions against him on the part of his kinsman, than any which a dream could have afforded to his father; and yet we must not wonder, gentlemen, that, in such superstitious times, old Tullochcarron's alleged vision had also its own effect upon the young man, when taken in combination with that strange new light that had recently opened on his cousin's character. The gallant youth was above all fear, however; but he had prudence enough to resolve to expose himself to no unnecessary danger. As to old Hamish, Duncan thought it better to gratify his father by allowing that faithful servant to be his companion at all times, save and except only when he went to meet her, of his attachment to whom he still thought it wise to keep Tullochcarron ignorant. Then, indeed, the god of love inspired him with so much ingenuity in escaping from his attendant, that he baffled every attempt at discovery.

It was upon one of these occasions, when he had an especial wish to have an hour or two of private talk with Anna Gordon, that he, in the first place, contrived to escape from old Hamish, and afterwards to steal her from her dumb brother and little sister. Away tripped the pair together laughing, and rejoicing in their own cleverness. Duncan had his angle-rod in his hand, but he wandered with Anna through the groves, by the margin of the Aven, without ever thinking of casting a line into its waters. The subject of their conversation was one of peculiar interest to both of them, for Duncan had sought this interview for the purpose of informing her that, from certain circumstances which had recently occurred, he was led to believe that their secret attachment might now be

safely divulged to the old laird his father, in the hope that
he might be brought to consent to the speedy solemnisation
of their marriage. The time they spent together was by
no means short, though to them it appeared as trifling.
At length they found out that it *was* time to part, and a
more than usually lingering parting took place between
them on the top of that *vurra* high and precipitous crag,
where now rests the northern extremity of the noble bridge
that spans the river Aven above Ballindalloch. When
they did at last sever from each other, Anna took her way
homeward by a footpath leading up the river through the
thick oak copsewood that covered the ground behind it,
and clustered to the very brink of the precipice where she
left Duncan.

The young man stood entranced with his own happy
thoughts for a moment after Anna had disappeared, and
then bethinking him that he must hasten to make the best
use of the time that now remained, if he would not return
empty-handed to his father, he stood on the verge of the
cliff, eyeing the stream below, and thoroughly occupied in
preparing his tackle with all manner of expedition, previous
to descending by a circuitous way to the water's edge to
commence his sport. He was alone, as you may think,
gentlemen; but there was an evil eye that watched him
with the tiger's lurid and unvarying gaze, aye, with such
a gaze as the tiger's fiery orbs assume when he has slowly
and silently tracked his unconscious prey through all the
mazes of the jungle, till he at last beholds it within his
reach. As the head of the traitor Lachlan Dhu appeared
from the thicket within three paces of the spot where
young Tullochcarron stood, a fiendish smile of eager
triumph gave a hellish expression to its features. It was
but one desperate spring. One piercing shriek was uttered
by the unhappy Duncan Bane, and in one instant his lifeless corse was floating, shattered and bleeding, on the
crystal stream of the Aven.

That scream was heard by Anna Gordon, and from the
moment it entered into her ears, it never left her mind.
As it reached her, she happened to be passing round a turn
of the river some little way above, whence the fatal crag
was still visible.

"Merciful saints!" she cried, as she turned quickly
round, "that was my Duncan's voice!"

She caught one instantaneous glimpse of the figure of Lachlan Dhu, as he fled from the summit of the crag. A dreadful suspicion shot across her mind. Winged by her agonising terrors, she flew back to the spot where she had parted with Duncan. There she met the poor dumb boy, her brother, pulling his little sister along by the arm. No sooner did he behold Anna, than with a wild animation of countenance, and with gesture so expressive, that no one but a creature deprived of the power of language could have employed, he imitated the action of one person pushing another over the face of the cliff, and then he ran down the path that followed the course of the stream. Anna rushed franticly after him; and when she had reached the margin of the Aven, her eyes rested on the lifeless corse of her beloved, which had been carried by the eddying current into a little quiet nook, where it lay half-stranded on a grassy bank.

It happened that old Hamish, who as usual had been anxiously seeking his young master, came a few moments afterwards accidentally to the same spot; and what a spectacle did he behold! Seated on the bank by the water's edge was the wretched Anna Gordon, with her lover's mangled and bleeding head upon her knee. Her eyes were fixed upon its livid and gory features, as if they had been gazing on vacancy. Not a tear flowed, not a groan nor a sigh was uttered. A monumental group could not have been more motionless or silent. Hamish was distracted. He tried to make her speak; for altogether ignorant of the powerful cause of interest which operated upon her, he viewed her but as an idle spectator, an indifferent person, from whom he anxiously desired to extract something that might enable him to guess as to how this dreadful calamity had occurred. His questions were rapid, urgent, and incessant; but still she minded him not, until he bent forward as if to attempt to lift the body from her knee. Then it was, that turning round with all the frenzied dignity of fixed insanity, she fastened the severe gaze of her unsettled eyes upon him, and spoke in a tone that froze his very heart.

"Begone, old man!" said she, "begone. What! wouldst thou rob me of my love on our bridal day? He is mine! he is mine! But hush," said she, suddenly lowering her voice and changing her expression, "hush! he sleeps!

He slumbers sweetly now. But he will awake anon with smiles, and then our bridal revels will begin. Go, go, old man! go, bid the guests! Bid all!—bid all, I tell thee!—bid all, but—but—the murderer!" A shrill shriek, graduating into a violent hysterical laugh, followed these wild wandering words; and a convulsion shook her delicate frame till she fainted away, as if life itself had fled from her.

I must leave this heart-rending scene, gentlemen, to tell you what soon afterwards took place in the old peel-tower of Tullochcarron.

"What!" exclaimed the laird, as he was in the act of sitting down to one of those many meals which the craving of his naturally enormous appetite rendered so essentially necessary for him. "What!" said he, "still no salmon? Hath Duncan not yet returned, then? Why, methinks the boy must have tyned his luck altogether. But I trow that the fish have lost the way into our waters, they are so rare to be seen. Ha! who comes there with haste so impatient? Is it thou, Lachlan Dhu?"

"Alas, uncle!" cried the murderer, rushing in without his bonnet, and with a frantic air, "alas, uncle! alas! alas! Duncan! Duncan!"

"What—what of Duncan?" exclaimed the anxious and alarmed father, starting from the table.

"Duncan," cried the traitor, "my poor cousin Duncan is no more?"

"What! Duncan? Villain! accursed villain! you lie," cried the old man half-distracted, and grappling his nephew by the throat with his powerful gripe. "You lie, most accursed villain!"

"Alas! alas! I wish I did!" said Lachlan Dhu, with feigned sorrow. "But I grieve to say that what I tell is, alas, too true. I was walking accidentally by the banks of the Aven, about a bowshot above the high craig, when, on looking towards it, I beheld him standing carelessly on the very brink of the cliff; and whether it was that his foot had tripped upon some of those roots that scramble for a sustenance over the surface of the rock, or whether some sudden gust of wind had caught him, I know not; but I saw him fall headlong thence; and after being dashed horribly against the projecting points below, I could perceive his inanimate body borne off by the stream.

Wild with despair, and scarcely knowing what I was doing, I ran directly home hither to tell thee the doleful news; and"——

"Villain!" shouted the old man in a voice like thunder. "Villain! thou art his murderer. Seize him, and drag him hence to the dungeon. He hath reft me of my boy! my only hope on earth! the solace of my old age! O fool! fool! Why did I not take the well-meant warning? Oh! I am now indeed bereft! But his murderer must die ere the sun goes down. Where is Hamish? He at least should have been at my poor Duncan's side!"

At that moment Hamish himself entered. He whose hypocritical acting I have just described, had taken so long to prepare it for exhibition that this old and faithful attendant had had full time to procure help to carry his young master's remains, and had now come on before the body, with the well-meant intention of breaking the afflicting intelligence as easily as he could to the bereaved father. He had been relieved of the task, as I have already told you; and the sad news had spread so, that all the vassals and dependants within reach had crowded to meet the body of their beloved Duncan Bane. The woeful wail of the pipes was heard at a distance. The old laird became dreadfully agitated. The sound drew nearer. Tullochcarron bit his nether lip, clenched his hands, and wound himself up to go through with the trying scene as he felt that Tullochcarron should do. He put on his bonnet with energy, wrapped his plaid tight around him, and descended with a resolute step into the court-yard. The clang of the pipes became louder; and yet a louder crash of their rude music burst forth, as they passed inwards from beneath the arched gateway. The old man strode two or three steps forcibly forwards, with his eyes fixed upon the spot where the rush of human figures came squeezing in. At length his sight fell on the bloody corse of his murdered son, his only earthly hope; and he became rooted to the ground he stood on.

And now a light airy figure appeared tripping fantastically beside the bier with her hair fancifully wreathed up with worthless weeds. She came dancing towards the old laird with gay smiles upon her face, and threw herself upon her knee before him.

"Thy blessing, father! thy blessing!" said she, "we

come to crave thy blessing, father! and now," continued
she, starting up, "let the feast be prepared!—and the
dance!—for Duncan, thine own dear Duncan, has made
me his bride, and I am the happiest maiden in all Scotland! See, see! look here, how gaily my head is garlanded!
Indeed, indeed, as all the neighbours were wont to say,
we were made for each other. And now I am Duncan's
bride! Aye, gentlefolks!" added she, curtseying gracefully
around, and then hiding her blushing face in her hands
for a moment, "and I shall soon be my Duncan's lady!
So, as the fair maid sings in the old ballad,—

> 'Oh! I shall henceforth be, my love,
>   As happy as a queen,
> For such a youth as thee, my love,
>   Was never, never seen—never! no, never!'

Father! father! thou art my father now as well as
Duncan's—hath not Duncan told thee all, father? Methinks
it was but to-day that we agreed to break the secret of
our love to thee; and Duncan, thine own Duncan Bane,
was to tell thee all! and thou wert to give us thy blessing;
and we were to be wedded—aye, wedded as man and wife,
never again to sunder—but my brain so burns with joy,
and my foolish heart beats so, that—but no matter—ha!—
I forget—I must go bid the guests!—I must away—I must
go bid the bridal guests, they will take it all the kinder that
I bid them myself. Hush, then!" added she, sinking her
voice, and approaching the bier upon tiptoe, and gently
stooping to kiss the cold lips of the corse. "Hush, then,
Duncan, my love, rest thee in sweet slumber till I return.
All good be with ye, good gentlefolks. Mark me, I bid
ye all to our bridal; but I have other guests to bid—I
must away!—I have many guests to bid—away, away!"
and so she hurried forth from the gateway, singing as
she went,—

> "And when that we shall wedded be,
>   All by the holy priest,
> Full many a knight and lady bright
>   Shall grace our bridal feast."

The true interpretation of the cause of Anna's frenzy
came palpably to the mind of the old laird of Tullochcarron. Whatever he might have thought of the attach-

ment of the lovers under other circumstances, he now
felt that the discovery of it had only come like a gleam
of sunshine to enhance the brightness of those earthly
prospects which were henceforth darkened for ever.   Yet
still with iron nerve he strung himself firmly up to bear
it all.   He gave one piteous glance of despair towards
the bier where lay the dead body of his son, his only child,
and then he suffered himself to be led passively up into
the hall of the peel-tower, whither the corpse was immediately carried and laid out.   Then it was that human
courage could no longer support him,—it yielded, and
he gave way to all a father's grief.   For a time he indulged
fully in this ; and then, drying up his tears, he summoned
his vassals, ordered in the prisoner Lachlan Dhu, and
instantly proceeded to hold a court upon him.

The murderer would have fain denied his guilt, but
little evidence was necessary to convict in those days.
In this case there was enough to convince all present.
An assize was set upon him—Ballindalloch's letter was
produced and read : at once his bold and resolute air of
innocence was shaken.   The prisoner's own statement
as to the point where he stood when he had witnessed
the alleged accident, was proved to be false by old Hamish,
who chanced to see him whilst running along a path
which led, not from that point, but directly from the
brow of the cliff whence Duncan Bane had met his death.
The dumb boy described and pointed out, with most
intelligent action, how and by whom the murder was
perpetrated; and his little sister distinctly told, that she
and her brother had seen Lachlan Dhu push Duncan Bane
over the crag.   Finally, the sheet was removed from the
body of Duncan, and then, they say, the wounds began
to well forth afresh; and the agitation of the murderer
was so great, that he called for a priest, confessed all, was
shortly shriven ; and as the sun of that day which had
witnessed his crime was preparing to disappear behind
the western mountains, its slanting rays were throwing
a horrible splendour over his powerful but now exanimate
frame, as it swung to and fro in the evening breeze from
the fatal tree on the gallow hill.

The afflicted Anna Gordon wandered wildly about with
maniac energy during all that day, no one knew where.
At last, her friends, who went in search of her, found her

on the mountain, and led her gently homewards. It happened that the path they took passed by the gallow hill. At some distance off she descried the figure of him who had so recently paid the penalty of his crime.

"Yonder is a guest! I will bid yonder guest!" cried poor Anna, with a frantic laugh, as she broke from her friends, and hurried towards the spot where it hung, ere anyone could arrest her. She stood for some moments with her eyes steadily fixed upon the ghastly visage, and then bursting out in a sudden fit of frenzy, "I heard my Duncan's cry!" she shrieked aloud, in a voice that pierced the ears and the hearts of all who heard her. "'Twas his last joyous cry to call me to our bridal! quick! quick! —let us away!—hark!—hark!—again!—again!—again!"

She rushed rapidly forwards a few steps, as if she had been flying to meet her lover. She tottered, and fell in a swoon, was borne home by her friends in a state of stupor, and placed in bed. But it would seem that some internal and vital failure had taken place, for the poor thing ceased to breathe; and the gentle spirit of Anna Gordon fled to unite itself with that of him she loved. Nor were their earthly remains sundered, for the father of Duncan Bane saw them consigned together to the same grave, and he wept over them both.

The old laird of Tullochcarron was but little seen beyond the court-yard of his peel-tower for many weeks after his son's murder; then, indeed, he did come abroad, as if to superintend his affairs as he was wont to do, but it was more because he thought that it was right for him so to do, than from any relish he had in the employment. It was this conviction of what was expected of him, that likewise made him force a false smile of cheerfulness over his good-humoured countenance, which, alas! was with him but as the sunshine that gilded the sepulchre of inextinguishable mourning within. One of the first visits that he paid was to the castle of his ancient feudal enemy, Ballindalloch. He was kindly received, for his severe recent affliction was sincerely pitied by his generous neighbour.

"Ballindalloch," said he, "I am come to thank thee for the friendly caution which thou gavest to a foolish old man, who, if he had taken it as it was meant, would have had his roof-tree still fresh and firm. But let that pass," continued he, with a sigh, and with the full tear rising

17

over his eyelid. "The obligation I owe to thee is not the less, that I, blinded man, refused to give more heed to thy caution."

"Talk not of this, sir," said Ballindalloch. "I must e'en confess to thee, Tullochcarron, that the advice came from so questionable a quarter, that had I been in thy case I might have spurned it myself. But say, sir, wilt thou not eat and drink with me?"

"Willingly," replied Tullochcarron.

"Wilt thou name aught that might, perchance, be most pleasing to thy taste?" said Ballindalloch.

"I know I need not ask for salmon," said Tullochcarron, "for such food is hardly now to be had."

"Though the fish have been somewhat rare with us of late," said Ballindalloch, "I think I can promise thee that thou shalt have as much of thy favourite dish as shall satisfy thee."

"Alas!" said Tullochcarron with a faltering voice, and with a tear rolling down his cheek, "salmon have, indeed, been rare with me since—since—but," added he, making a strong effort to overcome the feelings excited by the recollection of his son, and perhaps with the hope of hiding his agitation under a good-humoured jest, "I hear that the salmon are so bewitched, that they hardly ever come farther inland now than the Bog of Gight. In so great a scarcity, then, I much doubt whether the stock of fresh fish within the Castle of Ballindalloch will stand against my well-known voracity."

"Be assured that there is as much in the house, of mine own catching, too, as will extinguish thine appetite, and leave something to spare," said Ballindalloch.

"Thou knowest not what a cormorant I am," said Tullochcarron.

"I have heard much of thy powers," said Ballindalloch.

"And I am as sharp set at this moment as ever I was in my life," said Tullochcarron.

"All that may be; yet I fear thee not," said Ballindalloch laughing.

"Art thou bold enough to lay a wager on the issue?" demanded Tullochcarron.

"I am so bold," said Ballindalloch.

"Well, then," said Tullochcarron, "I will wager thee the

succession and heirship of my lands against thy grey
gelding, that I shall not leave thee a morsel to spare."

"Thou dost give me brave odds, indeed," said Ballindalloch; "thou hadst best bethink thee again ere we
strike thumbs on it."

"Nay, I require no more thought," said Tullochcarron;
"and, moreover, I grow hungrier every moment. Besides,"
said the old man with a sigh, that showed that all this
jocularity was only assumed to cover a broken heart; "I
am putting in peril that in which I can have no interest,
whilst, if I win thy gallant grey, I shall be sure of being
well mounted for the rest of my life. Art thou afraid of
losing thy steed? or wilt thou say done to the wager?"

"I do say done, then, since thou wilt have it so," said
Ballindalloch, and he accordingly gave the necessary orders
for having the matter put to the proof.

After a little time, a serving man entered with a covered
trencher, in which lay, smoking hot, one half of a small
salmon. When Tullochcarron lifted the cover, he eyed
it with something like contempt, and impelled as he was
by his irresistible disease, he fell upon it, and devoured it
with an alacrity that astonished every beholder. A whole
salmon, but of moderate size, was then brought in, and
was instantly attacked by Tullochcarron with as much
avidity as if he had not eaten a morsel. Wonderfully and
fearfully did he go on to clear his way through it; but as
he approached the conclusion of it, his jaws began to go
rather more languidly than before. Ballindalloch observed
this.

"Ho there! bring more salmon!" cried he aloud.

"No," said Tullochcarron, shoving the trencher from
him, and wiping his knife and fork in his napkin, and
sticking them into his dirk sheath. "No, no; I have
enough. Ballindalloch, my lands shall be yours the moment the breath is out of my body."

"Nay, then," said Ballindalloch, "I must in truth and
honesty confess that I called for more salmon but as
a bravado; for thou hast indeed finished all the salmon
that was in the house, and it is my grey gelding that is
thine, not thy lands that are mine."

"It matters not, Ballindalloch," replied the other.
"The lands of Tullochcarron are thine notwithstanding.
See, there are the writings which I had made out the week

after my poor Duncan was so foully murdered. Thou wilt find that thy name was then inserted therein. I but seized on this of the wager as a whimsical means of breaking the matter to thee; and now thou mayest make of Tullochcarron what it may please thee. I shall not stand long in the way, poor decayed sproutless stock as I am! and I have now known enough of thee to be convinced that thou wilt not see me kicked over before my time; but that thou wilt take care of me during the brief space that I may yet cumber this earth, and see me laid decently beside Duncan when I die."

Such then, gentlemen, was the way in which the lands of Tullochcarron came to be united to those of Ballindalloch,—ane union, the which I am told, did vurra much impruv the value of both, and which still subsists to the present day.

ANTIQUARIAN DISCUSSION.

Clifford.—Why, this is the best story I have heard for many a day, for it has both salmon and salmon fishing in it.

Author.—The secret is out now about the fairies and the peel-tower, and, for my own part, I shall never in future doubt the *prévoyance* and judgment of these good people. Aware, as they must have been, that fate had decreed the lands of Tullochcarron to be merged in those of Ballindalloch, and seeing that this coming event would render the commanding site of Ballindalloch's proposed peel-tower utterly valueless, as he would no longer have any enemy's territory to overlook, their regard for his interest induced them to drive him out of his fancy, and to compel him to descend into the delightful repose and shelter of the beautiful haugh below.

Dominie.—'Pon my word, sir, there is much reason in that observe of yours. That is, always premeesing that the story I told had been a tale of reasonable and probable fack.

Author.—But as you yourself remarked at the conclusion of it, Mr. Macpherson, the wild faery tale connected with the ancient foundations of the peel-tower may have some matter of truth wrapped up in it; and why may we not suppose then, that Ballindalloch, having commenced some small exploratory building there, had afterwards discontinued it when the prospect of his succession to the lands of Tullochcarron opened to him.

Dominie.—Troth, I'm thinking you have guessed it sir,—that *wull* just be it.

Grant.—The conjecture is at least as good as those of most antiquaries.

Clifford.—It would certainly seem to have some *foundation* in the old site.

Author.—If that was meant as a pun, Mr. Secretary, I think you should be immediately condemned to tell us a long story, in expiation of so grave an offence.

Clifford.—The first time, certainly, that I ever heard a pun called a *grave* offence; but, to *bury* all further controversy, I will tell you a legend which I learned when I was on a visit to some of my relations in Ross-shire; and since you think that my offence is so very heavy, I shall impose on myself a long penance, of which I pray the gods that you, my good auditors, may not suffer any share.

LEGEND OF CHIRSTY ROSS.

ABOUT the middle of last century, there resided in the burgh of Tain, on the eastern coast of Ross-shire, a poor shopkeeper of the name of Ross. The contents of that strange and multifarious emporium, which he called his shop, might have been well advertised by a handbill, like that which I once met with in Ireland, where, in the long list of miscellaneous articles enumerated, I remember to have seen "tar, butter, hog's-lard, brimstone, and other sweetmeats—brushes, scythe-stones, mouse-traps, and other musical instruments." You may easily imagine, that the profits arising from the sale of such trumpery wares as these, were barely sufficient to provide the necessaries of life for his numerous family, and to bestow on his children the common education which Scotland, very much to her credit, so readily and cheaply affords. Although Mr. Ross's enjoyments were not numerous, yet, by endeavouring to have as few wants as possible, he managed to live contentedly and happily enough, and he cheerfully struggled on drudging at his daily occupation, thanking God for the mercies which were bestowed on him, and looking forward with hope to the prospect of better days yet in store.

A circumstance occurred one afternoon, which led him to imagine that this prospect was nearer realisation than he could have believed it to be. A stranger, of a spare form and extremely atrabilious complexion, was seen to ride into the town at a gentle pace, and to go directly up to the principal house of entertainment for travellers, as if the way to it had been familiar to him. He had not been long housed there, when a waiter came across the street to Mr. Ross, with compliments *"from the gentleman at the inn,"* who requested a few minutes' conversation with him. The eager shopkeeper, anticipating some important sale of ls, waited not to doff his apron and sleeves, but d over the way directly, and, what was his astonishment and delight, when, after a few words of inquiry and explanation had passed between them, he found himself weeping tears of joy in the arms of an affectionate elder brother.

This man had left his father's house when very young, with little else but hope for his portion, and after being so lost sight of by his relations, that they had long believed him to be dead, he now most unexpectedly returned to them from India with an ample fortune. Wonderful were the visions of wealth which now arose in the mind of the poor shopkeeper, and, on his warm invitation, his brother, and his brother's saddle-bags, were quickly transferred from the inn to his small and inconvenient house, and the Indian was speedily subjected to the danger of being smothered in the embraces of his sister-in-law and her numerous progeny.

Narrow as was his apartment, and small as was his bed, the nabob felt himself in elysium in his brother's house. He had never before experienced the genial effects of the warmth of kindred blood. He was idolised by every one of the family, and imminent was the risk he ran of being killed with kindness. Nor was he the great object of attention to his immediate relations alone. He soon became the oracle of a large circle of kind friends and neighbours, who were seen crowding Mr. Ross's small back parlour, which many of them had never before condescended to enter. And not only was the Indian feasted by small and great, but his humble brother and his sister-in-law were also invited to parties by people who had hardly before been aware of the fact that such an individual as Mr. Ross, the grocer and hardwareman, existed in the place. But now Mr. Ross was not only discovered, as it were, but he was discovered to be a very sensible man, having much of his brother, the nabob's sound intellect, though wanting the advantages of cultivation. As to the nabob, he was a *rara avis in terris*,—an absolute phœnix, a creature a specimen of which is not to be met with in every age of the world. What the nabob uttered was considered as law; and even when he was absent, "the nabob said this," and "the nabob said that," and "that's the way the nabob likes it," were expressions continually employed by the good people of the town and neighbourhood to put an end to a debate; and they never

failed to be quite conclusive upon every question. All
this had a certain charm for the old Indian. It was
extremely pleasant thus despotically to rule over men's
opinions, aye, and over women's too, even in such a place
as Tain. But the copper of the gilded crown and sceptre
of his dominion soon began to appear through its thin
coating. His own origin had indeed been humble, but as
his wealth had grown by degrees, so had he been gradually
elevated above his original sphere, till he had at last risen
into familiar intercourse with people of rank and consequence, from whose society his address, and still more, his
ideas had received a certain degree of polish. This did not
prevent him from greatly enjoying the plain, honest, warm,
but very vulgar manners of his brother and his townsmen,
whilst they were as yet new to him. They pleased him at
first, precisely on the same principle of novelty, combined
with old association, which made him relish for a certain
time sheep's-head broth and haggis. But having unfortunately expressed himself rather strongly in his admiration
of these dishes, the good folks thought themselves bound
to give them to him upon all occasions, so that they soon
began to lose their charm; and just so it was that the
uninterrupted converse with the good, yet homely people
around him, to which he was daily subjected, very soon
became dull, tiresome, ennuyant, and, finally, disgusting,
until it eventually grew to be so very intolerable that he
altogether abandoned the thought he had entertained of
purchasing an estate in that neighbourhood which was
then for sale, and he quickly came to the determination of
bringing this visit to his native town to a speedy conclusion,
and of returning to London to take up his abode there
among people who like himself had known what it was to
live on curries and mulligatawny, and who could talk with
him of tiffins and tiger hunting.

How shall I describe that wet blanket of disappointment
that fell upon the shoulders of Mr. Ross, the grocer and
hardwareman, and his family, when the nabob communicated to them this change in his plans. All the poor
shopkeeper's splendid visions departed from him with the
same suddenness with which the figures from a magic
lantern disappear from a wall the moment its light is extinguished. He had already set it down in his own mind as
a thing absolutely certain, that his beloved brother would

live and die in his house; and he and his wife had been
calculating, that as every child they had would be as a
child to its bachelor uncle, every child of them would be
better provided for than another. Ten thousand cobwebby
castles had been erected in the air by this worthy couple,
who had already made lairds of all the boys, and lairds'
ladies at least of all the girls. "Out of sight out of mind"
was a proverb that came with chilling truth to their hearts;
and although the nabob had already shown much affection
to them, and had behaved generously enough in giving
liberal aid towards the improvement of his brother's
condition and that of his family, yet they could not help
considering his threatened separation from them as the
removal of the sunshine of fortune from the hemisphere of
their fate. Never was the anticipated departure of any
one more deeply or sincerely deplored. The nabob himself
had no such feelings. He looked forward to his escape
from his relatives and friends as to a period of happy relief.
Yet to this there was one exception.

Chirsty Ross, as his niece Christina was provincially
called, was then a very beautiful and extremely engaging
little girl of some five or six years of age.· From the first
day that the old Indian took up his residence in her
father's house, she had innocently and unconsciously commenced her approaches against the citadel of his heart.
Each succeeding hour saw her gain outpost after outpost,
and defence after defence, until she fairly entwined herself
so firmly around his affections, that he could not contemplate the approaching loss of her smiles, of her kisses, and
of her prattle, with anything like philosophy. He had
been naturally enough led to shower a double portion of his
favours upon her. She was already in the habit of calling
him "her own uncle," as if he had belonged exclusively
and entirely to herself, and to this she had been a good
deal encouraged by the nabob. It is not wonderful,
therefore, that when his departure was communicated to
her, she was thrown into an inconsolable paroxysm of grief,
and clung to his knees, giving loud vent to her plaints,
and sobbing as if her little heart would have burst.

"Take me with you! take me with you, my own dear
uncle! oh, take your own Chirsty with you!" cried she.

"I shall take you with me, my little dear!" exclaimed
the nabob, snatching her up, and kissing her. "I shall

take you with me, provided your father and mother will but part with you."

A negotiation was speedily entered into. The parents were too sensible of the great advantages which such a proposal opened for their child to think for one moment of throwing any obstacle in the way of its fulfilment. They, moreover, hoped that this arrangement might have the desirable effect of keeping up a connecting tie between them and their rich relative. However much they might have been disappointed in this last respect, they certainly never had any reason to accuse the nabob of any forgetfulness of those promises which he made to them at parting.

He was no sooner established in his house in town than he set about providing proper instructors for Chirsty, and a very few weeks proved to him that his care was by no means thrown away. The child's perception was quick, and her desire to learn was strong, so that things which were difficult to others were, comparatively speaking, easy to her. So rapid was her progress, that her uncle became every day more and more interested in it; and as she advanced, he was from time to time led to engage firstrate masters, in order to perfect her in all manner of solid acquirements and elegant accomplishments. With all this her person became every day more graceful as she grew in stature; and everything she said and did was seasoned with so much sweetness of manner, that she gained the hearts of all who had the good fortune to meet with her.

Not a little proud of what he had so good a right to call his own work, the nabob, on her fifteenth birthday, put the master-keys of his house with great but affectionate ceremonial into her hands, and with them he gave her the entire control and management of his household affairs. But she did not long continue to enjoy the distinguished situation in which he had thus placed her. Too close an application to the numerous branches of education she occupied herself with soon brought upon her that delicacy of health which is too often the produce of the similar over-confinement of young growing girls in our own days. A very alarming cough came on, her strength visibly declined daily, and her spirits began to sink. She was compelled to give up all her favourite pursuits. Books and music lost their charms for her, and her hours were spent in listless idleness, not unfrequently broken in upon by nervous fits of crying, which she could by no means account for. Then it was that in her moody dreamings her mind would revert to the innocent pleasures of her childhood, to the simple, the rustic, yet highly relished happiness she had enjoyed whilst surrounded by her brothers and sisters, when they wandered about the furzy hillocks in a joyous knot, inhaling the perfume of the rich yellow blossoms,— when they dug little caves in the sandy banks, or built their mimic houses, or planted their perishable gardens, with careless hearts, noisy tongues, and laughing eyes. The thought that she might never again behold them or her dear parents renewed her tears, and she pined more and more.

Her affectionate uncle became alarmed at this rapid and melancholy change. So far as gold could purchase the aid of the best medical skill he commanded its attendance. But even the most learned of the London physicians could discover no medicine to remove her malady. In their own minds they despaired of her, but as usually happens in such cases, to cover the deficiency of their art, they recommended her native air as the *dernier ressort.* Chirsty eagerly caught at this last remaining hope, so congenial to the current of her feelings at the time, and her uncle was thus obliged to yield to necessity ; and as certain matters in which he had engaged rendered it quite impossible for him to take charge of her himself, he was obliged to resign her to the care of her maid.

The doctors were right for once. Every breeze that blew on her from her native land as she proceeded on her journey seemed to be fraught with health ; her spirits rose, and long before she reached the place of her birth, she was so far recovered as to remove all fears of any serious termination of her complaint. How did her mind go on as she travelled, sketching to itself ideal pictures of the charms of home ! But alas ! how changed did every person and everything seem to her when she at last reached it. How pitiful did the provincial town appear to her London eyes ! The streets seemed to have shrunk in, and the very houses and gardens to have dwindled ; and when she reached her paternal mansion, she blushed to think how very grievously the fondness of her ancient recollections had deceived her.

The full tide of unrestrained affection which burst forth

the moment she was within its walls was so gratifying to
her heart, that for some time every other feeling or thought
was absorbed by it; but many weeks did not pass over her
head until the conversation and manners of her parents
and family, which had startled her even at the first interview, began to obtrude themselves on her notice in spite
of all she could do to shut her eyes against them, until
they finally became intolerably disagreeable to her. She
soon discovered,—and a certain degree of sorrow and self-
reproach accompanied the discovery, — that the refined
education which she had received had rendered it quite
impossible that she could long endure the mortifications to
which she was daily and hourly exposed by her vulgar
though affectionate and well-meaning relatives. Painful
as the thought was for many reasons, she became convinced
of the necessity of an early separation; and, accordingly,
she made her uncle's wish for her speedy return to him
an apology for fixing an early day for her departure. Yet
do not suppose from this that the ties of affection were not
strong within her. The parting scene was not gone through
without many tears and lingering embraces, that sufficiently proved the triumph of nature in her mind over the
arbitrary dictates of fashion. And after she was gone, the
large richly bound folio bible, out of which her father ever
afterwards read on Sundays,—the gold-mounted spectacles
which enabled him so well to decipher its characters, and
of which he was at all times so justly vain,—the cashmere
shawl that kept her good mother so warm, and the caps,
the bonnets, the gowns, the globes, and the books of prints,
with which her grown-up sisters and brothers were so
much delighted, and the dolls and humming-tops of which
the junior members of the family, down to the very
youngest, were so proud as having been the gifts of "the
grand leddy from Lunnon," for sister they dared hardly to
call her, were not the only marks of her affection that she
left behind her. Besides these keepsakes there were other
presents of a more solid nature bestowed in secret, which,
whilst they contributed to enable her father to hold his
head higher as he walked up the causeway of the main
street of Tain, compelled Chirsty herself to exercise a very
strict economy in providing for those wants which her own
style of life rendered essential to her, large as was the sum
which she had received from the bounty of her uncle.

Passing through Edinburgh on her way to London, she was visited and kindly invited by a lady of fashion who had known her in the metropolis, and she soon found herself deeply engaged in gaiety. Perhaps she did not enter into it the less readily that she had so recently returned from what might have been well enough called her life of mortification at Tain. Having once got into the vortex, she found it difficult to extricate herself from it, and this difficulty was not lessened by the admiration which her beauty and accomplishments so universally excited both in public and in private. She became the chief object of interest, and she was so caressed and courted by every one, that it was not very surprising if the adoration that was paid to her did in some degree affect so young a head. However this might be, three things were very certain,—in the first place, that she had been extremely regular in writing to her uncle during her stay at Tain; secondly, that before leaving that place she had heard from her uncle, who had warmly expressed his anxiety for her return to him; and thirdly, that whereas she had intended to stay in Edinburgh for two or three days only, she was led on from day to day by this ball and the other party to remain, till nearly a whole winter had melted away like its own snows, during all which time she had likewise procrastinated, and, consequently, had entirely omitted the duty of writing to her uncle.

The day of thought and of self-disapproval came at length, and bitter were her reflections. She resolved at least to do all in her power to repair her fault. She sat down immediately and wrote a long letter to her uncle, in which she scrupled not to blame herself to the fullest extent for her want of thought and apparent negligence towards so kind a friend and benefactor, and she declared her repentance and her intention of returning to him immediately.

Having accordingly reached London very soon after her letter, she was driven to her uncle's well-known door. Her impatience to behold him was such, that she could hardly rest in the chaise till the postilion dismounted to knock for her admittance. How intense were her emotions during that brief space! How eagerly did her eyes run over every window in the ample front of the house! How rapidly did the images of her uncle, and of Alexander Tod, his old and faithful servant, dance through her imagination whilst she gazed intently on the yet unopened door, prepared to catch the first smile of surprise and of welcome which she knew would illuminate the honest countenance of that tried domestic, the moment he should discover who it was that summoned him. As she looked she was surprised to perceive that the door itself had strangely changed the modest and unpretending hue which it had worn when she last saw it for a queer uncouth flaring colour, somewhat between a pink and an orange. Before she had time to wonder at this metamorphosis the door did open, and if its opening did produce any surprise it was her own ; for, instead of discovering the plain but respectable figure of Alexander Tod, whom she had been long taught to consider more as an old friend than as a menial, she beheld a saucy fopling, bepowdered, underbred footman, in a gaudy vulgar looking livery. The man stared when she asked for her uncle, and seemed but half inclined to consent to the hall being encumbered with her baggage, and, after having shown her with unconcealed petulance into a little back parlour, she had the mortification, through the door which he had carelessly left ajar behind him, to hear herself thus announced,—

"A young person in the back parlour who wishes to speak to you, sar."

And, chagrined as she was by this provoking delay, she could not help laughing, as she threw herself into a sofa to wait for her uncle's appearance. He came at last, and his joy at again beholding her was great and unfeigned.

"Welcome again to my house, my dear Chirsty," said he, with tears of joy, after his first warm and silent embraces were over; "Oh ! why did you cease to write to me ? But I need say no more, for what is done cannot be undone ; yet, if you had but written to me, things might have been otherwise."

"I ought indeed to have written to you, my dear uncle," replied Chirsty ; "but much as I have deserved your anger, things cannot be but well with me, whilst I am thus affectionately and kindly received by you."

Her uncle replied not ; but, with his eyes thrown on the ground, and with an air of solemnity which she had never seen him wear before, he led her upstairs to the large drawing-room, where she found seated a middle-aged and rather good-looking woman, with an expression of countenance by no means very prepossessing, and whose person was tawdry and very much overdressed. What was her astonishment, and what was the shock she felt, when her uncle led her up to this lady, saying,—

"Mrs. Ross, this is my niece, of whom you have heard me speak so much; and Chirsty, my dear, you will henceforth know and treat this lady as my wife and your aunt."

However little sensible people may think of those newborn and baseless dreams which have been recently blown up into something falsely resembling a science by the folly and vanity of man, and which I for one yet hope, for the honour of human intellect, to see burst and collapse ere I die, it must be admitted, that all are more or less Lavaterists; and that even the youngest of us will involuntarily exercise some such scrutiny on the features of a countenance, when we happen to be placed in such circumstances as Chirsty Ross now found herself thrown into. She, poor girl, failed not to bring all the little knowledge of this sort which she possessed into immediate requisition. The result of her investigations were most unfavourable to the subject of them, nor were these disagreeable impressions at all diminished by the profusion of protestations of kindness and affection which the lady lavished upon her with a vulgar volubility, whilst at the same time she seemed to eye the young intruder in a manner that augured but little for her future happiness. But although Chirsty perceived all this, she inwardly determined to doubt the correctness of her own observation,—at all events, sorrowfully as she retired to rest, or rather to moisten her pillow with her tears, she failed not to arm herself with the virtuous resolution, that as this woman, be she what she might, was the wife of her uncle, who had acted as a father to her, she would use her best endeavours to gain her affection, seeing that she was now bound to regard her as a parent. But yet she did not close her eyes, without having almost unconsciously exclaimed,

"What *could* have induced my uncle, with such tastes as he has, to marry such a person as this? Ah! if I had not fooled away my time in Edinburgh! or if I had only *but* written!"

Next morning she met her uncle alone in the library, and a single sentence of his explained the whole.

"What *could* have induced you to forget to write to me, Chirsty?" said the good man, kissing her tenderly, whilst his eyes betrayed a sensation which he vainly tried to hide. "We were so happy here alone together! But I have been a fool, Chirsty! : Blinded by momentary pique, I saw not the slough of despond into which I was plunging until too late! But she is not a bad woman, though not quite what I was at first led to believe her to be ; and so, all we can now say is, that she is your aunt and my wife, and we are both bound to make the best of it."

Chirsty assured her uncle that nothing should be wanting on her part towards her aunt ; and she kept her word, for, neglecting all other things, she devoted herself entirely to the task of pleasing her. For some little while her pious endeavours 'seemed to have succeeded ; but it happened that Chirsty, unambitious as she was to shine, so far eclipsed her aunt in every attraction that makes woman charming, that without intending it, or rather whilst intending the very reverse, she monopolised all the attention of those with whom they associated either at home or abroad. Compared to her Mrs. Ross was treated like a piece of furniture,—any table or cabinet in the room had more attention paid to it. : She could not shut her eyes to her own inferiority, and envy, hatred, and malice took full possession of her. Chirsty's efforts to please, though they had ceased to be successful, were still unremitting ; but her uninterrupted gentleness was met by perpetual peevishness and ill humour, always excepting such times as her uncle chanced to be present, when the lady's words and manner were ever bland, kind, and false. With such devilish tempers it often happens that the more they torture the more they hate, and so it was that the dislike of this woman towards her niece rapidly grew to so great a height, that she resolved to get her removed from the house.

Fondly believing that she had a stronger hold over her husband's affections than she really possessed, she first of all attempted to undermine her in her uncle's good opinion by sly insinuations against her truth, her temper, and what she called the girl's *pretended* love for him, which she declared was in reality no greater than her attention to her own self-interest required. : But finding that this line of attack only excited his anger, she with great art gradually

18

withdrew from it, and by slow degrees she began to confess that she now believed she had been altogether mistaken in her estimation of Chirsty, and every succeeding day heard her bestow more and more praise on her temper and disposition. This was a language that was much more congenial to the nabob, but he was not altogether the dupe of it. He however listened with seeming attention to his wife when she prosed on about the zeal she felt for her niece's interest, as well as when, after a long prologue, she finally proposed the grand scheme of sending Chirsty out to India to the care of a particular friend of the nabob's at Calcutta, that she might there make some wealthy match, so as to secure her a magnificent independence for life. Plainly as Mr. Ross saw through the motives that dictated all this apparent solicitude, he took care to appear to think it quite genuine. Nor did he refuse to entertain the project; for as he began shrewdly to suspect that his niece could now have but little happiness under the same roof with his wife, he resolved at least to put it in Chirsty's power to accept or reject this proposal. He accordingly sought for a private interview with her, and then it was that her tears, and her half confessions with difficulty extracted, satisfied him of the correctness of his suspicions, and the readiness with which she acceded to the plan which he laid before her at once determined him as to the propriety of going immediately into it. He therefore lost not a moment in securing everything that might contribute to her comfort and happiness during the voyage, and he presented her with a letter of credit for a sum of money amply sufficient to put her above all anxiety as to that matter on reaching the shores of the Ganges.

These substantial marks of her uncle's affection towards her, supported as they were by a thousand little nameless kindnesses, did not tend to allay the grief which she felt at parting with him. The reflection that she went because she felt convinced that her uncle's future domestic comfort required her absence, was all that she had to give her courage to bear it, and she was so much absorbed in this conviction, that she hardly gave much thought to the consideration of what her own future fate might be.

The gallant ship had gone merrily on its voyage for several days before Chirsty began to mix at all with her fellow-passengers. But when she first came upon deck, it

was like the appearance of the morning sun over the
eastern horizon of some country where he is worshipped.
All eyes were instantly bent upon her; and ere the people
had been familiarised to her beauty, the elegance of her
manners, and the charms of her conversation, soon made
her the great centre of attraction to all who walked the
quarter-deck. Above all others, she seemed to have made
a deep and powerful impression on the commander, whom
I shall call Captain Mordaunt, a very elegant and agreeable
man, of superior intellect and information. He soon
showed himself indefatigable in his attentions to her. His
command of the ship gave him a thousand opportunities of
manifesting a marked degree of politeness towards her, by
doing her many little courteous services which no one else
had the power to perform. He easily invented means of
keeping all other aspirants to her favour at a sufficient
distance from her. Her heart was as yet her own; and as
Mordaunt never lost any opportunity of engaging her in
conversation, and as his talk was always well worth listening to, it was no wonder that so many unequivocal proofs
of an attachment on the part of so handsome a man, in the
prime of life, and of address so superior, should have soon
prepared the way for her favourable reception of his
declared passion; and this having once been made, and
mutually acknowledged, it seemed to grow in warmth as
the days fled merrily away, and as the progress of the prosperous bark carried them nearer and nearer to that sun
which gives life and heat to all animated nature. Often
did Mordaunt gladden the artless mind of Chirsty Ross as
they sat apart together on the poop of the vessel, towards
the conclusion of their voyage, in the full enjoyment of the
fanning sea-breeze, by the enchanting pictures which he
painted of the happiness of their future wedded life.

"I have already realised a tolerable fortune," said he,
one evening carelessly, "so that by the time I return to
Calcutta from my trip to China, whither you know the
vessel is bound, I may safely claim your hand, in order
that we may sail home together as man and wife. You
can have no dread of spending our honeymoon on the wide
waters, my love, since they have yielded us so happy
a courtship, especially when you think that we shall
be on our way to some sweet rural residence in England,
where we shall be insured the enjoyment of tranquillity

and happiness for the rest of our days. And there, with what I have saved, added to the liberal allowance which your rich uncle will give you during his life, and with the certainty which you have of succeeding to his immense fortune at his death, we shall be able to live in a style altogether worthy of that exquisite beauty, and that angelic soul, with which Heaven has blessed you, and of those fascinating manners and brilliant accomplishments, which are calculated to make you the queen of any society you may be pleased to grace with your presence."

"Stay, stay, Mordaunt!" replied Chirsty, smiling playfully. "You are running too fast before the wind. I need not tell you what you have so often told me, that I am prepared to be thine on the wide ocean, in the populous city, or in the lonely desert, in sickness or in health, in wealth or in poverty! And well, is it, indeed, that you have so often vowed all this much to me, for I must needs disabuse your mind of some part of its visions of riches, so far at least as that share may have reached which your fancy has ascribed to me. I have neither claims nor expectations from my uncle, who has already done more for me than any niece in my circumstances had a right to expect."

"Haul taut that weather main-brace!" cried the captain, suddenly starting from her side; and although there appeared to be little change in the wind or the weather to warrant such activity, he became from that moment too much occupied in the care of the ship for any further conversation with Chirsty that evening.

In the morning the lovers met as usual, and then, as well as during the few remaining days of the voyage, Mordaunt was as full of affection and endearment to her as ever. Their last private interview took place ere she left the ship to go into the small craft that was to take her up the river, and then all their mutual vows were solemnly repeated. An understanding took place between them, that their engagement should be kept private, unless circumstances should arise which might render a disclosure necessary. Poor Chirsty gave way to all the poignancy of that grief which she felt at being thus obliged to part, even for a few months, from him to whom, in the then orphan state of her soul, she had given up the whole strength of her undivided affections. But hard as she found the effort to be, she was obliged to dry up her tears, and even to throw a faint and fleeting smile over her countenance as she left the ship, that she might not betray her own secret before indifferent persons; and it was only that warm and cherishing hope that lay nearest to her heart that kept the pulses of her life playing, and that enabled her to go through the trying scene of parting coolly with her lover, after he had deposited her under the roof of her uncle's friend, where they bid each other such a polite adieu as might have befitted two well-bred people who were separating with mutual esteem for one another, and who were, at the same time, very little solicitous as to whether there did or did not exist any future chance of their ever meeting again.

Mr. Gardner, as I shall call the gentleman to whose protection the nabob had consigned Chirsty, well deserved the confidence which had been placed in him. He spoke warmly of the many obligations under which he lay to Mr. Ross, and he declared himself to be delighted in having the opportunity which had thus been afforded him of proving his gratitude for those obligations. His lady entered deeply into all her husband's feelings, and both of them zealously occupied themselves in doing all in their power to promote the young lady's comfort and happiness. Numerous and brilliant were the parties which they made for the purpose of introducing their lovely protegé with sufficient eclat to the society of Calcutta., But not even the novelty and grandeur of Eastern magnificence, though produced for her with all its splendour, had any effect in removing that pensive air which their young friend wore when she landed, and which she continued to wear notwithstanding all the smiling new faces to which she was every moment introduced. One very natural result, however, was soon produced by these numerous public appearances which the kindness of her friends obliged her to make. She was immediately encircled by crowds of admirers; and before she had been many months in the country she had been put to the unpleasant necessity of declining proposals of marriage from numerous military men and civilians of rank so high as to make those with whom she lived wonder at the indifference she displayed. The more she was courted the more retiring she appeared to become.

Among the few who were admitted to a somewhat more familiar intercourse with Chirsty, was a Scottish gentleman of good family, whom I shall call Charles Græme. Though young, he had risen to a high civil situation, and he had already realised a very handsome fortune. He was a gentleman of enlarged mind and extremely liberal education; and as he was of manners much more retiring than most of those with whom she had become acquainted, she the more readily yielded to that intimacy which his greater friendship with her host and hostess gave him very frequent opportunities of forming with her. Like herself he was full of accomplishments; yet such was his modesty, that she had known him for a considerable time before accident led her to discover them. His mind was richly stored with the treasures of European literature; yet it was only on particular occasions that he allowed himself to give forth the sweets he had hoarded up, or to indulge in those critical remarks to which every one was prepared to listen with delight. As he became better known to her, and more at his ease with her, she discovered that his tastes, his acquirements, his sentiments, nay, his very soul, were all so much in harmony with her own, that she soon began to prefer his society to that of any other gentleman who approached her. Had her heart been unengaged, she might perhaps have had some degree of palpitation in its pulses, as she sensibly felt their friendship becoming every day more and more familiar; but, as the partridge believes that when its head is in the bush the whole of its body is secure, so she, knowing her own safety, owing to that secret cause which bound her to another, never dreamed that the accomplished Scotchman could be in any danger of feeling for her any sentiment one degree warmer than that of esteem. Thus it was, that with perfect unconsciousness on her part of the havoc she was working in his heart, she read with him, criticised with him, played with him, sang with him, or sketched with him, as the fancy of the moment might dictate, her heart being all the while filled with gratitude to him for so good-naturedly enabling her to pass, with at least some degree of rational enjoyment, some of those tedious hours that must yet elapse ere the return of him to whom she had pledged her virgin affections.

As for Charles Græme, he soon began to find that he existed only when his soul was animated by her bright eyes and her seraphic voice. When absent from their influence he felt like a walking mass of frozen clay. Her society became more necessary to him than food or air. He almost lived at the house of the Gardners, who, on their part, gave him every encouragement, being secretly pleased at what they believed to be the mutual attachment that was so rapidly growing, as they thought, between two individuals whom they had reason to love so much, and whom they knew to be so worthy of each other, and so well calculated to make each other happy for life. Day after day the infatuated young man drank deeper and deeper draughts of the sweet intoxication of love. At last the hour of wretchedness came. Seizing what he fondly believed to be a favourable moment, and with a bosom full of bounding hopes, he laid open the state of his heart to the idol of his soul. The scales fell, as if by magic, from her mental vision.

"What have I done, Mr. Græme," she cried, whilst her cheeks were suffused with blushes, and her whole frame trembled. "I have been blind! I have been thoughtless, most culpably thoughtless. Forgive me! oh, forgive me! but I cannot, I dare not, love you! I am already the pledged bride of another."

It would be vain for me to attempt to describe the kind of temporary death that fell upon her unfortunate lover as she uttered these terrible words, which, like the simoom of the desert, left no atom of hope behind them. Sinking into a chair, he uttered no sound, and he sat for some time quite unconscious even of those attentions which her compassion for him at the moment led her unscrupulously to administer to him. The friendship and the high respect which she entertained for him, as well as a regard for her own justification in his eyes, forbade her to allow him to leave her without a full explanation. It was given to him under the seal of secrecy, and the interview terminated with an agony of feeling and floods of tears upon his part, in which her compassion for that affliction which she had so innocently occasioned him compelled her, in spite of herself, to participate.

The young Scotchman tried for some time after this, to frequent the house where she lived as he had done previously. But her smiles fell upon him like sunshine upon a spectre. Reason and prudence at last came to his aid; and seeing that his heart could never hope for ease whilst he remained within reach of her attractions, he, to the great astonishment and disappointment of his friends, made use of the powerful interest which he possessed to procure another situation in a distant station, and he tore himself away from Calcutta.

And now came the time of misery to poor Chirsty herself, the season of hope deferred, of nervous impatience, and of sad forebodings. The period for which her fond heart panted in secret arrived—it passed away. Days, nay, weeks and months beyond it elapsed; and yet no tidings came of the gallant vessel that bore her betrothed husband. Delicately alive to the apprehension of betraying her secret by inquiry, she did not dare to ask questions. Fears, agonising fears, began to possess her, that some fatal calamity had befallen the ship, till, happening accidentally one day to cast her eyes over an old shipping list, she read, and her sight grew dim as she read, of its arrival from China, and its subsequent departure for England! How indestructible is hope! Even then she imagined it possible that all this might have been the result of accident, or might have arisen from the orders of superiors. But still her anxiety preyed terribly upon her mind, whilst she now looked forward to the new period of the ship's return from England. In vain did she try to occupy herself in her former pursuits. In vain did her friends endeavour to interest her with the amusements they provided for her. All were equally fruitless in their efforts; and the only explanation which the Gardners could find for her mysterious abstraction, was in the belief that the remembrance of Charles Græme was not altogether indifferent to her; and thence they cherished the hope that the matter between that young man and her might yet one day end as they wished it to do.

Months rolled on as if the days of which they were composed had been years, till Chirsty was one evening, with some difficulty, induced by her friends to go to a great public entertainment. She entered the room, leaning on Mrs. Gardner's arm; and they were on their way to find a seat at the upper end of it, when her eyes suddenly beheld him for whose return she had been so long vainly

sighing. Her heart beat as if it would have burst from
its seat in her bosom. She clung unconsciously with a
firmer hold to the arm of her friend, and her limbs tottered
under her with nervous joy as she moved forward. He
was advancing slowly with a lady; and as he drew near,
she held out her hand to him with a smile of happy and
welcome recognition. He started at sight of her; and then,
after scanning every feature of her countenance with calm
indifference, he bowed coldly, turned aside, and moved
away. Chirsty uttered a faint cry, swooned away, and
was carried home by her friends in a state of insensibility,
leaving the whole room in confusion.

Sufficient natural and ordinary reasons were very easily
found by a company in such a climate as that of India for
such an accident. But Mrs. Gardner had seen enough to
convince her that some deeper and more powerful cause
had operated upon Chirsty, than the mere heat of weather
or the crowded state of a room; and after she had successfully used the necessary means for recovering her from her
fainting fit, she insisted on being allowed to share con-
fidentially in the secret of her afflictions. Chirsty felt
some slight relief in telling her all; and strange it was
that she still clung most unaccountably to hope. He
might not have recognised her at first. He would yet
appear. But Mrs. Gardner's common sense told her there
was no hope; and she judged that it would be far better
that Chirsty should receive conviction, however cruel that
conviction might be, rather than remain in an anxiety
which was so agonising and destructive. A very little
time enabled Mrs. Gardner to collect all the particulars
of his treachery. To sum up all in one word, he had
arrived at Calcutta from England with a rich wife, with
whom he had already sailed on his last voyage home.

This overwhelming intelligence was too much for th
shattered frame of poor Chirsty Ross. She was attacked
by a most alarming fever, which finally produced delirium;
and even after the physicians had been able to master the
bodily disease, the mental derangement continued so long
unabated, that her friends the Gardners considered it
proper to write home to inform her uncle of her unhappy
state.

It pleased God, however, to restore her at length to her
right mind; and then it was that she was seized with an

unconquerable desire of returning to England. The most
that the Gardners could prevail upon her to agree to, was
to delay her voyage to a period so far distant as might
insure that fresh letters should reach her uncle, to inform
him of her perfect mental recovery, and to teach him to
look for her arrival by a certain ship they named; and
after impatiently waiting till the time destined for her
departure arrived, she bade her kind friends the Gardners
an affectionate farewell, and sailed with a fair wind for
Britain.

Who was it that arrived a week afterwards at the house
of Mr. and Mrs. Gardner in the middle of the night,
having come by Dawk from a far distant province? It
was the shadow of Charles Græme!

"Thank God! thank God!" cried he energetically, after
being told of her recovery, and at the same time bursting
into a flood of tears, which weakness and fatigue left him no
power to restrain. "Thank God for her restoration! But
oh! that I had reached Calcutta but eight days sooner!"

He took his determination, applied for leave, to which
the state of his health might of itself well enough have
entitled him, and went for England by the very first fleet
that sailed.

Chirsty Ross had a prosperous, but not a happy voyage.
Her bodily health improved every day that she was at sea;
but her thoughts having full time to brood over her
miseries, her spirits became more and more sunk. She
rallied a little when she beheld the English shore; and
when she arrived in the river, her heart began to beat
with affectionate joy at the prospect of again embracing
her dear uncle. Even the image of her aunt had had its
asperities softened down by length of time and absence;
and she almost felt something resembling pleasure at the
prospect of seeing her again. As the vessel arrived in the
evening at her moorings, a boat came alongside, and a
voice was heard to demand if there was a Miss Ross on
board? Readily did Chirsty answer to the inquiry; and
being told that it was her uncle's servant come to take her
home, she lost not a moment in desiring her black maid
to hand up a small box, containing a few things to be put
into the boat; and leaving the girl to follow next day with
her heavy baggage, she quickly descended the ladder. She
was immediately accosted by a stout, vulgar-looking man

out of livery, who announced himself to her as Mr. Ross's servant, and informed her that a carriage waited for her near the landing-place. She did accordingly find a post-chaise there ; but when the door of it was opened, and the steps were let down, she started back on perceiving that there was a man seated at the farther side of it.

"Only a friend of Mr. Ross, ma'am, whom he has sent to attend you home," said the fellow who held the handle of the carriage-door.

Surprised as she was at the vulgarity of the dress and appearance of the gentleman who was inside, and still more at his want of politeness in not coming out of the carriage to hand her into it, her heart was too full of home at the moment to admit of her inquiring very particularly into circumstances, and accordingly, without more ado, she entered the vehicle. But whilst she was yet only in the act of seating herself, the fellow who had passed himself as her uncle's servant, sprang in after her, pulled up the steps, shut the door, the side blinds were drawn up, and the post-chaise was instantly flying at the rate of twelve or fourteen miles an hour. She screamed aloud, but the ruffian hands of both the villains were immediately on her mouth and silence was inculcated with the most horrible and blasphemous menaces.

"We must have none of your Indian fury here, mistress," said one of the fellows. "Behave peaceably and quietly, and you shall be treated gently enough, but if you offer to rave and riot, the whip, the gag, and the strait-waistcoat shall be your portion."

"Merciful Providence !" said Chirsty Ross, "why am I thus treated, and whither would you carry me ?"

"As to your treatment, young lady," said the man, "methinks you have no right to complain of that *as yet ;* and as to the *why,* I should be as mad as yourself were I to hold any talk with you about *that ;* and, then, as to the *whither,* you have been already told that you are going to your uncle's residence."

"Mad !" exclaimed Chirsty, with a shudder that ran through her whole frame. "But, ah ! I see how it is. Mr. Gardner's letters have been received by my uncle, and not those which I wrote to him sometime afterwards. And yet how did he know to expect me in England, and by this particular ship, too, if my letters have not yet reached him? It is very puzzling—very perplexing—very distressing; but since I am going to him, I may thank God that all will soon be put to rights."

"Aye, aye," said both the men at once, whilst they laughed rudely to one another, "all will soon be put to rights, I'll warrant me."

Chirsty sat silently dreaming over this strange and most vexatious occurrence, yet hoping that her misery would be but of short duration, till the chaise suddenly stopped, when one of the men let down the window, and called to the postilion to ring the great bell at a gate, which he had no sooner done than the peal was answered by the fierce barking of a watch-dog.

"What place is this?" cried Chirsty, with new-born alarm. "This is not the house of my Uncle Ross."

"You will see that all in good time, ma'am," replied one of the men. "Postboy, ring again. What are they all about, I wonder?"

At this second summons the huge nail-studded leaves of the ponderous oak and iron-bound gate were slowly rolled back, and the chaise was admitted into a large paved court, where the lights that were borne by one or two men of similar appearance to those who accompanied her, showed the plain front of a pretty considerable brick building, the narrow windows of which were strongly barred with iron. The door, too, was of the most massive strength, and the whole character of the edifice would of itself have conveyed to her the heart-sinking conviction that she was within the precincts of a mad-house, even if those strange sounds of uncouth laughter, wild rage, and wailing despair that came from various parts of the interior, had been altogether unheard by her. Rapidly did her thoughts traverse her mind. The first natural impulse that possessed her was a desire to scream out for help. But Chirsty was not destitute of resolution and self-command; and as she immediately reflected that nothing but the calmest behaviour could afford her any chance of convincing the people of such an establishment that she in reality was sane, she at once resolved to restrain herself from everything that might look like excitement.

"Where is Sarah?" cried one of the men as he assisted Chirsty out of the vehicle. "Aye, aye, here she comes. Here is your charge, Sall."

"A tall, handsome young woman," said Sarah, surveying Chirsty from head to foot, whilst she herself exhibited a person in every respect the reverse of that which she was admiring, being almost a dwarf, though with a body thickly and strongly built. Her head was large, with harsh prominent features, and her legs were bowed, and her arms long and uncouth looking. Round her waist, if waist that might be called where waist there was none, there was fastened a leathern belt, to which was appended a large bunch of great keys. In the eyes of Chirsty she was altogether a most formidable looking object.

"A tall handsome young woman," said she. "In what sort of temper is she, I wonder?"

"She was a little bit riotous at first," said one of the men, "but she has been quiet enough ever since."

"Come this way, young lady," said Sarah to Chirsty, in a rough tone and sharp voice, and at the same time she stretched out her long arm, and grasped her wrist with her bony fingers, whilst with the other hand she held up an iron lamp, the light of which she threw before her.

"Treat me not harshly," said Chirsty gently. "I am ready to obey you. I am quite aware that, from the strange mistake that has occurred, it would be vain for me to attempt to convince you at present of my sanity. I must patiently submit, therefore, to whatever restraint you may impose on me, until my uncle comes to see me, and convince himself. But do not, I pray you, exercise any unnecessary severity."

"No, no, poor thing," replied Sarah. "No, no; no severity that is not quite necessary, I promise you. As to your uncle—ha! ha! ha!—no doubt you may chance to see un ere you leave this. Come this way."

Whilst this dialogue was passing, Chirsty was led by her strange conductress through some long passages, in which were several rectangular turnings, past many strongly secured doors, from within which issued strange discordant sounds of human misery, mingled with the clanking of chains; and up one or two flights of stairs, which induced her to believe that the apartment to which she was about to be introduced was in the upper story, and in a wing of the building. The door was like those she had seen in her way thither, of immense strength, and it was secured by a powerful lock, a couple of heavy bolts,

and a huge chain and padlock. It was the last door of the
narrow passage, which terminated about a yard beyond it
in a dead wall. The little woman pushed Chirsty past it
into the *cul-de-sac* which the passage thus formed, and then
quitting her arm, she planted the fixed gaze of her formidable eye upon her, and placing the lamp on the ground, she
selected the necessary keys, and using both hands she
exerted her strength to undo the lock and padlock, and
then drawing the bolts and removing the chain, she
opened the den within. Beckoning to her charge with an
air of command not to be misunderstood, she pushed
Chirsty into the place, and then standing in the aperture
of the half-closed door for a minute or more, with her
right hand on the key, she threw in the light of the lamp
so as fully to show the whole interior. It was indeed a
wretched place. A low narrow bedstead, with bedclothes
of the coarsest and meanest description, was the whole of
its furniture, and that occupied more than a fourth part of
the space contained within its four brick and stone walls.
The floor was of flags,—it had no fireplace, and one small
narrow iron-grated window was all the visible perforation
that could admit light or air.

"May I not be allowed to have the few things which
came in my travelling-box?" said Chirsty mildly, after
having seated herself on the side of the bed.

"We shall consider of that, young lady," said Sarah
sternly. "But in the meanwhile, to satisfy my mind that
you may be safely left for a little time, you must suffer me
to put those lily-white hands of yours into this glove,"
and setting the lamp on the floor, she drew from her ample
pocket a leathern bag, into which Chirsty patiently
submitted to have both her hands thrust together, after
which they were secured by a strap in such a manner as to
leave them entirely useless.

"Let me see now that you have got nothing dangerous
about you," said Sarah; and after searching her all over,
and removing from her a pocket-book containing such
small instruments as women generally use, together with
one or two other articles, and not forgetting her purse,
which she secreted carefully in her own bosom, she added,
"I shall be back with you in the twinkling of an eye, for
you must have food ere you go to rest; meanwhile, the
quieter you are the better it will be for you," and with

these words she lifted the lamp and retired with it, locking
and bolting the door with the utmost care.

It is needless for me to speculate as to what were
Chirsty's thoughts, left as she was in the dark, as she
listened to the retreating steps of her keeper until a
stillness reigned around her that was only interrupted at
times by the distant baying of the watch-dog in the court-
yard, or by some of those melancholy demonstrations of
madness that came every now and then upon her ear,
of different degrees of intensity, as they chanced to be
modified by circumstances. Notwithstanding all the
resolution which she had summoned to her support, she
shuddered to think of the vexatious confinement to which
she might be exposed ere her fond uncle might be able to
gather courage enough to come to visit her in the melancholy state of mind in which he probably believed her to be.
Whilst she was ruminating on such matters, she heard the
returning footsteps of Sarah.

"Here is some food for you," said her keeper, after
opening the door and entering cautiously, "and, see, I have
brought your night-clothes. I promised to use no needless
severity; and if you continue to behave, you shall have no
reason to complain of me. Let me help you to eat your
supper, for this night you must be contented with simple
bread and milk." And the first meal that poor Chirsty eat
after returning to her native Britain, was doled out to her
by spoonfuls from a porringer by the long fingers of her
dwarfish keeper, who after making down her bed, assisted
her into it, and then left her for the night.

And a strange night it was to her. Fatigue brought
sleep upon her it is true, but there was no refreshment in
it, for it was full of wild visions, and she started from
time to time, and awaked to have her mind brought back
to the full conviction of her distressing situation by the
maniac laughter or howlings that broke at intervals upon
the stillness around her. The only support she had in
circumstances so trying was derived from religious meditations and aspirations, together with the hope which never
forsook her, that her affectionate uncle might next day
visit and relieve her.

FRESH LIGHT UPON THE SUBJECT.

Grant.—Stop for one moment, Clifford, till we ring for
fresh candles, or we shall be in darkness before you have
uttered five sentences more.

Dominie.—Stay, sir, I'll run to the kitchen for them
myself. Preserve me ! the less time we keep Mr. Clifford's
poor lassie in such misery the better.

Mr. Macpherson soon returned with the new lights, set
them down on the table, and drawing in his chair, put his
elbows upon his knees, placed his cheeks firmly in the
palms of his hands, and sat with his eyes eagerly fixed
upon Clifford's countenance, with the most ludicrous
expression of earnestness. Clifford resumed as follows.

LEGEND OF CHIRSTY ROSS—*Continued.*

THE morning's dawn brought back the returning footstep of Sarah. She brought with her Chirsty's travelling-box with most of the things it contained.

"See," said she, as she set down the box, "I have kept my word. So long as you behave, you shall find me disposed to treat you well. I know that you have been quiet all night, and, therefore, we shall try you for to-day with your hands unmuffled. But mind !" added the old woman with a fearful expression of eye, "if you *should* change for the worse, there are worse punishments for you than this leathern glove."

"I thank you," said Chirsty meekly ; "I think you will have no occasion to resort to any such. I hope my uncle will be here to-day, and that a few moments of conversation with him will satisfy him that you may be released from any further trouble with me."

"Your uncle !" cried Sarah, with an uncouth laugh. "But we shall see. Meanwhile, here comes water for you, and, by and by, you shall have breakfast."

A little black-looking sharp-eyed girl now entered with a pitcher, basins, and towels. Sarah stood by to watch how her charge conducted herself, and, when the toilet was completed, the bed was made up, and the things removed, and soon afterwards breakfast was brought her, together with a common fir chair and a small table, and when she had finished her meal, she was again left to her own solitary meditations.

No sooner was all quiet, than Chirsty arose for the purpose of looking out of the window, that she might try at least to gain some knowledge of her position. She discovered that the walls of the building were extremely thick, that the window was powerfully barred with iron, and that a wooden shade projected over it from above, so as entirely to shut out any direct view outwards. By placing the chair near the window, however, and standing

19

upon it, she commanded a limited view dow
the sole and the lower edge of the wooder
from this she was enabled to satisfy herself t
was on one side of a narrow square court,
lower part of the buildings that inclosed
sides of it. Guessing from the windows t]
her view below, the court was surrounded v
to her own. The startling fact now arose i1
she had thus in one minute made he
acquainted with all the objects on which
her eyes to bear from this her place of con
could do were she to occupy it for half a
was something chilling in the reflectior
naturally began to pant in a tenfold de{
But that day passed away, and the next, a1
no kind uncle came to relieve her.

"Is there no message from my uncle ?"
as Sarah came to her one morning.

"None !" said the old woman, somewl
than usual.

"I would fain write a letter to him," sai

"I see no use in that," said Sarah q
hastily, as if to avoid further question.

She did not see the old woman again f
Nancy, the little girl already mentioned,
at the usual hours. In vain she tried to p
procure her writing materials. Her answ
had no means of doing so. She asked for
but the girl's answer was the same. At 1
appeared again.

"Any intelligence from my uncle, goo
Chirsty.

"None !" replied her keeper, in the sa1
used before.

"Then, I beseech you, give me the me{
cating with him by letter," said she earnes1

"Tush, I tell you it would be of n
Sarah.

"Nay, give me but pen, ink, and paper,
said Chirsty. "I am sure he would neve1
one moment here, if he could only see an
me. Oh! if I could but see him for fiv
harassing captivity would be at an end."

"Well, then!" said Sarah, after a silence of some moments, during which she appeared to be weighing circumstances in her mind. "Well, then, you shall see un. But see how you behave! Follow me, then, and I shall bring you to your uncle."

"Oh, thank you, thank you! a thousand and a thousand times!" cried Chirsty, almost embracing the old woman in the height of her joy. "Depend upon it, I shall satisfy you as to my behaviour."

Sarah now opened the door of the cell, and Chirsty followed her. Even the small additional motion of her limbs which she now enjoyed, was luxury to her after the narrow bounds to which she had been confined. The old woman led her along the passage for a considerable way, down one flight of steps, along another passage, to the very end of it, and there she stopped opposite a door, secured by little more than the ordinary fastenings used to any private chamber. Sarah opened it and desired Chirsty to enter. The light of heaven was permitted to pass fully in at the window, and she rushed forward to meet her uncle's embrace. But ere she had gone two steps into the room, her eyes caught a spectacle that effectually arrested her.

"Merciful Providence, my poor uncle!" she faintly cried; and, tottering towards a pallet-bed that was near to her, she sank down on the side of it, and gazed with grief and with horror on the miserable object before her.

Seated in a wooden elbow chair, she did indeed behold her uncle; but he was there as a mere piece of animated clay. His hair, which always used to be so nicely trimmed and powdered, now hung in long white untamed locks over a countenance so yellow and emaciated as to be absolutely fearful to look upon. Part of it fell over the eyes, which were seen within it like two bits of yellow glass, motionless and void of all speculation. The under jaw hung forward, and the tongue lolled out, as if all muscular power was lost. An old Indian dressing-gown, which Chirsty remembered to have been his pride, as having been presented to him by a great rajah, and as being made of the most valuable stuff that Cashmere could produce, but now begrimed by every species of filth, covered his person. A broad band of girth was passed around his breast under his arms, and attached to the

back of his chair, to prevent his weakness or his involuntary motions from precipitating him on the floor. His
feet were both occupied in drumming upon the ground,
and his hands were extended before him, with the fingers
continually crawling like reptiles on his knees, whilst he
was ceaselessly emitting a low muttering whine, that never
moulded itself into words. The very first glance she had
of him convinced Chirsty that her poor uncle was in the
last stage of confirmed and hopeless idiocy.

"What would a letter have done, think ye, to such a
clod as that 'ere?" demanded the unfeeling wretch Sarah,
"or what will you make of un, now you have seen un?"

"My poor unhappy uncle!" said Chirsty, starting from
her seat and going fondly towards him, and weeping over
him; "how sadly indeed hast thou been changed! When,
alas! did this awful affliction fall upon him? But why
has he been removed from his own comfortable home to
such a place as this?"

"Such a place as this, quotha!" cried Sarah. "Why,
what sort of a place would ye have un in? There is not a
more comfortabler room in the whole house. And see, if
I didn't bring down that 'ere old wardrobe, that we might
have summat to hold un's things in; though I must say,"
added she in an undertone, "that he hasn't much left now
that's worth the caring for."

"But why has he been removed to such an establishment as this?" said Chirsty. "Surely, surely, his malady,
helpless and unoffending as it has rendered him, could have
given no disturbance in his own house, why then has he
been torn from it? and how could his wife have agreed to
treatment so cruel and so unnecessary?"

"His wife!" exclaimed Sarah with a laugh. "It was
his wife who sent un here; and surely his wife has the
most natral right to judge what's best for un."

"Horrible!" exclaimed Chirsty, "his wife! There mus'
be some horrible villainy under all this."

"What!" exclaimed Sarah. "What is there horrible
in a gay woman like her ridding her house of such a filthy
slavering mummy as this? He would be a pretty orna-
ment, truly, to grace some of *the rich Mrs. Ross's splendid
routes*, as I now and then see the papers call them.
Besides, she pays well for his board here, and it is our
interest not to let un die."

"Rich!" exclaimed Chirsty indignantly. "Her riches are my uncle's riches; and if one spark of Christian feeling yet remained in her bosom, she ought to have employed them in relieving, so far as they could relieve, this most heavy affliction of a just and wise Providence."

"It's not for me to stand argufying with you here, Miss," said Sarah, in a tone of displeasure that led Chirsty to fear a coming storm. "Come, you see you have gotten all the good out of un you can; so you may as well leave un, and go quietly back to your cell."

"For the love of your Redeemer, and as you hope for mercy!" cried Chirsty, throwing herself on her knees before her keeper, "force me not to quit my uncle! To him I owe more than the duty of a child to a parent. Yield but to me the charitable boon of allowing me to watch by him, and to attend to him day and night, and you will render me so happy that I shall cheerfully and voluntarily submit to my present cruel confinement, without once inquiring by whose order it comes, or ever seeking to establish how unnecessarily it has been inflicted upon me. Oh! grant me but this, and may blessings be showered down upon you."

"I must think about it," gruffly replied Sarah. "In the meantime, you must back to your cell for this day at least. So bid un good-by for this bout. We shall see how you behave, and we shall talk more of the matter to-morrow."

Chirsty rose from her knees; and seeing that it was only through submissive obedience that she could hope to obtain what she so ardently wished, she went to her uncle, and taking up his unconscious hand, she kissed it, watered it with her tears, and then slowly left the apartment, and returned to her cell, where she was locked up as before.

She was no sooner left to herself, than so many circumstances and reflections occurred to her mind, that it had enough of occupation. She now remembered that after having had regular letters from her uncle for a considerable time, they had all at once ceased. But as the irregularity of Indian correspondence was even more common in those days than it is now, she had regretted this as arising from unfortunate accident, without being very much surprised at it. But much as she had had reason to believe that her aunt was a heartless selfish woman, she never could have imagined that she could have been guilty of conduct so unfeeling towards the unhappy man from whose affection she now derived all that wealth which it appeared she was spending so gaily. As to herself, a moment's thought was enough to convince her that she owed her present confinement more to the malice than to the care of her aunt. She remembered that the only communication from India that contained the intimation that she was about to return to Britain, as well as the name of the ship in which she was to sail, also conveyed the full assurance of the perfect restoration of her mind from its temporary malady. The person who knew to what ship to send for her on her arrival, therefore, must necessarily have known that she required no such treatment as that to which she had been so wickedly subjected. Villainy of the darkest dye, therefore, had been at work against her; and where or how it might end she trembled to think. But the thought of her poor uncle's melancholy situation banished every other consideration from her mind; and all her thoughts and wishes were now concentrated in the desire she felt to stay by him, and to watch over him to the last—the very idea of such a self-devotion being balm to her lacerated heart, as affording her the luxury of indulging that deep gratitude with which his unvarying kindness towards her had always filled her, and which she never hoped to have had any opportunity of repaying. She failed not, therefore, to employ all her meekness and all her eloquence to persuade Sarah to grant her request; and as the gentle drop by frequent repetition will at last wear through the hardest flint, so by repeated appeals to the best of the few feelings which that callous-hearted creature possessed, she at last succeeded in obtaining a limited permission to visit her uncle, which was extended by degrees so far, that she ultimately came to be allowed to go to his chamber in the morning, and to remain with him till he was laid to rest at night, when she was removed for the purpose of being locked up in her own cell. In this employment Chirsty forgot her confinement altogether, and weeks, months, nay even years rolled away with no other occupation but that and her devotions. There were times when she even flattered herself that the unremitting attention which she

paid to him was not without some material advantage
to his general state. She even thought she saw some
amendment in a seeming approach to a certain degree of
consciousness. Words, though altogether incoherent and
unconnected, would now and then break from him, as if
he was following out and giving utterance to some musing
dream; and on such occasions she would hang over him
with anxious fondness and intense interest, with the hope
of catching their meaning. Then she could distinctly
perceive that at such times his glassy eyes, which were
usually directed upon vacancy, would fix themselves upon
her, assume a strange and unwonted animation, as if the
dormant spirit had arisen for a moment and come to the
windows of its earthly house, to look out upon her,—
but alas! when she turned slowly away to try its powers,
there was no corresponding motion of the head to maintain
the proper direction and level of the eyes towards their
object, and she would weep at the cruel failure of her hopes
that followed.

It did happen, however, that one day whilst she was
sitting by her uncle, earnestly engaged in trying such
experiments as these, with the sunshine strong upon her
face, his lack-lustre eyes being fixed in her direction, they
seemed slowly to gather a spark of the fire of intelligence,
which went on gradually increasing like the light of dawn,
till suddenly they received such an animating illumination
as this earth does when the blessed orb of day bursts
from behind a cloud; and as all nature then rejoices under
the warm influence of his rays, so was the fond heart of
his niece gladdened when, as she moved her face slowly
from its position, and to this side and to that, the eyes of
the nabob followed all her motions with a growing expression, that speedily began to spread itself with a faint
glow over his hitherto frozen features. The lolling tongue
retreated within the orifice of the mouth, the under jaw
was drawn up, and the teeth were pressed together as if
with the increasing earnestness of the gaze. His niece,
with more than that degree of intensity of absorption of
attention with which an alchemist might be supposed to
have watched for the projection of the golden harvest of
his hopes, seized a hand of her uncle in each of hers, and
sat poring into his eyes, and over every feature of his
face in breathless expectation.

"Chirsty Ross," said he at length, slowly and distinctly, and in a manner that left no doubt that the words were not accidental.

"My dear, dear uncle, you know me then at last!" cried the happy girl, warmly embracing him, and sobbing upon his bosom. "Thank God! thank God that you know me!"

"Chirsty," said the nabob again, "why did you not write to me sooner? Why was you silent for a whole winter? I have been rash, perhaps. But what is done cannot be undone, and we must e'en make the best of it now. Yet, if you had only but written to me, Chirsty, my love, things might have been different."

"Oh, this is too heart-rending!" cried his niece, yielding to an ungovernable paroxysm of grief.

"How could you forget to write to me, Chirsty?" continued her uncle. "The woman, to be sure, is not so bad a woman after all; but you and I were so happy here alone together. But I have been a fool, Chirsty; yet she is your aunt, and my wife, so we must e'en submit, and make the best of it."

"Gracious Providence, support me in this trying hour!" cried Chirsty fervently.

"What!" cried the nabob, in a voice louder than she could have supposed his exhausted state could have admitted of. "What! is the ship to sail for Calcutta so soon? May the God of all goodness be with you then, Chirsty, my love! Keep up your spirits, my sweet girl, you will come home to me soon with a husband and pagodas in plenty. But forget not to write often to me. Your failing in that has already worked evil enough to us both."

"Oh, my dear, dear uncle!" cried Chirsty, quite overpowered by her feelings, and sobbing audibly.

"Nay, cry not so bitterly, my dear child," said the nabob. "Trust me, we shall meet again. And if we should not meet again here—if it should please God to remove me from this world ere you return, our sound Christian hope assures us, that we shall meet in another and a better. But, hold!" cried he with a more than natural energy, that seemed to be produced by some sudden and great organic change in his system. "The anchor is up—quick, aboard, aboard! God for ever bless and guard you, my love! my Chirsty!—farewell! Ha! the gallant ship, see how her sails swell with the breeze! —she goes—she goes merrily. But—but—how comes this sudden darkness over me? She is gone!—all is gone!— gone!—go—o—oh!" and his words terminated in a long deep groan.

Chirsty hastily dried up her tears, and anxiously scanned her uncle's face. His spirit had once more retreated from his glassy eyes—his face had again become deadly pale— his hands were cold, and their pulses had ceased. She shrieked aloud until help came, but it was too late—her uncle was dead.

Chirsty was no sooner made certain that all was over with her poor uncle than her nervous feelings, which had been screwed up to the racking pitch by this trying scene, gave way, and she fell in a swoon, that terminated in a repetition of that feverish attack which she had had in India, upon which delirium supervened; and when, after a period of nearly three weeks, she was again sensible of the return of reason, she found herself lying in bed with her hands muffled, as they had been the first night she had slept in the asylum. She awaked from a long, tranquil, and refreshing sleep; and little Nancy, who was seated by her bedside, immediately ran off for Sarah, who came directly.

"Aye," said that hideous creature, after surveying her countenance attentively, "she seems quiet enough now. The fit has gone off for this bout."

"I have been very ill," said Chirsty faintly, "but now, thank God, I am better."

"You have given me trouble enough i'facks," said Sarah. "But here is something that the doctor ordered you to drink; take this, and try to sleep again."

Chirsty readily swallowed what was given to her, fell asleep, and was soon well enough to quit her bed, and to be restored to that degree of freedom of person within her cell that she had enjoyed before the discovery that her uncle was under the same roof with herself. She was even allowed to go down once a day, for an hour, attended by Sarah, to breathe the open air, and to walk backwards and forwards in the narrow well of a court that was formed by that wing of the building which contained her cell. But this indulgence did little to relieve the insufferable tedium that seized upon her, now that the only object capable of interesting her had been removed. Her mind now recurred with augmented force to all the horrors of her iniquitous confinement. She resolved to try whether she could not move the compassion of her female Cerberus.

"Now that my uncle is gone," said she one day calmly to Sarah, "my confinement becomes so much more cruel and unnecessary, that I am sure you must feel for me. You have now known enough of me during the long period I have been under your care to be sufficiently aware that there never were any grounds for placing me in an asylum of this kind. If, then, I am shut up here for no other cause than that I may not give offence to Mrs. Ross by crossing her path, I am quite willing to give any security that may be asked of me that I will go down directly to live with my friends in Ross-shire, and that she shall never see or be troubled with me more."

"What!" exclaimed the wretch who listened to her; "what! and lose the good board which that worthy woman, your aunt, pays for you? No, no! Enough that we have already lost that which she paid for that mummy of a husband of hers. Yet, after all, he lived longer than one might have thought un like to have done. But you—an we but take care of you—you may long be a sure annual rent to us!"

"Can nothing move you?" said Chirsty, with a despairing look.

"No," said the wretch, with an iron grin. "I am not to be flattered from my trust. But what said you? No grounds for placing you here, quotha! Was it not but the other day that, strong as I am, it took all my power to hold ye down. Ha! ha! ha! The surest sign of madness is the belief that you are not mad."

"Then must my hope be in the Lord alone," said Chirsty, in a desponding tone. "But oh! if you would have me live, let me have books or work, or writing or drawing materials, or this painfully irksome confinement must soon kill me."

"No, no," said Sarah, shaking her head, "no, no. Writing or drawing materials might be used to send tales out beyond these walls, and books might be used as paper— aye, and work might answer the same end. Therefore content yourself, content yourself, child. I'll do all for

you that such a feeling heart as mine can do for a poor
fellow-creetur robbed of reason, as you have been. But I
must fulfil the duty I am paid for."

It happened that the very next day after this, as Chirsty
sat with her eyes cast down on the floor of her cell, some
small glittering body attracted her notice, and on stooping
to pick it up, to her great joy she discovered that it was a
needle, which had probably dropped from the sleeve of
little Nancy, who usually waited on her. She secured the
treasure about her person, as of infinite value, and the possession of it gave rise to a train of reflection that ended in
the formation of a scheme for ultimately producing her
liberation, which henceforward engrossed all her attention.
Provided as she had thus so fortunately been with a needle,
she was yet destitute of thread. But her necessity instantly
made her think of using her long black hair, with which
she resolved immediately to undertake the laborious task
of embroidering the outline of her melancholy story on a
cambric handkerchief, with the hope that some means might
occur to her of thereby communicating the place of her
confinement to her friends in Scotland. Eagerly did she
sit down to begin the task, but she wept when she discovered, what she had not hitherto been aware of, that the
first two or three hairs which she pulled were of a white as
pure as that of the handkerchief which was to be the field
of her work. Her miseries, however, had not as yet done
all the work of age upon her raven tresses; for enough still
remained of a silken and glossy jet to have embroidered a
whole volume. Such were her feelings at the time, however, that, dreading the change that might yet take place
she knew not how quickly, she rent forth such a quantity
of the precious material as might, at least, secure the com-
pletion of her purpose, and having carefully secreted it, she
went to work with an eagerness that seemed to promise to
lend her a new existence ; and, indeed, the occupation and
the hope it yielded her kept her up under all her afflictions
for the months and months that elapsed ere she stealthily
brought her work to a conclusion.

And after it was finished her heart sank within her, for
occupation was at an end, and now her dread arose that
the work would be fruitless ; for where was the hope, in
her circumstances, that she might ever find a messenger
fit to be entrusted with such a charge. Whilst employed

in the work her mind was tranquillised. But now it was thrown into a state of continued nervous excitement, which could not but have a tendency to wear it out. It did happen that, in her way down by the various passages and stairs that led to the little court whither she was daily summoned for exercise, she sometimes, though very rarely, met with strangers passing upwards to visit some unfortunate friend or relative. With none of these dared she to have communicated verbally; and if she had so dared, a word from her stern keeper to strangers in such a place would have turned the most sober expression of perfect sanity into the semblance of the mere utterance of hopeless madness. But if she could in any way manage to put her embroidered history into feeling and charitable hands, she trusted that the curiosity at least of the individual might save it from being either exposed or destroyed, and if so, hope might be interwoven with its living threads. Each time that her cell was opened, therefore, to allow her to descend to the little court her heart beat high. But, alas! day after day, and week after week, passed away, and no one came at the fortunate minute.

At length, as she was one day descending one of the flights of stairs, with Sarah close behind her, she met with an old gentleman having a particular lameness in one leg, who was limping up with a crutch. He stood aside to allow her to pass, and the pity, not unmingled with admiration, that seemed to animate his face as he earnestly looked upon her, made her almost accuse herself of folly for not having boldly risked the venture of putting the handkerchief into his hands. But a little thought told her that, if she had done so, all her labour and all her hopes would have been utterly wrecked, for she remembered that the keen eyes of Sarah had been close at her elbow, and detection would have been certain. Several other individuals passed her at different times, but the countenance of none of them gave her sufficient confidence to trust them, even if an opportunity had been afforded her, and every day her nervous excitement and irritability grew more and more distressing.

It happened one day, however, that as she was moving along a passage, she heard and recognised the particular *stump* of the lame gentleman whom she had formerly met. She could not be mistaken, and it was then entering on the

lowest step of a flight, down which she was about to turn.
She was then a pace or two ahead of Sarah, and contriving
to lengthen her stride as she approached the turn at the
stairs, she passed a keeper who was hurrying on to open
the various locks of a cell which the stranger he was con-
ducting was about to visit. Thus it was that, by fortunate
accident, she was brought alone and unseen into contact
with the gentleman for a few brief but precious moments.
Nerved up by the importance of the act, she expanded her
handkerchief before him, to show what it contained, put it
into his hand, and with an imploring look that spoke
volumes, she signed to him to conceal it, and as she passed
him by she quickly whispered him,—

"Hide it now?—read it at home—and, oh ! for mercy's
sake, act upon it."

Taken thus by surprise, the stranger held it for a
moment in his hand, and turned to look after her who
gave it him. Sarah appeared whilst he was still standing
thus. Chirsty stood on the lowest step, and looked up to
him in breathless and motionless dread.

"What stand ye there for?" cried Sarah roughly to her,
as she was descending.

The stranger seemed to recover his self-possession. He
quietly returned the salutation which Sarah gave him, and
wiping his face with the handkerchief, as if it had been
his own pulled forth for that purpose, he thrust it deep
into his bosom, and began again to climb the steps.
Chirsty, overpowered by her feelings, leaned for a moment
against the wall.

"What's the matter with ye?" cried Sarah impatiently.

"Nothing, nothing, good Sarah!" said Chirsty, "only a
sudden qualm of sickness, but it has gone off now;" and
so saying, she pursued her way with tottering steps.

If Chirsty was subjected to anxious excitement before
she had thus disposed of her broidered history, how much
greater were her nervous agitations, her eternal tossings
between hope and fear, from the moment she had thus
committed it to the stranger? Had he betrayed her?
nay, if he had, she must have heard of it from Sarah, or
gathered it from the harsher treatment with which she
must have been visited. He must have been so far her
friend. But, admitting all this, whether he would have
charity enough to act upon his knowledge of the facts it

contained, or whether he would treat it as the mere pseudo-rational statement of a maniac, were matters of doubt that agonised her by night as well as by day. She slept not,—she ate not, and her brain grew lighter and lighter every day. She became sensible of this. A most unconquerable dread came upon her, that even admitting that the stranger was doing all he could to inform her friends of her unhappy situation, her senses would be undermined before they could come to her relief, and, as time wore on, and hope grew fainter and duller, she began to yield herself up to despair, which gradually threw its damp and suffocating clouds over her soul.

Whilst she was in this gloomy state, she happened one day to think of the needle, which she had now so much reason to fear had been but uselessly employed; and the horrible idea crossed her mind, that even such a small instrument as it might readily enough produce death, and that thus there was yet another and a more certain way in which it might be made to effect her deliverance from her present imprisonment. She immediately drew it forth from the skirt of her gown, where she had concealed it. She looked at it for some moments with a steady but agitated gaze; and then, earnestly imploring Heaven for aid in the fearful struggle she was undergoing, she started up, with a resolution acquired from above, and threw it from the window of her cell, that such wicked thoughts of self-destruction might never again be produced by it; and then, on her knees, she poured out her humble and submissive aspirations of thanks.

And now despondency gave way to resolution, and she at length determined to take the first opportunity of making a desperate attempt to effect her escape. But to produce even a hope of success, she saw that it would be necessary to use much preliminary artifice.

It was the more easy for her to employ this effectually, that hope had hitherto made her behaviour so mild and so submissive, that all suspicion on the part of her Argus-eyed keeper had been for a long time put to rest. Recollecting what Sarah had said to her as to the important source of revenue which hung on the preservation of her life, she began by complaining of that for which she had, indeed, no inconsiderable grounds of truth, that her health was suffering deeply from want of pure air and exercise.

This was touching Sarah in the very point where she was most assailable. She of herself proposed to extend Chirsty's walk to a garden belonging to the place, to the existence of which she had more than once heard her refer. Next day, accordingly, she was taken from her cell, and conducted by Sarah and Nancy down through the same passages, and by the same flights of stairs with which she was already so familiar; but instead of being led into the small court which had hitherto been the utmost extent to which freedom had been permitted her, she was ushered into a large and high-walled orchard or garden, quite umbrageous with fruit-trees, and thickly intermixed with shrubs. Who can fancy, with any approach to the reality, the delight which Chirsty felt whilst wandering among the blossoming shades of this, to her absolutely, celestial spot, after the years of confinement which she had undergone? She leaped—she skipped—she threw her arms about, and laughed as if she had really been the poor unsettled maniac who might have required the restraint she had been so long kept under. She poured out her thanks to Sarah with strange volubility; and as she was guilty of no excess that could alarm her keeper, she was not only readily permitted to remain there for a considerable time under her watchful eye, but she was returned to her cell with a promise that she should be permitted to revisit the garden daily.

The effect of this leniency and indulgence was a renovated state of health, perfectly wonderful in itself, and highly gratifying to Sarah. But although the spirits of the patient rose from the blessed influence of a more frequent intercourse with the sun and the sky, her anxious mind was still deeply possessed with the sad conviction that every day made the hope of help from her friends in Scotland less and less probable. Her determination to attempt an escape, therefore, strengthened with the improvement and increase of her physical energies. She never made the round of the garden without scanning every part of its inclosure with scrupulous care. In the course of this daily examination, she one day discovered that a half-witted lad, employed in nailing up the fruit trees, had carelessly left his light hand-ladder leaning against the wall in a corner, where it was in a certain degree hid by a buttress, and as she saw it in the same spot the next

day, she became satisfied that it was for the present
unwanted and forgotten. The very thought of this
as a means for getting over the wall, brought her ingenuity
into play; and as she at once saw that any attempt
at escape in broad daylight must necessarily be unsuccessful, she began to work upon her keeper to procure a
change of the mid-day hour of airing to that of evening.
As the garden was used at all times of the day as a place
of exercise for the less violent patients, she occasionally
encountered them during her walks. She therefore pretended to be seized with an unconquerable alarm at their
uncouth appearance, and she declared that it was impossible for her longer to avail herself of the privilege
which she enjoyed.

"I feel all your kindness to me, unfortunate creature
that I am," said she, in a tone of despondency, to Sarah
one day, when she came as usual to take her out. "But I
cannot bear to have my path crossed by those melancholy
objects; and, since it is Heaven's will that I am so
condemned to misery in this world, the sooner I am
relieved by death, and dismissed to a happier the better."

"No, no," said Sarah, who was fully alive to the
important improvement of Chirsty's health from the
change of system already pursued with her. "We must
not let ye die,—we can't afford that,—so walk out you
shall. And, since you are frightened by the sight of
them 'ere creeturs, we shall walk in the cool of the
evening, when they are all locked up."

"Thank you, thank you, Sarah," said Chirsty, overjoyed
at the success of this first part of her scheme.

Anxiously did Chirsty look every evening as she returned to the garden to ascertain whether the ladder
was still in its place, for she was obliged to allow one or
two nights to pass that she might use certain management
with Sarah to ensure something like a probability of
success. Under pretence of giving greater exercise to
her limbs, she began to jump and dance with Nancy.
Some time afterwards she proposed to play a game of hide
and seek with her. These sports were renewed for several
evenings, so that Sarah was not only lulled into perfect
security, but, hard as she was by nature, she was even
so much amused by the merriment of the little girl,
who was her niece, that Chirsty easily contrived that

each successive evening should prolong their sports, until she one night succeeded in remaining in the garden till twilight had almost become darkness. Then it was that she wound up all her energies to make her attempt.

"Well, well," said she carelessly, "I am almost tired now, Nancy ; but come, I will give you one chance more;" and off she went by way of hiding again among the bushes.

But no sooner was she out of sight, than, forcing her way through the thicket, she darted down a long alley with the speed of a hare, mounted the ladder to the top of the wall, drew it up after her, and letting it down on the other side, she was beyond the hated precincts of the asylum before Sarah or the little Nancy had begun to suspect that she was gone. Already did her hopes bound over all intermediate obstacles, and transport her in imagination to her father's humble dwelling at Tain. Finding herself in a lane, with the garden wall on one hand, and another equally high on the opposite side, she sprang forward without knowing whither she went. Loud screams and shouts came from within the garden. On she ran wildly until she was terror-struck for a moment, and arrested by hearing cries of alarm, and beholding the flaring of lights in the very direction in which she was running. The loud baying of the great dog also reached her ears from the same quarter. Winged by fear, she was thus forced to double back, and bethinking her of the ladder, she rapidly retraced her steps to the spot where she had left it. Taking it hastily down from the garden wall, she dragged it across the lane with the intention of applying it to that on the other side. Whilst her trembling hands were in the act of doing this, the harsh iron screams of Sarah came all of a sudden loudly up the lane from the opposite direction to that in which Chirsty had first attempted to fly. A postern-door of the garden had given the old woman egress at about fifty yards below. Dreadful was now the nervous agitation of poor Chirsty. Her utmost strength was necessary to rear the ladder, light as it was, against the wall. She did succeed, however. Her enraged and baffled keeper was toiling up to her, with her wide mouth uttering shrieks and imprecations that might have well been called infernal. Chirsty climbed the ladder with a palsy in all her joints. She was already on the top of the wall,—one moment more would have enabled her

20

to pull the ladder up beyond the reach of the infuriated
dwarf, and she had succeeded in raising it a considerable
way from the ground, when the uncouth monster reached
the spot, and clutching at the lower end of it with her long
hands, she with one powerful jerk, not only dragged it
down, but she so destroyed the equilibrium of the unfortunate fugitive, that she fell from the top of the wall
into the lane, where the hideous countenance and de-
moniac eyes of Sarah frowned and glared over her, and
the horrible laugh of triumph, and the blasphemous
denunciations of vengeance and punishment which the
monster uttered, rang in her ears ere she was borne
off senseless to the asylum.

You are doubtless desirous to know something of the
history of poor Charles Græme, who, as you may remember,
left India for the purpose of following Chirsty Ross to
England? I shall shortly tell you, that on reaching
Britain, he made ineffectual inquiries for her at her uncle's
residence. Mrs. Ross denied having ever seen or heard of
her. He did find out her Indian maid; but from the little
that she told him, he could make out no clue to lead to the
discovery of her mistress. And after many ineffectual
attempts, repeatedly made for months, he at length yielded
to the advice of his friends, and returned to India, where
he vainly endeavoured to eradicate the sorrow of his heart
by fresh and intense occupation.

After the lapse of a good many years, accident led a
gentleman to visit a noble friend of his, who was proprietor
of a fine estate and residence in Ross-shire. The roads
thereabouts were then so bad for wheeled carriages, that,
tired of the slowness of his progress and of the jolting of
his vehicle, he left it at an inn to come after him at its
own rate by a somewhat circuitous route, and mounting
his servant's horse, he set off unattended. Following the
directions he received from the people of the house, he
took what was called the shortest way, hoping that he
might yet save his distance so far as to reach his friend's
house to a late dinner. Many was the long Scottish mile
of ground which he travelled over, however; and still as
he interrogated the peasants whom he met with, he found
that the way before him seemed rather to be lengthening
than diminishing. His horse began to manifest great
symptoms of fatigue, and as the night was settling down

v.iey fast, he was glad to meet with a man who pointed out tərsim a track leading by the sea-shore, which, as he assured h do would save him several miles of distance. At the same time he told him, that he would require to push on smartly, so as to reach a certain ford at the mouth of a river, before the flowing tide should render it quite impracticable. Stimulated by this information, and being, moreover, impatient to get to his journey's end, he put spurs to his horse and galloped on as fast as the tired animal could go.

He had not proceeded very far, when a vivid flash of forked lightning blazed amid the obscurity that brooded over the sea, and a tremendous peal of thunder rent the air. The waves, which were gradually rising upon tho beach, seemed every moment to swell more proudly, and to toss their snowy crests higher, and suddenly a deluge of rain began to be poured from the gathered clouds. The somewhat delicate traveller wished himself again within his old box of a carriage in defiance of its jolting; but now, both in mercy to himself and to the animal he rode, he was compelled to force the poor creature on to an accelerated pace, that they might the sooner reach some place of shelter. As if fully aware of the necessity of exertion, his horse bore him with tolerable rapidity for two or three miles amidst the lightning and rain and the thunder that at times deafened the sound of the advancing waves, till, as the darkness was just about to become complete, he dimly descried the huge mass of an ancient building rising before him from a low peninsula; and, on further investigation, he discovered that he had reached the river of which the peasant had spoken. A very cursory examination only was necessary to assure him that the stream was already so swollen by the rain and the tide as to take away all hope of his being able to ford. The river was a raging torrent, and the roar of its conflict with the swelling tide, was a terrific addition to the horrors of the storm. The gentleman had no alternative left, therefore, but to look for hospitality in the adjoining building.

Having dismounted then, he led his horse in at a gateway; and, having discovered a dilapidated outhouse, with a half entire roof, he contrived to fasten the animal by the bridal to a rusty iron hook that projected out of the wall. He then made his way across a court-yard so covered with tall docks and nettles as very much to discourage any hope which he might have previously entertained of finding inhabitants within the edifice ; but, as he groped his way towards the great door of the huge pile, he was cheered by beholding a light that glimmered through the unglazed and broken casements of what appeared to be a large apartment about two stories up, whence he distinctly heard the singing of a woman's voice. Somewhat encouraged by this circumstance, and guided by the faint gleam, he tried the ponderous old oaken door, but he found that it was firmly secured within. He was about to apply his hand to a large rusty iron knocker that hung upon it, when his attention was arrested by a wild laugh which echoed through the apartments above, died away, and was again more than once repeated with strange, sudden, and incomprehensible changes. Some of those superstitious feelings of which his infancy had largely partaken for a moment seized upon him, and he doubted whether the building was not tenanted by beings with whom those of this world could not dare to have intercourse. But a little thought, and a little more attention to the voice, soon reassured him against anything supernatural, and he then began to question himself whether he might not be about to rouse some body of lawless banditti or smugglers who might have taken possession of that which was evidently a ruined castle, as a place for their retreat or rendezvous. Was it prudent to proceed? But he was a man who never feared danger in youth ; and, now that youth was long past with him, certain bitter disappointments he had met with in early life, and the consequent sorrow which his heart had ever since endured, rendered him now much too careless about mere existence ever to allow any anxiety regarding that to influence his conduct, even if the deluge of rain which was then falling had not been enough to stimulate the faintest heart to the bold determination of making good an entrance at all hazards. Raising the knocker, therefore, he made a furious appeal to those within. But whether it was that the roar of the thunder, the rumbling of the river, the booming of the waves, and the continued plash of the rain, combined to drown his efforts, or to render the inmates deaf to his summons, he found it necessary to repeat his loud larum several times ere his ear caught the sound of a step descending the stair from above.

The stair was included in one of those curious thin round towers which are so frequently seen rising from the side of ᵗʰe doorway of these old Scottish castles, and a small window about half a story up seemed to have been placed there to enable the appearance of all applicants for entrance to be well reconnoitred before admission should be granted to them, whilst a small round arrow or musket hole on a level with their heads, enabled them to be easily and successfully assailed from below, if they were likely to be at all troublesome. A flaring light streamed suddenly out from the small window above, and threw a partial and fitful gleam over a part of the dripping weeds of the wet court-yard. It proceeded from a lighted torch of bog-fir, and the stranger's attention was instantly arrested by the apparition that brandished it aloft with a bare extended arm. It was a woman, whose countenance, though wasted, and tarnished, and rendered wiry, as it were, by exposure to weather, yet exhibited features of the noblest character, so that even a momentary glance at them and the dark eyes that flashed from them with a wild expression, as the torch which she held forth threw back its flickering light upon them, convinced the stranger that they must have been once beautiful.

"Who comes at this unseasonable hour to these my castle gates?" demanded the woman, in a haughty tone.

"A single traveller overtaken by night and by this pelting rain," replied the stranger, "from which, with your kind permission, he would fain find a temporary shelter."

"Aha!" exclaimed the woman again, with a curious expression of extreme and cunning caution, "dost think that these gates of mine ever turn upon their hinges to admit any guests but those who come in their gilt coaches, —aye, and with their running footmen and out-riders too?"

"I doubt not what you say," replied the stranger; "but I am at this moment acting the part of my own out-rider; I left my carriage to go by another road, whilst I came on this way on horseback. Pray, good madam, send down one of your people, and his inspection of my horse, which I have used the freedom to tie up in your stable, will no doubt satisfy you."

"My people! ha! ha! ha!" exclaimed she laughing wildly, "you look to be a gentleman, though, Heaven knows, looks are never to be trusted in this deceitful world.

But I will see you nearer," and having disappeared from
the window, he heard her step descending the lower flight
of the stair. After a few moments of a pause, the heavy
bolts were withdrawn, and the door was slowly opened to
about one-third of its extent. Although prepared to behold
something rather extraordinary, the gentleman was absolutely startled by the appearance of the woman who now
stood before him. He had already seen her countenance,
but now he could perceive that her hair was exceedingly
long and untamed, and whilst the greater part of it was
white or grizzled, as if from premature failure, it still contained what, if properly dressed, might have been called
tresses of the most beautiful glossy black, and the strange
effect of this unnatural intermixture of the livery of youth
and of age, was heightened by the wild combination of such
fantastical wreaths of heather and sea-weed, mingled with
sea-birds' feathers, as insanity is usually so fond of adopting
by way of finery. Her arms were bare to the shoulders,
and her bust was but imperfectly covered by a coarse canvas shirt. A red flannel petticoat that descended to her
knees, and which was confined at the waist by a broad
leathern belt, was the only other piece of drapery that she
wore. She stood before the stranger exhibiting the wrecks
of a form of the most exquisite mould, and her whole
appearance betraying the fact, that whatever the soul that
animated it might have once been, its reason was now obscured by the darkness arising from confirmed derangement.

"Enter my castle, sweet sir!" said the maniac in a
gentle and subdued voice, and at the same time courtseying
with a grace which might have better befitted the attire of
a court than that which she wore. "Enter my castle, and
I will speedily usher you up to the grand banqueting-
room. But stay," added she, with a sudden and wild
change of manner, after he had obeyed her invitation, "I
must make my gates secure against the wretches, they
might find me out even here. Bolt! bolt! bolt! there my
brave bolts," she continued, changing her speech into a
chant, as if addressing them in incantation,—

> "Keep your wards,
> Be faithful guards,—
> And you, master-key,
> Great warden shall be;
> To defend me from force and from traitorie."

"Come along, sir," continued she, again changing to a wild mood; "this way—I have a pride and a pleasure in personally attending on so distinguished a guest, as your whole appearance and manners declare you to be."

The gentleman followed his conductress up the half-ruined screw stair, which here and there exhibited fearful chasms, from the entire absence of two or three successive steps, over which she skipped without the least hesitation, whilst he was obliged to thrust his nails into the crevices of the wall to hoist himself over the difficulty. But after he had ascended two flights, he came to a landing-place where there was a doorway entering into that large hall, from which he had first heard the voice of the maniac. Into this she led the way, and as he was about to follow her, you may imagine his astonishment when I tell you he discovered that the whole flooring was gone except the bare oaken beams, and the apartments below being in the same state, his eyes stretched uninterruptedly downwards till vision was lost in the impenetrable darkness of the dungeons below. But his conductress hesitated not a moment, and went onwards from beam to beam, with as much indifference as she would have walked across a paved court, until she gained the great hearth, which, with a small portion of the planking in its vicinity, was still entire, and where a fire of wood was burning under the huge projecting chimney.

"Come, sir," said the maniac, smiling courteously, "never mind your wet boots; don't stand upon ceremony, I pray you, your long ride and the state of the weather are sufficient apologies. Here is a seat by the fire for you."

She then busied herself in placing an old rotten-looking chair, which appeared to have once had a back, and which seemed to have belonged to the castle in its better days, whilst she seated herself on an opposite stool, and began to arrange her head-gear, to run her taper fingers, with nails on them like eagle's talons, through her long hair, and to twist it round into certain curls that had now probably become natural from the art and care which had once been bestowed upon them. Meanwhile, the stranger, after bracing up his nerves and steadying his head, and balancing his person, with some difficulty and hazard accomplished the perilous passage.

"You must be hungry, sir, after your ride," said the

maniac, in the same mild tone. " I was about to sup when
you came in. Perhaps you will have no objections to join
me." And then suddenly changing in her tone, and bursting into an uncouth laugh, as she looked into a pot that
hung simmering over the fire—" Ha !—ha !—ha !—hah !—
see !—the water has boiled well. The lightning has helped
to do that for me. I am the favoured one ! The very
elements are my cooks ! Hah ! did you see where it came
again? flash—zigzag—zigzag. Now 'tis time to mix the
pudding," and, thrusting her hand into a large square hole
in the wall, she dragged out, first a bag of oatmeal, and then
a small wooden vessel full of salt, and with an earnestness
which for the time absorbed her attention from everything
else, she proceeded to put the ingredients into the pot, and
to stir them about with a large wooden spoon.

"Now for my silver dish !" said she again, as she pulled
forth a pewter basin from the same recess in the wall.
"Well is it for me that my gates are watched and warded,
else would robbers soon carry off this rare treasure of my
castle. See here now—ha ! ha ! ha ! let us begin the feast."
And as she said so, she filled the pewter basin from the
pot, by means of the wooden spoon, and set it between
them on an old box turned upside down, and drawing
forth a couple of pewter spoons from her curious cupboard,
she handed one to the stranger.

"Hah !" said she sternly, as she broke into a more
violent state of excitement than she had hitherto exhibited,
"do you see that mark ?" And as she said this, she drew
with her forefinger a line of division across the surface of
the mess that stood between them—" That's your half and
this is mine ; so take care what you do, for I'll have no
foul play—men *can* cheat !—but I'm hungry, and I must
have my food ; so see to it that you eat no more than what
is your own."

The mind of the traveller was too much filled with this
strange and distressing scene to admit of his appetite leading him to infringe on the rule thus prescribed to him,
even if the food itself had been much more inviting than
it really was ; on the contrary, he had hardly eat a third
part of his way up to the boundary line, when he found
that his hostess had scupulously given it a straight edge
upon her side.

"Come !" said she, in an angry tone of voice, quite

different from any she had hitherto used; "eat up your
share! do you think I want it? Come, there is no poison
in it. Come! come!"

"I do, I do," said the gentleman, pretending to eat;
and every now and then contriving to throw unobserved a
large spoonful down between the beams; until, partly by
eating, and partly by this occasional manœuvre, he at last
succeeded in emptying the dish.

"Now, sir!" said the maniac, resuming all the quiet and
decorous demeanour of a well-bred woman, " a little gentle
exercise after supper conduces to good repose. I shall be
happy to give you my hand for a minuet."

Pushing back the seats they had occupied, she seized the
stranger's hand, and took her position beside him on the
hearth. He offered no opposition to her proposal; and
she immediately began to sing with great brilliancy and
effect that minuet so well known to our grandsires and
grandmothers under the name of the *Minuet de la Cour.*
Following the example of his entertainer, the gentleman
was obliged to make his preliminary bows corresponding
to her preliminary courtesies; and had any eye looked
upon the couple as they were thus employed, it might have
been naturally enough supposed that he danced with some
handsome lady of quality disguised in a fancy dress, so
perfectly did the grace of her attitudes assimilate themselves to the various movements of the minuet. But the
gentleman had not altogether calculated the nature of his
present undertaking. The spot of terra firma on which the
dance commenced was by no means large enough for the
extent of one-tenth part of the figure of the minuet; and a
less bold man than he would have felt anything but
tranquillity of mind, when his insane partner, giving him
her hand, glided with him over the beams, amidst the half
light that proceeded from the decaying embers, like some
spirit from the other world. But if this was alarming,
what were his feelings, when, after the slow part of the
minuet was over, she began to carol the sprightly gavot
which follows it, with a clear voice, that made the lofty
vaulted roof ring again, whilst she darted off and called to
him to follow. So, indeed, he found himself compelled to
do; but whilst he, at the risk of his life, contented himself
with keeping up something like a semblance of the
figure, he was astonished and appalled to see his partner

go through the whole dance with all that activity which might have been exhibited on a common floor by the ablest professional dancer. Though he felt not for himself, his hair actually stood on end as he looked with trembling on her, whom he expected every moment to see disappear from his eyes into that abyss of darkness that lay below; and great was his relief from anxiety when the dance was at last terminated on the hearthstone where it began.

"And now, gentle sir," said the maniac, "you are doubtless well prepared for your night's repose after this healthful exercise. Let me see that your sleeping apartment is ready."

Had the roaring elements without permitted the stranger to have again ventured abroad, he saw that he could not have possessed himself of the keys of the outer door without the employment of force, which his feeling heart never could have allowed him to have attempted. He therefore sat patiently waiting until his hostess crossed the beams, and went into a small stone closet opening in the wall, whence she speedily returned, and lifting a lighted brand of bog-fir from the fire, she presented it to him with the same air as if she had been putting a silver candlestick, with a wax candle in it, into his hand; and taking up another for herself, she, with all the delicacy of the most refined lady, wished him a good night, and retired into a room on the other side of the hall similar to that which she had indicated to him. Before retreating to his dormitory, the gentleman took the precaution to rake the fire together, and to add to it one or two pieces of wood, which were piled up in the chimney near it, so as to keep up a certain degree of light in the place. He then moved across the beams to the stone closet, where he found a heap of ferns nicely spread over heather, and putting his cloak on, which had by this time become tolerably dry, he lay quietly down to try to procure a little repose.

He had not lain long until he was awakened by several rats running over him, and on looking out at the open door which gave him a view into the large apartment, he beheld swarms of these creatures gambolling about on the beams. Whilst he was lying watching their motions, he was surprised to perceive his hostess crawling silently forth on hands and knees from the small place she had

occupied. Suddenly she sprang upon the rats with all the
agility of a cat, flew after them hither and thither, with
wild and frantic yells, leaping at the walls in such a
manner that she absolutely seemed to scramble up a
portion of their height in the eagerness of her pursuit.
The chase lasted until all the rats had disappeared, but ere
it terminated, several of them had fallen victims to her
wonderful expertness in capturing them. Proceeding then
to the hearth, she seated herself on the stool by the fire,
in a state of great excitement, and inserting her long nails
into them, she stripped off their skins one after the other
with inconceivable expedition, and as she did so, she rose
up from time to time and suspended the bleeding reptiles
on tenter-hooks on one side of the chimney among many
others which the stranger had not till then observed,
whilst she attached their skins to a similar set of hooks on
the other side of the fire, amongst a corresponding number
of trophies of the same kind.

"This is for my winter beef," said she in a wild soliloquy,
"and this is for my winter cloak!" This she repeated as
every new occasion required, till all were stowed away.
After which the furious fit seemed to subside; and soon
afterwards she retired to her bed, where she lay so quiet
as to give no more disturbance to her stranger guest, till
both were roused by the early dawn.

The morning was a smiling one, and as if she had partaken of its peaceful nature, she was again in one of her
gentle lady-like humours.

"Will you walk, sweet sir?" said she to her guest, with
a profound courtesy. "Will you walk forth to see the
morning sun kissing the opening flowers and drinking up
the dewdrops from their lips? This way," continued she,
as she ushered him down the broken stair, and silently
opened the locks and bolts of the outer door.

"I thank you most sincerely for your hospitality, Madam,"
said the traveller to her whilst she was carefully locking
the door behind her. "I must now bid you farewell. I
see my horse has had the good sense to break out from his
stable during the night to feed on yonder rich bank of
grass, so that he must be well enough refreshed by this
time to be able to finish my journey."

"What," exclaimed the maniac with a sudden transition
to her highest pitch of excitement, and with great rapidity

of utterance, "are *you* going to leave me too? Did you not come to this my castle to woo me for your bride? And are you going to leave me too? But I forget, I forget," continued she, sinking into a low thoughtful tone of feeling, whilst tears came rushing to her eyes and rolled down her cheeks. "I must not forget that I am pledged in my own mind. There was but one that ever truly loved me, and him I lost by being true to a base deceiver."

"What said you?" exclaimed the stranger with intense interest.

"I say that men are deceivers!" cried she with her wildest tone and gesture; and then becoming gradually calm, she went on singing with great pathos,—

> " Sigh no more ladies,
> Ladies sigh no more,
> Men were deceivers ever,
> Men were deceivers ever,
> One foot on sea and one on shore——

Yes! yes! on sea!—how many vows did that false man of the sea utter! and how cruelly did he break them on shore!"

"What do I hear?" exclaimed the gentleman. "The very song! the very song we so often sang in duet together at Calcutta!"

"Calcutta!" cried the maniac, earnestly seizing his wrist, and in a tone of deep feeling; "yes, I sang that song often at Calcutta with one who tenderly loved me. How often do I think on that!"

"Merciful powers!" cried the stranger, as he suddenly observed a small Indian wrought ring on the little finger of that hand by which she had for a moment held his; "by all that is wonderful, it is the ring! the very ring! Let me see that ring!"

"No!" said the maniac, in a high, haughty, and determined manner; "it shall never be touched by you nor any one else. *He* gave it to me—I have worn it—I have preserved it through all my miserable sufferings, and it shall go with me," added she, fervently kissing it; "it shall go with me to my cold cold grave."

"Stop, stop!" cried the gentleman, as she was turning away from him; "avoid me not! I am he who gave it you!"

"You!" cried she, stopping suddenly in her retreat, drawing herself up to her full height, and looking back upon him with an air of the most sovereign contempt; "you Charles Græme!—Ha! ha! ha! ha!—you Charles Græme!—His face was fair, and with the expression of an angel; yours is sallow, withered, and wrinkled, like that of a baboon—his hair was lovely as the beams of the morning sun; yours is white, as the eternal snow of the Himala—his form was like that of the Grecian Apollo; yours is like that of winter. Go, traitorous man! I have had enough of falsehood! Come not near me! Chirsty Ross will wed no one now but Charles Græme or the grave!"

In an instant she darted from his sight, before he was aware of her intention, and she disappeared among the ruins. In the wildest state of agitation he rushed after her. He thought he heard a faint shriek, but he vainly sought her with unremitting solicitude for some hours. Believing at length that she must have got into the interior of the building by some secret passage known only to herself, he unwillingly gave up his search, and the sea having now ebbed, and the flood in the river having somewhat subsided, he mounted his horse, with some difficulty crossed the ford, and, oppressed with sorrowful thoughts, he slowly made his way to the castle of his noble friend, to whom he confided his sad tale. From him he learned much that was new to him. A cambric handkerchief, embroidered with Chirsty's story, had found its way to her friends, who, after many difficulties, succeeded in rescuing her from her confinement. But alas! they found her not till her sufferings had rendered her a confirmed maniac. For a time she felt soothed by the kindness shown her by her afflicted parents; and during the short time they lived, she amused herself by wandering harmlessly about the scenes of her childhood. But when her father and mother were both dead, and all her other relatives being likewise gone or removed, she abandoned her home and took up her abode in the ruinous building, of which she was for the most part left in undisturbed possession. Such was the melancholy outline of her history.

But Charles Græme was too feelingly alive to her unhappy situation to delay one moment in attempting to find her, that he might spend the remainder of his life in watching over and protecting her. Next day, therefore, assisted by his friend's people, he made his way into the ruins, and sought every part of them. But he sought in vain. Everything remained as when he had left them on the previous morning, and although the door was locked, the bolts on the inside were not fastened, showing that the wretched inhabitant had not returned.

But the mystery was cleared up towards mid-day by a fisherman, who, as he was landing from his boat, found her lifeless body on the sands, where it had been left by the receding tide. The supposition was that she had been drowned in attempting to ford the swollen river, immediately after the scene of her parting with Charles Græme.

COMPLIMENTARY CRITICISM.

Dominie.—'Pon my word, Mr. Clifford, you have given us good measure indeed; and of ane excellent *faybric*, too. As I shall answer, we are well on with the small hours.

Grant (pulling out his watch)—Is it possible? I declare I thought that it had been only about ten o'clock. Why, it is a good hour and a half after midnight.

Clifford.—I was resolved to reel you out a good long line while I was about it. I thought that it was but fair to give Mr. Macpherson an opportunity of being even with me, by enjoying as good a slumber as I had last night, but his politeness was proof against the soporific influence of my tale.

Dominie.—Your tale would have been as good as an *umberella* against all the drowsy drops that ever were shaken from the bough of Morpheus himself.

Author.—Perhaps it might; but now that the umbrella is taken down, the dewy balm of the god begins to descend very heavily upon my eyelids.

Grant.—Come, then, let us to bed.

The next morning's sun found us all later in bed than usual. After breakfast we left the village, and winding down through the forest of tall pines that lies between it and the river, and crossing the ancient bridge, we left the Spey behind us, and climbed the old military mountain road that leads towards Tomantoul.

Clifford (stopping and looking back over the valley)—What a grand Highland prospect!

Grant.—How proudly the grim old castle domineers over the extended forests, and the country of which it is the lord paramount! Let us sit down on this green bank of velvet grass, and enjoy the view. See how happily that single touch of bright light falls on the Cumin's tower.

Clifford.—Well thought off. Talking of the Cumins, we must not allow you to leave us, Mr. Macpherson,

without telling us the story of Gibbon More, to which
you alluded at Castle Grant.

Dominie.—I must tell it to you now then, gentlemen;
for I grieve to say that I must part from you at the top
of the hill a little way farther on. So, if you have a
mind to sit down and enjoy this refreshing breeze for a
little time, I shall give you the legend in as few words
as I can.

LEGEND OF GIBBON MORE CUMIN AND HIS DAUGHTER BIGLA.

If you will be pleased to remember, gentlemen, I already told you, that previous to the fourteenth century the whole of Strathspey was subjeck to that great clan or nation the Cumins. It was about that period, as I informed you, that the Grants, from Glen Urquhart, were, by royal favour, enabled to possess themselves of Freuchie, —a place of strength, so called from a certain heathery hillock near to which it stood. The Cumin's tower was probably part of that original building which, in the course of generations, has grown up into that great baronial pile which we now behold yonder. It is natural to imagine that the Cumins could not possibly regard this alienation of the property of their clan without its begetting their hatred against those who benefited by it, though they dared not always to show it by open deeds of violence. Their submission, however, was by no means owing to their weakness, for, notwithstanding that the Grants thus got a footing in this country, so powerful did the Cumins continue for a while, that many were the strangers that came from other clans to reside among them for protection, as was not uncommon in that olden time of trouble; these fugitives changed their own names for that of the people among whom they had thus found a safe retreat. But they were never admitted to a full participation in all the rights of the clan Cuminich, without submitting to undergo a very odd sort of an irreverential baptism, altogether worthy of the iron age in which it was practeesed.

Gilbert Cumin, Lord of Glenchearnich, as that country, watered by the river Dulnan, was denominated, was usually called Gibbon More, from his enormous size and strength. His chief residence was at Kincherdie, on the north-western bank of the Spey, on the brink of the river, just where there is now a ferry across to

21

Gartenmore, the vurra place, sir, where, as you have
recorded in your book of "The Floods," the worthy Mrs.
Cameron made her miraculous voyage upon a brander.
The old chronicler tells us, that the house stood on a
green moat, fenced by a ditch, the vestiges of which are
yet to be seen. A current tradition beareth, that at night
a salmon net was cast into the pool below the wall of
the house, and a small rope tied to the net, and brought
in at the window, had a bell hung at it, which rung
when a salmon came in and shook the net, so that the
beast was quickly transferred from the river to the pot.
What think ye of that, Mr. Clifford?

Clifford.—Very ingenious! but foul poaching.

Well, whilst Gibbon More Cumin flourished, the ceremony of Cumin-making was always performed by his own
hands. At the door of his castle there stood a huge
stone, which I have often myself seen when I was a boy,
and which, for ought I know, may be still in existence.
It was hollowed out in the middle like an ancient
baptismal font, and, indeed, it is by no means unlikely
that it had been originally formed as such. Be this as
it may, however, Gibbon More had it always filled with
water for the refreshment of his fowls. But, besides its
uniform devotion to the truly ignoble purposes of his
poutry, it was also employed by him in the unseemly
rites to which I have referred. When any of the strangers
of whom I have spoken had a desire to be metamorphosed
into a Cumin, he was brought incontinently to Kincherdie.
There the gigantic Lord of Glenchearnich, with the
observance of very great and decorous form, lifted him
up, and having slowly and solemnly reversed the natural
perpendicular position of the poor sinner, he held him
up by the heels, as Thetis did her infant boy Achilles,
and having dipped his head three times amid the pollutory
potation, as I may call the hen's water that filled the
hollow stone, he set him, gasping and gaunting, upright
on his legs again, telling him, in a stately tone, henceforward *to live and do like a Cumin as he now was.* But,
notwithstanding this cantrip of Gibbon More's, there was
a marked distinction still preserved between those who
were Cumins by blood and those who were thus manu-
factured by him by virtue of the chuckies' water, for these
children of adoption and their descendants had always

the degrading addition given to them of *Cuminich clach-
nan-cearc,* or *Cumins of the hen-trough.*

It happened, about the time I am speaking of, that
young Sir John Grant, son and heir of Sir Patrick Grant
of Stratherrock, now the Laird of Freuchie, did one evening
thus hold converse with a curious misformed waggish boy,
who had no father, and who went by the familiar name
of Archy *Abhach,* or Archy the Dwarf. Kicked and cuffed
as the youth had been about the castle, Sir John had
taken compassion on him, and had made him his page; and
the boy's gratitude and attachment were consequently great.

"Why look ye so sad, sir?" demanded the boy, gently
approaching his master, as he sat one evening on the
battlement of the bartizan, looking towards the setting
sun, with his head resting on the basket-hilt of his claymore, and his legs swinging about, as if he cared not
whether he should swing himself over the wall or not.
"Can poor Archy do nothing to rid thee of thy melancholy
mood?"

"Nay, boy," said the knight, kindly taking his hand,
"I doubt thy powers can scarcely reach my malady."

"As yet thou knowest not the extent of my powers,"
said the boy gravely, "nor can I show thee my remedy
till thou makest me to know thy disease. Yet, methinks,
my skill is such that I might dare shrewdly to guess at
it. Hast thou not ta'en a heart-wound from a pair of
bright eyes?"

"So far I must needs say, that, judging from this first
effort of thine, thy skill in divining is not to be questioned,"
said the knight.

"I will adventure further then, and say, that the slanting
beams of yonder declining sun are now gilding the casement
of thy lady-love," said the boy Archy.

"O Archy, Archy!" cried the knight, giving full way
to his feelings, "I have never enjoyed a moment's peace
since I beheld her at Whitsuntide at the church of Inverallan. She is an angel."

"Granting that she be so," said the boy, "for such they
tell me must, reason or none, be yielded to all lovers—yea
though the fair cause of their madness should be little less
than a devil—granting, I say, that she be an angel, surely
that should be no reason why thou shouldst thus mope
and pine, Sir Knight."

"Thou forgettest, boy, that the hatred naturally born between a Cumin and a Grant forbids all hope on my part," said Sir John despondingly.

"Methinks I could bring thee an instance where this hatred hath been exchanged for love," said the boy.

"Where? when? with whom?" cried the knight eagerly.

"Here—now—and with Sir John Grant towards Matilda or Bigla Cumin, as she is called in the country here, daughter and heiress of the big Lord of Glenchearnich," replied the boy laughing.

"Pshaw!" cried the knight, with a disappointed air.

"Nay, dear master," said the boy; "and if thou hast been able to get over this natural-born antipathy, why may not Bigla Cumin have been equally blessed by Heaven?"

"Ah!" cried the knight again, "would it might be so!"

"Wilt thou but give me leave to go to try what may be done?" demanded the boy. "Be assured I shall be better than most mediciners, for if I do no good, I shall take especial care to do no harm."

"Kind boy, thou mayest e'en do thy best," said the knight. "I well know thy zeal for thy master's good; but were thy powers somewhat more equal to thy zeal, I should count more on the success of thine efforts."

"Such as my poor powers may be, they shall be used to the utmost in thy service, Sir Knight," said the boy. "Good night, then, so please thee; and farewell, it may be for some time, for I go on mine errand by to-morrow's dawn, and the better I prosper, the longer, perchance, may be mine absence."

"Go, and may the Blessed Virgin guide thee and give thee luck," said the knight. "But see, boy, that thou bringest thine own person into no peril."

"Trust me for that," said Archy, as he disappeared from the bartizan.

The sun of next morning had scarcely well risen, and Gibbon More had just issued from his door to take a look at its face, that he might judge of the coming weather, when he descried an ill-formed dwarfish youth approaching, whose countenance, though ill-favoured, had a certain prepossessing expression in it.

"Whence comest thou, little man?" demanded the Lord of Glenchearnich.

"I come from the east," said the boy readily; "my name is Archy—other name have I none—and I would fain be a Cumin."

"Ha! ha! ha!—a Cumin, wouldst thou?" said Gibbon laughing. "By St. Mary, but our clan will be invincible when it shall be strengthened by such a powerful graff as thou! Tell me, what wouldst thou be good for, boy?"

"I could draw a bow at a pinch," said the boy. "But I must needs confess that I were better for the service of some gentle lady's bower. I'd willingly be thy fair daughter the Lady Matilda's page; and I'd serve her right faithfully."

"If Bigla should fancy thy ugly face, I care not if she should have thee," said Gibbon More, "for though thy countenance be homely, it would seem to be honest."

"Make me a Cumin, and the lady shall have no cause to complain of me," replied the boy.

"Thou shalt have thy wish then, boy, without further delay," said Gibbon More; and he straightway lifted up the youth, and, with more than ordinary gentleness, he performed the ceremony of the threefold ablution on him.

Archy Abhach, now converted into Archy Cumin, was speedily installed in his new office as page to the Lady Bigla, and, in his very first interview, he contrived to establish himself very firmly in the good graces of his fair mistress. But what might have been considered more wonderful, he made a no less favourable impression upon her handmaiden, a matter which jealousy might have rendered more difficult with any attendant of a less amiable disposition than the attached Agnes possessed.

"There is something more than usually interesting about that poor friendless boy," said the lady to Agnes, after her new page had been dismissed from her presence for a short time.

"A most interesting youth, notwithstanding the niggardly way in which dame Nature seems to have treated him," said Agnes archly; "but as to his being friendless, I shrewdly suspect that he is a rogue for making that pretence."

"What mean you, Agnes?" demanded Bigla.

"I mean that the varlet had no need to have come to Kincberdie to look for protection, seeing that he hath long been the favourite of one of the bravest young knights in all the country round," said Agnes.

" Of whom do you speak ? " demanded Bigla.

" Of a certain Sir John Grant, son and heir of old Sir Patrick Grant of Freuchie," replied Agnes, with an air of mock gravity; "but, perhaps, you have never seen nor heard of the man."

" O Agnes ! " cried Bigla, energetically clasping her hands, and throwing down her eyes and blushing deeply.

" You have heard of him, then, lady ? " said Agnes.

" A truce to your raillery," said Bigla seriously, "and tell me quickly all you know or guess of this matter."

" Why, all I know of the matter is simply this," said Agnes, in the same tone, "last Whitsuntide the Lady Bigla Cumin saw, for the first time, the handsome young knight, Sir John Grant of Freuchie, at the church of Inverallan. The knight, with becoming gallantry, stepped gracefully forward and lifted the lady to her saddle, sighing deeply as he resigned the precious load to her prancing palfrey. The lady's bower damsel, the quick-sighted Agnes Cumin, soon perceived that the said knight and lady had made a mutual impression on each other. With her wonted acuteness and ingenuity, the said damsel soon extracted the truth from the said lady ; and seeing that a misformed imp of a page, then in attendance on the said knight, hath now, without any apparent cause, left so good a master in order to undergo the ceremony of being baptized as a Cumin in the nauseous hen-trough, the said acute damsel ventures readily to pronounce that the flame burns as brightly and warmly at Freuchie as it does in my lady's bower at Kincherdie—that is all."

" But what *can* Sir John Grant mean by all this ? " demanded Bigla, blushing more deeply than ever.

" To seek and secure an interview to be sure," replied Agnes; "but I shall soon know what he would be at," continued she. " I shall soon be at the bottom of it all."

Without giving the Lady Bigla time to reply, the prompt and decided Agnes hurried away to hold converse with the page. Meeting, as they did, like two sharp flints, they were not long in striking fire enough to throw light upon the matter. Having mutually made one another fully aware of the position of affairs on both sides, they, without further hesitation, proceeded, like two able plenipotentiaries, to arrange plans for the future ; and it was finally agreed between them, without further ceremony, that the high contracting parties should meet in person, on the ensuing evening, in the bourtree bower, at the lower end of the garden, beyond the rampart, and the page was forthwith despatched on a secret mission to the knight to inform him immediately of this so happy an arrangement.

"Blessed Virgin, what hast thou done, Agnes !" cried Bigla Cumin, ere she had well heard her maid to an end ; and hiding her crimsoned face with both her hands, "What *will* Sir John Grant think of me ? "

"He will call you an angel, as Archy tells me he has already done," said Agnes coolly.

"Nay, nay, but this must not be !" said Bigla, starting from her chair. "Run, Agnes, and stop the boy from going on this most foolish and imprudent errand."

"Stop him," said Agnes. "You might as well ask me to stop Black Peter's arrow after it has left his bowstring. The boy is half way to Freuchie by this time. He knows too well how warmly his news will be received to allow the grass to grow at his heels."

"What will my father say to this strange arrangement, if it should come to his knowledge ?" cried Bigla, "to meet as a lover the son of the head of the very house with which we have ever held so great enmity."

"In the first place, your father, good man, must know nothing about this meeting," said Agnes. "It concerns him not; secondly, if there hath been ill blood for so long between the two clans, the sooner peace and friendship is re-established the better, especially after two of the principal persons have met together in a Christian church, as you and Sir John have done."

"Agnes, Agnes !" cried the lady, with emotions of vexation not altogether unmingled, it must be confessed, with certain tinglings of a more agreeable nature, "Agnes, Agnes ! thy precipitation in this matter hath brought me into a most distressing state of perplexity. I know not what to do."

But before the morning's sun had well risen, the page appeared in the lady's presence, with a perfumed billet, sealed with a flame-coloured silk ribbon, and filled with such professions of love on the part of Sir John Grant, as brought tenfold blushes into the lovely face of Bigla ;

and so touched her young heart as to leave her without
a chance of withstanding the powerful arguments of her
handmaiden Agnes, backed up as they were by the warm
descriptions of his master's sufferings, and the earnest
solicitations for her compassion on him, which were so
eloquently urged by the clever page. The result was,
that, attended by Agnes, she did go tremblingly to the
trysting place at the appointed hour—listened with a
pleasure she had never felt before to all the knight's
fervent vows; and both were made so happy by their
mutual confessions, that the prudential suggestions of
Agnes and Archy were repeatedly required ere the
tender separation could be effected. So well, however,
was that and several other interviews of a similar nature
planned and brought about by the two able auxiliaries,
that for a long time the easy Gibbon More had no suspicion
that anything of the sort was going on. But at length
it did happen, that as Sir John Grant was returning from
one of these meetings, he was rather unluckily encountered, not far from the house of Kincherdie, by Hector,
the confidential servant of Gibbon More. The man's
suspicions were so awakened by the circumstance of the
knight being on foot, that he scrupled not to follow him
at a distance, until he saw him join an attendant who held
a couple of horses in a grove about a mile off. Full of his
discovery, Hector went directly to Gibbon More ; and
there is no saying what the consequences might have
been had not the Lord of Glenchearnich been a person
of a temperament almost miraculously apathetical. So
wonderful was his disposition in this respect, indeed, that
it was only after his patience had been assailed and
battered, as it were, by repeated and most provoking
attacks, that he ever could be excited at all. But then,
indeed, when he was once roused, he became on the sudden
like a raging lion, and his enormous strength and fearless
courage being brought tremendously into action by his
fury, the effects were quite terrific.

"So you think, Hector, that the young Stratherrock
stripling has been here to look after Bigla," said Gibbon,
after hearing his man's story to an end. "Hum,—ha !
I did perceive that the maiden caught his eye at the
church of Inverallan on Whitsuntide. Ha, ha, ha !—
to think of a Grant being mated with her is too ridiculous.

But, for all that, I cannot blame the boy for bowing before the shrine of my daughter's beauty. I'll warrant the young goose came over here to try to get another peep, were it only of her robe as it might chance to sweep by her casement. Wiser folks than he have done as foolish things; I've done as much myself in my youth. But Bigla can know nought of this, so there is no harm done."

Whether Hector's renewed cautions did or did not succeed in making his master think something more of this matter than he was thus at first disposed to do, I cannot say; but certain it is, that the Lord of Glenchearnich was somewhat suddenly seized with the resolution of going some weeks earlier than he was wont, to spend the summer months on his hill-grazing property of Delnahaitnich, near the source of the river Dulnan. This was a most untoward event for the lovers, not only because the distance between them was thus immensely increased, but because Gibbon More's residence there was a small cottage, which might be called little better than a mere *shealing,** in or about which it would be next to impossible for them to meet without observation. And accordingly after this move was made, some weeks were vainly expended in fruitless attempts on the part of Archy Abhach to procure for his master Sir John, even the gratification of such a distant view of the Lady Bigla's robe as her father described in his conversation with Hector. Yet Sir John often hovered about the place, and lay for many a night wrapped up in his plaid among the heather of the neighbouring forest with no other shelter but a projecting rock and the thick foliage of the firs that grew over it. Archy Abhach was almost as much disappointed as Sir John himself at being so baulked. His ingenuity was put to the very rack, but all without effect; because it somehow or other happened that Gibbon More never went from home, and so his daughter was never left for one moment out of his sight. The knight had thus no comfort but in the frequent letters and messages which Archy contrived to carry between the lovers, and which they were fain to employ for want of those more interesting interviews, of which they were now altogether deprived.

---

* A dwelling only occupied in summer whilst feeding the cattle on the highest hill-grazings. The same word as the Swiss *chalet.*

It happened that Archy Abhach was one night sent
with one of those letters towards the place where his
master Sir John Grant was lying hid in the upper part of
the forest of Dulnan, which then spread much higher
over the hills than it now does. The moon was not yet
risen, and the dense foliage overhead very much increased
the darkness and the difficulty of his way. As he was
scrambling along past the narrow mouth of a small ravine
that opened on the course of the stream he was following,
he came suddenly upon two men who were seated beside
the dying embers of a fire which they seemed to have used
for some purpose of rude and hasty cookery. Curiosity
led him involuntarily to stop for a moment to observe
them; but becoming instantly aware of his imprudence
in doing so, he moved quickly away, and began to run as
hard as he could. But the consequences which he dreaded
were already incurred, and he had not gone many paces
when he heard footsteps hurrying after him. He fled as
fast as his legs could carry him, but the darkness was
such that he tripped and fell, and his neck was instantly
in the grasp of a powerful hand.

"I have him fast," said a rough voice in Gaelic; "it is
but a very small boy after all. Shall I whittle his craig
with my skian-dhu?"

"Not for thy life," replied another voice in the same
language. "Bring him along with thee, that we may see
what he is. Why wouldst thou hurt the creature till
we know something more about him?"

The man who had seized Archy now threw him over
his shoulder as he would have done a dead hare, and
groped his way back with him to the ravine, where a
blaze being produced by a dry bush of heather, the boy
was set down between them for examination. Archy on
his part was not slow in using his eyes also, and in a
much less time than I can tell it to you, he ran them over
the bulky rough figure of the individual who had seized
him, and then as hastily surveyed the compact well put-
together active-looking person, and intelligent countenance
of the other, who seemed in every respect to be the
superior. This last was by no means strange to him, and,
to the surprise of the man himself, he immediately addressed him by his name.

"Corrie MacDonald!" said he, "sure I am that thou

wilt never hurt any man belonging to Sir Patrick Grant of Stratherrock."

But I must now tell you that this same Corrie MacDonald was a certain hero who flourished in those days in Lochaber, and who made himself dreaded all through Morayland and its neighbouring districts by the periodical visits of plunder which he paid to them. Amongst other tracts of country, Strathspey and its tributary valleys were wont to be a prominent object of his attention. He had always a large band of followers at his command, who were equally expert in driving away herds of cattle, and brave in beating off the owners when they pursued with the hope of recovering them. Corrie was a reaver of no ordinary character; for, robber though he was, he had a natural fund of liberality and generosity about him; and he had so great a stock of native humour in him, that he was ever ready to indulge his waggish disposition at any expense; and no predatory expedition had ever half so great a relish for him, as that in which he could contrive to mix up a bit of a frolic. Many a cow and ox had Corrie Macdonald carried away from the extensive possessions of the Lord of Glenchearnich. But these trifling depredations never disturbed the good temper or overcame the patience of that most extraordinary man, the effect of whose unparalleled forbearance was to awaken in the inquiring mind of Corrie MacDonald a certain philosophic curiosity to ascertain by experiment to what extent it was capable of being stretched; and he had long panted for a favourable opportunity of bringing this investigation to a fair trial.

" Corrie MacDonald," cried Archy Abhach, in a whining tone, " sure I am that thou who hast never had quarrel with Sir Patrick Grant of Stratherrock wilt never hurt any man belonging to him."

" Thou art right," replied Corrie. " Not only shall I respect the safety of every man belonging to Sir Patrick Grant, but I will even respect thee, who art but a mannikin, if thou canst prove thyself to be his. I have had peaceable passage to and fro through his grounds on Loch Ness side for too many years to do otherwise."

" Then look ye here," said Archy, plucking from his bosom the letter of which he was the bearer, and straightway showing the address, which was—*To the honourable and gallant knight, Sir John Grant of Freuchie, these, mith speed.*

"That is all well," said Corrie. "But methinks, mannikin, that this is anything but the road to Freuchie, if I know aught of this country side."

"My master is up in the forest, a little bit above this, waiting for my tidings," said Archy.

"Aha!" cried Corrie, relaxing his features into a smile, "some love adventure, I warrant me. Awell! I am the last man to put hindrance in the way of any such matter, especially where Sir John Grant is concerned. Nay, I would willingly go a good way out of my road to help him on."

"Sayest thou so, Corrie MacDonald!" cried the urchin. "Then could I tell thee how thou mightest lend my master thy most effectual aid, and yet keep thine own road still, and that to thine own most abundant profit."

"How may that be, my small man?" demanded Corrie. "If thou canst make thy plans clear to my conviction, thou shalt find me ready, zealous, prompt, and decisive."

"Thou knowest Gibbon More Cumin, lord of these broad lands of Glenchearnich," said Archy.

"Know him?" said Corrie with a grin. "Well do I that."

"He is living here hard by at Delnahaitnich," continued the page. "He keeps home so close, that no one can even have a sight of his daughter, far less have speech of her. Couldst thou not carry away his cattle from the forest here, so as to furnish him with a reasonably rational object for travelling for a season?"

"By Saint Comb, but thou hast a wit larger than the tiny proportions of thy body might teach one to look for!" said Corrie. "The notion is excellent. I have long wished to work that lump of dough into a ferment. And, by Saint Mary, as the *creach* will be carried off from under his very nose, I shall stir up his temper now, if it is to be stirred up at all by mortal man. So speed to thy master, and keep him advised to watch his time; and if I don't by and by clear the way for him, by giving Gibbon More and his people a chase of a day or two through the hills after me and my men, I shall wonder of it."

"Master, master," cried Gibbon More's man Hector, as he came running in to him next morning quite out of breath, "Corrie MacDonald has been in the forest last

night, and he has carried away every stot he could find on
this part of your lands."

" Has the rascal taken the cows too ? " demanded
Gibbon coolly.

" No—sure enough—he has not taken a single cow,"
replied Hector, " I counted the cow-beasts myself, and they
are all safe."

" There was some civility in that, however," said Gibbon
laughing. " The fellow is a thief of some consideration ;
for if he hath left us the cows, thou knowest, Hector, that
we shall have plenty of stot beasts by and by."

" Ou aye, surely, sir," said Hector as he retired, very
much disappointed by the manner in which his intelligence
had been received.

Corrie was not without his spies ; and the oxen were
hardly well so far over the hill, on their way to Lochaber,
as to be fairly considered beyond all reach of recovery,
when he returned with some of his people to prowl about
Delnahaitnich. There he soon learned from Archy Abhach
the manner and speech with which Gibbon More had
received the news of his loss.

" I'll try him again," said Corrie. " The fellow must be
the dullest stirk that ever was calved."

" The cows are all gone now, master ! " cried the same
ill-omened messenger, as he entered Gibbon More's apartment next morning before he was out of bed.

" A plague upon the plundering thief," cried Gibbon
More, " has he taken the young beasts too ? "

" No ! " said the man, who was much disappointed to find
that this, his second piece of bad news, was just as unsuccessful in rousing his master's ire as his first had been.
" He has not ta'en a single young beast, but, on my conscience, I'm thinking he has ta'en enough."

" The villain robs by rule, I see," said Gibbon ; " but
since the young beasts are safe, Hector, we shall have
plenty of both cows and stots again, anon, you know."

Corrie MacDonald, who was curious to find out how
this second loss was to affect Gibbon, was absolutely piqued
beyond endurance when he heard of the quiet manner in
which he had taken it. Withdrawing a handful of his
people from the large body of them who were then in
charge of the second prey he had taken, he lay in ambush
for a third night.

" We're altogether harried now then !" cried Hector, as he appeared the third morning with a face like a ghost. " Every young beast upon the place is gone."

"What !" cried Gibbon More, starting up to hurry on his clothes in a state of the fiercest excitement, " does the caitiff make a butt of me ? I can bear to lose my bestial, but to be played on thus by a thieving scoundrel is more than man's patience can suffer. I'll teach these ruffians to crack their jokes upon me ! Where is my two-handed sword ?"

" Father, father ! dear father, where are ye running to ?" cried his daughter Bigla, as she met him raging out at the door like a roaring lion. " Where are you running without your bonnet ?"

" I have no time to speak now," replied the infuriated Gibbon. " I'll tell you all about it when I come back."

" I fear he has gone on some rash and dangerous enterprise," said Bigla, "run, run, Hector, and gather the people, and be after him with help as fast as you may."

Hector was not slow; but he must have been active indeed, if he could have caught Gibbon More at the pace he was going. He rushed up the steep hill in front of his dwelling, and was soon out of sight.

Gibbon had no sooner reached the summit, than, throwing his eyes abroad, he espied his young cattle feeding on the south side of the hill called the *Geal-charn*, or the Hoary Hill ; and from the smoke which he observed curling up from a ravine at a short distance from the spot where the animals were scattered about, he at once conjectured that the robbers had chosen that concealment as a fit place for cooking their morning meal. He was right in this supposition ; for, judging from his former apathy, Corrie MacDonald had not quite calculated that this third act of depredation would lead to so speedy a pursuit.

"What a pity it is that Gibbon More Cumin has no more beasts left in Delnahaitnich," said Corrie MacDonald to his people, with an ironical laugh, as they sat in a circle round the fire, devouring one of the young beasts they had killed.

" We need not come back here for a while, till he sends up some more stock from Kincherdie," said one of his men.

" We have done not that much amiss in these three

turns," said another. " I'm thinking we may be content
to free him of *blackmail* for a season."

" By the beard of St. Barnabas, but we'll come back
again and again, until we drive away every beast the
cowardly loon has between this and Spey," said Corrie.
" What should we do with such a lump of butter, but keep
melting at it as long as it will run."

" Surely, surely," replied several of them.

" It will make our broth all the fatter," said Corrie,
laughing again.

" Villains, do ye dare to laugh at me at the very
moment when you are feeding at my cost ?" cried Gibbon
More, rushing suddenly and unexpectedly among them,
like a raging wolf into a flock of penned sheep. " I'll
teach you to make a fool of me."

The immense blade of his two-handed sword gleamed
like a meteor in the air, flashed in the sun, and shed lightnings into their terrified eyes. Each of them tried to
scramble to his feet as he best could ; and one or two were
shorn of their heads ere they could rise from the ground.
Bonnets with heads in them fell to right and left, as I have
seen ripe apples scattered from their parent bough by a
violent gust of wind, or by the inroad of some thieving
schoolboy. No one thought of anything else but flight ;
and the actions of all were as quick as their thoughts.
But Gibbon More's enormous double-edged weapon was
quicker in the repetition of its sweeping cuts than even
thought itself. On he went, slashing right and left after
them as they fled, till he had strewed the ravine and the
hill-side with about a dozen of their carcases, and then,
breathless and overcome with rage, haste, and toil, he sat
himself down to rest on the heather. The remainder of
the robbers were thus allowed to escape ; and as he did not
know the boasting Corrie MacDonald personally, that hero
contrived to get safe away among the rest, and went home
to Lochaber, somewhat less disposed to try experiments on
the temper of Gibbon More Cumin, than he had declared
himself to be before this his terrible and unlooked for
onslaught.

Gibbon More's people, with Hector at their head, arrived
too late to share with him in the glory of his victory. But
they were useful in burying the slain. A few tumuli,
which are still to be seen raising their green heads among

the heather on the southern declivity of the *Geal-charn*, were thrown up by them over the dead bodies; and they then had the satisfaction of driving home their master's young cattle in safety to their native pasture, where the animals afterwards grew to be cows and oxen, entirely free from any further alarm from Corrie MacDonald.

I need not say that the sharp-witted page took good care that his master should profit by the temporary absence of Gibbon More. Sir John Grant was at the cottage immediately after the Lord of Glenchearnich had left it. But the knight had little advantage after all from an adventure which had cost Corrie MacDonald so dear. He had indeed the satisfaction of again beholding and conversing with Bigla; but, filled as she was at the time with alarm and anxiety about her father's safety, she could talk about or listen to no other subject. The time of the Lord of Glenchearnich's absence fled like a short dream. His anticipated travel of a few days had, by his own extraordinary activity and courage, been reduced to a few short hours, and the wary and watchful page had barely time to warn his master away, ere Gibbon More's voice was heard calling to his people, as he returned to the house begrimed with the blood and soil of his recent conflict.

But Sir John's more frequent opportunities of meeting with Bigla were soon afterwards again happily renewed by the return of Gibbon More to Kincherdie; and, by the ingenuity of the page, these stolen interviews passed over undiscovered even by the lynx-eyed Hector, whose energies were by this time somewhat diverted from their wonted watchfulness, by a certain newborn affection which had recently possessed his bosom for the fair maid Agnes.

It happened on one occasion that Gibbon More chanced to go to a fair or market at Inverness. The streets were crowded with people, as well as with horses, cows, and oxen of all sorts. There might have been observed the eagle-winged bonnet of the chief, followed by his tail of clansmen and dependants; and chieftains were seen promiscuously mingled with cattle-boys, gillies, and serfs of every degree and denomination, thronging the public way. Many were the friendly salutations, and many the flashes of hostile defiance that passed among the various personages who, coming from distant parts of the country, chanced on that day to meet each other. Often was the authority of

the provost, the bailies, the sheriff, and other officials called
into operation to quell embryo quarrels, and sometimes it
was all that the united forces of these public functionaries
could do to keep the restless and bloodthirsty dirks and
claymores in their sheaths.   Rarely did the mantled and
well-wimpled damsels venture forth amidst the complication of dangers that were to be encountered at every step
from the prevalence of those quarrels, as well as from the
horns of the cattle and the heels of the horses.   They contented themselves with saluting their friends from their
open lattices; and many were the warm though distant
acknowledgments that took place between the young and
the fair ladies, who, whilst they were ostensibly occupied
in gazing at the marvels in the street,—at the jesters and
mummers who jingled their bells, or grinned with their
painted faces, and trolled their rude and threadbare rhymes
to ditties as unpolished, the pretty creatures were in reality
altogether overlooking these vulgar absurdities, and were
holding interesting conversations by signals, only known
to themselves, with their handsome Highland lovers in the
street.

Bigla Cumin was an heiress of consequence, but she was
moreover very beautiful, so that many were the eyes that
sought her as she sat at a lofty balcony in the house of a
burgher friend of her father's, and not a few were those
who endeavoured, and endeavoured in vain, to obtain one
glance of recognition from her.   I do not mean to say,
however, that the lass was haughty, but she bore herself
with the modesty befitting her years and her sex.   There
was but one on whom she did vouchsafe to look with an
eye of yespecial favour, and that was Sir John Grant.
Her heart beat in double time when he and his father, Sir
Patrick the Lord of Stratherrock, passed by in their gay
red and green tartan, which, except in its broad blue *lysts*
and in its want of those pure white *sprainges* which enliven
that of the Cumin, had so general a resemblance to it, that
at a little distance they might have been easily mistaken
for each other.   When the rays from her bright eyes shot
across the street in a condescending smile in return for the
more than merely courteous reverence which he made to
her, their sunshine was concentrated, if I may so express
myself, as if it had been met by the burning glasses of that
most wonderful man Archimedes, and it was returned to
her in one melting focus of adoration.

22

"Angel that she is!" said Sir John to his father.

"She is an angel, indeed, boy!" replied the elder knight; "and, moreover, there be angels enow in her father's coffers, not to mention those broad acres of his which would give to the Grants so pretty a little principality in Strathspey. Stick to her, boy! She is well worth the winning."

"Would I could but have an interview with her, freed from all chance of interruption from her old father!" said Sir John in a tone of vexation.

"Trust to me, dear master," said Archy Abhach in a whisper, as at that moment he plucked the knight's sleeve. "Watch well thy time! I have seen some one in the town here to-day who will be right willing to lend thee a helping hand."

Gibbon More was not wont to go without the following of a chieftain on such occasions as this; and he generally bore his portly person over the crown of the causeway with a dignity which, when at home, he laid aside with his best bonnet, doublet, and plaid. The recognition between him and his new neighbour, as he called him, was remarkably warm and friendly on the part of Sir Patrick Grant, and very stately and condescending on his own side. His eyes were offended at the sight of the two Grants and their followers, and he sought relief from them in looking at a beautiful black palfrey which a West Highland gilly was leading down the street. The prancing, the caracoling, and the menage of the animal showed that it had been bred of the gentlest Arabian blood in some far away English pasture.

"Ho!" cried Gibbon, stopping the man. "Who is the owner of that beautiful creature?"

"I am the owner, sir," replied a sharp-eyed little man, right well accoutred both as to his arms and garb, but having no remarkable signs of any great rank about him.

"Are you for parting with the pretty creature?" inquired Gibbon More.

"I should not care much to part with him to a good customer," replied the other.

"Is he young, gentle, sound, and sure-footed?" demanded Gibbon.

"I'll answer all your questions by and by," replied the West Highlander, "if you will only do me the favour to satisfy me as to one point."

"What is that?" asked Gibbon More.

"Will you tell me what part of the country you come from?"

"From Strathspey, to be sure," replied Gibbon.

"I guessed as much," said the other. "I see, moreover, from the set of your tartan that you are a Cumin, and by your attire, bearing, and following, I can guess that you are a gentleman of some note. Do you happen to know Gibbon More Cumin of your country?"

"Know Gibbon More Cumin!" cried he, laughing good humouredly; "if I know anyone, I should know him, seeing that he always lives in the house with me, and that we never eat a meal asunder. I love him better than a brother. But not to keep you any longer in doubt—I am Gibbon More Cumin!"

"I am truly glad to see you," said the West Highlander, seizing his hand and shaking it heartily. "You are the man, of all others alive, to whom I am most obliged."

"Ha, friend!" replied Gibbon, looking hard and seriously at him, "I cannot say that. I recollect having ever seen you before; how then have I happened so to have obliged you?"

"Well!" said the other, "if you cannot remember that you ever saw me before, the greater was your kindness to me—unsight unseen, as we say. It is not every man that keeps such an easy reckoning as you do of the benefits for which his friends are indebted to him."

"But what benefit have you had from me?" demanded Gibbon.

"I'll tell you that," said the West Highlander. "I'll tell you that in a moment. You see, I have no less than three strapping lasses of daughters. I have married all the three, and to each one of them I gave a tocher which you provided."

"Tut!" cried Gibbon laughing, "the man is demented. When did I ever give a tocher to daughter of yours? By St. Mungo, I have a strapping lass of a daughter of my own to portion. I have little ado therefore to portion those of other people."

"What I say is nevertheless true," replied the other. "And so sensible am I of the obligations I owe to you, that by way of a small return, and to show my gratitude, I must ask of you, as a favour, to accept of this horse of

mine as a present for your daughter; and if you will go to
the inn with me, I shall be happy to give you a pint of
French Claret, if such be to be had in the town, to drink
good luck to the young lady and her new palfrey."

"As I am a Cumin you are an honest fellow!" cried
Gibbon More, shaking him again heartily by the hand.
"But I prythee explain—I cannot accept either your present or your wine till .you tell me who you are, and until
you expound your riddle to me."

"I am not sure how far I am safe to do that," said the
other archly, "especially here, on the High Street of Inverness; and you standing there with so many pretty men
at your back."

"If I have done you kindnesses heretofore," said Gibbon,
"what fear can you have of me now, stand where I will,
or let me be backed as I may?"

"Why, then, you see," said the other, with a certain
degree of comical hesitation, "I must confess that I did,
on one occasion, presume somewhat too far on your liberality, and in your anger you gave me such a fright, that
I am not sure that I have just altogether got the better of
it yet."

"Ha! ha! ha! why, you give me more riddles every
time you open your mouth," replied Gibbon. "When did
I ever give you a fright?"

"Ou! troth sudden and terrible was the fright you gave
me!" said the man, "and surely after tochering of three
daughters, each of them with twelve beautiful milch cows
and a bull, all of which came from your pastures, I should
have been contented. But I'm thinking that if I was a small
thing over greedy, the fright I got from Gibbon More's
two-handed sword, as it flashed behind me on the Geal
Charn, was enough to put all greed out of my head, so far
at least as he was concerned."

"Hoo!" exclaimed Gibbon with a long whistle, "ha!
ha! ha! Corrie MacDonald! as I am a Cumin, you are
a most merry conditioned rogue as ever I met with! Your
hand again! I accept your handsome present, and I will
go drink your pot of wine with you, with all my heart, to
my daughter's health, and to a better acquaintance between
you and me. Ha! ha! ha! By St. Mary, but I am sorry
now that I killed your men and so grievously frightened
yourself. But, though the poor fellows are past all hope

of recovery now, I am resolved that your dread of me shall
be drowned in your own flagon. Lead on then, my brave
fellow, to your hostel."

Gibbon More had too much enjoyment in this unexpected meeting and merry-making to allow it to terminate
very soon; but Bigla Cumin was in some degree recom-
pensed for the tedious time she had to tarry for her father
by the long interview which she enjoyed with Sir John
Grant, as well as by the sight of the beautiful prancing
palfrey, which was led out for her to ride home upon.

It was not very long after this occurrence that poor
Gibbon More Cumin was seized with a sudden malady, of
which he died after a few days' illness, and he was carried
by his friends and dependants to be laid to sleep in the
tomb of his fathers. Jealous of the Grants even in his
dying moments, he left Bigla, his orphan daughter and
heiress, under the guardianship of some of the chieftains of
his own clan, with earnest injunctions above all things to
" keep her out of the *fremyt** hands of Freuchie."

There was no one more anxious to fulfil this dying order
of Gibbon's than one of the Cumins, who at that time
possessed Logie, which, in later times, became the patri-
monial property of that more recent branch whence
proceeded the worthy family which is now so designated.
This gentleman had been for some time one of Bigla's
suitors; and his pretensions had been always favourably
looked upon by her father. The days of mourning for the
old man were not yet expired, when Logie came to Kincherdie, gaily apparelled, and well appointed and attended,
and urging the authority of a father's dying wish, he
signified to Bigla his desire of taking her with him on the
ensuing day to his residence on the banks of the river
Findhorn, where, as his guest, and under the protection of
his aged mother, she should find a safe and comfortable
asylum. Though satisfied that there was more of the
warmth of the lover in the language in which this invitation was conveyed, than altogether befitted the character
of a guardian, yet the young maiden, in her present lonely
state, could not well find any reasonable excuse for refusal,
and accordingly she was compelled, however unwillingly,
to accept his offer, and she issued orders to her people to
prepare for the journey.

* Strange.

The prospect of so soon leaving that home where she
had spent her whole life under the fostering care of her
doting father, filled her heart with a double portion of
sorrow; and after artlessly communicating her feelings to
Logie and his friends, she craved their pardon, entreated
them to entertain one another, and to make themselves at
home, and then she sought the retirement of her chamber,
where she spent the remainder of the day, and the greater
part of the evening, in giving way to that affliction which
had more than one exciting cause.

"My dear mistress," said her faithful maid Agnes
Cumin, breaking in upon her as she sat in silent abstraction, with her moist cheek resting upon her hand, "why
should you cry your eyes out thus? The night is soft and
balmy, a little fresh air would do you good. Do let me
throw this plaid over you, and be persuaded to step out a
little, were it only as far beyond the walls as the bourtree
bower at the lower end of the garden."

"I cannot, my good Aggy," replied Bigla, with a fresh
flood of tears; "in sooth I have no heart."

"Come! be persuaded to try the air," said Agnes.
"Who knows what sighs and tears may be at this moment
idly fanning the leaves and watering the rosebuds of your
own bonny bower."

"What say you?" cried Bigla, starting up with a
suddenly acquired energy. "What say you, Aggy? is *he*
in the arbour?"

"Hush, my lady!" said the cautious girl, "he *is* there;
and from his tears and sighs I should judge that his heart
is well attuned to thine at this moment."

"Let me fly to him!" exclaimed Bigla, "the moments
are most precious;" and throwing her plaid hastily around
her, she stole out beyond the barbican; and, having
reached the garden, she ran on tiptoe to the simple elder-
bush bower at the farther end of it, leaving Archy Abhach
to keep watch against intrusion.

The scene between Bigla and her lover was tender and
melting. For a time they did little else than weep and
sigh together.

"Aggy tells me that you go with Logie to-morrow,"
said Sir John at last. "How could you suffer yourself
to be persuaded to agree to any such arrangement?"

"It was with no good will that I did so," replied Bigla;

"but as Logie was armed with my dear departed father's delegated authority, and as his proposal was backed by a parent's dying wish, I could not withstand his request."

"Holy Mother, then art thou lost to me for ever!" cried Sir John passionately. "Canst thou thus coolly resolve, even for such a cause, to throw thyself into the very jaws of those from whom I can never hope to reclaim thee but by force of arms!"

"Force of arms!" said Bigla. "I question much whether any force of arms from the Grants could prevail against the men of my clan, who will have the keeping of me. But fear not, for the time is not far distant when the law will give me guidance of mine own affairs; then mayest thou reclaim me from myself with full assurance of a ready compliance on my part."

"But what if these clansmen of thine should basely coerce thee to a hated union with one of themselves?— with Logie, for instance, who is old enough to be thy father!"

"I have no such fears," replied Bigla.

"By the rood, but I have!" cried Sir John hurriedly. 'You forget the old saying,—*Whilst there are leaves in the forest there*—a—a—a "——

"Nay," said Bigla playfully, "do finish your proverb, Sir Knight. *Whilst there are leaves in the forest there will be guile in a Cumin.* Did your worship mean that as a compliment to me, or do you forget that I, too, am a Cumin?"

"Nay, nay, nay! my dearest Bigla, you are truth itself," replied Sir John eagerly. "Pardon me, my love, for quoting this old saw; but, seriously, you are too valuable, too tempting a prize to be risked in any hands but—but— but "——

"But *yours*, as I presume thou wouldst say, good Sir Knight," replied Bigla, interrupting him in the same playful tone.

"Thou hast said it, angel of my life!" exclaimed Sir John, rapturously kissing her hand. "I can and will resign thee to no one! Thou art my pledged, mine affianced bride!"

"I am, I am, indeed I am," said Bigla tenderly.

"Then why shouldst thou put our mutual happiness to peril?" cried Sir John. "Why not secure it by flying

with me this moment? My horses and people are within
a whistle of where we now are, and in half an hour's
riding or so we shall be safe within the walls of Castle
Grant."

"No, no, no!" replied she, "a stolen marriage would
neither be for the credit of Sir John Grant nor for that of
Bigla Cumin. Besides, I should be but a poor offering at
Castle Grant were my broad lands not well buckled to my
back."

"I care not for thy lands," said Sir John, "'tis thyself I
would wed, and not thine estates. And if that be all, let
us to horse forthwith. Better for me to secure thy precious
self, though with the chance of losing thy lands, than lose
thee in trying to save thy lands."

"'Tis gallantly resolved of thee, Sir John," said Bigla;
"but I cannot allow thy chivalrous ardour to do us both
so serious an injury. All I ask of thee, then, is to trust
everything to my discretion and resolution, and, depend
upon it, thou hast nothing to fear."

The parting between the two lovers was tender and
prolonged, and it was only at length finally effected by the
interference of Agnes and the page, who came running to
tell them that the revellers in the hall were breaking up.
And what he told them was true, for Bigla found that she
required the exertion of some degree of ingenuity to effect
her retreat to her chamber unnoticed.

An early hour of the next day beheld the cavalcade,
formed by the united trains of Bigla Cumin and her kinsman the Laird of Logie, winding away from her paternal
mansion, amidst the mingled lamentations and benedictions
of her people. Bigla was mounted on her favourite palfrey,
the beautiful and fleet courser of Arabian blood which was
presented to her by Corrie MacDonald. Her maid Agnes
rode by her side on an animal of mettle little short of that
which carried her mistress. Logie and his friends, all well
armed, surrounded both in a sort of irregular phalanx,
which Bigla could not help thinking had more the appearance of a guard to prevent the escape of a prisoner, than
that which might do her honour or give her protection.
Her own followers were but few, and they were mixed up
with those of the Laird of Logie. In the midst of them
was the faithful page Archy, to whose care was committed
the charge of a small iron-bound oaken chest, which con-

tained her family charters and other important documents. This Logie had especially insisted that she should carry with her, in order to secure its safety. The strange mis-formed urchin sat like an ape, mounted on a very remark-able milk-white steed, of noble courage and beautiful proportions, and whose action was in no degree inferior to his beauty. As this fine animal had been accustomed to carry Gibbon More himself for some years before his death, it was not wonderful that Bigla should have ridden up to caress him ere the march began, and whilst she did so she contrived to give some secret orders to the rider, which did not appear to have been poured into a deaf ear.

The sun was nearly in the meridian before the party reached that point on the edge of the high plain, imme-diately over the double valley of the rivers Findhorn and Divie. There, as you know, a grand and extensive view of these romantic twin glens is to be enjoyed, together with the broad, rich, and beautiful vale that is formed by their union, with the majestic combined stream winding away through it, between its rocky, irregular, and wooded banks, till it is lost amidst the vast extent of forest stretch-ing widely along both sides of it, as it proceeds on its course towards the fertile plains of the low country of Moray, and its distant firth, the whole being bounded by the blue mountains of the north. Bigla had seen this glorious prospect more than once before, but she was an enthusiastic lover of nature, and, consequently, she was not sorry when she heard the Laird of Logie propose that they should alight for a few moments to rest themselves, and that they might enjoy it, at greater leisure, and with more ease to themselves. Logie did not make this proposal without private reasons of his own. Having contrived to seat himself apart with Bigla, he began to urge his passion with an energy which he had never ventured to employ before, and after using every argument that he thought might be most likely to prevail on her to yield to his suit, he seated her again on her palfrey, and as he rode down the wooded steeps by her side, he continued to press her eagerly on the same subject, without taking the trouble to use the delicacy of speaking in a tone which might have rendered their conversation private from those with whom they travelled.

" If you will only consent to be mine, fair Bigla," said

he, "I will make you mistress of as much of the bonny land of Moray as your bright eyes can reach over."

"I knew not that thy patrimony had been so ample," said Bigla coldly.

"Put your fate and mine upon the peril of this condition then," said Logie eagerly.

"I trow I might safely do so, were I to bar all trick," replied Bigla.

"Nay, then, thou art pledged to stand to the bargain," said Logie.

"I am pledged to nothing," replied Bigla haughtily.

"Ha, look there now, gentlemen!" cried Logie. "My fair ward and kinswoman Bigla Cumin here hath pledged her own pretty person to me, on condition that I shall make her mistress of as much of bonny Moray-land as her beauteous eyes can reach over. Now, how say you? Let her cast her eyes forward, and you will all bear me witness, my friends, that she can now see nothing of which I am not the undoubted owner."

By this time, you must know the cavalcade had descended from the high grounds through the winding hollows of the steep wooded braes, till all the distant and more extended part of the landscape was lost by the rise of the opposite high grounds, and certainly from the umbrageous recess where they now stood, nothing was to be seen before them but the lands of Logie.

"The joke is very well," said Bigla, not a little piqued, and reddening considerably at the liberty which had been thus taken with her before the men-at-arms who followed them; "but though Moray-land was all thine own from Ness to Spey, I would not have thee if thou wouldst lay it all at my feet."

"Talk not so proudly, mistress!" said Logie, very much nettled. "There are many maidens more than thy marrows, who would be happy to mate with me, though I had nothing but this good claymore for my portion."

"I doubt it not," replied Bigla; "but as I am not one of these, it may be as well perhaps that we talk not again on any such subject."

"A little less haughtiness would have better become thee," said Logie. "You forget that you are not now on Dulnan side; and, moreover, you forget that I am your guardian."

" Nay, it is you who forget that you are my guardian,"
replied Bigla. " I do feel, indeed, that I can never forget
that thou art so; and, moreover, that there is a cruel
difference between an unfeeling guardian and a fond
father."

"I am armed with thy father's authority," said Logie
hastily ; " and I will exert it."

" By basely taking advantage of it to proffer thine own
vile suit," said Bigla.

" To see, at least, that Freuchie's son proffers no more
suit to thee," replied Logie. "If he took leave of thee last
night beyond the barbican, I trow it shall be his last leave-
taking of thee."

" Last night !" said Bigla with surprise.

" Aye, last night," said Logie bitterly. " Dost think I
have not found out your secret meeting? Had I caught
the caitiff his blood should have paid for his impudence."

" 'Tis well to boast now, fair sir !" said Bigla, " now that
thou hast no chance of any such encounter. Oh, would I
were on my bonny Dulnan side again ! but I trust that
my foot shall soon be on its flowery turf."

" That shall be when thou hast my permission," said
Logie, allowing his passion to get the better of him.

" What ! am I so in restraint then?" said Bigla taking
a scarf from her neck, and waving it behind her head
in such a way, that it was hardly perceived to be a
signal by any one but Archy Abhach. He no sooner
observed it, however, than he began to rein his steed
backwards, until he fell behind the line of march.

" Aye, bold girl, thou shalt obey me ere long as thy
husband as well as thy guardian !" continued Logie.

" Sayest thou so?" said Bigla, putting on her Arabian
to a gentle canter over the meadow towards the ford of the
Divie, whither they were then going, so as to rid herself
in some degree of the throng by which she had been
surrounded. Then turning in her saddle, she shouted
aloud—" Ride, Archy, for thy life, man ! Ride ! ride !
Men of Glenchearnich, follow your mistress. Come, Aggy,
spur with me, and may Saint Mary be our guide !"

And with these words she and her maid boldly dashed
their steeds, breast deep, into the ford, and quickly
stemmed the stream of the Divie, whilst the well-tutored
Archy Abhach wheeled his horse suddenly round at her

word, and, drawing his dirk, he pricked his milk-white sides till the red blood spurted from them, and the noble animal darted off, with his flea-bite of a burden, towards those wooded braes, down which they had so recently come. The Laird of Logie and his followers stood for some moments astounded on the mead, before they could determine what to do. On the one hand fled the lady; and on the other hand the charters of her lands, her bonds, and her wadsets were already winging their way upwards through the woods; and the question was, which of the two objects of pursuit was the most important. Even after he had gathered his scattered recollection, Logie stood in doubt for a time. At length, seeing that Bigla Cumin had taken the direction of the house of Logie, so that he was still left, as he reckoned, between her and her own country, he quickly made his selection.

"After that miscreated devil on the white horse!" cried he. "Take the caitiff and the *kist* he carries!—take him dead or alive!—but, at all hazards take the kist!"

Off went the laird and his people helter-skelter after Archy Abhach, whilst the followers of Bigla Cumin were left at liberty to become her followers indeed. The waters of the Divie frothed and foamed again as they dashed through after her. I need not tell *you*, gentlemen, who know the *carte de pays* so well, that although Bigla rode off at first in the very direction in which the laird had wished her to go, I mean towards his own house, she had no sooner forced her way up the steep narrow path leading from the ford, than she found herself in a position where she had it in her power to choose between two ways— one stretching straight onwards towards the house of Logie, and the other leading directly back over the hills to the eastward of the Divie towards her own country, by a route different from that which she had travelled in the morning. There she stood for some moments on a conspicuous point overlooking the valley. But you may easily guess that she stopped not from any doubt that possessed her as to which of the two ways she should take—she only waited till her panting followers had clustered around her; for they had no sooner gathered than she waved her scarf again, and, amidst the shouts of her men-at-arms, she turned her horse's head to the hill, and began to breast it most vigorously. Logie beheld her manœuvre, and it shook his purpose for an instant. He gave hurried and contradictory orders, which only had the effect of slackening the pursuit after the urchin page, and Bigla had the satisfaction of seeing that faithful creature shooting far up among the bowery braes ere any final decision had been taken by the laird. At length, a small plump of horsemen were sent off towards the ford to pursue Bigla, whilst the remainder, with Logie at their head, renewed their chase after Archy Abhach and his precious casket.

"Who is he, think you, that rides hither with so much haste from the pass of Craig-Bey?" demanded Sir John Grant of the man-at-arms on watch, as he stalked along the bartizan of his castle to take a look over the country, about the time that the sun was hastening downwards to hide himself below the western horizon.

"If mortal man it be who looks so like a speck on the saddle, he either rides with hot news to spur him on, or he has some enemy after him," replied the man.

"By'r lady, but you have guessed right well," said Sir John; "for see! there comes a straggling line of some dozen of horsemen rattling like thunder through the pass."

"Methinks that the elf who flies bears some strange burden behind him," said the man-at-arms.

"He doth so, indeed," said Sir John.

"Some common thief, I'll warrant me, who hath carried away a booty from some usurious burgher of Forres," said the man-at-arms.

"Be he what he may, his white horse is no carrion," said Sir John. "How the noble animal devours the ground!"

"He is as like old Gibbon More's favourite horse as one egg is to another," said the man-at-arms as he drew nearer.

"Gibbon More's, saidst thou?" exclaimed Sir John; "and, by all that is good, he that rides is like my faithful page; but see, he turns this way. Let's to the barbican," and, taking three steps down the narrow stair at each stride, he was at the barbican in a few moments.

"What, ho!" cried Sir John, as the horse came galloping up to the gate. "What, ho! Archy Abhach, is it you? What news of thy mistress?"

"I have neither time nor breath to speak of her at present," cried Archy, leaping from his horse, and hastily unbuckling the little charter-chest from behind the saddle of his reeking horse; " but here —catch !—there you have her charters and titles, being that which I reckon some of the people who are after me would think the best part of herself. There,. catch, I say !" and with that, he threw the precious box clean over the top of the wall.

"Soh !" continued Archy, taking a long breath—"I have done my lady's bidding like a true Cumin, and now I must draw to defend mine own head, like a true Grant, for the knaves will be upon me."

" Thou shalt not long lack help, my brave little fellow !" cried Sir John, and in a moment, a party of armed Grants came crowding out from the gate at the heels of their young chief. And, as Archy's pursuers came up one by one, they collected into a knot on the top of the heathery hillock, and then filed off without ever daring to come within bowshot of the walls.

" Now, tell me what has befallen the Lady Bigla ?" cried Sir John Grant, impatiently addressing the page.

The faithful Archy Abhach gave him a brief outline of all he knew.

" To horse ! to horse !" cried Sir John, hardly waiting till he had finished. " Holy St. Mary ! she may be lost if we tarry."

*A very few minutes only were expended ere Sir John and his troop were mounted and away. They galloped after the retiring Cumins, but they could see nothing of them anywhere. He had got to the side of the hill of Craig-Bey, and was stretching his eyes in all directions, when the distant clash of conflict came up through the woods that sloped away into the glen to the right. Sir John gave the spur to his horse, and dashed down through the thicket, calling to his men to follow him. In a grassy holm, by the side of a small stream, he found Bigla Cumin surrounded by her faithful but small band of followers, who were bravely defending her against a superior body of assailants. His sudden appearance immediately dispersed her enemies, and, overpowered by the fatigue occasioned by her long wearisome and rapid flight, as well as by the alarm which she had endured, she slipped from her palfrey, and sank exhausted on the ground. Sir John Grant was soon on his knees beside her, to support her weakness, and to calm her agitation. She had owed her escape, in the

first place, to the swiftness and endurance of her favourite
Arabian blooded palfrey, together with her own wonderful
hardihood as a horsewoman, which, much surpassing that
of the Lady Juliana Berners herself, had carried her over
mountain and moss, through bog and stream, in a manner
altogether inconceivable ; and, secondly, to the appearance of Sir John Grant, just as she had been attacked by a
quickly formed ambush of the retreating Cumins, whose
onset had given time to those who pursued her to come up,
by which means she and her people being hemmed in on
all sides would have been speedily overcome.

Ere the evening closed in, Bigla Cumin found herself
safely housed within the walls of Castle Grant ; and
the very next day the priest's blessing gave to Sir John
Grant her fair hand, and with it her fair lands too.

VELVET CUSHIONS.

Clifford.—Well done, Bigla Cumin! If ever I marry, I am resolved to have a fearless wife who can gallop across a country. But hey!—(*stretching himself as we arose to proceed*)—I protest I am quite stiff. Confound your green velvety grass! commend me rather to your velvet cushion of Genoa. Your story was too long, Mr. Macpherson, and by far too interesting for a breezy hill-side and a dewy bank like this.

Dominie.—It will grieve me sore, Mr. Clifford, if you should in any way suffer from my prolixity.

Clifford.—Tut, man, I'd sit in a snow-wreath, or on a glacier, to listen to you. But, hark ye! what was that you muttered, before you began your story, about leaving us?

Dominie.—Really I cannot speak it without vurra great pain, Mr. Clifford; but my path disparts from your road a little way on here. I have to wend my way through the whole extent of these wild forests, which you see below us there, stretching across the intermediate country between us and the misty Cairngorums yonder. I am journeying to visit a brother of mine, who, as the elegant author of Douglas hath it,

> "Feeds his flocks,
> A frugal swain,"

on the slopes of the mountains beyond.

Clifford.—Nay, nay, we cannot part with you so. Had it been a lady, indeed, that you were going to visit, I should not have said a word. But for a brother merely.

Dominie (with the tear swelling in his eye).—Pardon me, Mr. Clifford, pardon me; but I have an affection for my brother which few can estimate. We were twin bairns. Ewan and I alone remain of all our family. I make a yearly journey to visit him.

Clifford.—I venerate you for your feelings, and I

sympathise with them from the bottom of my heart. But if I may make a guess at the geography of the country before us, I should conceive that if we could persuade you to go with us to Tomantoul to-day, your walk from thence to your brother's to-morrow would be but short.

Dominie (hesitating).—Hu—um!—that may be, sir. I am sure I am vurra happy in your company; but, may I ask gentlemen, what your plans are?

Clifford.—We tie ourselves to no plans. For aught we know we may be in Switzerland or Sweden before this day month. But, at present, we propose to proceed up the Glen of the Aven to-morrow, on our way to Loch Aven.

Dominie.—It is a wild place, and the way is not easy to find.

Author.—Wild enough, indeed. I once wandered all round it; but I never approached it by its own glen.

Dominie.—I would have fain gone with you as your guide, for well do I know every mountain, moss, rock, and well by the way. But I cannot mistrust my brother, who is expeckin' me about this time. Albeit, as I cannot go all the way myself with you, I would fain, before I quit you, put you into the hands of one who is well acquainted with all the mountain tracks and passes, that there may be no risk of your losing yourselves amidst those savage Alpine solitudes.

Clifford.—Ah! that would be kind of you indeed.

Grant.—Had you not better consent to spend this night with us at Tomantoul, then, Mr. Macpherson.

Dominie.—I was just thinking in my own mind that I behooved so to do. I can then see you as far up Strathdaun to-morrow as Gaulrig, where old Willox the Wizard lives, and there——

Clifford.—What! a wizard, said you? You don't mean to put us under the guidance of Satan, I hope. That would indeed be sending us to the——

Dominie.—No, no, Mr. Clifford; but there is a friend of mine, who lives near to old Willox, one Archy Stewart, a retired sergeant, who will be just the man for your purpose, if we can find him at home. He knows every inch of the mountains, and, moreover, he is as full of old stories as an egg is full of meat.

Clifford.—The very man for us. But what can you tell us of old Willox the Wizard? I hope we shall see him.

23

Author.—I have often heard of him. His name is MacGregor, is it not? I should like much to see him.

Dominie.—You will be sure to see him if you call at Gaulrig, for, as he is now above ninety, he is too old to leave home. He is worth the seeing too; for although, as I need not tell you, gentlemen, he never possessed any supernatural power, yet his cleverness must have been great to have enabled him to make the whole country, far and near, believe, even in these more enlightened days, that he can divine secrets and work wonders by means of his two charmed instruments—*the mermaid's stone* and the enchanted *bridal of the water-kelpie.*

Clifford.—How the deuce did he get hold of such articles? and what sort of things are they?

Dominie.—You will easily persuade him to show them to you; and it will be better for me to leave him to tell his own story about them. But, as I have now made up my mind to go on with you to Tomantoul, gentlemen, I can tell you a short anecdote or two of him as we journey on our way, which will show you that all his fame as a warlock really rested on his own natural acuteness.

Clifford.—I could have guessed as much, methinks, without being any great conjuror myself. But let us have your anecdotes, if you please.

Dominie.—I had much information about Willox from the Rev. John Grant, late Minister of Duthel, who was acquainted with him for many years. For, notwithstanding the warlock's reputation for the possession of uncanny qualities, he was uniformly consorted with and treated as a gentleman by all the gentry of this Highland country. My old and worthy, and kind and benevolent friend, Mr. Grant, was a man of too much wisdom as well as learning to believe in the supernatural powers of Willox, or any such pretender. Mr. Grant, indeed, was a man of vurra enlarged mind and sound judgment, a deep divine, a classical scholar, such as is seldom to be met with in our poor country of Scotland, an admirable critic, and an elegant poet; and although what I may be stating regarding him has little to do with what I am going to tell you about Willox, yet, as you may have a chance to hear more of Mr. Grant from my friend Sergeant Archy Stewart when you come to make his acquaintance, I may be allowed to complete my sketch of this remarkable man by saying that,

whilst he was pious and regular in his duties, as became a
clergyman, he was, nevertheless, cheerful and convivial,
and extremely fond of a bit of humour ; and, moreover, as
he was often called upon to give his opinion pretty strongly
in argument, he was equally ready to back it up at any
time by his courage and bodily vigour against the brute
force or the insults of his opponents, in days, now happily
gone by, when even the sacred character of a minister of
the gospel did not always proteck his person from injury.
To enable him to defend himself the more effectually in
such chance encounters, nature had given to him a stout
and athletic frame and a nervous arm, in addition to which
he did himself furnish the hand of that arm with a great
hazel stick, which he facetiously called his *Ruling Elder*,
and so armed, no man nor set of men in the whole country
side could make him show his back. He was a capital
preacher; but many doubted whether his sermons or his
cudgel wrought the most reformation in his neighbourhood.

It was observed that Mr. Grant was always peculiarly
unfortunate in losing his cattle. Not a year passed that
some of them did not die of a strange and unaccountable
disease which quite baffled the skill of all the farriers and
cow-leeches in the district. But on one occasion the
mortality was so great as seriously to threaten the utter
extermination of his stock. As this calamity seemed to
affect none of his neighbours, and to fall upon him alone, it
was not unnatural for his superstitious servants to say that
his cattle were bewitched. In their opinion nobody but
Willox could cure such an evil.

"If you don't send for Willox, sir, you'll lose every
nout beast in your aught," said the minister's hind.

"Saunders," replied the minister, "although I have no
faith in any such wicked and abominable superstitions as
would gift Mr. MacGregor with superhuman powers, I am
willing enough to give him credit for more than ordinary
shrewdness and sagacity as a mere man. You may, therefore, send for him with my compliments, as I believe that
he is more likely than any one to discover the natural
cause of these my losses."

Willox came accordingly; and after the usual salutations he took the parson aside.

"Between you and me, Mr. Grant," said he, "there is

no use in my making any pretence of witchcraft. But you know we may find out the cause of the death of your cattle for all that. Your losses, I think, always happen at or about this particular season of the year?"

"They do," replied the parson.

"Come, then, let you and me take a quiet walk together over your farm."

Mr. Grant and Willox patiently perambulated the farm, and especially the cattle-pastures for some hours together, Willox all the while throwing his sharp eyes around him in every direction, until they came to a hollow place where the warlock suddenly stopped.

"Here is the cause of the evil," said Willox, at once pointing to a certain plant which grew there, and nowhere else in the neighbourhood. "If you will only take care that your man Saunders never allows your cattle to get into this hollow until the flower of that plant is withered and gone, you will find that you will never again lose a single beast in the same way."

I need not tell you, gentlemen, that Mr. Grant took care that the warlock's advice was strictly followed; and the result was perfectly satisfactory.

Clifford.—A most invaluable wizard! I wonder whether one might hold a consultation with him on the mysteries of fly-fishing.

Grant.—I have no doubt he could advise you well.

Clifford.—Nay, it was not for myself that I was asking. I manage to do well enough by means of mine own conjuring rod; but to you and my friend there some little aid of magic might be useful, seeing you can make so little of it by your own simple skill. But come, Mr. Macpherson, what more of old Willox?

Dominie.—A great alarm was created at Castle Grant, in consequence of a strange madness that frequently seized upon the cattle at pasture in the grounds. At such times they were observed furiously running in all directions, with the tips of their noses and tails in the air, and bursting over all the fences. The easiest solution of this phenomenon was to say that they were bewitched; and all the servants about the castle, especially those who had the broken fences to mend, believed that it was the true one. Even Sir James Grant, worthy man, when brought out to judge for himself, could not deny the grounds at least of

this general opinion. To satisfy those who held it, he
allowed the aid of Willox to be called in.

"Some trick has been played here," said the warlock,
after inquiring into all the particulars, and minutely
examining those parts of the pastures where the animals
were in the habit of lying most frequently. "Some wicked
person has thrown some disagreeable odour among the
beasts."

The probability of this was doubted by every one present.
Nay, every one declared that such a thing was impossible.

"Well," said Willox, "*I* know that what I say is true;
and I'll soon convince *you all* that it is possible. Drive
the cattle into the fold."

The cattle were folded accordingly, and Willox walked
into the very midst of them. There he took certain
ingredients from his pocket, and putting them on a small
bundle of tow, he prepared to strike fire with a flint and
steel.

"Now, gentlemen," said he, "I advise all of you who
have any regard for your own safety to look sharp to it."

The fire was struck, the tow was kindled, a most offensive stench arose, and no sooner had the cattle winded the
fumes of it, than they darted off in twenty different directions, as if the burning tow had been the fuse that discharged
them from some vast bomb-shell. The poles and other
barriers of the fold were shivered and levelled in a moment
as if such an inclosure had never existed. Down went the
astonished spectators one by one in detail, as they chanced
to come into the diverging lines of flight of the scattering
herd. Smack, crash, and rumble went the nearer fences,
as the several flying animals went through or over them,
like cannon-shot; and by the time the poor wounded,
maimed, and crippled people had gathered themselves to
their legs, such of them, I mean, as had legs left to stand
upon, they beheld, to their utter dismay, the cattle scour-
ing the distant country in all directions.

I need hardly add, that a little further investigation
enabled Willox, without the aid of witchcraft, not only to
satisfy every one that his first suspicions had been well
founded, but also to prove that they had been so by discovering the offender.

Grant.—Depend upon it, this warlock must be no
ordinary man.

Dominie.—I have another anecdote of him. A certain farmhouse in Strathspey was said to be haunted, and dust and rubbish were thrown into the middle of the family apartment, and no one could discover whence or from what hand they came. Mr. John Grant, the minister of the parish, was sent for to lay the ghost; and to the great comfort of those to whom the house belonged, he came accompanied by Willox.

"While I am engaged in going through the evening family worship," said the parson to Willox, "do you keep your eyes on the alert, and try to ascertain whence the missiles appear to come."

The minister began the duties of the evening. A psalm was sung. During the time the people present were singing it, the volleys were discontinued; but the moment the psalm was ended, the discharges again commenced.

"We had better sing another psalm," whispered Willox to the parson. Mr. Grant immediately gave out some verses accordingly. The disturbance ceased as before; but they were no sooner concluded, than it began again with redoubled fury. The sharp eyes of Willox shot like lightning into every part of the chamber. In an instant they were arrested by one of those great clumsy wooden partitions so common in our Highland farmers' humble dwellings, which, being boarded on both sides, rise up a certain height only towards the bare rafters above, leaving the vast vacuity below the roof undivided from end to end of the building. Willox gave a preconcerted sign to the parson.

"My friends," said Mr. Grant, "I insist that the boxing of that partition be immediately opened up."

His orders were obeyed, and no sooner were the boards removed than the ghost was discovered. A little black Highland herd lassie sat cowering within, her face filled with dread of the punishment that awaited her. The creature had managed from time to time to creep in there by lifting up a loose plank, and from that concealment she had contrived to throw her missiles over the open top of the partition into the apartment, all which she had done to revenge herself against the family for having been whipped for some piece of negligence of which she had been guilty. The parson had no sooner learned these particulars, than he pounced upon the trembling culprit, like a great mastiff on a mouse, and dragging her forth, he, without the least delay or ceremony, gave her, to use his own phrase, a good *skegging*.

Clifford.—Had Mr. Grant and Willox been sent for, the celebrated ghost of Cock Lane would have had but a short reign of it.

Dominie.—I have but one story more of Willox to plague you with. William Stuart, a farmer in Brae Moray, was led, by his father's persuasion, and very much against his own inclination, to marry a woman whom he could not like, all because she possessed a certain tocher. He went to his marriage like a condemned thief to the gallows, and from the very first moment he treated his wife as an alien. A certain worthy lady in the neighbourhood, who felt interested in Mrs. Stuart, firmly believed that her husband's dislike to her was occasioned by witchcraft. She accordingly sent for Willox, and entreated him to exercise his skill in the poor woman's behalf, and the warlock undertook to do all in his power for her.

Having contrived to pay a visit at Stuart's house, when he knew that he should find him at home, he accepted his invitation to stay to dine with him, and after they had had a cheerful glass together, Willox ventured to begin his attempt by drinking Mrs. Stuart's health.

" You are the only man, Stuart, that does not admire your wife," said Willox, in a half jocular tone.

" May be so," said Stuart dryly.

" If you were not bewitched, as my skill tells me that you are, you would find more happiness at your own fireside than you do," continued Willox.

" Maybe I am bewitched," said Stuart, from the mere desire of being civil.

" I tell you I know you are," said Willox, " and if you will allow me I shall soon show you the people who have bewitched you."

" Ha! ha! I should like to see them," said Stuart with a forced laugh ; " but if you do show them to me, you are even a greater conjuror than I take you to be."

Willox, with great solemnity, now took forth the mermaid's stone from his pocket. It was semi-transparent, circular, and convex, like an ordinary lens, and it filled the palm of his hand. Placing the back of his hand on the table, and keeping the stone in the hollow of it, he solemnly addressed Stuart.

" If you would know those who bewitch you," said he, "look downwards through the mermaid's stone."

" I see nothing," said Stuart, following his direction.

" Do you see nothing now ?" demanded Willox.

" Yes," replied Stuart, "I see something like a red spot."

" Look again, do you see nothing more now?" demanded Willox.

" Yes," said Stuart again, "I see something like a black spot, a little way from the red spot."

" Listen, then !" said Willox. " These are the heads of a red-haired lass and a black-haired lass, and it is they who bewitch you from your lawful wife."

" If you are not a great warlock, you are at least a great rascal," cried Stuart, losing all temper; " but by the great oath, I'll soon know which you are." And saying so, he suddenly seized on the wizard's hand before he was aware, and turning it up, he extracted two pins from between the fingers, the head of one of which had been dipped in red wax, and the head of the other in black wax.

" You scoundrel," said Stuart, preparing to assault him, " you have been unjustifiably prying into my secrets, but I'll teach you to use greater discretion in future."

" Approach me at your peril !" cried Willox, stepping back towards the door, and brandishing a dagger which he drew from his bosom. " I have done or said nothing but what is friendly to you, and if you have the folly to attempt anything of a different nature towards me, you must take the consequences," and so saying he immediately took himself off. So ended the Dominie.

Our walk to-day had little beauty in it, except in its distant prospects, which, when we looked over the vast extent of fir forests towards the Cairngorum group of mountains, were always grand. The scenery of the Aven indeed, and especially at the spot where we crossed it, delighted us all. The fragment of the ruined bridge of Campdale still stood, a sad monument of the ravages of the fearful flood of August, 1829; but the stream now sparkled away along its customary channel like liquid crystal.

Clifford (stopping mechanically to put his fishing-rod

together).—It is certainly the clearest stream I ever beheld.
Yet shall I try my skill to extract some trouts from it
for dinner.

*Grant (as we ascended the path that led us up from the
deep glen of the Aven where we left Clifford fishing).*—Anything to be seen at Tomantoul?

Author.—Nothing that I have ever been able to discover.
The sight is one of the dreariest I know,—a high, wide,
bare, and uninteresting moor, quite raised, as you see,
above all the beauties of the river, which are buried from
it in the profound of the neighbouring valley; nor has
the village itself any very great redeeming charm about it.

Grant.—How comes it that all the cottages and walls
are built of sandstone in the very heart of this primitive
country?

Author.—You may well be surprised, but you will
perhaps be still more astonished to learn that the place
stands on a great detached isolated field of the floetz strata,
four miles in length by one in breadth, which has been
raised up on the very bosom of the primitive granite.

Grant.—A curious geological fact.

Author.—It is a fact which I learned when I was here
formerly from a very intelligent gentleman who is the
clergyman here, to whom I was also indebted for much
valuable information during my inquiries about the great
flood. I shall be happy to introduce you to him.

Grant.—I believe similar instances occur elsewhere in
this part of Scotland.

Author.—Yes, at Kildrummie Castle, in the Glen of
Dollas, and also near the borders of the primitive in the
vale of Pluscardine.

Dominie.—To what strange changes has this earth of
ours been subjeckit!

Grant.—Tell me, I pray you, what nice looking house
is this?

Author.—It is the residence of the clergyman; perhaps
you would like to call on him now, while our friend here
goes on to the inn with our man to secure beds and
entertainment for us all.

Grant assented, and, entering the manse accordingly, we
remained talking very agreeably there, until the whistling
of Clifford, as he marched up the street with his rod in his
hand, and his fishing pannier on his back, made us suddenly

terminate our interesting colloquy, in order to run after him. As we got into the inn we found him in the act of admiring his trouts, which filled a large trencher.

Clifford.—See what noble fellows! There is one of three pounds and a half if he is an ounce. I hooked him in the pool above the broken bridge, and I called to you as you were going up the hill to come back and witness the sport he yielded; but you were too intent on your own conversation to hear me, and so you lost it all. What *were* you talking about?

Grant.—Geology.

Clifford.—Geology!—fiddlesticks. By all that is good, you deserve to dine upon fossil fishes.

Author (*to the landlady*).—Well, ma'am, I hope you can give us something good for dinner.

Landlady.—We shall see, sir; we'll do the best we can.

Author.—You will at least be able to give us an omelet, after the instructions I gave you when I was last in your house.

Landlady.—That I can; I made one for the Duke when he was up here at the fowling, and he said that it was just famous.

Clifford.—Can you give us any soup?

Landlady.—Na, sir; I'm dootin' that I hae na time for that.

Clifford.—Pooh! If you will give me a large smooth white pebble, such as is called by my geological friends here quartz, but which you know better, I believe, by the name of a *chucky-stane*, I'll make some capital soup out of it in a very few minutes.

Landlady.—Odd, sir, I'm thinkin' ye'll be clever an ye can do that.

Clifford.—Be quick, then, and fetch me such a stone as I have described. Remember it must be quite clean, and large enough to make soup for four gentlemen,—and recollect that we are very hungry.

Landlady (*entering with a stone in one hand*).—There it is. It's quite clean, for I washed it wi' my ain hands.

Clifford.—So, that is all right. Now, fetch me a pan with clean water in it. Oh, you have it there, I see. Well, put in the stone, and put the pan on the fire. Now, you see, my good woman, I am a pupil of old Willox the Warlock, therefore you need not be astonished at anything I do. Go get me a spoon to taste the soup with. (*Whilst her back is turned, slyly dropping a cake or two of portable soup into the pot.*) Aye, now, let me see; taste it yourself. It already begins to have some flavour.

Landlady (*astonished*).—Have a care o' huz a', so it has!

Clifford (*stirring it*).—But, stay a moment; taste it now!

Landlady (*taking a spoonful of it*).—Keep me, that *is* just awthegither maygics indeed!

Clifford (*tasting it*).—Oh, it will do now. Bring me an iron spoon to take out the stone with. Now, here take it away, dry it well, and lock it carefully up in your larder; for, you perceive, that it is but very little wasted, and, consequently, it will make some good tureens of soup yet; and though such stones are plenty enough, yet you know it is always good housewifery to be economical.

Landlady (*taking away the stone*).—That's true, indeed, sir.

Grant (*after we had dined*).—Well, thanks to Clifford's chucky-stone soup, his delicious *fritto* of trout, our landlady's excellent mutton-chops, and your omelet, we have dined like princes.

Clifford.—I am now hungry for nothing but a narrative. Come, Mr. Macpherson, as we are to lose you to-morrow, I must remind you that you are still in my book for some story about Old Stachcan, the man with the pistol, I mean, whose portrait we saw at Castle Grant. Pray do not hesitate to clear off your score.

Dominie.—I need not say, Mr. Clifford, that since you and your friends here are so good as to accept of such poor coin as my bit stories, in return for all the kindness and condescension which I have received from you, it is well my part to pay it readily, and without a grudge. But what I had to tell you about Old Stachcan was more an account of the man than any very parteeklar story about him. Now, as you will pass by the very bit where he lay concealed, I would rather leave it to my friend Sergeant Archy Stewart, who knows more about him than I do, to give you his history on the spot.

Grant.—Well, since that is the case, Mr. Macpherson, I shall undertake to tell a story for you. And instead of that which you were to tell us about *one* Grant, I shall give you a legend which I have heard of *two* lairds of that name.

Clifford.—Provided you do not on that account make your story twice as long as Mr. Macpherson's would have been, I for one am contented.

Grant.—If I should do so, you have your resource, Clifford, you may go to sleep, you know; and if you do, I shall perhaps have the pleasure of singing, in the words of Scott's Water Sprite,—

"Good luck to your fishing."

! *Clifford.*—No more of that, an thou lovest me, Hal.

LEGEND OF THE RIVAL LAIRDS OF STRATHSPEY.

SOME time previous to the Reformation a venerable priest, of the name of Innes, lived at Easter Duthel, in Strathspey, and superintended the spiritual concerns of the people of the surrounding district. He was a benevolent old man, whose heart was devoted to the duties of his sacred office, and to those deeds of Christian benevolence which he inculcated upon his flock by example as well as by precept.

The only other occupation which the good man had was the watching over the nurture and education of his orphan niece, Helen Dunbar, who had been early left to his care by the death of her mother, his only and much beloved sister. Helen was a beautiful young creature. Her features were of the most perfect regularity of form and arrangement, her complexion was the fairest imaginable, the lustre of her dark eyes was softened by their long eyelashes, and her jet-black hair fell in rich abundance over her person, which was in every respect most exquisitely and symmetrically moulded. But what was better than all this, she was as good as she was beautiful. Her whole time and thoughts were occupied in finding out objects for her uncle's benevolence, and, like his ministering angel, she was ever ready to fly to the cottage of the poor, or the bed-side of the sick, to bear thither such comfort or consolation as he had to impart, when the infirmities incidental to his declining years rendered it impossible for him to bestow them in person. When he was able to go upon his own errands of charity he never failed to do so; and on such occasions it was a pleasing sight,—a sight that might have furnished a fine subject for a painter—to have beheld her acting as the crutch of his old age, and the ready auxiliary of all his beneficent actions. You may easily believe that so amiable a pair as Priest Innes and his niece could not fail to secure the love and admiration of every one who knew them.

When they appeared in church, the grey hairs, and the thin, pale, spiritual countenance of the old priest, were looked up to by his flock with reverential awe, as if he had been some being who was only lent to them for a brief season from another and a better world, and who might every moment be called on to return thither. But whilst there was enough of heaven in the young and healthful face and form of Helen Dunbar, she was regarded by all with an affectionate attachment which savoured more of the kind and kindred feelings of humanity, and the good folks were thus satisfied through the niece that the uncle was allied to the earth. Fathers and mothers regarded her and loved her as a daughter, young maidens looked upon her with the warmest sisterly affection, and the youths of the district, with whom modesty naturally made her less familiar, beheld her with that respectful adoration which was due to so angelic a creature. I speak, of course, of those of humbler rank; for there were many among the young knights and lairds of the neighbourhood who would have willingly robbed the old man of his treasure by carrying her home as a bride.

Of this latter class there were two, who, as they were the most remarked of the admirers of Helen Dunbar, were also believed to be the most formidable rivals to each other. These were Lewis Grant, the young laird of Auchernach, and John Dhu Grant of Knockando. The first of these was a tall, handsome, fair-faced young man, universally believed to be open, brave, generous, and warm-hearted. He had the art of making himself beloved by all who knew him, and people thought that he had no fault in life but a certain degree of hastiness of temper, which, as folks said, might flash out violently upon particular occasions, and yet would pass away as harmlessly as a blaze of summer lightning, leaving everything peaceful behind it after it was gone. The other was a dark swart man, properly conducted, and calm and cold looking, whom it somehow happened that nobody knew sufficiently either to like or to dislike. Both of these gentlemen were observed to be very assiduous in their attentions to Helen Dunbar upon all occasions where they were seen in her company. But the talk of the country was, that if either of them met

with encouragement at all, Lewis of Auchernach was
rather the happier man. As the fact, if it was a fact,
could have been known to himself and the lady alone, this
suspicion probably arose partly from the circumstance that
Auchernach was the general favourite, and partly because
his place of residence was nearer to the parsonage of Easter
Duthel by some fifteen or twenty miles or so than that of
his rival. But I, who as a narrator of their story am
entitled to arrogate to myself a perfect knowledge of all
their secrets, and in virtue of such my office, to be present
at, and to describe scenes witnessed by no eyes but those
of the actors themselves, I will venture to assure you,
upon my own authority, that public opinion, however
rarely it may be correct, was in this instance the true one,
and that Lewis Grant of Auchernach had really for some
time been the favoured lover of the fair Helen Dunbar;
that they had already plighted troth to each other, and,
moreover, that their mutual love was neither unknown nor
disapproved of by the lady's venerable uncle.

You will easily guess, from what I have already told
you of the good priest of Easter Duthel, that he was not
one of those sour sons of the church who think that it is
their duty to keep as much aloof from their flocks as they
possibly can, and who would consider it as quite unclerical
to appear capable of participating in their harmless amusements, who think it better to allow rustic enjoyment to
run into what riot and excess it may, than to hallow and
temper it by the sacredness of their presence. Priest
Innes and his niece were always invited and expected to
be present at all merry-makings; and the consequence was,
that he kept many such scenes within the bounds of
innocence and propriety, which might have otherwise gone
very much beyond their limits. A word from their pastor
indeed was at any time sufficient to bring the liveliest and
most exciting revel to a decent close.

It happened that a joyous meeting of this sort occurred
one night at the mill of Duthel, occasioned by the marriage
of the miller's daughter. As the miller was a wealthy man
and well known by all ranks, and the bridegroom was
highly respectable, the assemblage was graced by many of
the lairds and better sort of people along the banks of the
Spey; and, amongst others, both Auchernach and Knockando were there. The matrimonial rite was performed by

the good Priest Innes with all due ceremonial. But when the company adjourned to the long granary, where the sports of the evening were to be held, and when the harps and the bagpipes began alternately to give animation and joy to the scene, he did not consider that the jocund dance or the merriment that ensued brought with it any just or reasonable argument for his departure. On the contrary, seated in the chair of honour, his venerable and benignant countenance was lighted up with smiles of pleasure from the inward gratification he felt in beholding the chastened happiness of all around him.

His niece, Helen Dunbar, sat in a chair by the old man's side, that is to say, she sat there during such intervals as she was allowed to rest from the joyous exercise in which all were participating. These indeed were few and short, because she was of all others the partner most sought after. She danced often with Auchernach, and not unfrequently with Knockando; and from that desire, natural enough to maidens, to veil the true object of her affections from prying eyes around her, she was, if possible, even more gracious that night in her manner and conversation to the latter than she was to the former. The cold dark countenance of John Dhu Grant was flushed and animated more than it had ever been before, by the seeming preference which was thus shown to him. Presuming upon that which his passion magnified, he persecuted Helen with attentions which she now began to see the necessity of repressing. She could not well do this without throwing more of her favour into the scale of him whom Knockando so well knew to be his rival. This alteration on her part inwardly galled and irritated the disappointed man beyond what his habitual self-command allowed his countenance to express. Lewis Grant of Auchernach, on the other hand, satisfied with his own secret convictions, went on joyfully through the mazes of the dance, perfectly heedless of all those minor changes on the face or manner of Helen which had so touched John Dhu, whose equanimity was not the better preserved because he perceived how little that of his rival was affected.

"These weddings are mighty merry things, Auchernach," observed Knockando with seeming coolness, as they accidentally stepped aside together at the same moment to take a cup of refreshment.

"When or where can we expect mirth, Knockando, if we find it not on a wedding-night?" said Auchernach, after courteously pledging to his health. "The happy union of two devoted young hearts, as yet unscathed by the blasts of adversity, smiling hope dancing before them, gilding with sunshine all the brighter prospects of life, whilst her friendly hand throws a roseate veil over all its drearier and darker changes."

"Thou speakest so warmly that methinks thou wouldst fain be a bridegroom thyself, Auchernach," said Knockando.

"So very fain would I so be, Knockando, that I care not if this were my wedding-night," replied Auchernach with great animation.

"Ha! ha! ha! art thou indeed so desirous to barter thy sweet liberty?" said Knockando. "Well, then, I suppose that I may look for a spice of thine envy now, should I perchance submit to my fate, and yield to those blandishments which have been so skilfully used to catch me."

"I envy no one," said Auchernach carelessly, "and sooth to say, very far indeed should I be from envying thee, Knockando; trust me, no one would dance more heartily at thy wedding than I should."

"Since thou art so fond of dancing at weddings, depend on't thou shalt not lack an invitation to mine," said Knockando; "nay, out of my great friendship for thee, I have half a mind to sacrifice myself and to hasten my fate, were it only to indulge thy frolicsome propensities."

"Kindly said of thee, truly," replied Auchernach, laughing good humouredly, "then sudden and sweet be thy fate, say I."

"If I mistake not greatly, my fate is in mine own hand," continued Knockando, throwing a significant glance across the room towards the place where Helen Dunbar was then sitting beside her uncle.

"What!" exclaimed Auchernach in amazement, hardly daring to trust himself with the understanding of what seemed thus to be hinted at by his rival.

"Thou see'st how her eyes do continually rest upon me as if I were her loadstar," continued Knockando. "Her solicitation could not be more eloquently expressed by a thousand words."

"Whose eyes? whose solicitation?" cried the astonished

24

Auchernach, his countenance kindling up with an ire which it was impossible for him to conceal.

"Whose eyes? whose solicitation?" repeated Knockando. "Those love-encumbered and pity-seeking eyes yonder, which are now darting glances of entreaty towards me from beneath the dark-arched eyebrows of the beauteous Helen Dunbar. The girl loves me to distraction; and if no other motive could move me, feelings of compassion would of themselves urge me to show some mercy towards her, and to make her my wife."

"Villain!" cried Auchernach, at once losing all command of himself, "thou art a base traducer, and a lying knave to boot!"

The previous part of this dialogue had been overheard by no one; but these last words were thundered forth by Auchernach in a voice so loud that they shook the whole room, stopped music, dance and all, and attracted every eye towards the speaker, just in time to see him fell Knockando to the ground by a single blow.

The confusion that ensued was great. Knockando was raised from the floor by some of his dependants who chanced to be present. Dirks might have been drawn and blood might have flowed, had not the good priest immediately hastened, with what speed his tottering steps enabled him to exert, to interpose his sacred person, and to use his pious influence to allay the growing storm. By his authority he now put an abrupt termination to the festivities of the evening. Ashamed of his violence, Auchernach came forward to entreat a hearing from the priest, and at the same time to offer that support to his feeble frame in his homeward walk which, in conjunction with his niece, he was not unfrequently allowed to yield him, and of which the agitated and trembling Helen Dunbar had hardly strength at that moment to contribute her share. But he was shocked and mortified to find himself rebuffed, and his proffered services refused in a manner at once resolute and dignified.

"No!" said the priest, waving him away, "until thou shalt humble thyself, and make thy peace with Knockando, thou canst have no converse with me; and to prevent the chance of his suffering further insult or injury from thine intemperance, he shall be my guest for to-night. Give me thine arm, Knockando."

"Old man! look that thou dost not pay dear for thy favour to that new guest of thine!" cried Auchernach aloud, and gnashing his teeth in the vexation and bitterness of his heart.

"What! dost thou threaten?" said Knockando coldly, as he left the place. "This way, reverend sir, lean on me, I pray thee."

"Villain! villain!" muttered Auchernach, striking his breast with a fury which now knew no bounds, and, rushing out like a madman, he hurried homewards to spend a sleepless and agitated night.

The miller's guests departed to their several abodes, wondering at Auchernach's strange and unaccountable conduct, talking much of it, and no one blaming him the less that his furious and apparently uncalled for violence had so rudely and so provokingly put an end to their evening's merriment.

John Dhu Grant was hospitably entertained and lodged by the priest; but Helen Dunbar allowed him to mount his horse next day, to ride home to Knockando, without ever permitting him to be once gladdened by the sunshine of her countenance. As she had wept all that night, so she sat all the ensuing morning in her chamber, brooding over the distressing scene of the previous evening, and anxiously listening for the footsteps of Auchernach, in the hope that he might come to give her some explanation of the cause of the strange ungovernable fury to which he had given way. But he came not.

"I had hoped to have seen our friend Auchernach here in tears and repentance," said Priest Innes mildly to his niece, when they at last met: "I fear he hath hardly yet come to a due sense of his error."

Helen was silent and sorrowful. She still trusted, however, that he might yet come. Her ears were continually fancying that she heard his well-known step and voice, and they were as perpetually deceived. The whole day and the whole evening passed away, and still he came not. With a sad heart she accompanied her uncle to his chamber, to go through those religious duties with him in which they never failed to join before they separated for the night. Her voice trembled as she uttered her responses to the prayers of the priest, and the old man, participating in her feelings, and fully sympathising with her, was little less affected. But her self-command altogether forsook her, when, after the prescribed formula of service was at an end, her uncle again kneeled down reverently on the cushion by his bed-side, and prayed fervently for her and for her future happiness, and that the Almighty protection might be extended over her when it should please Heaven to remove him from this earthly scene. And when, as connected with this dearest object of his heart, he put up earnest petitions for him who was already destined to be her husband and protector, she hid her face on the bed, and sobbed aloud. He besought his Creator so to deal graciously with the erring youth, as to make him deeply sensible of the wickedness of so readily yielding, as he had recently done, to the violence of passion; and he implored the Divine Being to render his repentance sincere and enduring, so that he might never again be led to sin in the same way.

"I forgive him already!" said the good man, as he gave his niece his parting embrace; "I forgive him, and so will you, Helen. And if I have been too hasty in judging *him*, as in mine erring nature I may have been, may God forgive *me!* Bless thee, my child! and may the holy Virgin and her angels hover over thy pillow! Good night!"

Helen's tears prevented her from speaking, and after partially composing herself, she arranged the simple uncanopied and uncurtained couch which her uncle used, in obedience to his rigid rule, smoothed his pillow, placed a carved ebony crucifix, with an ivory figure of the Redeemer attached to it, on the little oaken table that stood by his bed-side, and after trimming his night-lamp, she set it before the little image, and having laid his breviary and his beads beside it, she placed the cushion so that he might the more easily perform those religious rites which his duty prescribed to him, and which he regularly and strictly attended to at certain watches of the night, and having done these little offices, she again tenderly embraced him, and retired to her own chamber.

The good priest's mind was so filled with distress about Auchernach, that he could not close an eye. For several hours he lay turning over and over in his thoughts those prospects which his niece had before her from such a marriage—a marriage the contemplation of which had so recently laid every anxiety of his heart regarding her most satisfactorily to rest, all of which were now again awakened afresh by the unfavourable view which last night's experience had given him of her future husband. In vain he tried to court slumber. At last when nearly worn out with watching, he arose and kneeled before the emblems of his faith, to perform his midnight orisons. When these were concluded, he took up the crucifix with veneration, reverently kissed the image of our suffering Saviour, and, laying himself again down in bed, he covered himself with the clothes, and, placing the crucifix length-wise upon his bosom, he committed himself in thought to the protection of his patron-saint, and composed himself confidently to rest, under the conviction that he should now be certain of enjoying sweet slumber.

And the good man was not mistaken. Sleep immediately weighed down his eyelids, and his senses were soon steeped in the deepest and most perfect oblivion. If you will only fancy to yourselves his venerable and placid countenance, pale as the sheet which partially shrouded his chin, and rendered yet paler by its contrast with the black cap which he wore, his motionless form disposed underneath the bed-clothes, with the crucifix lying along over it, you will be ready to admit that his whole appearance might have well suggested the idea of a saint.

But the devil was that night abroad. The priest's habitation was humble, and, though partly consisting of two low stories, the roof was composed of a simple wattle, covered with heather thatch. His chamber was above, and away from those of the other inmates, at one end, where a lower shed was attached to the back of the building. Suppose yourselves, for a moment, invisible spectators of a scene which was alone looked down upon by that eye which sees all things. Listen to that strange deafened sound above, as if some one was crawling over the outside of the roof. What noise is that as of a cutting and plucking up of the heather? Ha! did you see that dirk-blade glisten through the frail work of the wattle?—again, and again, it comes! It rapidly cuts its way in a large circle through the half rotten material of which the roof is composed. The fingers of a hand now appear under it, as if to prevent the piece which is about to be detached from falling downwards, and alarming the sleeper. He hears not the noise, for he sweetly dreams that as he prays on his knees, the clouds are opened, and the beautified countenance of his patron-saint smiles upon him from the skies, and beckons to him to throw off his mortality, and to join him in the heavens. He awakes with the effort which he makes to obey him; and, immediately over his bed he indistinctly beholds, by the feeble light of his night lamp, the stern and remorseless features of a man,—the eyes glaring fearfully upon him. He is paralysed by the sight: and, ere he can move, nay, ere he can utter one shriek of alarm, the murderer drops upon his bed, and, crouched across him, he, with his left hand, lays bare the emaciated throat of the old priest, and with his right he strikes his dirk blade through it, till it pierces the very pillow underneath. No sigh escapes from the murdered man. If groan there be at all, it comes growling from the ferocious heart of the fiend who does the atrocious deed; who, as he sits for a moment to satisfy himself that his victim is really dead, shudders to look upon his own bloody work. To shut it out from his eyes, even for the instant, he replaces the bed-clothes over the chin, and, adjusting the crucifix as he found it, he makes a precipitate retreat through the orifice in the roof by which he entered.

If you have well pictured to yourselves the particulars of this most revolting murder, you will be the better able to imagine the scene that took place next morning when, at the hour at which she usually went to awake her uncle, to receive his kiss and his blessing, to inquire how he had passed the night, and to administer to his little wants, his affectionate niece softly entered the apartment of the good Priest Innes. Her eyes were naturally directed at once to the bed, so that the hole in the roof above escaped her notice.

"How tranquilly he sleeps!" whispered she; "I almost grudge to awaken him to the recollection of that distressing event of the evening before last, which so disturbed him, and which hath ever since so tortured me. I see, from the crucifix being laid on his bosom, that the earlier part of his night hath not been passed with the same composure as he now enjoys. But it is late, and he may chide me if I allow him longer to slumber. Uncle! dear uncle!

it is time for you to be up. Ha! still he answereth not! can he be unwell?"

Snatching up the crucifix with one hand, and gently removing the bed-clothes from her uncle's chin with the other, the harrowing spectacle that presented itself told her the fatal truth. She stood for one moment petrified by the sight, uttered one piercing shriek that penetrated into every part of the humble dwelling, and then she fell backwards on the floor in a swoon, where the old woman, Janet, who waited on her, and James, the priest's man, both of whom came running to her aid at the same moment, found her lying, with the crucifix firmly and spasmodically embraced over her bosom.

You all know how fast ill tidings travel. The particulars of this horrible transaction, multiplied and magnified, quickly spread far and wide, and the whole neighbourhood was instantly in a ferment. The lamentations for their priest, their father and their friend, were loud and heart-felt, and the execrations which were poured out on his murderer were deep, and were mingled with unceasing cries of vengeance. But, on whom were they to be avenged? Who was the person most likely to have committed so foul a deed?—a murder in every respect so unprovoked, and so perfectly without any apparent object, committed on an innocent and pious man, who could never have been supposed to have had an enemy! It could have been the work of no common robber, for the few small articles of value which the priest's chamber contained were left untouched. The outrageous conduct of Lewis Grant of Auchernach on the evening of the previous night, at the wedding at the miller's—conduct which had already been talked of and discussed with no inconsiderable degree of reprobation by every one who had seen or heard of it, now came fresh into the minds of all. The vengeful threat which he seemed to have directed against the innocent and pious Priest Innes, in return for his calm and fatherly rebuke, was now remembered by every one. The very words had been treasured up by many of them, and were repeated from mouth to mouth—"*Old man! look that thou dost not pay dear for thy favour to that new guest of thine!*" Uttered as they had been with the gnashing teeth of frantic passion, and with rage and revenge flashing from his eyes, they were too plain to be mistaken. High in favour as Auchernach was well known to have been with the pure inhabitants of the priest's dwelling, his violence was very easily explained by the jealousy which it was natural to suppose must have been excited in him by the visible preference which had been that evening given by Priest Inues to his rival, John Dhu of Knockando, a circumstance to which his threat had so distinctly pointed. The grounds of suspicion against him, therefore, were too evident—too damning to be for one moment doubted ; and he who, two short days before, had been respected and beloved by all who knew him, was at once condemned by every one as a cool, deliberate, sacrilegious murderer. A hue and cry was immediately raised for his apprehension, and off ran the whole population, young and old, and of both sexes, to secure, or to witness his capture, leaving no one to attend to the afflicted Helen Dunbar but her old woman Janet.

But strange as it may seem, after the people had been gone for some considerable time in hot search of the felon, Lewis Grant himself rode slowly up to the priest's house. For some reason which he best knew, he came by a road quite different from that which should have brought him directly from Auchernach. He seemed gloomy and thoughtful—his head hung down—and as he walked his horse up to the stable and dismounted, as he was often wont to do, to put the beast with his own hand into the stall with which it was sufficiently familiar, his eyes glanced furtively in all directions from under the broad bonnet that shaded his brow. Having disposed of the animal, he shut the stable door, and, with a downcast look and chastened step, very much unlike that which had usually carried him over the same fragment of ground, and with a sigh that almost amounted to a groan, he presented himself at the little portal of the house. With a hesitating hand he lifted the latch, and with his limbs trembling beneath him, he moved softly along the passage that led to the priest's parlour. He halted for a moment irresolutely at the door of that little chamber where he had passed so many happy days and hours. At last he summoned up courage enough to open it, and he stood on its threshold with his eyes thrown upon the ground. Silence prevailed within, till it was broken by a deep convulsive sob. He looked up, and he beheld old Janet, with her back towards him, kneeling beside a low couch placed against the opposite wall ; and upon its pillow, and stretched out at length upon it in a state which left him in doubt whether she was dying, or already dead, lay the grief-worn countenance and the form of Helen Dunbar. He was struck dumb by this spectacle. He stood amazed, with the blood running cold to his heart. But recollection soon returned to him—his whole frame shook with the agitation of his feelings, and, clasping his hands in an agony, he rushed forward and threw himself on his knees before the couch. The humble domestic was terrified to behold him, and started aloof at the very sight of him.

"Helen!—my life!—my love!" cried he in a frantic tone; "can I—can I, wretch that I am—can I, murderer that I am!—can I have brought death upon my beloved! Oh, answer me!—gaze not thus silently upon me with that fearful look! Am I then become in thy sight so accursed? Oh, mercy!—mercy!—look not so upon me!"

He tried to take her hand. His very attempt to do so seemed instantaneously to rouse her from the stupor in which she had hitherto lain. She recoiled from him back to the wall as if a serpent had stung her, whilst her fixed eyes stared, and her lips moved without sound, as if she could find no utterance for the horrors that possessed her.

"Is there no mercy for me?" cried Auchernach again. "Hast thou doomed me to destruction? Am I to be spurned by thee as I was by thine uncle Priest Innes?"

A prolonged and piercing shriek was all the reply that his frantic appeal received from Helen Dunbar. It was echoed by her old attendant, and mingled with loud cries for help. Steps were heard pattering fast without— Auchernach started up to his feet. The steps came hurrying along the passage—several men burst into the chamber —they stood for a moment in mute astonishment. Then it was that Helen Dunbar seemed to regain all her dormant energies. She sprang from the couch—retreated from Auchernach—and gazing fearfully at him, with her head and body drawn back, she pointed wildly towards him, with both her outstretched arms and hands—and whilst every nerve was convulsed by the torture which her soul was enduring, she at last found words to speak.

"Seize him! Seize the murderer of mine uncle!" she cried in a voice which rang shrilly and terribly in the ears of all who heard her; and altogether exhausted by

this extraordinary effort, she would have fallen forward
senseless on the floor, had she not been, caught by some
of the bystanders, who carried her in a swoon to the
couch from which she had so recently risen.

Auchernach stood fixed and frozen, as if her words had
suddenly converted him into a pillar of ice. He was
immediately laid hold of by some of the men, who hastily
bound him, and he submitted to be led away, as if utterly
unaware of what had befallen him. His horse was taken
from the stable ; he was lifted powerless into the saddle,
and strapped firmly to the animal's back. The crowd of
people who had collected, some on horseback, and some
on foot, looked upon him with horror, mingled with awe.
But no one uttered a word, either of pity or of condemnation. He sat erect, it is true, but it was with all the
rigidity of a stiffened corpse, for not a feature nor a muscle
exhibited the smallest sign of consciousness. That night
found him, after a wearisome journey, of the scenes or
events of which he had no knowledge, chained, on a
heap of straw, on the floor of one of the deepest dungeon-
vaults in the Priory of Pluscarden.

The simple and unpretending funeral of the good Priest
Innes had a larger following than that of any person who
had been buried from that district for many years, and
the silent sorrow which was exhibited by all who beheld
it, was not only more sincere, but it was likewise far more
eloquent than those louder lamentations, and those otherwise more obtrusive expressions of woe which had arisen
around the bier of many a departed knight and laird of
Strathspey. His corpse was carried the same road as they
had taken the wretched man who stood charged with his
murder. It was met at some distance from the Priory by
its monks and their superior, who accompanied the procession, chanting hymns before the coffin, till it was carried
into the church. There the services were performed for the
dead, and he was laid to rest in his last narrow house,
within the cemetery of that religious establishment, where
the requiem masses that were sung for his soul went
faintly, and with anything but consolation, to the ears of
the wretched Auchernach in his subterranean prison.

Most of the gentry of the neighbouring country were
present at these obsequies, and John Dhu Grant was there
amongst others. It was especially remarked, that although

his house of Knockando lay directly in the way between
Easter Duthel and the Priory, and about equidistant from
the two places, his desire to show respect to the memory
of the deceased was so great that he appeared at the
priest's house early on the morning of the funeral, and
rode with the procession all the way to the place of inter-
ment. He, moreover, took a very prominent part in the
whole ceremonial. From these pregnant signs the good
people naturally argued that there had been a gross mistake in the belief that had hitherto so currently prevailed
as to which of the rival lairds had been really most
favoured by Helen Dunbar and her uncle; and the wiser
gossips now shook their heads, and looked forward to the
time when John Dhu Grant would probably dry up the
orphan's tears, and establish her in the arm-chair at the
comfortable fireside of Knockando. The laird himself
never did nor said anything which might have contradicted
any such supposition; on the contrary, he always spoke
and acted as if it was tolerably well-founded.

A good many days passed away after the loss of her
uncle, before the tide of Helen's grief had gushed from her
eyes in sufficient abundance to afford any relief to her deep
affliction. Many were the kind hearts that came to condole
with her, but some of her more intimate friends of her
own sex only had as yet been admitted to her presence to
share her sorrows. John Dhu Grant had made repeated
journeys to call at the house, but his urgent entreaties for
admission had been always met by courteous refusals. He
came at length one day, and as he stated that he was the
bearer of an especial message from the Lord Prior of
Pluscarden, Helen could no longer decline giving him an
audience. She received him, however, not only in the
presence of old Janet, whose long services in the priest's
house had given her most of the privileges and indulgences
of an old friend, but also in that of an elderly matron, who
had kindly agreed to spend some time with her to cheer
her loneliness. You will not be surprised when I tell you
that Helen was deeply affected and much agitated when
the laird entered. After she was somewhat composed,
and the first preliminary civilities were interchanged,—

"I come, lady, from the Lord Prior of Pluscarden," said
Knockando, "and I am the bearer of a message to know,
with all due respect and godly greeting, on his part,

whether thou art as yet sufficiently restored to be able to undertake a journey to the Priory, that thou mayest give evidence against him who now lieth in a dungeon there, charged with the crime of the most sacrilegious murder of thine uncle, Priest Innes ?"

"I beseech thee, sir," said Helen, much affected, and with a trembling and scarcely audible voice, "I beseech thee to tell the reverend father, that I do, with all humility, abide his command, and that when he shall see fit to demand my presence, I shall be ready to obey."

"I doubt not that thou art by this time most eager to see vengeance fall speedily upon the foul murderer," said Knockando.

"Alas! no vengeance can restore him to me whom I have lost," said Helen, bursting into a flood of tears.

"But his blood crieth out for vengeance, and it lieth with thee to see it done upon the murderer," said Knockando.

"When the Lord Prior calleth for me, I shall speak the truth, and let vengeance rest with that Almighty Being who alone beheld the cruel deed!" said Helen, throwing her eyes upwards as if secretly appealing to Heaven. "As for me, I can but weep for him that is gone, and pray to have that Christian feeling supplied to me which may enable me to forgive even—to forgive even his murderer."

"Forgive his murderer!" cried Knockando, with a strange and wild expression. "Canst thou indeed think that thou mayest yet ever be brought to forgive him? But no! no! no!" continued he calmly, and with his usual cold manner and unmoved countenance, "it cannot surely be that thou couldst ever bring thyself to *save* the monster who could allow one passing word of just reproof to wipe out so many years of kind and hospitable intercourse, and who could revenge it by so barbarous and unheard of a murder."

"I said *forgive*, not *save*," replied Helen, in a half choked voice. "The laws of God and of man alike require that the murderer should die; and I shall never flinch from the dreadful but imperious duty which now devolves upon me, to see that justice is done upon the guilty person. But our blessed Saviour hath taught me to *forgive* even him; and ere he be called on to expiate his crime on earth, may the Holy Virgin yield me strength to pray sincerely for his repentance, so that his unhappy soul may be assoilzied from an eternity of torment."

"What!" cried Knockando, with a recurrence of that wildness of expression which he had already exhibited, "canst thou even contemplate so much as this regarding a wretch, who, lighting down like some nocturnal fiend upon the sacred person of thine uncle, ánd, reckless of the emblem of Christ which lay upon his bosom "——

"Ha!" exclaimed Helen, suddenly moved as the horrors of the spectacle she had witnessed were thus so rashly and so rudely recalled to her recollection by this ill-timed speech. "What saidst thou?"

"Nay," continued Knockando, "I wonder not that thou shouldst start thus, as I stir up thy remembrance of the bloody and most inhuman act. Methinks thou wilt hardly now deny me that the man who could put aside the holy image of Christ, that he might plunge his dirk into the innocent throat of his sacred servant, must not only die the death of a felon, but that he can never hope for mercy from Him whose blessed emblem he hath outraged."

"Give me air! give me air!" cried Helen faintly, as she motioned to her companions to open the lattice; and then falling back into the couch, she covered her face with both her hands, and was seized with a long hysterical fit of laughter, followed by a convulsive shudder, from which she was relieved by a deluge of tears.

"This is no scene for a stranger to witness," said the lady who sat with her, "nor is the subject which thou hast chosen to dwell on so circumstantially by any means suited to the weak state of this poor sufferer. I must entreat of thee to withdraw."

"Madam," said Knockando coolly, "I am no stranger. I am here as the messenger of the Lord Prior, and as the friend of the deceased. As that friend to whom the good Priest Innes did manifest his last most open act of confidence. I am here, as it were, by his posthumous authority, as the avenger of his foul murder, and as the protector óf his desolate orphan niece; so that hardly even might the orders of the lady herself induce me to quit this apartment whilst my duty may tell me that I ought to remain."

"Thine arm, Janet," said Helen feebly; and, with the old woman's support, she slowly arose and moved towards the door.

"Stay, stay, I beseech thee, my beloved Helen!" cried Knockando, eagerly rising to follow her. "Stay, I entreat thee, or say at least when I may return to offer thee my protection, that legitimate protection which thine uncle authorised me to yield thee, that substantial protection which can alone be supplied by him who hath the rights and the affection of a husband."

"A husband!" cried Helen, turning suddenly round and gazing wildly at him,—"Husband!" and being again seized with the same involuntary laugh, she was hurried away up stairs to her chamber by the women.

Knockando then slowly left the apartment, called for his horse, and departed.

Helen Dunbar kept her bed all next day, and no one was admitted to her chamber but the lady I have mentioned, and her old and faithful Janet. With these she had long, deep, and private talk regarding all that had passed the previous day. On the ensuing morning the Laird of Knockando again came to the house. Janet was immediately despatched to refuse him admittance. He now came, he said, with a letter from the Lord Prior of Pluscarden, which he trusted would be a passport for him to the lady's presence. Leaving him below, Janet carried it up stairs to her mistress. It was tied with a piece of black silk ribbon, but it had no seal. It ran in these terms :—

"To Helen Dunbar, these,—It being our will and pleasure that the vengeance with the which it doth behoove us to visit Lewis Grant of Auchernach, the murderer of thine uncle, Priest Innes, shall no longer tarry, but descend quickly upon his guilty head, so that the air of our sacred precincts may cease to be poisoned by the foul breath of his life, we do now, by these presents, call upon thee to appear before us here on Tuesday next at noon, to give thy testimony against him. And as the way hither is long and lonely, we do further give thee our fatherly advice to avail thyself of the kind offer about to be made thee by the bearer of this, our friend, that worthy gentleman, John Grant of Knockando, who promises to shorten thy travel by lodging thee in his house on the previous night, and to guard thee hither. And so we greet thee with our holy blessing.

"DUNCANUS PRIOR. PLUS."

Helen was much agitated by the perusal of this letter, but after a little consultation, her friend took it upon herself to go down to tell Knockando that the Prior's summons should be obeyed ; but that the laird's offer of protection and hospitality were with all civility declined. After much vain solicitation on his part, Knockando left the house with great unwillingness.

He had not been gone an hour when the tramping of a horse again sounded in their ears.

"Holy Virgin !" exclaimed Janet, as she looked from the lattice to ascertain who this new visitor might be. "As I hope to be saved, it is the lay brother who rides on the Lord Prior's errands. What can he want, I wonder ?"

Janet hastened down, and soon returned.

"He came the short way over the hills with it," said Janet, putting another letter into Helen's hands.

It bore the large seal of the priory over the black silk ribbon by which it was bound.

"What can this mean ?" said Helen, as with trembling hands she applied the shears to divide the ribbon. "Again a letter from the Lord Prior ! But, as I live, in a very different, fairer, and more clerk-like hand, and, methinks, in better terms."

"*To our much afflicted and much beloved daughter Helen Dunbar—these :*

"Deeply do we and all our brethren grieve for thy cruel affliction. By ourselves, or our sub-prior, we should have ere this visited thee with heavenly comfort, had not weighty affairs hindered. But deem not thyself desolate ; for we do hold that our brother, thy much beloved and greatly lamented uncle, the umquhile Priest Innes (whom God assoilzie !) hath left thee to our guardianship, and, as a daughter of the Church, thou shalt be watched with our especial care. We have made it known to all, that, *but* further delay, we shall, God willing, proceed on Wednesday . next, after the hour of tierce, to look earnestly into the mysterious case of the good priest's wicked and sacrilegious slaughter. We beseech thee, therefore, to do thy best, to render thyself at the priory on the forecoming day, that, assured of the best hospitality that we can provide for thee, thou mayest rest and prepare thee for the trial of the following morrow.   Till then we commend thee to the care of God, the blessed Virgin, and Holy Saint Andrew ; and with this, our consolatory benediction, we bid thee farewell.

" DUNCANUS,

"Monach. Ordinis, Vallis Caulium, Plus. Prior."

"Haste thee, good Janet," said Helen Dunbar, after she had read the prior's letter ; "haste thee, and see that the honest lay-brother and his beast be well looked to for this night."

Left to themselves, the ladies compared and canvassed the two letters, one of which was so evidently a forgery. They had little difficulty in determining which was the true one.   After some consultation, Helen proceeded to pen a proper answer to that which she had last received ; and having sent orders to old James to get his steed ready, she despatched him with it forthwith by that short route over the hills which the lay-brother had taken to bring the prior's letter to her.   And a few lines of reply, which James brought her next day from the reverend father himself, assured her of the safe delivery of her communication.

During the interval which elapsed before the day on which she was to set out for Pluscarden, the Laird of Knockando made two more ineffectual attempts to gain admittance to Helen, and on both of these occasions he sent her urgent messages to come to his house on her way, and to allow him to be her escort on the journey.   To these courteous but resolute refusals were given by the matron, who was then her companion, and on both occasions Knockando left the house with a degree of disappointment and mortification which he could not altogether conceal.

The day fixed for her journey at last arrived.   Aware of the stern necessity that existed of arming herself with fortitude to undergo all that she had to encounter, she kneeled down, and fervently prayed to God and to the Virgin to aid and to support her.   She arose with the conscious conviction that her prayers had been heard, and she met her friend with a quiet and composed countenance.

As that lady and Janet were to be the companions of her journey, she calmly issued her directions for getting ready the animals which were destined to carry them. The table was already spread for their morning's meal, when suddenly a loud trampling of horses was heard, and ere they were aware, they saw through the casements that the house was surrounded by about a dozen of mounted men-at-arms. Before they had time to recover from their astonishment, their leader threw himself from his saddle, and entered the house and the apartment.

"Knockando!" cried the ladies in astonishment and alarm.

"Fear nothing," said John Dhu Grant, advancing and bowing with his usual imperturbable manner. "I have merely ridden up hither with a handful of brave fellows to guard thee. Ha!—what's this?" continued he, surveying the ample table which was liberally spread with trenchers, flagons, and drinking cups, and provisions of all kinds much beyond what the moderate wants of the two ladies could have required. "It was kind, indeed, to be thus hospitably prepared for our coming. But think not, I pray thee, of my fellows without there, for their hound-like stomachs are already provisioned for the day's toil. As for myself, indeed, I shall make bold to benefit by thy kindness to me, for I rarely eat at so early an hour as my spearmen do."

"John Grant of Knockando," said Helen Dunbar, drawing herself up with an effort to summon all her resolution, and speaking with great determination, "I lack not thine aid, and I reject it as insulting to me! And touching my hospitality, I tell thee that it is to be given solely to such as it may please me to bestow it upon—not taken, as thou wouldst have it, by a masterful hand. That board was never spread for thee, and thou shalt never partake of it with my good will!"

"These are strong and hard words, lady," said Knockando, coolly seating himself; "they are hard, yea, and sharp too—harder and sharper, methinks, than anything that I have unconsciously done to offend thee may well have merited. Hadst thou not better unsay them? if not with thy lips, at least by silently seating thyself here beside me, to do me the honours of the table."

"Again I tell thee, that table was never spread for

25

thee!" said Helen firmly. "Begone, then! and leave.
it untouched for me, and for such other guests as I
may judge to be most fit to seat themselves there."

"Tush, tush, lady!" said Knockando frigidly. "The
good old Priest Innes never meant that this table should
be spread for thee without my sitting at it with thee.
That very last night we passed together, the worthy
man told me that he should leave thee to me as a legacy
together with all his little means. So, lady, I have e'en
come to claim thee, and I have brought these rough but
staunch spearmen with me, that we may guard thee safely
to Knockando as we would a treasure. There a priest
waits to make thee even yet more securely mine own.
After which we shall ride together, if it shall so please.
thee, to Pluscarden, that we may draw down the blessing
of holy mother Church upon our union, by seeing condign
punishment swiftly done on the murderer who now lieth
there. Come, lady! break thy fast, I pray thee, with
what haste thou mayest, for thy palfrey waits by this
time. Ha! what stir is that among my people?"

"Thanks! thanks to Heaven, they come at last!" cried
Helen, clasping her hands together with fervour.

"Who comes?" said Knockando, turning to the lattice,
and growing deadly pale as he looked out. "What! the
sub-prior of Pluscarden!—ha! and the bailie too with
him, and a strong force of mounted men-at-arms! What
means all this?"

The small plump of men who had come with Knockando
were smothered up, as it were, by the long train of horsemen who now filed up and crowded the confined space
formed by the modest front of the priest's manse, and
the humble out-buildings which were attached to it at
right angles. The heads of the houses of Cistertian monks,
of which the brethren of Vallis Caulium were but a sect,
seldom travelled in later times without all those external
emblems of religious pomp which their rules allowed
them. Upon the present occasion, the sub-prior and
his palfrey were both arrayed in all the trappings to
which his official dignity entitled him. Before him appeared a monk bearing a tall and splendidly gilded crucifix,
that glittered in the morning sun, and some dozen of
the brotherhood came riding after him, two and two,
with their white cassocks and their scapularies covered

by the black gowns in which they usually went abroad.
These carried banners, charged with the arms of the
Priory—the figure of Saint Andrew their patron saint—
and various other devices. And a strong body of men-at-
arms, who, as belonging to the regality attached to the
Priory, owed service to it as vassals, preceded and followed
the procession, under the orders of the seneschal or bailie.
A monk dismounted to hold the stirrup of the sub-prior as
he alighted at the door, and singing a cross in the air, the
holy father forthwith entered.

"The blessing of Saint Andrew be upon this house!"
said he, as he stepped over the threshold. "Benedicite,
my child of sorrow!" continued he, as he entered the
apartment. "Soh!—the Laird of Knockando here! I
thought as much. How camest thou, false and lying
knave, to use the sacred name, and to forge the sign-
manual of our most reverend Lord Prior, to further thine
own vile frauds against this innocent daughter of the
church? Surrender thyself forthwith into the hands of
this our bailie, that he may take thee prisoner to Pluscarden, where thy delicts may be duly dealt with."

"What ho, there, men-at-arms!" cried the bailie aloud.

In an instant the followers of Knockando were disarmed,
and the apartment being filled with the men-at-arms belonging to the Church, Knockando was made prisoner, led
out, and bound upon his horse.

"It was well, daughter, that the blessed Virgin gave
thee wit to discover and to foil the base tricks of this false
man," said the sub-prior.

"Nay, reverend father, but rather let me say, thanks be
to the Virgin, and to thy timely succour," replied Helen.
"One moment later, and my fate had been sealed. But
will it please thee to partake of our humble Highland fare?
and whilst thou dost condescend to taste of the poor refreshment we have ventured to provide for thee, we women, as
beseems us, will withdraw."

"Nay, nay, fair daughter!" replied the sub-prior, "thou
shalt by no means depart. Were it a meal, indeed, we
might see fit rigidly to insist upon our rule. But we shall
but taste thy viands, and put our lips to thy wine-cup for
mere courtesy's sake. Therefore disturb thyself not.
Marry, as we broke our fast scarcely two hours since
before leaving Inverallan, where we sojourned last night,

we can have but small appetite now. Yet thy board
looketh well, and this upland air of thine, in truth, is
sharp and stimulating; and, moreover, we should never
refuse to partake—moderately I mean—of the ·blessings
which are furnished to us by a bountiful Providence, yea,
even when they are set forth on a table spread, as thine
may be said to be, in the wilderness."

Saying so, the good sub-prior seated himself, and set an
example to the rest by cutting off and placing on his own
trencher the leg and wing of a large turkey, relished it with
some reasonably large slices of bacon, and filled himself a
cup of wine from a flagon on the table, adding as much of
nature's fluid to it as might, with due safety to his conscience, enable him to call it wine and water. The rest
of the holy fraternity were not slack in imitating their
superior ; and after he had thus shown how much the deeds
of the Church were better than its promises, by doing much
more justice to the provisions than his preface had led his
entertainer to hope for, Helen and her companions were
mounted on their palfreys, and the sub-prior, and his
monks and their escort, having got into their saddles, the
prisoner was sent on before them well guarded, and they
proceeded on their way. The sight of the Priory of Pluscarden, as its picturesque ruins now prove, was like that
of all the monasteries of the same order, beautifully retired,
lying at the foot of the hills that abruptly bound the
northern side of its broad valley. It was surrounded by a
square inclosure of many acres, fenced in by a thick and
high wall of masonry, the remains of which are still visible.
As the day was departing, the setting sun that shed its
light athwart the motionless foliage of those woods that
hung on the face of the hills behind the Priory, and gilded
the proud pinnacles of the building, which arose from the
tall grove in the middle of the large area I have described,
threw a last ray of illumination on the glittering crucifix
as the long dark line of the procession wound under the
deep arch of the outer gate, and as it threaded its way
among the small gardens into which the area was parcelled
out for the several members of the fraternity. By the
kind and hospitable care of the Lord Prior the ladies were
soon safely and comfortably lodged in one of the detached
buildings on the outside of the wall inclosing the precincts
of the Priory, whilst the Laird of Knockando was thrown,

a solitary prisoner, into one of the subterranean dungeon vaults within.

Helen Dunbar was that night blessed with sweet and refreshing rest after the fatiguing journey of the previous day. As her gentle spirit began to return to her towards morning from that world of unconsciousness where it had been laid by the profoundness of her sleep, pleasing visions floated over her pillow. The saint-like figure of her venerable uncle, surrounded by a resplendent glory, hovered over her, and smiled upon her from above. Saint Andrew then appeared beside him, and bore him slowly upwards, till both gradually melted from her sight amidst a flood of light in the upper regions of the sky. She awaked in a transport of delight to which her bosom had been for some time a stranger. She arose and attired herself in the sad and simple habit of mourning which she wore, and she threw herself on her knees to ask again for aid from above in the trying circumstances in which she was placed ; and then, having partaken of the refreshment which was liberally provided for her and her companions by the hospitable orders of the prior, she sat patiently waiting for the moment when she should be summoned to attend the chapter.

The brethren of the Priory had no sooner performed the *tierce,* as those services were called which took place at nine o'clock in the morning, than the convent bell rang to call the chapter to assemble. The chapter-house in which this convocation took place was a beautiful Gothic apartment, of about thirty feet in diameter, lighted by four large windows, and having its groined roof supported by a single pillar. Arranged on one side were the seats of the members of the holy tribunal. That of the Lord Bishop of the diocese, who had come from his palace at Elgin on purpose to preside over the investigation which was about to take place, was a high Gothic chair raised on several steps. Arrayed in his gorgeous episcopal robes, he sat silent and motionless, as if oppressed with the painful subject of the inquiry in which he was to be engaged. On the steps where his feet rested, two handsome boys of his choir were seated, one of whom held his mitre and the other his crosier. On his right sat the Prior, and on his left the Sub-Prior of Pluscarden, attired in their full canonicals, and the other chairs on both sides were filled with those dignitaries and brethren who were members of the chapter.

The area of the place was crowded by the monks in their flowing white draperies, together with the lay brothers in their attire, the extreme interest of the case having prevented every one from being absent who was not in the sick-list of the infirmary, or occupied with duties from which they dared not to absent themselves. A deep silence prevailed. At last the sound of arms was heard echoing through the lofty aisles of the adjacent church, and a body of spearmen, retainers of the monastery, headed ·by the seneschal, entered, guarding in two prisoners.

One of these was the wretched Laird of Auchernach, who appeared with his arms loaded with heavy chains. The captivity.which his body had endured in his dungeon, and the mental agony which he had undergone, had manifestly done sad havoc upon him. He took up the position assigned to him by the seneschal with a subdued yet indifferent air, as if the stream of his life had been poisoned, and that he cared not how soon he should now be called upon to pour out its last bitter dregs.

The black visage of the Laird of Knockando, who was the other prisoner, seemed also to have undergone a considerable change since the morning of the preceding day. It was haggard, and his eyes were bloodshot, as if he had had but little repose during the night. There was a certain expression of mental uneasiness about it, which his habitual air of cold and motionless placidity could not altogether conceal. The two prisoners were placed near to each other in a position a little to one side, and at some distance in front of the tribunal that was about to investigate their respective cases.

"John Grant of Knockando," said the Bishop, whilst a subdued hush ran round among the spectators, "thou hast been brought hither as a prisoner, charged upon very undoubted evidence of having most feloniously forged the sign-manual of the reverend superior of this holy priory, and this for the base purpose of wickedly circumventing an innocent orphan maiden, whom, for her pious uncle's sake, we have been pleased to take under the .especial protection of our holy mother Church. But as thy delict is one with which we as churchmen may deal in our own good time, we shall for the present postpone.and continue thy case, and proceed straightway to our inquiry into ·the graver. and deeper charge touching that crime of a deeper

dye, to wit, the most sacrilegious murder of our pious
brother the Priest Innes, of the which he who now stands
on thy left hand is accused,—I mean thee, Lewis Grant of
Auchernach. But as thou, John Grant of Knockando,
wert present at the last interview which the murdered
man had with his suspected murderer only the night
before, where that unjust 'cause of offence would seem
to have been taken which whetted the cruel blade of
the assassin for its purpose, we would first hear what
evidence thou hast to give upon the matter."

' "My Lord Bishop, and you most Reverend Fathers,"
said Knockando, his eye having brightened up as the
speaker had proceeded, and who had by this time regained
all his wonted coolness and self-possession, "I now stand
before this holy tribunal under circumstances the most
distressing that can well oppress a human being. I shall
at present pass entirely by those charges which have been
made against myself; and regarding which I trust I shall
afterwards have little difficulty in giving ample satisfaction
to my venerable accusers. I shall pass these charges by,
I say, because I could not, if I were willing, find room in
my mind for anything touching myself, filled, as it at this
moment is, with the awful and heavy charge made against
the unhappy man who now stands beside me,—him whom
I once called my friend, and for whom, in the weakness
of my nature, and in despite of the unjust outrage which
he did me on a recent occasion, I still cannot help being
agitated by the same friendly anxiety with which I was
ever moved on his account. Such being my feelings, I am
sure that no one who now heareth me but must pity me,
compelled as I thus am to bear an unwilling testimony
the which, I am aware, must grievously tend towards
fixing on him the guilt of one of the most unnatural, cruel,
and deliberate murders that ever fouled the page of the
history of man, and that done, too, on the sacred person
of a servant of God, with whom the murderer had for long
companied in habits of the strictest intimacy, and in whose
hospitalities he had so long and so often shared. But my
duty to mankind,—my duty to this venerable tribunal,—
and my duty to Heaven, all combine to compel me to speak
out the truth, which I shall now do as briefly as I can.

"It is already well known, most Reverend Fathers,
hat a merry meeting took place at the mill of Duthel on

the occasion of the marriage of the miller's daughter. There all who were present can bear testimony, that Lewis Grant of Auchernach did, without any cause of provocation on my part—though it may perhaps be well enough urged in his exculpation, that the violence he did me arose from jealousy because Helen Dunbar took greater pleasure in my converse than in his—yet certain it is that then and there he did most grievously assault me at unawares. The good Priest Innes, who was my most especial friend, and who is now, alas! so much lamented by me, bestowed a quiet word of reproof on the enraged Auchernach, such as a pastor or a father might have well given upon such an occasion. But instead of taking his rebuke with that humble submission with the which it doth alway become a layman to receive the admonitions of the Church, Auchernach in the ears of all uttered fearful denunciations against the good old man as he was in the act of leaving the place, leaning, as he was often compelled by his infirmities to do, upon the stay of this arm of mine. It sorely wounds my heart to be thus forced to repeat the very words which he used, seeing that they are of themselves enow to condemn him; but if I should fail of so doing, there is not a person of any age or sex who was present that night who could not repeat them. They were these,—'*Old man! look that thou dost not pay dear for thy favour to that new guest of thine!*' Thus carrying his bitter and most unjust rage from me to the good priest, who was about to show me that hos- pitality which, for that night at least, had been denied to himself. He could have made no successful attempt against the good man that night, for I was in the house to act, under Heaven, as his shield from all harm. But the very next night, when I was no longer there—would I had!—to defend him, the murderer comes, and"——

"Thou hast now gone as far as thy knowledge as an eye or ear-witness may bear thee, Knockando," said the Bishop. "When the subject of thy testimony hath been taken down, our brother the sub-prior may go forth to bring in the lady who is our next evidence."

In obedience to the Bishop's order, the sub-prior with- drew, and soon afterwards returned, ushering in Helen Dunbar. As she entered, she was so overcome by the feelings naturally excited by her situation, as well as by the

solemn and impressive spectacle before her, that she did
not very well know how she found herself seated in the
chair that was placed for her a little to one side, and at
such an angle to those of the members of the chapter, so as
to permit a full stream of light to fall upon her from a
window. Her eyes were thrown on the ground, and she
put up a secret aspiration for aid from Heaven during the
interval of silence which the judges charitably allowed to
give her time to compose herself.

"Helen Dunbar!" said the Bishop, at length slowly
addressing her in a deep-toned voice, but with an encourag-
ing manner; "thou already knowest but too well, and to
thine unutterable grief and affliction, that thy uncle,
Priest Innes, a godly, and now, it is to be hoped, a sainted
son of the Church, was, upon the night of the twenty-ninth
day of the last month, most cruelly and barbarously
murdered, by some one at present unknown. What canst
thou say touching that strong suspicion which doth attach
to the prisoner, Lewis Grant of Auchernach, who now
standeth yonder?"

"My lord," said Helen Dunbar, looking fearfully round,
whilst every fibre of her frame seemed to quiver with
agitation, as she caught her first view of the wasted form
and countenance of the unfortunate prisoner, and met his
eye, which was now filled with a flitting fire of anxiety
which it had not before exhibited. But she seemed yet
more affected by the glance of the Laird of Knockando,
who stood beside him. It quite overcame her for some
moments. "My lord!—my lord! I—I"——

"Take thine own time, daughter!" said the Bishop
cheerily; "and begin, if it so pleaseth thee, with thy
recollection of what befell at the wedding at the mill of
Duthel. The prisoner Auchernach did then and there
strike down John Grant of Knockando without cause of
provocation, did he not?"

"My lord, he did strike down Knockando," said Helen;
"but as I chanced to watch them standing for some time,
as if in talk together, I observed their looks; and, were I
to judge from what I saw, I should hold that John Grant
of Knockando had by his words so chafed Auchernach,
and worked upon his dormant ire, as to fret it into the
sudden outburst of that flame, the which blazed forth so
openly to the senses of all who were then present."

" Was he not rebuked by the good priest, thine uncle, for the outrage of which he was then guilty ? " demanded the Bishop.

" He was, my lord," replied Helen ; " and in a sterner tone than he had ever heard the priest use before. But ere mine uncle went to bed, on the evening of that very night in which he was murdered, these ears did privately hear him express a doubt whether he might not have been too hasty in judging him, and he then uttered a fervent ejaculation to Heaven for pardon if he had so erred."

" Heard ye no threat from the lips of Auchernach against thine uncle ? " demanded the Bishop.

" I did hear words which in mine agitation at the time I could not well interpret," said Helen. " After the murder of mine uncle, I did, in my distraction, recall and connect these words with the cruel deed which had so swiftly followed them. But certain circumstances did afterwards occur to satisfy me that the words,—' *Old man ! look that thou dost not pay dear for thy favour to that new guest of thine !* " were meant by Auchernach as a friendly warning, and not as a threat."

" Against whom then dost thou believe that Auchernach's friendly warning was given ? if so thou judgest it to be," said the Bishop.

" Against him who now standeth beside the accused," said Helen Dunbar ; and rising from her chair as she said so, she turned round, and drawing herself up to her full height, she regarded the individual she was addressing with a firm and resolute look, and added in a clear, distinct, and solemn voice,—" The warning of Auchernach was kindly meant, and would to the holy saints that it had been taken as it was intended! The warning of Auchernach was meant to guard against the false arts of John Dhu Grant of Knockando there, whom I do here fearlessly accuse as the real murderer of mine uncle ! "

The murmurs of astonishment which ran through the assemblage at this most unlooked for accusation may easily be imagined, as well as the change that took place on the respective countenances of the two prisoners.

" My guardian angel ! " cried Auchernach, clasping his hands fervently, and looking tenderly and gratefully towards Helen, his face suddenly flushed with joy.

" Some deep conspiracy against me," murmured Knock-

ando, his countenance changing alternately from the deadly
white of guilty fear to the black expression of fiend-like
ferocity. "A deep compact between the murderer and
his paramour! Where can the veriest shadow of proof be
found against my perfect innocence of this foul deed?"

"Let the sacred dignity of our tribunal be respected!"
said the Bishop sternly; "and let all such unseemly
interruptions cease. Proceed maiden! proceed to offer to
us the testimony on which thou art bold enough to make
so strange and so determined an accusation."

"My lord," said Helen, still standing, and betraying
deep agitation, as in her modest and respectful address to
the Bishop she recalled the appalling circumstances; "I was
the first person who entered mine uncle's apartment on the
morning which followed the fatal night of his murder.
When I did approach me to the bed I fancied that he
slept; for, as was not uncommon with him, he lay with
the blessed crucifix over his bosom. I lifted the holy
emblem in my left hand, whilst with my right I did
remove the bed-clothes from his chin—when—when—when
beholding, as I did, the bloody work which had been done
upon him, I fell backwards on the floor in a swoon, and so
firmly did I grasp the crucifix to my bosom in mine
unconscious agony, that those who came to mine aid,
called thither by my scream, found it so placed, and it was
carried with me to mine own apartment, and I so found it
when my senses were restored to me. That the crucifix
had ever lain that night upon mine uncle's breast at all,
therefore, could have been known only to myself alone;
and to him who, during that fatal night, removed it from
his bosom for the purpose of doing the murder on him, and
who replaced it there after he had wrought the cruel deed."

"But how can this touch the Laird of Knockando?"
demanded the Bishop earnestly.

"My lord," said Helen, "some days after the murder,
the Laird of Knockando did force himself into my presence,
under the false pretence of bearing a message from the
reverend lord prior. His object seemed to be to whet my
vengeance against the person who then lay accused of the
murder of mine uncle. It was then that, in the presence
of my friend and my servant, who are both now within the
call of this tribunal, prepared to support this my testimony,
then it was, I say, that he used expressions, the which

were, for greater security, taken down after he was gone,—
'*The wretch*,' said he, 'The wretch who, lighting down
like some nocturnal fiend upon the sacred person of thine
uncle, *and, reckless of the holy emblem of Christ which lay
upon his bosom*, could put it aside, that he might plunge
his dirk into the innocent throat of his sacred servant,
must not only die the death of a felon, but he can never
hope for mercy from Him whose blessed emblem he hath
outraged.' None but the murderer could have so circumstantially described this most barbarous deed. John Dhu
Grant of Knockando did so describe it. Therefore is John
Dhu Grant of Knockando the murderer! On his head the
blood of my murdered uncle doth loudly call for that
justice which it doth behoove man to do upon it. And
may He that died for us all, grant that mercy hereafter to
his guilty soul which his own relentless sentence would
have denied to another."

As Helen Dunbar finished speaking, she fell back into
her chair, exhausted by her exertion to fulfil that duty
which she had wound up her mind to discharge. The
murderer gasped for breath as if he was undergoing suffocation; and his eyes started from their sockets with the
terrors which now overwhelmed him. The murmurs
which burst from those who were present being checked
by the seneschal of the court, the Bishop ordered Helen's
servants, James and Janet, and also her friend, to be all
three severally called. Each of them were examined. The
members of the chapter conferred together for a few
minutes apart; and after they had resumed their seats on
the tribunal, a death-like silence prevailed, and the Bishop
putting on his mitre, and leaning on his crosier, began thus
to speak :—

"After the full and patient probing which we have given
to this most mysterious case, it must be clear to all men
who do now hear us, that this holy tribunal hath before it,
as its bounden duty, to dismiss Lewis Grant of Auchernach,
discharging him as free from all taint or suspicion of any
participation whatsoever in the foul and barbarous murder
of our pious brother, Priest Innes. And as it is beyond
our power to shut our eyes to the miraculous proof which
the Almighty in his wisdom hath caused the very murderer
himself to bear towards his own proper condemnation, we
have no choice left but to direct our bailie, the which we

now hereby do, forthwith to return John Dhu Grant of ·
Knockando to the dungeon whence he was taken, thence to
remove him by to-morrow's earliest sun, and to convey
him, under a strong guard of our men-at-arms, to Elgin,
there to be delivered into the hands of the king's sheriff,
that he may take measures to see that the prisoner be
submitted to the knowledge of an assize, to be by it clenged
or fouled of the crime laid to his charge, as the evidence
laid before it may determine. This we do without all
prejudice to our own claims to the full right of pit and
gallows which belongeth to us ; but because this crime of
murder, when not fresh and redhanded, being to be considered as more especially one of the pleas of the Crown,
we do think it more seemly to leave it to the judges of the
King's Grace to execute justice upon the murderer."

The Laird of Knockando's countenance was all this time
working like that of a fiend, especially whilst the Bishop
was delivering this appalling judgment against him. He
had no sooner heard it to an end, than, putting his hand
into his bosom, he plucked forth a concealed dirk—that
very weapon with which he had murdered the good Priest
Innes. He raised it aloft. Helen saw it glancing in the
air, and uttered a piercing shriek that rang in the groined
roof of the chapter-house. It saved her lover; for, as
Knockando brought it down, aimed with a desperate plunge
at the heart of his rival, his intended victim threw his
body back, and so he most wonderfully escaped from its
fatal blade. But it fell not innocuous—it cleft the very
skull of a wretched lay-brother, who sat with his tablets
below noting down the minutes of the procedure, and the
man dropped lifeless upon the pavement. The perpetrator
of this second murder was seized and pinioned, and, being
instantly tried red-handed as he was—his guilt was established—he was carried out for shrift—confessed that his
first crime was done for the wicked purpose of revenging
himself against Auchernach by fixing upon him the guilt of
the murder. After which the convent-bell tolled dismally.
A long procession of monks chanting a hymn, followed
by the criminal and the bourreau, guarded by the seneschal
and his men-at-arms, was seen winding from the gate of
the Priory, and after a few short moments of prayer, he
was forthwith executed, without further mercy, on the
gallow-hill.

I need not tell you that the Laird of Auchernach performed the part of protector to Helen Dunbar during her homeward journey, and that so soon as the days of mourning for her murdered uncle were fulfilled, he received from her the right to act as her protector throughout the longer journey of life. And if he had ever been supposed to be apt, when provoked on certain occasions, to yield too hastily to that indignation which chanced to be excited within him, the recollection of the terrible events which I have narrated to you had the effect of arming him ever afterwards with a degree of control over himself which few men since his time have been known to possess.

THE END.

GLASGOW: PRINTED BY BELL AND BAIN, 41 MITCHELL STREET.